# FAN FIC
# THIRD KIND!

**O**nce "fan fiction" meant stories written in imitation of ordinary published fiction — usually by struggling science-fiction writers not good enough to sell yet.

**T**hen there was fan fiction written by fans of some commercial series like *Star Trek*, devotees who couldn't get enough of their favorite show and wrote their own stories about it (and darned lucky not to get their pants sued off).

**B**ut lurking in the shadows was a *third* kind of fan fiction — fiction written *about* fans!

**C**omics fandom dates back to the early 1960s, science-fiction fandom is decades earlier yet. Every once in a while, somebody would realize that fantastic stories about amazing adventures on other worlds were all very well and good — but the people with the imagination to appreciate those stories were *themselves* interesting characters who often had adventures of their own, if a little closer to home.

**A**nd so a few writers tried their hand at putting just such tales down on paper. In-jokey, in-groupy, published in a few obscure amateur magazines printed in basements on primitive home duplicating machines like the messy mimeograph and the odiferous "ditto," seen by only a scant few readers before now... well, these are some pretty rare stories, folks!

**F**unny and satirical, historical and hysterical, capturing the spirit of comics fandom in the '60s as well as the independent comics of today, reflecting the possibly somewhat skewed personal vision of one author in particular, the stories collected in *Dancing with the Squirrels* explore a world like no other!

# DANCING WITH THE SQUIRRELS

## TALES FROM COMICS FANDOM AND BEYOND

### DWIGHT R. DECKER

*For Mike! and to think this book began one summer upstairs at 128 W. FAIRGROUND!!! Cheers! — Dwight R. Decker 2-15*

Vesper Press

Northlake, Illinois

Cover by Sam Kujava
(Originally published in 1984 as the cover for *Tales of Fandom Past*:
Volume 1, by Dwight R. Decker, a pamphlet reprinting some of the
first few fan fiction stories in the series.)

Coloring by Jesse Kujava

ISBN: 1507578520
ISBN-13: 978-1507578520

*V*Vesper Press

Northlake, Illinois

# ACKNOWLEDGEMENTS

Thanks for help, support, and encouragement to the Gaff, Hurricane Heeran, Mike Hough, Tony Isabella, Rick Johnson, Jesse Kujava, Sam Kujava, John C. LaRue, Jr., Irene Maschke, John J. Pierce, Richard Pryor, Mike Raub, Bill Schelly, Craig D. Smith, Rick Spanier, Jeff Wasserman, and a host of others over the years.

# DEDICATION

In memory of

## Joan Hanke-Woods

(1945 – 2013)

Artist, friend, fellow voyager

# CONTENTS

# QUOTES TO PONDER
## BY DR. FREDRIC WERTHAM

### (Or, How Wrong Can a Man Be?)

I have known many adults who have treasured throughout their lives some of the books they read as children. I have never come across any adult or adolescent who had outgrown comic-book reading who would ever dream of keeping any of these "books" for any sentimental or other reason.

*— Seduction of the Innocent* (1954)

When *Seduction of the Innocent* appeared in the middle fifties, it started a grass-roots social reaction... A change occurred. Murder in comic books decreased, and so did the number of crime-comic-book publishers. Within a few years after the publication of *Seduction of the Innocent,* twenty-four out of twenty-nine crime-comic-book publishers went out of business. But it was only a partial victory. We now meet some of the child comic-book readers as parents of the "battered child" or in similar roles. Moreover, very many of the old comic books are still around at reduced prices.

*— A Sign for Cain* (1966)

Comic-book collecting which started as a nice nostalgic hobby is in some danger of becoming an overpriced, overcommercialized transaction ...

*— The World of Fanzines* (1974)

# INTRODUCTION

## FAN FICTION OF THE THIRD KIND

It was the summer of 1969. The Moon landing. Woodstock. I was 17, a newly minted high-school graduate, and just back home from a cross-country trip to California for a science-fiction convention. I had been an active comics fan for two years, collecting comic books, writing articles about them for fanzines, and even publishing an issue or two of my own fanzine. The Westercon had broadened my horizons a bit, and I had some sense that I could be doing more, or perhaps something different.

Then inspiration struck. I had tried my hand at writing stories, but never with much success since I didn't know what cowboys, detectives, spies, or starship captains actually did in real life. (Okay, nobody else knew what a starship captain did in real life, but *Star Trek*'s creator Gene Roddenberry could extrapolate from military experience I didn't have.) The answer seemed to be that old writer's dictum — *Write what you know*. And what *did* I know? Comic-book fans! It seemed only natural to write stories about fictional versions of the kind of people I knew best and the scrapes they got into.

It was all strictly for my own amusement, of course, and that of a few friends and fellow comics fans. There was absolutely no chance of professional publication for something so in-groupish, so the stories could only appear in fanzines with circulations well below even a hundred copies.

What I didn't know at first was that my inspiration was hardly unique, and the genre of fiction about fans had long been invented in science-fiction fandom. There it was called "faan" fiction (pronounced with a kind of bleat) to distinguish it from fan fiction of the more usual sort, or retina-

1

scarringly bad stories written by a would-be author not good enough to sell yet in imitation of professionally published science-fiction. (The later definition of fan fiction, highly unauthorized amateur stories written by devotees of commercial properties like *Star Trek*, exploring a given series' fictional universe and continuing the characters' adventures, hadn't emerged yet.) "Faan" (and the adjectival form "faanish") was science-fiction fandom jargon for someone who was more interested in fandom and its associated activities for their own sake than in the thing the fandom was a fandom of. The term seems so cutesie and incomprehensible to the non-initiates outside the innermost inner circle that I've preferred to refer to the stories here as simply a third variety of fan fiction rather than as faan fiction and have to explain it every darned time.

It was only after I had written a few stories in that vein that my attention was called to the fact that fan fiction of the third kind already existed. I particularly remember somebody lending me an actual novel from 1965, about the members of a science-fiction club in England, printed on a mimeograph machine and bound with staples and tape: *The Meadows of Fantasy* by Archie Mercer, which may be read at:

http://efanzines.com/Meadows/index.htm

Then there was John Stockman, who had taken fan fiction into some downright strange directions with his fanzine *Tales of Torment*. Stockman was so monumental in this remote backwater of creative endeavor that this book includes a full chapter to pay him tribute.

Though my first story was intended strictly as a one-shot, I found I couldn't leave the characters in limbo, and more stories followed as a full-fledged series developed. Then came a fanzine to put them in, called *True Fan Adventure Theatre*, printed by my own hands on the duplicator in my basement. A few buddies answered the call and wrote stories of their own in the genre for both my zine and others. My stories reflected my own experiences in fandom, but other writers had different stories to tell, widening the variety. In all, I published seven issues of *True F.A.T.* during my first couple of years in college, and the whole thing came to an end as summer wore into fall in 1971 mainly because I went off to Austria to spend my junior year on a study-abroad program. I still remember the last-minute rush of trying to get #7 out before I left, stuffing copies into envelopes and mailing them at the post office less than 24 hours before my plane was due to take off.

After that, I just never seemed to have time or ambition to get back to the old level of fan writing and publishing. A couple of further issues of *True F.A.T.* were published by other hands, for which I wrote stories, but the old zing was gone. The time-consuming bother of earning a living in the real world got in the way and neither revival effort lived past an issue apiece. Fan fiction had been something fun to do once, but time had marched on.

Some years later, in the 1984/1985 period when my life was stable and my income steady, I took up fan fiction again out of some sort of nostalgia for my lost youth, reprinting some of the old stories and even writing a few new ones, notably "TV Comics" and "The Old Abandoned Warehouse." That effort also faded out, but in the last few years, yet another yen to write some stories in a fannish vein overcame me and the other stories in this book resulted. It's a little astonishing to realize that I've been writing about some of these characters for 45 years. (To be honest, Jack Tremaine is probably something of what I would have liked to have been at that age — the background stated for how he got into fandom is pretty much the same story as mine — while Bob Trent is more what my despairing parents and teachers would have liked me to be. Since both Jack and Bob get good grades, however, neither matches the sad reality. Pam's age doesn't seem to match up with the dates given for things like her college graduation, so she may have skipped a grade somewhere.)

Recently, with new possibilities opening up for publishing books of highly specialized interest, it occurred to me that it might be worthwhile to dust off some of the old stories and make them available to anyone inclined to take a look. I did put some time, effort, and thought into them, and it seemed to me that they capture a time and a place that might otherwise be forgotten. Besides, with *The Big Bang Theory* the most successful show on TV at the moment, it may be that the woes and tribulations of comics fans are not as mysterious for a wider audience as I once might have thought.

Selecting the book's contents was the next consideration. The earliest stories were written over several years by a young writer with varying degrees of eptitude. They were not written according to any organized plan, they contradict each other, they meander hither and yon as my enthusiasms waxed and waned, the characters aren't consistent, and some stories had to be retroactively declared outside the canon. In the end, the Early Period petered out without any real conclusion as I went on to other things.

For this book, it seemed best to use Middle and Late Period stories in which the Author had matured about as much as he was ever going to, just to be able to present the stories straightforwardly without having to apologize for the lunkheaded teenage-boy excesses or explain all the dated references to fandom controversies long forgotten. The Prologue to "TV Comics" covers three previous stories' worth of continuity to bring the reader up to speed about the characters. Even at that, there is a lot of background detail that might be puzzling for a non-comics fan, if any should chance to open the pages of this collection, and even younger fans might not be fully versed on what comics and fandom were like in 1967. For their edification, I've included some supplemental features covering the history of comics and fandom that explain what the references are to, which older fans already familiar with it all can skip at their option.

That one of the main characters in several of the stories was a girl was perhaps a fantasy in itself, as there weren't too many more female comics fans in real life than there were starship captains. There were thought to be around 2000 active fans in comics fandom in the late '60s ("active" defined as people who got fanzines, basically the subscription list of the *Rocket's Blast/Comicollector*, the one fanzine almost everybody got, plus a couple hundred more who had let their subscriptions to the *RBCC* lapse), and of them maybe four were known to be female. It wasn't *quite* as though comics fandom was a little boys' tree house with "NO GIRLS ALLOWED" painted on the side (with a backwards "S"), and most teen-boy comics fans at the time probably would have loved it if there had been more girls who shared their hobby. Female comics fans later began to appear in greater numbers, but at least into the '70s, it seemed that most of the girls inclined to fan-type activities were over in *Star Trek* fandom (where they invented today's best known form of fan fiction, the one about unauthorized versions of commercial properties that I still don't understand why people don't get sued for writing). Between the lines of the story "Dancing with the Squirrels," which is more or less contemporary, there are signs that more women are involved in comics now.

When I started writing fan fiction *about* fans at 17, I hadn't traveled much and the stories reflect my Midwestern small-town boyhood. In a way, that highlights one of the better parts of comics fandom: As high school wore on, I was feeling pretty lonely as the one serious comic-book collector I knew of in my town, although I did pick up a couple of collections from kids who had lost interest and wanted to sell out. Through fandom, on the other hand, I had friends who shared my interests all over the country.

And that, really, is what this book is about.

—DRD

# DANCING WITH THE SQUIRRELS

It was the biggest comics convention in the country. For a few days each summer, everybody who was anybody in the comics business gathered there, as well as every nobody who wanted to be somebody. The convention had been running for so many years that a few legends had grown up around it.

One was that every year, some aspiring comic artist or writer would be discovered — someone's dreams would come true and the doors would open to professional advancement and even stardom.

*It's not going to happen to this guy*, Ethan Standish thought gloomily, flipping through the portfolio.

Ethan had been minding his own business, sitting by himself at a small table in the mezzanine snack bar as he sipped a Coke and looked over the day's purchases. He was thin with a scraggly beard and a little way to go yet before he hit 30. Behind him, a huge glass window looked out over the vast convention floor below where swarms of people jammed the aisles between endless lines of booths and displays. Then someone had said, "Mind if I sit here?"

A man of about 40 stood in front of the table, carrying a worn and battered brown portfolio. Shrugging, Ethan replied with an indifferent, "Go right ahead."

The man sat down, wiping the sweat off an expanse of glistening brow exposed by a receding hairline. He was a little overweight from perhaps a few too many years behind a desk and not in the best of shape for an entire day of walking the aisles of the mammoth convention center. "Big show, isn't it?" he said, sounding out of breath. "It's my first time. I'm pretty overwhelmed."

5

"I think it's my ninth, but I've lost count," Ethan replied absently, more intent on trying to remember if he already had a copy at home of an old comic book he had just bought.

"Oh, so you're an old hand. You in the business?" It was now painfully obvious that the man had something on his mind and wanted to talk to someone, anyone.

Ethan looked up. "Yeah," he said warily, not knowing quite where this was going. "I'm an animator."

"Like for Disney?"

"Not quite. A studio you've never heard of, probably. We do commercials. If you remember the one where the guy's crabgrass turns into a giant green monster that eats his lawn, I storyboarded that."

"Hey, I've seen it! You're an artist, then?"

"I'll admit to it."

"So am I. Well, kind of. Er... could I show you my stuff, see what you think, since you're a professional and all? I'd really appreciate it, getting a professional opinion, if you don't mind."

*I really shouldn't,* Ethan thought, *but this guy isn't a starry-eyed kid, either. Oh, what the heck.* "Okay, sure, I'll take a look."

As Ethan flipped through the sample pages and came to his pessimistic conclusion, he half-listened to the man's life story. His name was Arthur D. Claymore, he was a college graduate with a business degree and now some kind of middle manager in a white-collar office somewhere, married with two children — all while nursing a lifelong unfulfilled dream of breaking out of the cubicle farm and becoming a famous cartoonist. He drew evenings and on weekends as a hobby, with enough skill that friends and neighbors were constantly after him for free art for their posters for local events, but he had always yearned for the big-time. As in being the next Charles Schulz with a comic strip that was the next *Peanuts*. Unfortunately, he had next to no idea how to get there.

"Were you ever in comics fandom?" Ethan asked. "Contribute to fanzines or small-press comics?"

Claymore looked blank. "What are those?"

So he hadn't served any kind of apprenticeship. Still, he had been able to figure out that comic strips were syndicated and that he could find the addresses of the syndicates somewhere. He had sent them proposals and sample packages, but all he had to show for it were printed rejections months later.

"They get thousands of submissions," Ethan said, trying to be consoling. "Very tough to break in that way."

Finally, Claymore's wife had gotten tired of him spending so much time at the drawing board on something that was getting him absolutely nowhere, and gave him a near-ultimatum to stop playing around at it and either show some progress or give it up. Seeing a clip about the convention on the news and hearing someone in his local amateur artists' Wednesday evening coffee get-together say that it was the place where stars were discovered, he had decided to go for broke and make a trip halfway across the country to show his samples.

So far, though, the trip had been a bust. The convention was huge and he didn't know where to go or whom to talk to. The low-level twenty-somethings manning the booths at the big comic-book company exhibits had brushed him off with the assurance that their bosses would have no interest in his stuff. Based on what he saw in the portfolio, Ethan decided they were probably right. Beyond that, Claymore was clueless as to what to do next, except maybe give up and head for home a day early.

"This kind of strip really isn't my area of expertise," Ethan said diplomatically, deciding he wasn't the one to give the man the bluntly honest appraisal he really needed, "but I might be able to give you a suggestion."

"Oh?" Claymore looked at him, suddenly expectant and hopeful.

Ethan gestured vaguely to the sprawling convention floor behind him. "Down there is a booth for an outfit called Psi Press. It's just a little publisher of independent comic books, what they call 'small-press comics.' The big companies are all superheroes and that kind of thing, nothing like what you do, but Psi Press will publish almost anything if they think it looks interesting. The downside is that they mainly sell to a few loyal fans, and you won't make much money if any. The publisher is a guy named Tedd Wicke who does it as kind of a hobby, and probably makes up for the losses out of his own pocket. That's the man you should talk to."

Claymore now didn't look nearly so hopeful. More like dismayed. "Why should I go to him if it's such a small operation? A comic book nobody reads isn't going to get my characters on lunchboxes or my wife off my back."

"Because you have to start somewhere," Ethan said flatly, "and Tedd will look at things nobody else will. They published one of my books years ago, and it opened some doors for me. Not many people bought the book but it was something for me to add to my portfolio and show around. Just getting your work out there is a big step forward and you never know who might see it. It's a place to get your feet wet, anyway."

Claymore smiled in weary gratitude. "Thanks so much. You're the first person I've talked to who's given me even that much advice. I'll go talk to the people at this, er... Cypress, was it?"

"Psi Press," Ethan said, emphatically pronouncing the initial "p" in Psi. "You can find where the companies' booths are in the program book index. Let's see... Ah, here we go. Psi Press, Aisle M, Booth 24. Good luck," he added as Claymore got up to go.

*And forgive me, Tedd,* Ethan thought, glancing back at the convention floor. *After you gave me my break, I'm repaying you by sticking you with the job of killing a man's dreams!*

At first glance, Psi Press looked less like a comic-book company and more like an anarchic collective of artists. Two or three even smaller operations with their own logos seemed to have temporarily linked up with it to combine their booth space into one large sales area, not to mention a couple of very likely self-published artists who couldn't even be called publishing companies.

Several artists sat behind the tables sketching — there seemed to be more of them than paying customers — and had there been very many eager customers, they would have had to push their way through the hangers-on, friends of the firm perhaps, loitering in front of the tables and chatting with the people on the other side without any evident intent of actually buying something.

The curtained back wall of the booth was hung with a large cardboard disc replicating the company logo: a roughly trident-formed evergreen tree in a circle, representing a cypress shaped like the Greek letter "psi." Underneath, a sign was emblazoned with the words: **PSI PRESS**. It seemed to Claymore that somebody had given the symbolism almost a little too much thought.

As for the wares themselves, Claymore saw swathes of comic books with brightly colored covers arranged in rows on the tables. He noticed that many of them, perhaps the majority, featured talking animal characters, which perhaps meant he might have a chance here with his own strip. He managed to squeeze into a space between the non-buying kibitzers in front of a table and picked up a comic book at random. The title was *Fur God and Country* and the cover was a parody of the famous photo of the raising of the flag on Iwo Jima with animal characters as soldiers. He leafed through it, and to his surprise only the cover was in color — the inside pages were plain black and white. The comic books he remembered from his boyhood had been all in color. The story was about anthropomorphic animal characters in a military setting, and not the least bit funny. In fact, it was equal parts insane technical accuracy in depicting weapons and gruesome realism in depicting war. Suddenly his little comic strip about a dog and a bird wryly philosophizing about life from a backyard fence seemed very, very tame and old-fashioned.

He felt more out of place than ever but he had come this far, so he might as well do like that animator had suggested and at least talk to the man in charge.

Finding him wasn't hard. Tedd Wicke, a short, middle-aged man, stood behind the table and at the moment, he was talking to some tall, cadaverously thin old man with a thick manuscript in his hands.

"I'm sorry," Tedd was saying, "but just because our name is Psi Press doesn't mean we publish books about ESP and psychic powers."

The man mumbled something complaining about the bad vibrations in the air preventing anybody from even looking at his great work, then turned away to find some other potential publisher down the aisle.

Tedd smiled as Claymore came up to the table in turn. "We get that a lot," he said conversationally, glancing at the departing would-be author, "but it's too late to change our name now." Noticing the portfolio Claymore was carrying, he added, "I take it you have something to submit, too?"

Claymore nodded. "If you don't mind? It's called *Woofer & Tweeter*, and it's about a dog and a bird and—"

Tedd waved off the explanations. "If it has pictures and tells a story, I'll be glad to take a look. Inscrutable 600-page theories of the universe, not so much." Tedd motioned to a twentyish assistant behind him who was just then pulling some comics out of boxes to put on the tables. "Take over separating the customers from their money, Josh. It's portfolio review time."

"Again?" Josh wailed.

Tedd had Claymore step inside the booth area and they sat down on a couple of empty folding chairs by the back wall. After introducing himself, Claymore opened his portfolio and handed Tedd the samples he had spent so many evenings and weekends working so hard on. He felt strangely tense. Somehow this was even more nerve-wracking than a performance review at work. He did his job well enough that it was pretty much routine anymore and hardly more than an annual formality, but this was like a judgment on deeper, even embarrassingly more personal parts of his self that were seldom exposed so nakedly.

"Please be honest, Mr. Wicke," he said.

"I'm never anything but," Tedd replied as he looked through the pages. He gave the drawings a critical eye and frowned. "All right, to start with, it seems to me your *Woofer & Tweeter* is basically recycling *Peanuts*. Later *Peanuts* at that, when the strip was past its peak."

The tense feeling changed to disappointment. This was not going to be good. "I guess that was when I was reading it..."

"And your basic situation... It's a bird and a dog commenting on things. The dog never gets out of the backyard and the bird never gets off the fence. It's the same thing strip after strip after strip. It's Snoopy and Woodstock if Woodstock could talk. You've also got a size problem. The dog is so much bigger than the bird that it's hard for them to interact in the same panel. You're constantly having to play games with perspective, like having the bird in the foreground, to get them the same apparent size."

"I'm surprised you picked up on that right away."

"It's kind of obvious. I'm sorry, Mr. Claymore, but there's nothing here people haven't seen a thousand times before. *Woofer & Tweeter* just isn't Psi Press, I'm afraid."

"So what exactly are you looking for?"

"You can tell by what we publish. You want to draw funny animals? Take a look at *Nutz 'n' Squoilz*. The artist is a woman named Kaelynn Larrabee. That's her over there."

Tedd pointed to a blonde woman of about thirty sitting nearby, next to a display of her comics on the table. She was short and thin, attractive in an almost ethereal sort of way. Just behind her, a pony-tailed man of about the same age — boyfriend? husband? — was sitting on a folding chair and reading a book, his job apparently to keep her supplied with bottles of water as well as any art supplies she happened to need that were in a nearby case.

As Claymore watched, a young woman and her approximately eight-year-old daughter approached Kaelynn from the aisle side of the table.

"I jus' *wuvv* your squoilz!" the little girl burbled. "They're so cute an' funny!"

"I'm glad to hear it, honey," Kaelynn said. "Here, I'll do you a sketch and autograph it for you! How's that?"

"Gweat!"

"You'd never notice her sitting on the bus as anything unusual," Tedd told Claymore, "but give her a sheet of paper and a pencil and she starts drawing squirrels. Crazy squirrels like nothing you've ever seen before, getting into crazy situations nobody ever thought of before. She has a sense of humor that has to come from Mars — there's no other explanation — and it only seems to come out when she draws. We've published five issues and it's getting something of a following, as you have just now seen spontaneously demonstrated before you. If your strip had the same kind of demented verve hers does, we might be able to talk." Tedd leaned over and grabbed a random copy of *Nutz 'n' Squoilz* off the table.

Claymore paged through it in something like appalled awe. "I can't do crazy. Not like this, anyway."

"We publish other kinds of stuff, too." Tedd pointed to another comic book on the table. "Here's *Lt. Vogelmann*. It's by another woman — she's probably at her own table over in Artists' Alley just now — who happens to be a real Germanophile. Her book is sort of an alternate history of World War I, about a man who can fly because he was born with a pair of wings growing out of his back and he joins the German air corps."

"That's a little... beyond my grasp, too."

"It's a little beyond a lot of people's, but let me tell you, the book's got the best letter column in the business because the fans who are really into it come up with all kinds of technical and historical information."

Tedd showed him a few more books, even gave him samples of several to peruse at his leisure. Claymore went away realizing that he didn't understand these comics in the least. *I can't do that stuff!* he thought bleakly. He had the uncomfortable feeling that there were decades of comics history he knew nothing about, and there was no place in this strange new world for him and his gentle little comic strip about a dog and a bird in a backyard.

It had been a long and tiring day. Claymore had learned something about the business, had spoken with a couple of people who had been friendly and even helpful, but he had still gotten nowhere. He wasn't any closer to his dream of cartooning fame and success than before. If anything, the only result was that he now had a somewhat clearer idea of just how enormously far away the dream actually was.

He had no interest in the evening convention activities listed in the program book. For most of them, he would have had to have been about twenty years younger. Like an all-night movie room showing non-stop anime, something else he knew little about and had even less interest in, although his kids would have loved it. About all he could do after a lonely dinner in the hotel restaurant was go up to his room, call his wife back home to report in, and then make an early night of it. But first, maybe a drink — just one — to drown his disappointment and salute the death of a dream...

Standing at the counter in the dark and noisy hotel bar, he was about to order something when he happened to overhear what someone next to him was saying.

"I'm looking for some fresh new characters for this!" a pudgy middle-aged man with thick glasses was insisting to a non-descript companion of about the same age. Both were wearing suits and loosened ties, and struck Claymore as executive level. He hadn't spent some eighteen years in corporate America without acquiring an instinct for identifying the type.

*Fresh new characters...?* Claymore unobtrusively moved a little closer.

"Something kids will really go for," the pudgy man went on, jabbing the air with the forefinger of his free hand while he took a sip from the glass he held in the other. "Zany, you know? The higher-ups want talking animals because they're traditional, but other than that they have to be different. Not *too* different, though. They have to be cute and lovable as well as zany. But so far I've got nothing. Nada. We have to go into production soon and here I am with absolutely zilch. The studio in Korea is screaming that they need character designs and model sheets yesterday and I've got utter zippo to send them. Nobody I've talked to at this show has anything. I've looked at proposals until my eyes bleed and it's been hopeless. Nobody's got what I want and I'm getting desperate. Lemme tell you, America's next big hit doesn't come up to you at a convention and say howdy..."

*Oh, thank you Lord!* Claymore thought and raised his hand to attract the man's attention. "Excuse me, but could I talk to you for a moment?"

They went out of the bar to the lobby where the light was better and they could talk normally without being drowned out by music and other people's loud conversations. "My name's Peltier," the pudgy man said. "I'm a producer for the Toonorama Network. You know, All Toons, All the Time."

"Sure," Claymore replied. "My kids watch it a lot."

"Okay, so you know what we do. Anyway, what I'm looking for are characters for bumpers."

"Bumpers?"

Peltier seemed surprised Claymore didn't know. "Short gag bits running between the cartoons and the commercials. If you've got what I want, your characters will be all over the network all day long, they'll be in all our advertising — you'll be *made*. And make a ton of money, too, I might add. So let's see what you've got."

Feeling more hopeful than he had all day, Claymore pulled the sample pages out of his portfolio. "It's a strip called *Woofer & Tweeter*," he added helpfully.

As Peltier looked through the pages, Claymore felt even more hopeful. He tried imagining what Liz would say when he called her later and told her *this* piece of news. And his kids would be heroes at their school if the characters really caught on—

"Cripe!" Peltier suddenly blurted. "Charles Schulz is dead and he could *still* do better than this!"

It was a two-by-four across the nose. "But... what? What's so bad?" Claymore managed to gasp as the last of his dreams shattered.

Peltier exhaled impatiently. "I'll be blunt. The characters are just plain lame. I want zany and different, not warmed-over Snoopy. I'm not even sure you know what a gag is, let alone how to set one up." He handed the pages back to Claymore and softened slightly. "Look, I'm sorry, but this is a business, and I've got to go with what will sell."

"I understand," Claymore said, his voice a little thick.

As he jammed the pages into his portfolio, Claymore's hand brushed something — the sample comic books Tedd Wicke had given him earlier. Something clicked in his mind, a connection was made.

For a long time afterwards, he would wonder why he did what he was about to do. After being turned down and humiliated all day long, he had accidentally run into a producer looking for something. What were the odds? By a miracle, he had been given one last chance. And he still got a flat door-in-the-face rejection. Anybody else might have just said the heck with it and quit right then and there. But even though he had lost his own chance, even though he had no more hope for himself, he had one second left when the producer was still paying attention to him. And there was one last thing he could do.

All his life, he had wanted to be a part of this world. In that moment, he was.

"Wait," Claymore said as Peltier started to step away. "How about this?"

He handed him a copy of *Nutz 'n' Squoilz*.

"Eh...?" Peltier leafed through it. Something caught his eye. He looked at it for a long moment, then glanced up. "You know the artist?"

"No, it was just something the publisher gave me as a sample."

Peltier leafed through some more pages. "Damn. Damn! *Damn!*" He shook his head, as though he couldn't quite believe what he was seeing, then grabbed Claymore's arm. "C'mon, I'll buy you a drink! And you can tell me where you found this!"

The convention opened at 10:00 the next morning. At the Psi Press booth, several of the artists had already trickled in and were sitting in back of the tables and sketching while waiting to greet any fans and customers who might materialize in front of them. So far, only a few people were strolling the aisles between booths, but by afternoon the convention floor would probably be wall-to-wall protoplasm.

At the moment, Tedd and Josh were bending down and opening a box of freshly printed comic books that had just been delivered.

"Excellent!" Tedd exclaimed. "The new issue of *Funky Skunk*! I was afraid it wouldn't get here in time."

"If Barry had turned in the art when he was supposed to," Josh reminded him, "it wouldn't have been late in the first place!"

Tedd sighed theatrically. "The price we pay for publishing the work of talented non-professionals."

That was when a pudgy middle-aged man wearing a suit and tie appeared in front of the booth, seeming to want something.

Leaving Josh to take care of emptying the box of comics, Tedd stood up and went to talk to the man.

"Can I help you?" he asked, wondering what it was about. This was not a typical Psi Press customer.

The man held up a copy of *Nutz 'n' Squoilz*. "Is this yours?"

"Well, yes. We publish it, anyway." *Is this guy a lawyer? Kaelynn didn't do something to get us sued, I hope!* That hadn't happened yet, but Tedd remembered with a shudder an amateur artist who hadn't been clear on the concept that plagiarism is a bad thing, and Josh, who had seen the source somewhere, only caught it just before the book went to the printer...

"My name's Peltier. Here's my card." He explained.

Tedd's eyebrows went up. There had always been a chance of something like this happening. Publish enough books long enough and eventually somebody might notice. It was something every artist and writer dreamed of, even if most of the Psi Press regulars had long ago scaled their dreams down to a more realistic level and contented themselves with just doing what they liked for any readers who liked what they did. On the other hand, a few actually had gone on to bigger things over the years, like that animator Standish who as a result was now about four years overdue delivering the promised second issue of his comic.

But nothing like this. This was lightning striking.

Tedd swallowed hard and said, "Well, you can talk to the artist herself." He led Peltier to where Kaelynn sat sketching.

Peltier spoke a few words to Kaelynn, gave her his card, told her what he wanted.

It was a shriek heard five aisles away.

She sat there with both hands pressed against her mouth, her eyes wide.

Startled, her boyfriend looked up from where he was sitting on the floor just behind her and unpacking a box. He scrambled to his feet. "Kae' — what's wrong?"

She couldn't say anything. She just leaped up and hugged him, crying and laughing at the same time. Peltier stood back, smiling a little bemusedly, and let the scene play out.

The news spread quickly through the Small Press section and suddenly everyone in Artists' Alley was talking about it. Kaelynn Larrabee, an artist everyone had known for years as a regular fixture in the legion of amateurs with a low-circulation book that was well-regarded by the few who read it but otherwise considered a little too eccentric to be taken seriously as having commercial possibilities — Kaelynn Larrabee, an artist just like any other artist in the non-professional scene — had gotten the break of a lifetime.

Everyone wanted a copy of *Nutz 'n' Squoilz* to see what the buzz was about, and the Psi Press booth, already depleted after selling a dozen copies of each issue to the Toonorama reps for their production staff, sold out fast. The few other dealers on the convention floor who carried the book also sold out.

It was just the beginning.

And it would add to the legend of the convention. Aspiring comic artists and writers would tell each other that there was something magic about the convention, that every year, somebody would get their big break.

"Remember *Nutz 'n' Squoilz*? That was discovered there!"

"You're puttin' me on!"

"No! It really happened! Some producer saw it at the con and wham! Just like that! And it could happen to us!"

It usually didn't, but the dream never died completely, either.

"I guess she's an overnight success now," Josh said that afternoon, putting up the **NUTZ 'N' SQUOILZ SOLD OUT** sign over the front table of the booth, "if several years of hard work drawing that comic counts as overnight. Good thing that producer saw the latest issue instead of her first. It was pretty rough at the start, but as usual you saw something in her samples. And now look what happened. How do you do it?"

Tedd shrugged. "I liked it, that's all."

"I just hope the Toonorama people give her a good deal and don't rob her blind," Josh added a little darkly.

"I'm not worried. She's got her boyfriend to negotiate for her, and he's good at that. I know — he negotiated her deal with me."

This late in the day, the crowds were thick in the aisles. As he emerged from the mass of humanity and stepped to the front table, Arthur D. Claymore looked a little frazzled from fighting his way through the mob halfway across the convention floor to get to the Psi Press booth. As he went over to talk to him, Tedd noticed that he was carrying his well-worn portfolio, perhaps nursing one last forlorn hope that something might yet turn up.

"You were pretty decent to me yesterday," Claymore said, "so I felt I should stop and say good-bye before I head out."

"You were pretty decent yourself," Tedd replied. "That producer told us you referred *Nutz 'n' Squoilz* to him."

Claymore looked puzzled. "He did? I don't remember giving him my name. Oh wait — I guess I did. They're supposed to be paying me some-thing for pointing them to the squirrel comic. Of course, things got a little blurry after about the third drink."

"It wasn't hard to figure out. I don't think there are two artists who draw *Peanuts* imitations carrying our books around."

"How did things turn out, by the way?"

"Off the Richter scale. Kaelynn's in a meeting right now with the Toonorama people. You did her such a huge favor that I'm actually at a loss for words for how to thank you. I don't know what made you think of her book when you were talking to that Peltier guy, but..."

Claymore shrugged. "It just seemed like the right thing to do."

"I'm glad you felt that way. This isn't just big for her — it could be big for us, too. I've already gotten queries about reprint rights and distribution deals for the *Squoilz* book."

"So, are you going to expand and go big-time?"

Tedd shook his head. "Nahh, I like things the way they are. I might not be thanking you if this deal gets too big. Most likely, though, one of the major publishers will snap her up and we'll stick with the same oddball books we've been putting out all along."

"But why do you do it?" Claymore asked.

"I just like it. It's fun to find people who would never get published anywhere else and give them that little break they've never had. I like to be surprised, too, to see something in a submission I've never seen before, and I like to share it with the world. And I like the convention. Being a publisher gives me an excuse to come here every summer and get together with all the friends I've made over the years."

"And making a little money probably isn't bad, either."

Tedd winced slightly. "You may be right, but I wouldn't know. The only way to make a small fortune doing this is to start with a large one. But it's fun and I like it, so I keep doing it."

Claymore nodded. "I think I'm starting to understand."

"Like I said," Tedd added, "Kaelynn's in a meeting somewhere, but I'm sure she'd want to thank you, so I'll thank you for her." He paused, looked uncomfortable, then said, "I gave *Woofer & Tweeter* some thought. Your drawing isn't bad, but it's a little uninspired and derivative, and your gags aren't much to write home about. Later, though, it struck me that there was a hint of something deep down, a certain absurdity in your approach that would be kind of charming if you could bring it out. But you're trying so hard to be like the strips you see in the papers that you're squelching what's good about yours. I'll tell you what... Here's my card. Throw out all your old samples and draw new ones, come up with some new characters, and work on that absurd quality. Let the strip find its own way that's all your own. All I can promise is that if you do that and send me a submission, I'll take another look at your stuff."

Claymore glanced at Tedd's card, then tucked it into his shirt pocket. "I'm not sure I can convince my wife it'll be worthwhile — I'm not even sure I'm going to tell her I gave my break to a woman I don't even know — but maybe I'll give it a try. This is it, then. So long and thanks for everything."

They shook hands and Claymore left feeling a little better about things. Still, given the domestic climate back home and the daunting challenge of thinking up some new approach that was somehow "absurd" — what did Tedd mean by that, exactly? — he had a bad feeling that his comics career was already done. Unless he had some brilliant inspiration in the next few months like none he had ever had before, he doubted if he would ever take advantage of that second chance Tedd had given him.

After Claymore had gone, Josh stepped to Tedd's side. "You weren't serious about giving him another crack at it, were you?" he asked. "That was just your way of thanking him, right?"

Tedd looked thoughtful. "Both, actually. Normally, I'd stick with what I said about his stuff yesterday. It's clichéd, it's tired, and he would have been laughed out of any syndicate's office even in 1954 if he'd shown up with those samples. I'd say that if that's the best he can do at his age, it's too late for him. But think of what he did. When his own strip got turned down, he knew enough to guess what that producer might like instead. The man's got comics in him. Somewhere, anyway. I thought he deserved another shot just for that."

On his way through the convention center lobby, Claymore passed a trash bin just outside the men's restroom. He jammed his portfolio into it — old and battered as it was, he would need a new one anyway and there was no point in carrying it around empty after tossing his samples. It didn't fit in the bin very well and part of it still protruded conspicuously, but never mind. Then, realizing it was a long walk back to his hotel, where he would pick up his suitcase, check out, and catch a cab to the airport, he decided that he might as well make a pit stop while he was here.

When he came out of the restroom, he noticed that the portfolio was already gone.

*I hope whoever found it can get better use out of those characters than I could,* he thought. He went on out the doors to the street, adding to himself, *Goodbye, Woofer and Tweeter.*

# WEEKEND IN HOLLYWOOD

Chapter One: CALIFORNIA SCHEMING

Hollywood had always seemed a little bit like Mars to me.

It was big and bright, and you could see it from where I lived in the middle of Ohio... but you couldn't get there from here.

Well, welcome to Mars, Jack.

It was the summer of '67 — touted as the "Summer of Love" somewhere but that was nowhere close to the part of the country I was living in — and Dad had decided to go to Los Angeles for a doctors' convention.

Of course, there was no way Dad would be going by himself. If he was headed out to California, Mom would be going with him. Since Dad found it hard to get away from his practice, the family hadn't gone on a real vacation in years other than for a few short trips to visit relatives. I'm sure there must be plenty of interesting things to see in Toronto, but mostly we saw my grandparents' house and not much else. So Mom wasn't about to pass up a vacation in sunny California. That left the problem of what to do about the kid.

I was all for going along, if I could somehow skip the convention part of it. Presentations by medical equipment companies about the latest in stethoscopes weren't my idea of a fun-filled vacation in the state where Disneyland was just down the road. On the other hand, most of the convention would probably be restricted to members of the profession anyway, and there would be tours and other activities for the wives (and husbands, in the case of lady docs), so what was I supposed to do — sit around the hotel room all day? I'm sure Los Angeles TV was a considerable improvement over the Cleveland stations, but I couldn't park myself in front of the tube the whole time. Even bringing a suitcase full of books along would get old kind of quick.

I could just stay home, of course, and keep the place looking lived in so nobody would rob us while the parents were gone. Now that I had just turned 16, I thought I was old enough to be trusted not to burn the house down, and it wasn't like I'd have all my buddies over for wild parties every night. I didn't have that many buddies to begin with, and the ones I did have thought an exciting evening was a six-hour chess marathon. In fact, me staying home was the general direction of the way opinion was headed around the Tremaine homestead, and much as I might like to go to California, I could enjoy the holding down the fort scenario, too. I was even looking forward to it.

But Mom and Dad suddenly changed their minds.

It was a cloudy night, so I was in my room stretched out on the bed and reading a book instead of outside with my binoculars learning which dark splotch was which on the Moon. Dad knocked, then came in. Known in some circles as Dr. William S. Tremaine, he was a tall, broad-shouldered man, a bit craggy in the face, his hair still dark on top but graying at the temples, and almost old enough to be my grandfather.

"I was just talking with your mother," he began. His voice was resonant and he could give good speeches, but every once in a while some slight inflection would bring out his Canadian boyhood. Like the way he pronounced "out" almost as "oot." "She thinks we should make this a family outing. You'll be off to college in a couple of years, so we won't have too many more opportunities for all of us to do something together..."

"So I'm going?" I finished.

"I suppose if you really *want* to stay home instead of go to California, we could manage something," he conceded, "but I'd doubt your good sense. Of course, there's still the problem of how you can occupy yourself while we're at the convention itself. They do offer a babysitting service for attendees with young children, but I doubt if that's quite the right option for us."

I had a sudden vision of me as the one big kid sitting on the floor of a playroom in a circle of four- and five-year-olds while babies in diapers crawled around and a nice lady read to us from a Little Golden Book. Nope, that wouldn't fly.

As it happened, though, I'd actually given the matter some thought in case it came to this. "Well, I know some guys out there. Maybe I could go visit them during the day?"

"You know people in California...?" Dad seemed baffled that such a thing was possible. Then he remembered what I had been involved with for the last year or so. "Oh, right, that, er, hobby of yours."

Oh yes, that, er, hobby of mine... I suppose my story is typical enough. Like every American boy my age, I had grown up reading comic books. In my case it was mostly Superman because I liked the stories where he went into outer space and even at five I was a big-time astronomy buff. Eventually, comic books started seeming like kids' stuff and I drifted out of them towards regular science fiction and amateur astronomy. Then, when I was 14 or so, a kid at school showed me some Marvel comics and I was hooked again. Something new and exciting was going on that appealed to me even though I was a teenager and supposedly too old for comics. That led to writing a letter of comment to *Spider-Man*, it was printed in the letter column with my full address, and that led in turn to somebody sending me a sample copy of his amateur fan magazine, or fanzine, about comic books, especially Marvels, and before I knew it, I was writing articles for fanzines, exchanging letters with other fans all over the country—

"That's right," I said. "In fact, there's one guy I've been writing to a lot lately, a guy named Mel. In his last letter he even invited me to drop in and see him if I ended up going to California with you and Mom."

"Is he your age?" Dad asked.

"Well," I said, trying to remember what he'd said about himself in his letters, "I don't think there are too many fifty-year-old men still in high school."

"Does he seem responsible?"

"Pretty much. He's really smart, seems to know everything about anything, he's in all kinds of activities… He's even the president of his local comic-book club!"

That last didn't quite have the effect I had hoped in convincing Dad that Mel was a good gander from a mellow egg, to quote Donald Duck. Somewhat the opposite, actually. (My parents weren't exactly thrilled about me taking up with comic books again, and had occasionally hinted gently that perhaps my time could be more profitably spent on other pursuits, but they didn't really press it, probably hoping I'd grow out of funny-books on my own.) Dad changed his tack. "What about his family? Do you know anything about his parents?"

"I think he mentioned once that his father works for the IRS."

Dad choked slightly. I knew from years of dinner-table discourses what Dad thought about taxes in general and the IRS in particular. If evil had a name, if Hell had a branch office in Washington DC, the Internal Revenue Service filled the bill on all counts.

*But…* that was all theoretical stuff. Arguing politics out in the ozone was one thing, but down on the level where real people lived, Mel being the son of a respectable government official meant he probably didn't live in a broken-down trailer with a moonshine still out back.

Thus assured, Dad had an idea. I'd go along with him and Mom to California, but while they were at the docs' convention, I'd go see my friend during the day. Then, when the convention was over, Mom and Dad and I would spend a few days seeing the sights and hitting the high spots as regular tourists before getting on the plane back to Ohio. It sounded like a good plan, but the slight sticking point was having to invite myself to visit somebody I had never met and only barely knew from writing letters back and forth.

"The main thing," Dad said, "is that I want to make sure you aren't completely on your own in a strange city and somebody knows where you are. Give him a call and see what you can work out."

So I went to the phone in the living room and called Information. I didn't know Mel's father's name, but asking for the number of the Endicott family living at the address I sent letters to got results in the form of a phone number for a Mr. Leonard Endicott. Then, with full paternal approval to make a long-distance phone call all the way to California, I dialed the number. I was a little nervous since I didn't know Mel all that well, and long distance phone calls were pretty unusual. And expensive.

A woman answered the phone. "Hello?"

"Is this the Endicotts'? Is Mel there?"

"Not right now. He and his friend are down the block putting on a birthday party for one of the little neighbor boys. Should I have him call you when he gets in?"

"Er… no need," I replied, thinking it would be asking a lot to expect him to make a long-distance call just on the basis of our short acquaintance. "I'll call back. Thanks!"

I waited until the next day, then called again.

"Is Mel there?"

"No," the lady — probably Mrs. Endicott — told me, "he's over at the park district office, arranging for a place to hold the comic-book club meetings. Something about a car wash, too, but I didn't get all of it. Can I take a message?"

"Thanks, but I'll call back later."

Meanwhile, time was ticking away and nothing had been settled about where I was going to spend my days in California. Dad was getting a little antsy about it and urged me to hurry up and get the details nailed down, but it was starting to look like I might stay home after all. I tried again that evening, which would have been in the afternoon California time.

"Is Mel there?"

"I'm sorry," Mrs. Endicott said, "but he's out with his father making the rounds of all the used bookstores. Uhm… this isn't about the burping record, is it?"

"The *what*?" I blurted.

"Oh, pardon me. It's a record with somebody burping on it. Mel plays it at the children's birthday parties he puts on, and it seems to be a very popular part of the show. I don't know why he went to the trouble of learning all those magic tricks when he can just play that record. Anyway, every other day somebody calls wanting to borrow the record or have Mel play it at a birthday party, and I just thought..."

Now I knew exactly what record she meant. It was called "It's a Gas" and had come as a freebie with a special issue of *Mad* Magazine, and featured someone (supposedly the magazine's mascot character Alfred E. Neuman himself) belching along with some jazzy instrumental tune. If you were an eight-year-old boy, it would be hilarious, so I could see why it would be a popular item at kids' parties.

"You've called before, haven't you?" Mrs. Endicott went on. "Maybe you'd better leave your name so he can call you. He's always in and out, so he can be a little hard to catch..."

I started to explain that I was calling from out of town — *way* out of town — and he might not want to call long distance, but then she interrupted. "They're coming in the front door now. Wait just a moment — I'll put him on."

Pause. Then, "Hello?" He was a little younger than I was, still fifteen, but his voice sounded mature and he could have passed for quite a bit older.

"Mel? This is Jack — Jack Tremaine! Long distance from Ohio!"

"Yes, it certainly is." If there was any surprise on the other end, I didn't register it. "So, what's up?" He was polite but businesslike, perhaps mildly puzzled by why I would call him out of the blue from across the continent. Even if we already knew each other to some extent from our letters, this was upping the ante quite a bit.

I explained that I would be coming out his way in a couple of weeks and suggested that maybe we could get together while I was in the area. Even before I had fully clarified the point, he knew I was looking at a period of about three days so far unaccounted for and that my parents would like to see me put in safe hands. "No problemo!" he assured me. "You can stay here for the weekend! My folks won't mind and it'll be a heck of a lot easier than you having to commute every day all the way out here from downtown."

"Er... sure! Okay!" I was so surprised that I hardly knew what to say. Staying at his house would certainly solve the problem of where to park me for the weekend. I just hadn't expected an offer like that.

Mel seemed to consider the matter settled and changed the subject.

"Hey, did you see my letter in the new issue of *Detective*? They only printed half of it and it wasn't even the half where I talked about Bob Kane's ghost artists!"

Somehow we had gone off on a tangent talking about comics, but then that was the common interest that had brought us together in the first place. (As usual, I could only wonder how Mel *knew* the behind-the-scenes stuff about comics he did. Was there some secret newsletter that only the well-connected could subscribe to?) Dad, however, had heard enough of my end of the conversation to know that the immediate problem had been solved and I was now just running up the phone bill talking about comic books at his expense. He stepped into my field of view and tapped his wristwatch. So I switched the conversation back to getting some of the details of my forthcoming meeting with Mel finalized.

After hanging up, I explained to Dad what we had come up with. He seemed uncomfortable with the idea of my not only visiting a perfect stranger I had never met before but staying a few days with him. Actually, Mel wasn't *that* perfect of a stranger — we probably already knew each other better through the letters we had exchanged than we did a lot of people we knew in person — so it wasn't a total leap in the dark. Dad suggested a possible compromise: maybe I could get a motel room near Mel's house and just go over during the day so I wouldn't have to put his parents to any bother by spending the night or taking my meals there. In the end, keeping things simple won out, and I would take my chances with Mel's hospitality.

I went off to my room humming "California, Here I Come."

Chapter Two: GO WEST, YOUNG FAN

Now that the trip had been planned, the only thing left was to do it.

We caught a westbound plane on a Thursday morning at Cleveland's Hopkins Airport, and I spent the next few hours in a window seat on the longest plane ride of my life watching America slide by far below and change from the green of the Midwest to the brown of the West.

It occurs to me that these memoirs have so far lacked a physical description of mine own 'umble self. Not much to say, really. I was topping out at a little under six feet, about 5'10" or so, and I was a bit on the lanky side though filling out from my skinnier younger days. My hair was light brown and a little shaggy in this post-Beatle era, but that was more from being slow to get down to the barber shop now that school had let out for the summer than to follow the dictates of Fashion. As for my face... hmm. I was used to what looked back out at me when I looked in a mirror and I suppose it was reasonable enough, but if you saw my picture even without knowing me, you'd probably say, "This kid reads a lot of books!" Or at least I've been told by impartial third parties that was the impression my picture gave.

After we landed at Los Angeles International and picked up our luggage, Dad rented a car and set about navigating the dreaded Los Angeles freeways. The TV comedians were always joking about the freeways, making them sound like deathtraps, especially for sadly unprepared and pathetically doomed out-of-towners, but Dad found the traffic in the early afternoon light and the drive even pleasant.

While he drove and Mom puzzled over the city map that had come with the car, I sat in the back seat and looked out at the scenery. It was a hot, clear summer day under an achingly bright blue sky without even a trace of the legendary Los Angeles smog.

We weren't in Ohio any more. In the distance to the north was a line of low mountains — there was nothing like that back home. Where downtown Wadsworth, O., was just a couple of intersecting main streets, Los Angeles was huge, with wide boulevards that went on seemingly forever. When we left the freeway and came onto the surface streets, I saw few high buildings. Most were one or two stories, modern and new-looking, not like Wadsworth, where the buildings downtown mostly dated to something like 1910. At intervals along the streets, palm trees stood tall against the sky. Even the landscape around us was different: not as lushly green as the Midwest in the middle of summer, but drier and browner.

Mel lived in West Los Angeles, seven or so miles north of the airport. As Mom and Dad figured it out from the map, the way the streets worked was commercially zoned thoroughfares in a rough grid pattern and fronted by stores and other businesses, while narrower streets between the main avenues were zoned residential and lined with houses. We found Mel's address on a quiet street just a couple of blocks over from West Pico Boulevard. It was a relatively small one-story stucco house with a tile roof, one of many such up and down the street on both sides, with a lawn out front that probably took a lot of watering to keep green in the Los Angeles climate. The street ended in a T-intersection with a cross street some distance to the west, and beyond that was the lot of the 20th Century Fox movie studio. Now I *knew* I wasn't in Ohio any more — there certainly weren't any movie studios in *my* neighborhood.

As we pulled up at the curb, a casually dressed teenage boy came out of the house to meet us. I got out of the car and found myself shaking hands with somebody taller than I was. "You must be Jack Tremaine!" he greeted heartily. "If you aren't, boy, do you have the wrong house!"

I had just had my first sighting of Mel Endicott in person. He was a big guy with short, dark hair. Not fat, just big. He reminded me a bit of a young Elvis merged with Paul McCartney and enlarged.

The purpose of the stop was just to drop me off, but then Mrs. Endicott came out and invited Mom and Dad to stay for a few minutes and have some coffee. While Mel led me inside, kindly carrying my suitcase for me, and on to his room in the back of the house, Mom and Dad sat with Mr. and Mrs. Endicott in the front living room. Since they'd all just met, I think everybody was checking each other out, the Endicotts making sure I wasn't some juvenile delinquent being foisted on their hospitality and likely to disappear one night with the silverware, and Mom and Dad assuring themselves that I wouldn't be kidnapped and forced into a life of crime. Actually, I can't think of four more respectable, middle-class people than Mel's and my parents. Their conversation probably ended up commiserating over how it happened that no matter how normal and respectable *they* were, their sons had mutated in some strange directions.

What little of the conversation I did overhear suggested that Dad could find common ground even with a tax man — they seemed to be discussing the respective fortunes of the Dodgers and the Indians. There were also points where they didn't have common ground: Dad had trouble

taking a day off, let alone several, while Mr. Endicott was home on a week-
day because he had some vacation time he had to use or lose. They probably also discussed matters concerning my care and feeding. I think Dad
had some idea of contributing some cash to cover the damage I'd likely do
to the Endicotts' larder, but whether the offer was accepted or waved off
with an informal agreement that we'd return the favor if Mel ever found
himself out our way, I don't know.

Mel's room was furnished about like you might expect, with a bed, a
desk and chair, and a TV set on a stand. What made it a little different from
most were the walls lined with shelves. Lots of shelves. All filled with
comic books. Stacks and stacks of comic books.

To the left of a second door leading into the kitchen was some of the
little open wall space in the room, with a bulletin board hung to it. Catching
my eye was a sheet of heavy paper with drawings of Superman on it pinned
to the board. I took a closer look and realized it was more than that — it
was a page of original artwork for a Sunday newspaper *Superman* comic
strip. I even recognized the artist, who had drawn most of the stories in the
*Superman* comics I had read growing up. I couldn't remember his name,
but his eccentric style could not be mistaken for anyone else's. He was the
artist who drew Superman striding through the sky like a god instead of
flying horizontally like on the *Superman* TV show. The only question I
had was how Mel had even come by such a thing. Maybe I just hadn't been
in comics fandom long enough to find out the sources of supply for the
more esoteric collectibles like original artwork, but I couldn't even
imagine owning something like that myself. Mel did, though.

Before I could ask about it, Mel launched into a tour of the comic
books. He had *everything,* all meticulously organized. Not just superhero
comics, which were about the only thing most of us serious teenage fans
cared about, but funny animal, western, war, even off-brand hot-rod and
romance titles. If there was a comic book that got published and put out
on a newsstand somewhere, no matter how low its print-run or spotty its
distribution, Mel had it. My own collection would have easily fit into a
corner and never been noticed.

About the time we finished the tour, it sounded as though the parental
conclave in the living room was breaking up. Mom and Dad still had to
drive all the way to downtown Los Angeles and check into their hotel, so
they couldn't stay very long. I went out to settle the last few details about
when they would pick me up Sunday evening and say goodbye. Then they
were gone and it was back to Mel's room.

While I took a seat on the edge of his bed, he settled into his desk
chair and got down to business.

"So what would you like to do while you're out here?" he asked.

"Let's see…" I gave it some thought. "I definitely want to see the Griffith Observatory and the La Brea Tar Pits, but Dad wants to see them, too, and we'll be staying a few days after his convention to do the tourist stuff like that. Go to Disneyland?" Mom and Dad wouldn't be thrilled about something that would seem too much like kid stuff I was theoretically too old for, but going with Mel might be just the ticket.

Mel sighed. "I see you don't know Los Angeles geography. Disneyland is in Anaheim, *way* south of here. Since neither of us drive, we'd have to take the bus, and it would take hours and all the transfers would be a nightmare. Save it for your next trip. Any other ideas?"

"How about attending a meeting of the legendary Southern California Comic Book Club?"

"You can go if you want, but I won't be there — I told the guys I had somebody coming in from out of town so Solly, my VP, will be standing in for me. Besides, it'll just be a few die-hards anyway. There's a movie convention in Hollywood this weekend, which is where most of the members will be, including me. And you, too."

I perked up. "A movie convention…? With real movie stars and everything?" This sounded interesting. And it was actually something I could tell my friends back home about, since they were at least familiar with movies while they'd yawn over travel stories involving a comic-book club meeting.

Mel was quick to lower my expectations. "Actually, it'll be mostly dealers selling stills and lobby cards and posters, but they're supposed to be getting in some guests to sign autographs. Probably nobody really famous, though, but I never thought the big stars were all that interesting. Most were too wrapped up in their own careers to have any perspective. It's the old-time character actors and bit-players who saw it all from the inside, and they're the folks who'll talk to you."

"Maybe so," I said, "but I wouldn't know who most of those people are." It wasn't as though I hadn't watched my share of old movies on TV, and I had been known to spend a Friday evening or Saturday afternoon at the movie theater in downtown Wadsworth, so I wasn't completely unaware of who the brighter stars in the Hollywood firmament were. I just hadn't taken it to the extent Mel obviously had.

"Hmm…" he mused, as though he had never been confronted with a hard case quite this dense before, then said, "Lack of knowledge is curable. We can start on your education after dinner. Then, for the advanced course, the Silent Movie Theater is having a laugh show tomorrow night."

"A laugh show…?"

"Every few weeks the guy who runs the place does a program that's just a collection of comedy shorts, no features. It's a good way to get a sample of what's out there. Have you seen many silent comedies before?"

"Just what they show on *Fractured Flickers*..."

Mel almost fell over backwards in his chair. He stood up and raised his arms towards the ceiling beseechingly. "Oh, great Jay Ward, what hast thou wrought? I loved *Rocky and Bullwinkle*, but what moved you to mock a great art form by chopping up classics, making great stars look ridiculous by dubbing in silly modern dialogue and narration, and not even running the films at the right speed?"

I blinked, a little started by the dramatic performance. "Er... I take it *Fractured Flickers* wasn't the best introduction?"

"Hardly." Mel sat back down and took a deep breath to recover his composure. "Unfortunately, that *is* what folks think of the silents nowadays — quaint, ancient, antique, not worth saving except as scraps to laugh and sneer at... Well, I can see I have some work to do with you—"

We went on talking, mostly about comics, where I was on at least somewhat familiar ground, and he showed me some interesting things from his collection to illustrate his points. Before I realized how much time had passed, there was a knock on the door. It was Mrs. Endicott announcing that dinner was ready. Had the entire afternoon flashed by just like that?

After dinner and back in his room, Mel dove into his closet and hauled out an 8mm movie projector and a large assortment of movie reels in little boxes. I recognized the brand — Castle Films — since I'd seen them for sale in the camera department at Sears when I went in to ogle the telescopes, but I'd never known anybody who owned any. With a couple of expensive hobbies already, movie collecting was something I hadn't looked into.

"We'll start with this one," Mel said, holding up a box labeled *Have Badge Will Chase*. "It's cut down from *Abbott & Costello Meet the Keystone Kops*."

"I can't say I ever really cared for Abbott & Costello—" I started to say.

Mel looked at me like I'd just said I thought the Mona Lisa wasn't all it was cracked up to be, but left it at saying, "That's not the point. It was kind of a tribute to the old silent comedies made long after they were gone, so it makes a good introduction from a modern viewpoint. Once you get the lay of the land, you can start exploring."

He set up a screen, threaded the projector, turned off the light, and away we went. I can't say I got a whole lot out of a feature film cut down to four minutes and with no sound, but I began to see some possibilities here. Wouldn't it be great if you could go into a store and buy a copy of any movie you wanted and take it home so you could watch it any time you liked? Not chopped up like this, but the whole thing, complete? But a four-minute silent Castle film cost $6.00 retail, so a whole movie with sound would probably cost so much that most people couldn't afford to own even one, let alone a whole collection, and I gave up on the idea.

After a few more films with running commentary, we spent the rest of the evening talking about this, that, and the other thing. Eventually, Mrs. Endicott appeared in the doorway to suggest that since I must be tired after such a long trip, it might be time I thought about going to bed. I had to admit that it had been a long day, and as far as my Ohio body was concerned, it was several hours later than whatever the California clock might have been showing. Mel and his mother dug a rollaway bed out of a closet and set it up in his bedroom (not that there was a whole lot of open space for it to fit but they squeezed it in).

I may have gotten ready for bed, but there were no signs that Mel was within even an hour of following my example. He sat at his desk working on some project or other, and after saying good night, left me to get the sleep I suddenly realized I desperately needed.

I conked out at once. I woke up in the middle of the night a time or two, though, and noticed Mel was still stirring. I found out later that before he went to bed, he handwrote for later typing three letters of comment to as many different comic books (all published a few months later in the letter columns of *The Flash*, *Action Comics*, and *Batman*), wrote two fanzine articles (both also published, one in *Concussion*, the other in *Fan Focus*), and worked out a detailed itinerary for us for the next couple of days, all while he was half-watching an old movie on his TV with the volume turned down low so it wouldn't disturb me. The birds must have been chirping in the trees by the time he finally went to bed, but I can't say for sure he ever actually did. I drifted back to sleep with a gloomy feeling that I had been wasting my life up to now. I had thought my days were busy and filled with activities, but Mel's example showed me I hadn't been doing half the things I could have.

Maybe it was all a matter of organization…

Chapter Three: THE SOUND OF SILENTS

After breakfast the next morning, Mel and I walked a couple of blocks to Pico Boulevard. This was a main artery, several lanes wide and thick with traffic, lined with stores and other commercial establishments on both sides. The sky was clear again today, and the climbing sun shone down hot and bright. The mostly low, glass-fronted buildings along a street that went on until it was lost in the distance were almost blinding in the dazzling sunlight. An occasional palm tree waved in the slight breeze, and I felt as though I was under some vast blue dome arching high overhead.

Mel took me to a drug store called (what else?) Pico Drug to see what new comics had come out the day before since new issues showed up on Tuesdays and Thursdays, and I picked up a couple of Marvels I hadn't had a chance to buy in the rush to get to the airport the day before. I also bought some postcards to send to a couple of my buddies while I was at it. And unless I did it today, there was a strong chance the cards would arrive after I got back home, which would defeat the purpose of the whole thing.

From there we went to a local post office branch so I could scribble some notes on the postcards and send them on their way. When we came out, Mel announced, "Oh, and we have to stop at the market. Mom asked me to pick up a few things for her."

The "*market*"? Maybe I was thinking Ohio, but what first came to mind was a farmers' produce market, or a Medieval European-style marketplace, with people selling various odds and ends from individual stalls. It turned out Mel meant a regular grocery store, what we called a *supermarket* back home. I didn't know if it was a dialectical difference between California and Ohio, or maybe a generational thing Mel had picked up from his parents (a supermarket would be an improved version of a market, after all, so maybe people did used to say "market" for the old Mom & Pop corner-store type places). I had just never heard anyone use the word for a big modern chain grocery store before. Or since.

As we came into the store, I noticed a sign hanging overhead that read: "If we don't carry what you're looking for, we will gladly special-order it for you."

"That's a lie," Mel said, grabbing a cart and pushing it down an aisle. "They won't. Not gladly, not even grumpily."

There must have been some story behind it. Maybe he'd come to grief trying to special-order some off-brand of orange juice or something. But before I could ask him to elaborate, we came to the soft-drink section.

"What kind of soda do you like?" he asked.

"*Soda?*" I echoed blankly. "Isn't that what Moe sprays Larry and Curly with?"

Mel sighed. "No, that's *seltzer*. I mean soft drinks. Coke, Pepsi…"

The dawn broke. "Oh, you mean *pop!*"

Mel looked at me like I'd grown a straw hat and overalls. "*Pop?* You call it… *pop?*"

"Well, why not? That's what it is, isn't it?"

"Oh, brudder," he said resignedly in a Bugs Bunnyish voice and started picking up things to put in the cart.

That afternoon, Mel and I took the bus to Hollywood Boulevard so we could look in on the old comic-book stores and some lesser points of interest. I had to admit that Mel was going all out to show me the town and willingly giving up a couple of days of his busy schedule to play host. I also had to wonder what I could possibly do in return if he ever came to Ohio. I could show him my home town in fifteen minutes, and even throwing in everything worth seeing in Cleveland would leave a lot of weekend left over.

During the ride, Mel explained some of the finer points of Hollywood history that hadn't been covered in school back in Ohio. For one thing, Hollywood didn't even exist as a separate town, but was a district of Los Angeles. For another, Hollywood was more a metaphor for the movie business than the reality these days. With MGM's studio down in Culver City, 20th Century Fox's out in West Los Angeles where Mel lived, and Disney and Warner Brothers up in Burbank, Hollywood the movie industry was considerably more spread out than Hollywood the place.

The day was a little hazy but still bright and warm when we got off the bus. I looked around and saw gleaming storefronts, the usual palm trees along the street, and star-shaped plaques honoring Hollywood's great and famous embedded in the sidewalk. The traffic passing us along Hollywood Boulevard was light, but I noticed a lot more convertibles than I'd ever seen back home. On a lazy summer Friday afternoon, there were mostly tourists around us as we walked up the street, but I also saw an occasional local character, and even… *hippies!* I'd only seen them on TV before this, but there they were, long-haired guys in clothes that looked like war surplus from both sides of Little Big Horn, not to mention long-haired girls in headbands and lots of fringe. I gave that fad about another six months and then they'd be as forgotten as beatniks.

A car went by out on the street, a red '57 Thunderbird with the top down. A beautiful blonde girl wearing sunglasses was driving, and I had a sudden thought — *Is that Nancy Sinatra?* Mel was looking in that direction, too, though more at the car, it seemed, as though someday owning a '57 T-Bird himself was his greatest dream, never mind whether or not the blonde came with it.

In that moment, however, something at the corner of my eye caught my attention. Considering the driver of the T-Bird, it would have taken a lot to distract me just then, but some distance down the sidewalk stood a strange old man in an old-fashioned black suit, staring at me with piercing dark eyes over a sharply pointed nose. Our gazes met for a few seconds and I suddenly felt weirdly cold even in the warm sunlight. I blinked, and the man was gone, seemingly melted into the crowd although there wasn't really that much of a crowd on the sidewalk to melt into just then.

*That was odd*, I thought, wondering why the old man had thought I was worth staring at. I was going to mention it to Mel, but now that the Thunderbird had gone on its way without a chance to see if its gorgeous driver was really who I thought she might be, it was back to business and he proceeded to lead me to the nearest bookstore. I wasn't sure what I could say, anyway. Just a brief glimpse of one of the colorful local characters, no doubt, eccentric but hopefully harmless...

What interested me was the whole idea of stores that sold old comic books, where you could actually see the timeless treasures before forking over your hard-earned for them. This was practically unimaginable out in the backwoods where I lived and we had to go through the hassles of answering mail-order dealers' ads, hoping that the goods were still in stock when our money arrived and that they were as described in the ads when we got them. Having one store in your town like classy Collectors' Bookstore, which was right on Hollywood Blvd. at Highland and looked like it had been a bank in a former life, would have been heavenly, and having two more like the more lovably down-to-earth Cherokee Books a couple of blocks east and around the corner or the nearby Bond Street Books would have been next to Nirvana.

The eyes of any non-fans reading these memoirs would quickly glaze over if I described what I saw in any detail, so I'll just say that I feasted my optics on more classic 1940s-era comic books in beautiful condition on display in those stores than I had ever beheld before in my life, but then I hadn't beheld that many to begin with. I saw titles I had only read about, had only dreamed of, had known only from bad cover reproductions in fanzines... Unfortunately, I came out of the stores still dreaming. My stock of ready cash was limited, so I couldn't go crazy with the purchases on this trip. Dad had given me a little extra money in case of an emergency, but I doubted if I could have convinced him that seeing a copy of *Superman* #1 that I just had to have and for only a hundred dollars would have qualified as exactly urgent.

Back outside, a man passed us on the sidewalk. I didn't get a good look at him, but Mel certainly seemed impressed. "Do you know who that was?" he asked me after the man was well on his way down the street.

I shook my head and Mel told me it was somebody named Sutton, though I didn't quite catch the first name. If it was Frank Sutton, he was the actor who played Sgt. Carter on *Gomer Pyle* and I just missed seeing somebody I might have recognized. Then again, it may have been Grady Sutton, who was somebody else and I wouldn't have known him. Forgive me for not being up on minor actors.

"Does this happen to you often?" I had to ask. "Running into famous people on the street?"

Mel shrugged. "Hey, it's L.A. They live around here. Of course you see them on the street. What I like is spotting the old guys everybody else has forgotten. I even saw Billy Gilbert on the bus a month or two back. The trick is knowing whether you should say anything to them or not. There's a fine line between letting them know they're still remembered and appreciated, and just being a pest."

Good advice, I suppose, but I didn't know who Billy Gilbert was and wouldn't know him if I saw him, so I wasn't at much risk of making a pest of myself by saying something.

In between bookstores, we took in the Hollywood Wax Museum and walked past the exhibits of all the great Hollywood legends, like Marilyn with her dress billowing up, Bela Lugosi as Dracula, John Wayne, Clark Gable, and many more. I was hoping for Raquel Welch, too, but maybe she was too recent to be considered a screen immortal. We also squeezed in a walk around the courtyard of Grauman's Chinese Theater down the street to the west to see the handprints and autographs of the stars preserved in cement on the pavement. I realized that it had to be painfully basic tourist-trappy stuff for Mel, but he wasn't doing it for himself. It was part of furthering my education.

The afternoon was wearing on, so we decided to call it a day and went back on the bus to West Los Angeles. We had just enough time to clean up a bit when the doorbell rang at about five-thirty.

As he'd promised the day before, Mel had penciled in the Silent Movie Theater for the evening's entertainment. One of his friends, a slightly older guy named Dave Steiner who was already driving, had come by in his (or his parents') car to pick us up.

Dave was even taller than Mel, but amazingly skinny — I think I've seen clothesline poles with more meat on them — and topped with a thatch of brown hair that hadn't seen a comb in a week or two. He was an interesting guy to listen to, in small doses anyway. I think he knew more about old movies than even Mel did, but Mel had lots of different interests, like comics, while Dave didn't seem to be interested in anything *but* movies.

We hadn't eaten dinner yet, so the first item on the agenda was a stop at Farmers' Market. (For once Mel was calling something a market that really was a market.) We picked up our food from the vendors at the various stalls and took it to one of the many tables out on the open courtyard. This was "dining out" taken a bit literally, but hardly unpleasant since it was a warm and clear evening.

Mel and Dave talked as we ate. Much of it was movie trivia way over my head, but I gathered that Dave helped out now and then at the Silent Movie Theater and kept Mel informed of what new movies the owner had gotten hold of. "New" is relative, of course, since everything the theater showed had been made before 1930, but the owner was always tracking down old films he had never shown before and sometimes were thought to be completely lost until they turned up in some dusty warehouse or forgotten vault somewhere. Since it was the only theater of its kind left, private film collectors often donated their dupes as a way of showing support and to help keep the old silents alive by letting them be shown to appreciative audiences again, the way they were meant to be.

However, what Dave was telling Mel through mouthfuls of a barbeque beef sandwich sounded like it was unusual even for this place. "Like I told you over the phone the other night, it was the darnedest thing. The film just showed up the other day, left on the doorstep in its original packing crate. An anonymous donation, I guess, since nobody can figure out where it came from. And it's in great shape, too, no frames missing or anything."

Mel glanced at me. "You lucked out, Jack. You showed up just in time to see a real find."

"What is it?" I asked.

"A Chubby Dale short nobody knew even still existed."

I tried to express the appropriate reaction of awe-struck amazement at hearing such astounding news, but to be honest, I hadn't even known Chubby Dale had existed.

The Silent Movie Theater was a plain white building on Fairfax just south of Melrose, and across the street from a high school. Although a big sign across the front read **OLD TIME MOVIES**, the place looked less like a theater and more like just any other building along the street. I thought at first it might have started out as a flower shop or something along that line, but Mel assured me that it had been originally built in 1942 as the theater it still was. Anyway, there was a feeling of a kind of friendly shabbiness to it.

The doors opened at 7:00 but people were already milling around on the sidewalk out front when we arrived at 6:30. They were apparently regulars since Mel seemed to know most of them, ranging from kids our age or younger to old people who had probably seen the movies when they were current, and even a couple of families.

Then, standing off to one side of the crowd, I noticed an old man with a hawk nose and weirdly piercing eyes under massive brows. If I was sure of anything, it was that he was the same old man I had seen on Hollywood Boulevard earlier that day. Just like before, he was staring at me a bit too obviously for my liking. I blinked and looked again but he was gone, perhaps having slipped behind somebody standing between us. A minute or two later, I caught another glimpse of him, some distance away from where I had seen him the first time, still staring at me. I moved to get a better look at him, wondering why anyone would even want to look at me, but I lost him. *Was that weird or what?* I certainly couldn't explain it, so with a shrug I left the inexplicable to twist in the wind on its own.

Meanwhile, I had come up to the front of the building where a row of hand-made posters was hung up. Pinned to a board next to the box-office window were faded old stills and lobby cards illustrating the evening's program. Even I had heard of Charlie Chaplin, but who was this droopy-moustached guy named Snub Pollard? Another home-made poster, with an obvious rushed look to it, billed Chubby Dale, showing a young fat man in a vest with a star on it and a big-brimmed black hat something like a cowboy's chasing a couple of overall-wearing farm boys with a butterfly net.

"We're in for a treat, folks," I heard Mel announce to the crowd, and he launched into an impromptu lecture about the life and career of Chubby Dale. People gathered around him, many apparently assuming this was an official part of the evening show, not only sanctioned but organized by the management to warm the crowd up and give them a little background about what they were going to see so they could better appreciate it. But no, it was just Mel's voluntary contribution to the proceedings.

I wish I could have tape-recorded his lecture for posterity, but it would have been obsolete in a couple of days anyway. As nearly as I can remember what he said, though, to understand Chubby Dale, you first have to understand Roscoe T. Arbuckle, better known as Fatty. Back about 1920, Fatty Arbuckle was one of America's top stars in those distant bygone days of really ancient silent comedy, with a salary of a million dollars a year when that was some serious money. That kind of success attracts imitators, and so some long-forgotten studio called Ganton Lumiscope found a similar-looking performer in vaudeville named Eddie Grimes, renamed him Chubby Dale, and put him in a series of two-reel comedies shamelessly mimicking the Fatty formula. That is, they featured a boyish, good-looking young fat man who was light on his feet and fairly acrobatic despite his weight and girth. Like Fatty, he projected a good-natured persona, easy-going but quick-thinking when the situation was dire. There was enough room in that particular niche for both Fatty and Chubby to prosper, and some said Chubby's comedies were actually better. The problem was that Fatty had gotten there first and his films had much wider distribution, so Chubby was always a distant second even though still reasonably successful.

Then came 1921. Fatty Arbuckle was caught up in a terrible scandal involving a hotel room, a wild party, and a dead girl. Fatty was eventually cleared of any guilt for the girl's death, but by then his career had been destroyed. Meanwhile, at Ganton Lumiscope's studios, it looked for a moment as though their time had come. With Fatty's movies being banned everywhere and the newspapers making Fatty Arbuckle hated throughout the country and the world as a fiendish murderer, the way was clear for Chubby Dale to take his place as the reigning comedy star.

It didn't happen. Chubby looked too much like Fatty. In a lot of places around the country, people had the idea that Chubby *was* Fatty. Either they thought the depraved monster had simply changed his name in a cynical attempt to fool the public or else they had just never been clear on the difference in the first place. It was 1921, movies were still fairly new, and not much was understood about them out in the hinterlands. Even where the public knew perfectly well that Chubby wasn't Fatty, people now hated Fatty so much that they didn't want to buy tickets to see somebody who looked like him, either, and theaters refused to show Chubby's films as well. Ganton Lumiscope's own cynical attempt to fool the public by making Chubby just like Fatty had backfired disastrously. By early 1922, Chubby's career was in ruins right along with Fatty's.

The collapse was so sudden that it caught Chubby flat-footed. His vices were probably mild by most standards, but he did have a gambling habit that he had been able to support comfortably when he was making a good income. When the inbound flow of cash was abruptly cut off, he might have been considerably in debt and now had no likelihood of ever being able to pay it.

In the spring of 1922, somebody murdered Chubby Dale in a restaurant parking lot. No one was ever charged. To the extent that anybody even remembered Chubby Dale afterwards, there was some speculation that his gambling debts had been what led to his death. It was even said that given what happened to Fatty Arbuckle as the scandal dragged on, Chubby had been the lucky one.

And then Chubby Dale was forgotten.

About the time Mel wound up his lecture, the theater's doors were opened and we lined up to buy our tickets.

Inside, we found a cramped, stuffy little auditorium with about 150 hard wooden seats facing a screen. Small-town theaters in the Teens and early Twenties had probably looked something like this, which did add to the atmosphere. We would be seeing silent movies the same way people back then did. On the way to our seats in the third row, the best spots in the house based on Mel's years-long experience with the theater, I thought I saw the strange old man again, on the other side of the room, but I couldn't be sure.

When everyone was seated, the lights dimmed and the show began with a rattling projector. A Felix the Cat cartoon was first up on the laugh show program, but I can't say I really enjoyed it. Silent, black and white, more weird than funny. Then, as a scratchy jazz record played as accompaniment somewhere, Snub Pollard, the droopy-stached comedian whose poster I had seen outside, appeared as a wacky inventor in a live-action short called *It's a Gift* (1923). It was a look into a vanished world with funny old cars, somehow ghostly and unreal since it was silent and in black and white, the shadows that were all that was left of yesterday. Snub's inventions were pretty clever, though, even if there was a lapse of logic at the end concerning the propulsion of his "magnet car."

Mel leaned over and muttered in my ear, "Snub's real name was Fraser. He wasn't Daphne Pollard's brother like a lot of people think."

That was no doubt a good piece of information to know, so I tucked it away in my mental archives on the chance that it might come in handy someday. Like when I found out who *Daphne* Pollard was.

Snub was followed by a Charlie Chaplin short (*By the Sea*, 1915), which just seemed like twenty minutes of overexposed black and white silliness shot at some California beach. It was so primitive that I couldn't really get into it. "A lot of people have that reaction now," Mel assured me, "but if you compared it to what other comedians were doing in 1915, this was way ahead of the game."

Then came a Chase Brothers short (*Excuse Our Crust*, 1926). Even I had heard of the Chase Brothers, since their '30s era sound shorts were occasionally shown along with the more typical *Our Gang* shorts (same distribution package most likely) on kiddie shows on TV where I lived. Mel's whispered lowdown: "After Harold Lloyd left in 1923, the Hal Roach studio was really hard up for new stars. *Our Gang* was the biggest series Roach had. The Chase Brothers — who really were brothers, Charley and Jimmie, though their real name was Parrott — were about as good as he could get, and they transitioned to sound nicely, but they just weren't the major success Roach needed. Comedy shorts were pretty much dead by 1936 anyway, killed off by double features, though a few series like the Three Stooges lasted a lot longer. The Parrott boys both had their own problems, and neither lived very long after that."

After that, we saw the long-lost Chubby Dale comedy, probably its first public showing in 45 years or more: *Chubby's School Daze* (1921). Despite its age, the film was in perfect condition, every frame a clear window on a diamond-hard world of black and white, an astonishing contrast to the worn-down old films we had just seen. This must have been how the first-run audiences back in 1921 saw it. Chubby played some rural county's truant officer, rounding up wayward little boys in a truck that was probably modeled after a dogcatcher's. When he'd accumulated a good-sized load, he'd drop the boys off at the one-room schoolhouse presided over by the sweet young teacher who was also his girlfriend in the film. As Chubby kissed her goodbye in the school doorway before going back out on the road to look for more truants, some boys were seen in the background slipping out the window, so his work was never really done. Two boys in particular eluded his butterfly net, and even cooked up all kinds of dirty tricks to play on him. In the last part, however, the boys got into trouble with their rowboat and were about to go over a waterfall, and Chubby had to save them. But saving the boys left Chubby about to go over the falls himself, and the boys had to save *him,* leading to some tentative handshakes and sheepish thanks and apologies all around... and in the end Chubby and the boys were sitting on the riverbank fishing together. Fadeout.

The film was certainly interesting, especially considering the circumstances of its rediscovery, but whether it was a long-lost masterpiece of movie history... that I wasn't so sure.

The rest of the show was probably the usual Silent Movie Theater fare, one short film after another, often scratched with frames missing, and featuring comedians mostly long forgotten. Who even remembered *Lord Limey*, let alone the name of its star, the short-lived series that replaced Chubby Dale's on the Ganton Lumiscope roster, about a perpetually baffled English aristocrat who could never quite figure out American customs?

Mel knew something about every short we saw. Like: "Watch Billy Bevan trying to eat oyster stew with a live oyster in it. Curly redid this scene practically frame for frame in a Three Stooges short about twenty years later." Again, I could only wonder — How did Mel *know* this stuff?!

When the show was over, we all filed out of the theater and Mel and I went with Dave back to the car. I didn't see the old man again, but somehow I knew he was there, watching me. Don't ask me *how* I knew. I just… knew.

By this time, I wasn't even disturbed by it. Just curious as to what it was all about, not that I was ever likely to find out. I did mention the old man to Mel, though not without wondering if that would just make him think his Buckeye buddy was *completely* nuts. I hadn't needed to worry.

"I've seen him around for the last couple of weeks, too," Mel said. "Sometimes old guys like that are silent actors who come by to see their films again, but if he is, I can't place him."

"Who are you talking about?" Dave asked.

Mel explained. "Skinny old guy wearing a suit that looks like he bought it in 1928, always sits way in the back, stares at you like he's trying to drill a hole through you by sheer power of concentration."

"That's funny," Dave replied a little blankly. "I spend a lot of time at the Theater, but I've never seen anybody like that."

Mel and I glanced at each other. For once he seemed just as puzzled by something as I was, with no immediate answer. But rather than continue trying to explicate the inexplicable, we let it drop. "So, what did you think of the show, Jack?" Mel asked.

I was still sorting that out, but managed to answer the question with, "It was great. I've never seen this stuff before. It was a whole new world."

Actually, though, it had been almost too much of a good thing, and maybe too much all at once. Besides, even if I did get inspired to become a fan of silent comedy, where would I go to see more films like that back home? The world may be full of wonderful things, I decided, but what it doesn't have is enough time or opportunity to do all of them justice even though Mel certainly seemed to be giving it a good try. Seeing a show at the Silent Movie Theater looked like it would be just one more interesting thing I did on my summer vacation, but I seriously doubted if it would lead anywhere.

From there it was back to Mel's house. After Dave dropped us off, Mel and I hit the hay early. Tomorrow was the convention, so it would be a big day.

Chapter Four: CONVENTION OF BROKEN DREAMS

We got an early start the next morning. On the way from the front door to the street, Mel waved to his next-door neighbor, an attractive woman in her 30s who was out working in a flower bed by her house. She was an actress, he told me, and had a small but regular part on a current TV show. It was a show I didn't watch, though, and I promptly forgot which one it was, so I couldn't brag about seeing her to my friends later. Once again I could only marvel over how *immersed* Mel was in TV and movies. I certainly didn't have any TV stars for neighbors.

We caught a bus down on Pico and headed back to Hollywood. This time we ended up at some ordinary-looking building on a side street that seemed to be a women's club that rented itself out to groups wanting a hall when the ladies of the club didn't need it for their own meetings.

Today, it was the venue of MovieCon, my first fan convention of any kind, though I had read enough about comics and science-fiction cons in fanzines to have some idea of how they worked. At the door, we paid the price of admission to a bored-looking woman who was probably the organizer's wife, sitting by herself at a small table with just a cash box and some pin-back badges on it.

Once we were inside, I looked around and at first I was a little disappointed. This was not the extravaganza of Hollywood glitz and glamour I would have expected for a movie convention. It was just a big room, like the American Legion hall back home, with a lot of dealers selling their wares from rows of tables. The fans I saw ranged from teenagers my age to adults well advanced in years, mostly male. There were a few females of various ages, but the odds wouldn't have been good for making a date. The number of attendees barely outnumbered the dealers, and I had a bad feeling that neither the organizer nor the dealers were going to be happy with the day's receipts.

*This isn't a convention*, I thought, *it's a flea market!*

But taking a closer look at what was on sale, like movie-themed magazines, books, and toys, records of soundtrack music, and other memorabilia, even reels of film, I started to have second thoughts. Colorful movie posters were hung up everywhere, while fans flipped through boxes of lobby cards and stills on the tables. What flea market back home would have stuff like *this?* That alone made up somewhat for the slightly seedy look of it all.

Along with the dealers' tables and a room off to the side where movies were being shown, there was an additional, sectioned-off row of tables in the back. Here sat the guests, ready to sign autographs, sell pictures of themselves, or even chat about their careers.

"Let's go meet some of the folks first, before things get too crowded," Mel said, pinning his badge to his shirt and leading me past the dealers' tables to the guests' area. On the way, we passed several people Mel knew. We even saw Dave Steiner, though he was too busy just then poring through a box of lobby cards on one dealer's table in the hope of finding display material for the Silent Movie Theater to more than mumble a quick "Hi" to us.

We started at the far right end of the guests' tables, where a black man in later middle age sat by himself at a two-man table by the wall. Apparently whoever was supposed to sit next to him and share the table hadn't shown up. A card identified him as:

**RUSSELL BALDWIN**
**("I. B. TOOTIRED / DEUCES WILDE")**

As we came up, a twentyish black college student (I guessed) with an enormous Afro was arguing with him: "Man, how could you play parts like that?"

To which Mr. Baldwin replied mildly, "That was just how times were back then, and I had a wife and kids to support, so I had to take what I could get. Besides, watch some of my pictures again. I usually had things figured out before anybody else, and if I didn't want to go into the mummy's tomb where people had already been killed, who was showin' he had some common sense? I wasn't a fool."

As Mel explained it in a low voice, Baldwin was best known for his I. B. Tootired character, which was a stereotype that was no longer popular, to say the least. (The name came from his trademark catchphrase: when asked to do the least bit of work, he'd protest: "I'm like a bicycle!") He might have been completely forgotten if it hadn't been for the recent rediscovery of a stash of films long believed lost. It turned out he'd had a second career in the '40s as *Deuces Wilde, Harlem Detective*, in a series of feature films made for black audiences and seldom shown outside the inner cities or the rural South. The movies made up for their low budgets with snappy dialogue and tight plotting, and judging by the publicity photos he was selling of himself in his younger days, Russell Baldwin could wear a fedora and a trench coat with the best of them. Film historians were showing him some respect now, and one critic said the movies gave new meaning to the term "*film noir*." There was even talk of a major studio doing a new *Deuces Wilde* movie with a decent budget, though Mel had some five-minute lecture on how few proposed movies ever actually saw the light of a projector bulb and not to believe any rumors about a movie being made until you were actually waiting in line at the box office to buy a ticket for it and maybe not even then.

Meanwhile, Mr. Baldwin's critical fan had gone elsewhere and Mel stopped briefly at the table.

"Hi, Russ."

"How y'doin', Mel?"

Some tinny soundtrack noise from the movie room drifted into the main hall, with gunshots, screeching tires, and the grunts and thuds of a fistfight. Mr. Baldwin jerked a thumb in that direction. "They're playin' one of *my* pictures," he said, smiling proudly, and somehow I knew it wasn't a movie with I. B. Tootired.

"I shouldn't have to ask this," I said when Mel came away, "but... you know each other?"

"Sure," Mel replied matter-of-factly. "It's like I told you the other night, character actors like Russ tell the best stories. He worked for years with *everybody*. Someday I've got to sit him down with a tape recorder!"

According to the card on the table next to Mr. Baldwin, the no-show was somebody named Johnson. "Too bad you missed him," Mel said. "That's the Johnson of Epke & Johnson, an old comedy team from the '30s. After Epke retired, Johnson went solo doing a ventriloquist act with a dummy named Mr. Mumbles. It's the only ventriloquist act I've ever seen where it's the *dummy* who drinks a glass of water while he talks. Wonder why he didn't show up today?"

Mr. Baldwin overheard us. "He called — said he couldn't make it because Mr. Mumbles wasn't feelin' good."

I had to think about that for a second, but Mel cut me off before I could say anything. "Ventriloquists get really attached to their dummies," he said with a shrug.

At the next table sat a sixtyish woman named Polly Zinger. Mel informed me that she was the last surviving member of the Zinger Brothers, who had been something like the Marx Brothers back in the '30s, only without the extreme characters and not nearly as well-known. Brought in as a replacement when one of the Brothers had to drop out in the middle of filming a movie for unspecified "health reasons" possibly related to alcohol, she was known thereafter as Polly the Zinger Zister. I thought that should have made them the Zinger Ziblings, but Mel said "Zinger Brothers" had already been trademarked and "sibling" wasn't exactly a word that rolled off the tongue. Besides, there was a girl in the *X-Men* comic book, wasn't there? The act might have been better known, Mel added, if it hadn't come to an early and sudden end with everybody suing each other, their agent, and the studio in some complicated dispute over who owed whom how much.

Mel paused long enough at the table to say "Hi, Polly," and she replied, "Oh, hi, Mel. Call me when you want to do that interview."

Next to Polly Zinger sat a woman of about forty. She was overweight and overly made-up, with way too many rings and bracelets, and her hair was bleached beyond recovery and a little too bouffant. She had probably been beautiful once but the ravages of a hard life had left lines in her face and drooping jowls, and her constant smoking didn't help.

"That's Sweet Little Arlene," Mel muttered to me.

Even I knew something about her. Whatever her real name was, she had been known as Sweet Little Arlene since she was about four and was a former child star who had never gone on to adult roles. She seemed like such an icon of the distant past that it was a little surprising to realize she wasn't all that old and was actually younger than my mother.

In front of not so little Arlene's table, a rather intense-looking girl with long dark hair and glasses and a camera dangling on her chest from a neck strap held out her autograph book. "What an exciting childhood you must have had!"

Arlene glared sourly at the girl, as though she had heard it all a hundred times before and hadn't much liked hearing it the first time. The girl didn't see the storm clouds gathering on Arlene's face and brightly burbled on. "All that Hollywood glamour and all the fame and money — I wish I could have been you!"

"You do, do you?" Arlene leaned over forward, smiling. Her voice was deadly cold, the smile about as friendly as that of a skull on a poison bottle. "I never even *had* a childhood! I always had to work instead!" Her voice rose. "My mother and the studio stole my childhood from me! And then, when I wasn't quite so cute any more, the studio dumped me! I was a has-been before I had my first bra!" By this time she was just about shrieking. "I wish I could have been *you!*"

"Well, I'm sorry!" the girl exclaimed, not sounding very, and bolted off in near terror.

Arlene settled back in her chair, arms folded across her chest, and looked so angry that no one dared approach her for some time after that. I had no doubt that Mel knew her, but even he gave her a wide berth for the time being.

The next guest down had the only table where fans were crowding around. At first we couldn't see who it was through the mob, but Mel knew most of the fans as members of the comic-book club. "If I had my gavel," he said, "we could have today's meeting right here." Then we had a glimpse of the man behind the table, and even a jaded fan like Mel showed some distinct if faint signs of excitement. "I need to talk to him because I want to interview him for an article," he explained.

The celebrity in question was a local TV horror movie host, and of course I was familiar with the concept since until just recently we'd had Ghoulardi doing the same sort of thing on Cleveland TV. He was a tall, gaunt-looking man in dead-white facial makeup and wearing a threadbare black suit and a top hat, with a tied ribbon for a necktie. Behind him was a big sign with his picture and the words:

# DR. M. BALMER.
# He puts the FUN in FUNERALS!

The effect seemed to be trying for faded elegance, like a 19th Century undertaker who wasn't any too prosperous, but overdoing it by making him creepy and kooky, mysterious and all together ooky. It was a little lost on me since I knew a girl back home who was a funeral director's daughter, and her father wasn't at all creepy, kooky, mysterious, or even ooky. In fact, he looked just like any other small-town businessman, not like this character. Then again, Victoria was a horror and mystery buff, and she probably would have preferred it if her father *had* looked like Dr. M. Balmer.

"I think I'll go take a look at some of the dealers' tables while you do that," I said to Mel, thinking I could afford a still or two from some favorite movie as a souvenir of my trip.

Mel nodded, probably realizing I wouldn't be all that interested in somebody who only appeared on Los Angeles TV. "Fine. I'll catch up with you when I'm done here and introduce you to some of the guys."

While Mel went up to talk to the fun-loving funeral director, I turned to go—

And came face to face to face with the old man. *That* old man. The one I had seen at the Silent Movie Theater and before that on Hollywood Boulevard. His blazing eyes were barely a foot away from mine, seeming to burn a hole right through me.

"Come with me!" he said in a resounding voice I heard in my mind, not with my ears.

Startled, I stumbled back a step.

In fact, I took one step backwards too many — and fell off the world.

Suddenly I was floating over a vast sea of lights. Hundreds of feet above Los Angeles at night was my guess. Dark, brooding mountains to the north, an empty blackness to the west where the Pacific would be, beneath me an endless gridwork of brightly lit city streets — it had to be L.A. Around me were a few scattered clouds lit from below, and above me was a black sky sprinkled with the few bright stars I could see in the glare.

I flailed in panic for a moment, then realized I wasn't falling and relaxed. I wondered how I had gotten here just like that, especially since it had been broad daylight a few seconds ago. I felt very much alive — I was still breathing, and I could feel my heart beating when I put my hand on my chest, so it wasn't as though I had dropped dead at the movie convention and my soul was on its way to the next world. Despite being half a mile high at night, I felt warm, even comfortable. No matter how impossible it seemed, it was too real to be a dream. I should have been worrying about how I was going to get back down from way up here, but all I could do was wait to see what happened next.

Before very long, I became aware of a presence next to me. It was the old man, taking shape from the surrounding atmospheric vapor. I could see him clearly in the light shining from beneath us — first he was just a misty form, then he was human but transparent, and within moments he was solid.

"I suppose you can explain this?" I said.

"Certainly," he replied now that there was enough of him to talk. He floated alongside me and waved his arm at the lightscape below. "There is an anomaly down there," he said in an elegant voice and diction that made a simple statement sound as though he was delivering the State of the Union address. "It must be corrected."

"Oh?" I looked down at the lights. "Looks all right to me…"

The old man glared at me. "It would hardly be apparent from a superficial glance. No," he went on, looking down again, "there is a disruption in the flow of time and events. It can be sensed on a much higher level than this as a disturbance in what should be an orderly pattern. It must be corrected to prevent further damage that might accumulate to the point of being irreparable." He looked back at me, his eyes burning with a fierce determination. "Someone must correct the error, and I have chosen — *you!*"

I would have fallen off my cloud if I had been sitting on one — and *if* I could have fallen. I seemed to be firmly stuck in that one spot in mid-air, however, and all I could do was gasp. "*Me?* But… who… why… *what* do you want me to do?"

"The full ramifications are lost in the fine detail and are not apparent even to me," the old man said, "but I can say this much. Chubby Dale should not have died. You must prevent his murder."

45

I gulped. He planned to send me back in time something like 45 years, just so I could get involved in a violent incident involving criminals and gunplay? I was just barely 16... I didn't feel up to this.

"Hey, wait a minute! Who says I have to do anything? Just who are you, anyway?"

"I have no name," he replied quietly. "I do not even exist as you see me. You might think of me as the avatar of a higher level entity entirely outside the universe as you conceive it. My function is to maintain the order of things."

It sounded as though he was saying he was "from another dimension," but even if he'd had a name, I doubted if making him say it backwards would get rid of him for 90 days. It was more that he existed on a scale where human beings were no more than just interesting patterns in a tiny corner of the overall immensity of a super-cosmos I couldn't begin to imagine. Concepts like justice, fairness, or compassion had nothing to do with it — if Chubby had to be saved, it was only to make some abstract pattern come out right.

"So why do you need me?" I asked, in a tone that was probably a little more surly than was proper in addressing a being with the power to squash me like a bug if he felt I was wearing out my usefulness. "If you're so powerful, why can't you do the job yourself? Can't you just wave your hand and make it so?"

"There is a certain difficulty of fine-degree focus," the old man replied with somewhat strained patience.

The best I could make out from the explanation that followed was that what I was seeing wasn't a physical body in the usual sense, or even the higher level entity itself, but some kind of projection, with the old man the infinitely fine tip of a very long extension and his form a copy of some real person observed somewhere. Imagine a scientist probing the interior of a single cell with a needle honed to such near-infinite sharpness that he could inject something into the nucleus, but the slightest jiggle at his end would send the needle tip flying far away, relatively speaking. Something like that was going on here. I was on the level of the cell nucleus talking to the tip of the needle, while the being controlling the needle was inconceivably vast and distant. The old man could do some things in manipulating events and time, but he didn't have the fine-tuned control for the really close-in work that required finesse and on-the-spot judgment by somebody who lived down here and knew the territory. Since he had limitations, he wasn't God, or even *a* god, but still, in back of the old man was something so unthinkably colossal and awesome that it hurt my brain to even try to think about it.

"That is why I require your assistance," he finished.

"But why did you pick me?" I demanded, though I really wanted to ask why something that had happened 45 years ago was suddenly a problem that had to be solved *right now* — but I just figured that cosmic entities move on a different time scale than we do and complaining about it wouldn't get me anywhere. "Why didn't you get somebody like Mel Endicott, who actually knows all about this stuff?"

The old man's expression and voice showed some human-like signs of irritation. "What makes you think he was not in fact my first choice? Unfortunately, he insisted on correcting me on minor matters of fact, and he had the insufferable habit of usually being right. Because there is a certain degree of imprecision at this extent of projection, I am not always the omniscient being you may think I am, and I am not entirely immune from error, but I prefer not to argue with my delegated agents about trivial details. I decided to start over and so I expunged his brain of all memory of his encounter with me, reasoning that someone else with little or no knowledge at all would be more amenable to instruction."

"Thanks for the compliment." I muttered.

The old man nodded but didn't pick up on my sarcasm. "Still, the agent had to be trained. Young Mr. Endicott did well in teaching you the basic history of the cinematic artform."

That made me feel a little uneasy. Had Mel's friendliness and hospitality all been merely the result of robo-mind control from on high? And what about Mom and Dad's sudden insistence that I had to go with them to California? Had everything that happened so far on this trip been planned from the start? "You *made* Mel tell me all that stuff and take me around places…?"

"Not at all. He did that entirely on his own. He *enjoys* sharing his remarkably extensive knowledge with others. I am merely taking advantage of a suitable subject he was accommodating enough to prepare for me, however unwittingly, and I was certain such a subject would appear if I observed him long enough. Now that you know the background, it is time to set you about your task."

Before I could remind him that he had forgotten about the part where he asked me if I even wanted to do this task in the first place, the lights beneath me began to spin — I was dropping towards them — I tried to yell but couldn't even breathe — and some of the lights down below were going out, large black areas were appearing, other lights were turning dim — Los Angeles was contracting as time ran backwards — and then I was *there*.

Chapter Five: ONCE UPON A TIME IN HOLLYWOOD

I stood in a small circle of weak light on a street corner, next to a very old-fashioned lamppost. It was night, clouded over with a light drizzle, and a little chilly, probably sometime in the spring, and early spring at that.

A car chugged past me on the dimly lit street. It was a car straight out of all those ancient films I had seen the night before, from back when cars still looked like motorized farm wagons, a car that I wouldn't have seen back home outside of some classic car show. A couple walked by on the sidewalk, the man in a hat and a long coat, the woman wearing a close-fitting cap and a long coat with a fur collar. I looked up the street, shivering in the cool air since I didn't have a coat to wear over my short-sleeved shirt. It was a commercial district, but the buildings were small and widely spaced, with few lit signs and only some sparse and ineffective streetlamps on the corners. Wherever I was, it was not the year 1967. This had to be Los Angeles in 1922. Not the dreamlike shadows of an old black and white movie, but hard and *real* — not only in color and sound but in 3-D. Unfortunately, it was also cold and damp. The weather in southern California wasn't always warm and clear.

I had read about things like this happening to dauntless heroes in comic books and science fiction, but they just accepted it as a matter of course and did their heroic deeds without too much thought over the why and how of it. Now that it had happened to me in real life, some part of me wanted to run around screaming that it was impossible — but I was here just the same, and all I could do was get on with things.

I had materialized in front of a white, one-story wood-frame building. Above the porch roof was a starkly lighted, painted board sign reading: **VITO'S ITALIAN RESTAURANT**. What was it Mel had said in his lecture the night before…? Chubby Dale had been murdered in a restaurant parking lot? This was a restaurant, but it had a front porch that was right on the sidewalk. Maybe the parking lot was in the back. This was 1922 and cars were just now becoming common, so business establishments might not have completely adjusted yet.

Since I had been set down here at this particular place and moment,

Chubby was probably inside the restaurant right now. All I would have to do, it seemed, was go inside, find him, and warn him that there was trouble, and my job would be done. Besides, it was getting cold outside without a jacket, and it would be warm inside. I could have used Deuces Wilde's trench coat right about now. Heck, I could have used Deuces Wilde. Solving crimes and preventing murders was a detective's job, not a teenager's...

*Is this trip really necessary?*

The sudden thought brought me up a little short as it finally began to sink in where I was and why I was here. Chubby Dale was an obscure, forgotten comedian who had died thirty years before I was born. The old man had said his death was an anomaly, but the world had seemed perfectly able to get along without Chubby anyway. He may have been a most excellent fellow who hadn't deserved to die so young, but if you wanted to right the wrongs of history, why start with him? I could think of any number of far more important people whose deaths I'd rather go back in time to prevent. Why did I have to save *this* guy's life? What if I refused? That may have sounded a little cold, since I didn't really *want* Chubby to die, but what if I just said, *Get yourself another boy for this job because I won't do it?*

The answer came as a voice I heard inside my head: *You would like to return to your own era, would you not?*

I couldn't tell if it was my own voice of reason or if the old man could read my mind and had sent me a friendly little message of encouragement, but I turned and started up the steps to the restaurant.

A well-dressed couple was on the porch ahead of me. The man opened the door for the woman and I caught a whiff of warm and savory spaghetti-enriched air from inside. The couple were met by a host in black tie and coat, and I realized the place was fairly swanky. That meant that dressed like I was in a casual shirt and slacks, without a tie or even a jacket, I wouldn't be allowed in, or at least not through the front door.

*Then let's try the back.* I turned and walked around to the side of the building. There was a wide yard between the restaurant and the next building, with a sidewalk leading to the back and lit by a couple of not very bright outside lights. Light shone through the curtained windows as I passed them.

In the rear was a graveled lot between the restaurant and an alley. The light wasn't much better here than in the side yard despite the back windows and a porch light. Several parked cars filled about half the lot and some garbage cans stood along the alley.

Not wanting to be seen if the bad guys were already here and waiting, I kept to the shadows and scouted the premises. No lurking figures were obviously in sight, and no one was in the flivvers except for a man and a woman sitting in the dark in the front seat of one, apparently just talking, and they seemed harmless. Waiting for friends to arrive, maybe, or engaging in a little making out. It wasn't something I cared to watch, so I turned my attention elsewhere. The bad guys hadn't shown up yet, it looked like.

The restaurant's back door opened, revealing a brightly lit kitchen within. A man in a white apron and chef's hat came out, dumped something in a garbage can on the porch, then went inside and shut the door again.

I wouldn't be going in that way, either. If anything, it would be worse than the front door, where I'd only have to dodge one host. If I tried to go in the back door, I'd have to pass through a kitchen filled with cooks and waiters who would take exception to non-staff wandering in without a good reason for being there.

As I wondered how I could possibly get inside the restaurant, two cars with shining headlights came up the alley, turned into the lot with a crunch of gravel under the tires, and parked next to each other. The headlights and motors were turned off, the doors opened, and four adults and several kids of various ages piled out. They all seemed to be members of the same party and gathered into a single group, then started up the sidewalk towards the front.

Now I had it. I emerged from the shadows and followed the last of the kids. The group went up the steps, onto the porch, and through the front door, filling the foyer with a large crowd. While the host was distracted trying to get a count from the adults of how many members were in the party and figure out where to put them, I slipped around the edges and into the dining room.

I glanced around and saw straightback wooden chairs and small tables covered with tablecloths almost to the floor. The room was dimly lit with a drippy candle stuck in a fat wine bottle on every table, and there was a haze of smoke and the smell of tobacco mingling with spaghetti sauce while a live band in a corner played some accordion-y and Italian-sounding tune that I didn't recognize.

The place wasn't crowded and a number of tables were empty, so it wasn't hard to spot Chubby even in the semi-darkness, sitting alone at a table in the corner and eating spaghetti by candlelight. He was young, a little short of thirty, an amiable-looking fat man with plastered down black hair, wearing a napkin like a bib over his suit coat. Several different feelings were running through me right then, mostly of the queasy variety. He was somebody I had just seen in an ancient black and white film and now here he was in real life and in living color (red in particular — there was a lot of sauce splashed on that napkin he was wearing), and not only was he doomed to die in a short time, he *had* died in the world I knew.

I went over, unsure what to say or even how to address him. I remembered Mel saying his real name had been Grimes, but was he legally Mr. Dale now? And how *do* you tell somebody that you're from the future and you've got the inside scoop on how he's going to die in the next ten minutes? Or maybe fifteen… that was a pretty big dish of spaghetti there.

But if I didn't tell him, I'd be stuck in 1922 with no usable money. Trying to spend what I had in my wallet would just get me arrested for counterfeiting. Unless I wanted to ask Vito if he needed a busboy, I'd better get this over with.

I stood in front of Chubby's table. "Mr. Dale—" I began, thinking that calling him by his real name might be a little much. I knew a lot more about him than I really wanted to, but he didn't know me at all.

He looked up, a little puzzled. "You a fan? You want my autograph?" he mumbled through a mouth of pasta.

"Well, not exactly—"

Suddenly, I felt a very heavy hand on my shoulder. A human hand shouldn't have been able to cover as much of my shoulder as that one did… and it started squeezing. I tried to look back but caught only a glimpse of a human mountain of flesh wearing a black waiter's jacket and a white apron, well over six feet tall and able to look down and see if my part was straight. My first thought was of Lurch the butler, but this guy was even bigger.

A smaller, older, and rather round man with curly hair and a mustache stood next to him. "This boy bother you, Chubby?"

"It's okay, Vito," Chubby said. Now that he had swallowed and his mouth was clear, I could hear his natural speaking voice. It wasn't just deep but downright gravelly. Mel would be the one to ask for an expert opinion, but I had my doubts that his career would have survived the coming of sound even if he had lived long enough to see it. "Let him stay. It's not like I've had a lot of fans pestering me lately…" he added a little wistfully, then glanced at me. "You eaten yet? Have some spaghetti, best in town. It's on me. Bruno, put your mitt somewhere else and bring a plate and some silver for… for…?" He looked at me questioningly.

"Jack," I said as I sat down in the empty chair, feeling relieved as the human vise-grip came loose from my aching and probably bruised shoulder. "Jack Tremaine."

Vito scowled. "Your tab already plenty big, Chubby, but okay this time."

I turned to Chubby. "Well, it's like this — gack!"

Somebody grabbed me under the armpits and hoisted me upright. I glanced back. Bruno towered behind me, glowering down. Meanwhile, another aproned male waiter started tying a tie around my neck, fumbling with my collar as though he hadn't expected it to be part of the shirt. Vito hovered nearby, saying, "You can stay, but you eat in my place, you dress up!" He turned away.

When that was done and I had a chance to yank on the tie so it was loose enough to allow me some vital bodily functions like breathing, Chubby remarked, "Hey, Vito runs a classy joint. You have to dress the part."

I started to sit down again. "As I was saying — awp!"

The tie wasn't enough for Vito's dress code. I had to have a coat, too. Bruno jerked me upright again and the other waiter worked my outstretched right arm into the sleeve of what was probably a spare black waiter's jacket, then my left arm. Once the jacket was on, I was shoved back down into the chair and the waiters left.

As I wheezed, still not completely certain if my windpipe was open for business again, Chubby attempted to make conversation.

"Have you seen many of my pictures?" he asked.

Just the one, but no need to go into my scant knowledge of his filmography. "I saw *Chubby's School Daze* last night," I told him.

"That one's been out for a while," he said, giving me a puzzled look as though he couldn't imagine where it might be playing at the moment. "I had to kiss Dorothy Hollister in it…" He grimaced at the memory.

"What's so bad about that?" I had to ask, even though I was being distracted from my mission. "I thought she was pretty."

"She is, but she's also the producer's girlfriend. You probably think it'd be fun kissing those tomatoes all day long, and I can't say I don't enjoy it… but when it's the boss's private property you're smooching with and you're caught between making it a good show for the customers and not letting the boss get the idea it might be more than all in a day's work, it can get you in dutch. Besides that, though, did you like the picture? *Somebody* must have liked it… I heard a copy was stolen from some theater back East. One of the few theaters that still plays my pictures and then one just up and walks away."

No, it hadn't walked off by itself — it probably had help from beyond space and time. Suddenly I had a glimmering of an idea as to where the copy that mysteriously turned up at the Silent Movie Theater had come from. Intended as part of Mel's training, perhaps, then I had been thrown into the game as a last-minute substitute….

One of the normal-sized waiters arrived just then with a dish filled with spaghetti and meatballs as well as the utensils to eat with, and set it all down in front of me. As long as I was here and as long as the spaghetti was here, I might as well eat it. I hadn't had breakfast all that long before, but this would be a nice early lunch. Lord only knew where or when I'd be eating supper… Even if it did stretch things out a little, the only people waiting for us were the guys planning to do Chubby in, and certainly there was nothing wrong with making *them* wait a little longer. Besides, it really was good spaghetti.

As we ate, we talked a little more about *Chubby's School Daze* and what I thought of it, but Chubby realized I must have come here for some other reason than to bask in the radiance of my favorite star. Finally he asked, "So what was it you wanted to talk to me about? If it's a job in pictures you're looking for… well, I can't help you there. I could use one myself now. I've had it. I'm dead."

His blunt language startled me. "Not *yet*, anyway," I said, "but… well, that's why I came in here. To warn you. Somebody's going to be waiting for you in the parking lot out back when you leave. He — or they — are going to kill you."

Chubby gave a slight start but continued winding a thick, stringy mass of spaghetti around the tines of his fork. "Who would want to kill *me*?" he asked without showing much or any alarm. "And *why*, for God's sake? I'm hardly worth bothering with. Not anymore…" He raised the dripping glob to his mouth.

"I'm not sure who they are," I admitted, trying to remember what Mel had said in his lecture, "but I think it has something to do with your gambling debts."

Chubby's eyes went a little wide and he let the fork drop to his plate with a splat of pasta and sauce. "That's ridiculous!" he exclaimed, and turned serious. "Nobody would kill me for that! Look, I saw trouble coming months ago when the thing with Fatty Arbuckle blew up, and I knew nobody would want to see my pictures anymore, either. So I quit gambling and paid off everything I owed as much as I could while I still had money coming in. Heck, I owe Vito more than I owe anybody for gambling, and you don't see him trying to rub me out. It'd be stupid — I'd never be able to pay my tab if I was dead. Sorry, kid, your story doesn't wash. Some garlic bread? Fresh-baked."

It did smell good, but… "You've got to listen to me. I was sent here to stop you from being killed, and I can't go home until I make sure you aren't."

"You don't know who wants to do me in or why, so what makes you so sure somebody's after me? Who sent you?"

"Never mind who sent me because you'd never believe it, but… well, I'm from the future. You aren't supposed to be dead and it's causing some kind of problem, so I was sent to straighten it out."

"You're right. I don't believe it. Got any proof?"

I thought for a second, then fumbled in my back pocket and hauled out my wallet. My library card wouldn't prove anything and I didn't have my driver's license yet, but I did have a learner's permit. I extracted a folded sheet of paper and handed it to Chubby. "Look at the dates," I said.

He unfolded the paper, held it by the candle flame, and squinted. "John Wesley Tremaine... Wadsworth, Ohio... long way from home, ain'tcha? Wait... what th—? Date of birth, June 10, 1951? And you're sixteen?"

"Right," I said. "I'm from 1967, and I'd really like to go back there, so would you please make sure you don't get killed tonight?"

He slapped the learner's permit down on the table. "It's just a piece of paper. Anybody could type it up."

I took the permit back and fished a coin from my wallet. "Well, look at the date on this quarter."

I passed it across the table to him and he looked at it critically. "1966, huh? Since when do quarters have pictures of George Washington on them? Heck, it's not even real silver. It's a fake." He tossed it back.

"Er... they just started making quarters and dimes out of copper and nickel. The silver in them got to be worth more than the coins were and people were melting them down."

"Aw, go on, tell me another!" Chubby laughed. "You're just full of stories, kid!"

Vito walked past just then and stopped at our table. "Everything fine, Chubby?" he asked with a disapproving look at me.

"Listen to this!" Chubby asked, still laughing. "This kid thinks somebody's laying for me out back! I don't have an enemy in the world who'd think I'm worth the powder to blow me away, but Junior here thinks my number's up! Can you beat that, Vito?"

Vito actually showed some consternation. "What's this you saying? Somebody wants to kill you, Chubby? Who? How you know this?"

Chubby laughed some more. "Junior says he came from the future to warn me! Don't need a crystal ball with him around! Ha ha!"

Vito went from consternation to extreme annoyance, and glared at me. "So you think this is April Fish day?"

"Look," I said a little desperately, "maybe it does sound crazy and you don't have to believe me if you don't want to, but can't you at least call the police or something? Just in case?"

"Maybe I call the police on *you!*" Vito snapped. "Your welcome just about wear out. Finish your spaghetti, then get out of my place *subito*. But make sure you leave that coat!"

Vito left and I stared down at my spaghetti for a moment. Suddenly I didn't have much of an appetite. Chubby seemed perversely determined to walk right into an ambush and there wasn't a thing I could do about it.

Maybe it really was impossible to change history, even for all-powerful cosmic super-beings and their somewhat reluctant helpers. I scooted my chair back and stood up. "Well, I'm glad to have met you, Mr. Dale," I said, taking off the jacket and draping it over the back of the chair. I could have used the jacket outside but I'd probably be stripped of it on my way out anyway. "Just be careful, all right? Even if you don't believe me?"

Chubby held up his glass of red wine and contemplated it in the candle light. "Sure thing, kid. Next time you come back from the future, how about bringing some horse racing results for the next couple of years?"

"I'll try to remember to." I said goodbye and left Chubby to his Chianti or whatever it was.

Outside in the dark and the drizzle again, I took stock of things. Chubby wasn't dead yet, so maybe I could still do something even if I wasn't sure what. I went back to the parking lot to see if anyone had shown up yet. Keeping to the shadows, I looked around. The lovey-dovey couple were still in their car, but otherwise no new guests had arrived at the party.

I saw the back door open. A hulking figure stepped outside, and it wasn't hard to recognize Bruno from his silhouette against the bright light of the open doorway. He picked up a garbage can — even though it looked like it was made of cast iron and probably mostly full, he lifted it as easily as I would an empty aluminum can — and carried it across the parking lot to the alley where he set it down next to the cans already there. He paused for a moment, looked around, then walked back to the building and closed the door behind him.

I doubted if taking garbage cans to the alley was part of Bruno's regular duties. Despite what he said inside, maybe Vito had taken me seriously enough to send Bruno out to look things over. And of course he wouldn't have seen anything the least bit suspicious. It looked like I was still on my own.

All I could do was wait to see what happened next. I found a car parked in the shadows where I would be out of sight but had a good view of the back of the restaurant and the sidewalk, and I sat down on the running board. Handy thing, that — too bad modern cars didn't have them.

Several minutes ticked by. The drizzle had subsided to a faint mist, but that still left me cold and damp. *What's keeping him?* I wondered through my acute discomfort. I could just imagine Chubby having a leisurely dessert of spumoni ice cream, then lingering over a last glass of wine and maybe a cigar. *Hurry it up, will you?* On the other hand, another part of my mind was arguing the other way. *Take your time!* After all, the sooner he came out, the sooner the trouble would start.

Then I saw somebody coming down the sidewalk towards the back, and I started to rouse myself from my chilled lethargy — but it just turned out to be an anonymous man and woman. They got into one of the cars and drove away.

Chubby certainly was taking his time. I was just getting colder, and I was sure I'd come out of this with a bad cold at least if I had to wait much longer...

No, wait — here he came now.

Chubby was alone as he walked along the side of the building towards the parking lot. *That idiot!* Even if I thought a goofy kid was making up some wild story, I would have at least had Bruno see me to my car to play it safe. Just having Frankenstein's Italian cousin at my side would have discouraged any number of bad guys from getting too close to me.

Speaking of whom... the bad guys still hadn't shown up yet. Chubby was now in the parking lot, with one particular car obviously in mind, and so far, he and I were the only people around. *Don't tell me the old man sent me here on the wrong night...!*

Then I heard a door open a couple of cars down. Somebody got out, and I heard footsteps on the gravel, heading towards Chubby's car.

Now I realized my mistake. I had been expecting hoods and gangsters to be coming for Chubby and I'd forgotten about the couple in the car. Nobody sits in a car for the better part of an hour unless they're waiting for somebody. I took a quick look from the shadows.

It was the woman who was approaching Chubby. The man had also gotten out of the car, but he had quietly slipped out of sight into the surrounding darkness. Although I had no idea what, something dirty was in the offing.

The woman wore a long, plain coat, and either it had a very lush fur collar or she had wrapped a dead animal around her neck. Over her short, dark hair — long hair must have been out and blondes weren't in yet — she wore a wide-brimmed, close-fitting hat that covered her forehead, probably fancy for the era, if not quite all the way to that bell-shaped hat I'd seen women wear in pictures and movies from the later '20s.

I hadn't recognized the woman in the dim light, and probably wouldn't have known who she was even in a good light, but I heard Chubby exclaim, "Dorothy? What are you doing here?"

Dorothy — Dorothy Hollister — Chubby's co-star — the "tomato" he had been kissing in his films — the producer's girlfriend... Things were adding up fast, and I could already see that gambling had very little to do with Chubby's demise.

"It's my car," I heard her say. "It won't start. Could you see if you can do something about it?"

I was still at a loss. This was obviously a set-up of some kind, but I couldn't make any sense out of it. I also had no idea what to do. Run out and tell Chubby that the car not starting bit was a lie and there was somebody hiding in the shadows waiting for him? That would disrupt the flow of events so that whatever happened next wouldn't be what had happened the first time around. It also might get both me and Chubby shot, though, if the man had a gun, which I had no doubt he did, and didn't take kindly to meddlers and potential witnesses…

I followed as best I could, keeping to the shadows and gingerly trying not to make any noise in the crunchy gravel, as Chubby and Dorothy walked to her car. "I can't say I know much about motors," he was saying, "but I'll take a look."

I was just a few feet away, crouching in a pool of darkness by the neighboring car's front wheel, when they stopped at Dorothy's roadster, and I could hear every word.

Chubby bent down to lift the handle of the hood covering the motor just as the man stepped into the light. "That won't be necessary, Chubby." He wore a hat and it was hard to see his face under the shadow of the brim, but I guessed he was middle-aged, and he looked as though he had a burly body under that long coat.

Chubby stood up, an astonished expression on his face. "Boss…?" he blurted.

"Now, Chubby," the man — presumably named Mr. Ganton — said, "get in the car and we'll take a nice ride somewhere and talk."

"I ain't budging," Chubby shot back. "I've got a perfectly good car of my own and I don't need a ride anywhere. What's this all about?"

Ganton sighed in resignation, as though to say, *You won't make it easy for us, will you?* He motioned to the woman. "Keep a lookout."

With her head held back in a sign of haughty contempt — or else she had to hold her head back to be able to see out from under that hat — Dorothy stepped a few feet away and stood with an eye on the restaurant and the parking lot in case anyone might inopportunely show up.

Chubby crossed his arms over his chest and glared at Mr. Ganton. "Besides, I told you this morning when we had our little argument — I think you've been holding out on me and I'm not going to talk to you birds any more until I see a lawyer. Not here, not in your car. I'm not going anywhere."

"That's just it, Chubby," Ganton said. "You aren't going anywhere. Your career's ruined. You're done for in pictures."

"Then just fire me. I'll even quit if you want me to. I've been thinking about quitting anyway. I don't like the way you and your brothers have been treating me."

"That wouldn't solve anything. You see, Chubby, you've ruined *us*, too. You were our top star, and when the theaters stopped showing your pictures, most of our income dried up."

"I knew it!" Chubby blurted as several things clicked in his mind. "You told me my pictures didn't make all that much money so you couldn't pay me a whole lot, but I knew that couldn't be right! Maybe my pictures aren't making any money now, but they had to be making more money last year than you were letting on!"

"Do you think we'd tell somebody what he's really worth?" Ganton demanded as though he thought it was the dumbest idea he had ever heard of. "It might give him ideas the next time contracts come up for renewal. Dorothy knows a thing or two about accounting and she figured out some interesting angles for keeping the hired help in the dark about what they should be getting. I don't doubt but they'll be standard practice in the movie business before long."

Chubby glanced at Dorothy with a pained expression. "And you're in on this too? *Why?*"

"I just got tired of having to kiss those fish lips of yours and knowing millions of people were watching me do it," she shot back. Judging by the shocked and stung look on Chubby's face, that one had really hit home. Had he been cherishing some fond hopes for her if she were ever to get tired of her present boyfriend?

"You were our golden boy, Chubby," Ganton added, "but you're through. Let's face it, you aren't worth a dime to us now — alive. Dead… well, we took out a nice little insurance policy on you. If something happens to you, we get a big payoff, and we can keep the doors open. We're negotiating for a new boy who'll put us back on the map, and he's got a lot more going for him than you ever did. All we need is the dough to hire his Limey lordship, and that'll come out of your hide. That's all your fat carcass is good for." He pulled a small pistol from his coat pocket and aimed it at Chubby.

"Holy—!" Chubby exclaimed. "Some kid tried to warn me just now that somebody was out to kill me, but I didn't believe him! I never suspected *you*, of all people, would—!"

"Some kid…?" Ganton echoed vaguely. "Who could have known about what we were planning…?" Then, suddenly suspicious: "Dorothy, you didn't spill the beans to anybody, did you?"

"Of course not!" Dorothy snapped. "But I thought I saw somebody sneaking around the parking lot a while ago! Maybe he overheard us talking or just guessed too much?"

"It doesn't matter," Ganton said quickly. "We'll be out of here before anybody can do anything. "

His deep voice cracking with indignation and scorn, Chubby demanded, "Does your father know anything about this scheme or did you come up with it all on your own?"

Ganton winced, as though Chubby had also managed to find a tender spot to jab. "What Dad doesn't know won't hurt him. He'll just think we finally had some luck blow our way, and when I turn the studio around, he and my brothers won't think I'm the family idiot they can laugh at behind my back anymore. The only thing that's keeping all these wonderful things from happening is your continued breathing, and Dorothy was the one who pointed out that interesting fact to me!" Hearing that, Chubby just looked more distraught than ever.

Dorothy snorted impatiently. "That's one credit I don't need on the screen. Just get this over with before somebody comes, would you?"

Ganton shrugged. "Well, I guess that's it. So long, Chubby!"

*Now!*

I lurched forward from out of the shadows — surprising even myself, since I had never thought of myself as a man of action, but I had never been in a situation like this before where the chips were really down and I had to do *something,* and besides, I realized I'd gotten to *like* Chubby, and I couldn't let this happen to him — and threw myself at Ganton.

I knocked his arm to one side, but he didn't drop the gun — he fired out of reflex and the shot went wild. As the bang of the shot faded away, there was the tinkle of falling glass in a nearby car's windshield.

Momentum carried me on into him, and I tried to shove him off balance to keep him from taking another shot with better aim at Chubby. But he was bigger and heavier than I was, and threw me aside with a sweep of his arm.

I was the one off balance, and I went flying into the gravel. I scrambled to a sitting position, only to see a pistol pointing down at my nose from a few feet away.

"That must be the kid I saw nosing around!" Dorothy exclaimed.

"I don't know who you are, kid," Ganton snarled, "but you should've kept your nose out of this!"

For a second, I had a cold feeling that I was about to die right then and there, nearly thirty years before I was born, but then Chubby leaped at Ganton and jerked his arm away. Ganton fired a second time, though uselessly into the air. They grappled, Chubby driving Ganton back by his sheer mass. I pulled myself to my feet and waded in to help Chubby before Ganton could point his pistol at something fleshy, then Dorothy jumped on all of us with a scream of rage probably prompted by knowing there were now two living witnesses to Ganton's confession and her part in the

plot. There was a mad tangle for several moments, I barely dodged Dorothy's fingernails as she tried to scratch my eyes out—

Then an irresistible force eased its way in between us and pushed us
apart. It was Bruno, with some very strong fingers wrapped around the
wrist of Ganton's gun hand. Ganton shrieked, as though Bruno had only
to squeeze just a smidge more and his hand would pop off his wrist.
Screaming, Dorothy pounded futilely on Bruno's back, but he hardly knew
she was there.

Suddenly we were caught in the glare of bright headlights. A police
car pulled into the lot and two cops got out. They wore officers' caps with
visors, not helmets like the Keystone Kops had in that movie with Abbott
& Costello. We froze in the light for a long moment, like a living snapshot,
then Chubby, Dorothy, and I untangled ourselves and stepped back from
Bruno and Ganton, all of us flushed and breathing hard.

"Drop the pistol!" one cop ordered.

Ganton did, looking as though he was in excruciating pain. Bruno
continued holding on to his wrist.

"Now what's going on here?" the cop demanded.

Dorothy looked imploringly at Chubby, as though begging him to
come up with some story that would get her and maybe her boyfriend off
the hook, and she might reconsider her wicked ways and perhaps even be
nicer to him from now on...

Chubby shook his head. "Attempted murder and insurance fraud," he
said to the policemen.

She shot him a poisonous look.

"You shouldn't have made that crack about 'fish lips,'" was all he
had to say about that.

Meanwhile, I stood a little apart, trying to catch my breath and cool
down from the adrenalin rush, and did a little imploring myself. Looking
up at the featureless black sky, I thought, *If you're out there, old man, now
would be a good time to pick me up!* If I stayed here much longer, I'd be
taken to a station house for questioning about what I knew about this affair,
and things would really get sticky when my lack of credible identification
came to light.

Unfortunately, my prayer went unanswered, and I remained right
where I was with a depressing lack of any signs of imminent demateriali-
zation.

Now Vito was on the scene, having heard the gun shots, and he was
in a lively discussion with one of the cops, while the other was trying to
get some kind of statement from Chubby and a very sullen pair of suspects.
Some restaurant patrons were showing up, too, and I heard a howl of dismay from the owner of the car with the shattered windshield. No safety

glass in 1922 — a bullet through a windshield just smashed it. In the end, the police took Mr. Ganton and Dorothy to the station house in their car, while Chubby followed in his, with me next to him in the front seat and Bruno sprawling in the back. I certainly didn't look forward to being questioned, but I didn't see any way out of it.

On the way through the wet, dark streets of Los Angeles, we talked and I got the story somewhat straight. Bruno's English wasn't the best and he tended to grunts anyway, but I gathered that Vito had started thinking after I left. Some gut feeling told him something really was wrong. Chubby had shrugged off any suggestion of Bruno accompanying him back to the parking lot, but after he was out the door, Vito worried some more, then finally told Bruno to follow him anyway. He also called the police and asked them to send a couple of boys over just in case of trouble, and everything came together all at once.

That was easy enough to understand. What got me was what had led up to it.

"Fine way to run a business," I said. "I've heard of firing unwanted employees, but not firing *at* them."

"It fits, though," Chubby replied. "I always heard the Gantons originally made their money raising cattle in Texas before coming out to California. Wouldn't be surprised if their grandfather started out by rustling — and getting into pictures was one way to keep up the family tradition. I saw enough of how they operated to know they wouldn't be too fussy about laws or how they got rid of people they thought were in their way. Still, this was pretty low even for them."

"What will you do now?" I asked.

Chubby sighed. "Get a lawyer and sue them if I can for what they still owe me, but the Ganton boys aren't just greedy and crooked, they're all stupid, so there might not be much left. Besides that... go back on the road in vaudeville, maybe, or just hang around here and see if I can get parts at other studios, though I dunno if anybody will still want to touch me after this. 'He was so bad, his own studio tried to kill him!' Not a great recommendation.

"Anyway," he went on, "whatever happens, I owe you a lot of thanks. I'd be lying in the gravel right about now if you hadn't come along. I still can't believe a word you told me about where you came from or that somebody in the future would think I'm worth saving, but I'm plenty grateful just the same."

"Don't forget Ganton was about to take a shot at *me* until you charged into him," I pointed out. "I'd say we're about even. It's kind of like you and the kids in *Chubby's School Daze*. You saved them, then they saved you. Only we did it the other way around. "

"Sure enough — though it's a stretch. What happens to *you* now?"

"My job's done, so I guess I just wait to get picked up and sent back. Don't know when or how, though. Or even *if*, for that matter." My confidence was fading badly as time wore on without any further word from higher spheres, and it probably showed in my tone.

"If you end up stuck here," Chubby said, "you can always bunk with me until you get settled. It's the least I can do for you for saving my—"

It was a kind offer, but the problem was suddenly solved.

Chapter Six: WHEN WORLDS RUN RIGHT SMACK DAB INTO
EACH OTHER

With an abrupt transition from one second to the next, I found myself
back in the women's club hall. Evidently the super-cosmic powers that be
weren't much for expressing thanks or appreciation. No reward, no farewell appearance by the old man to tell me, "Well done, my good and faithful servant." I had done what I was supposed to, so as far as the higher
entities were concerned, I was no longer worthy of further attention. I
probably should have been glad that they had bothered to return me to my
own place and time instead of just leaving me back in the past, but even
that might have been done out of cold-blooded necessity rather than con-
cern for fairness or my well-being. Just knowing what I did at 16, I could
have changed history but good if given a few years.

Or had it all been a dream? If it had, it had been a darned realistic one.
I was still a little damp from the drizzle of a wet night 45 years before and
I still had some fresh scratches and bruises on my short-sleeved arms from
my tumble in the gravel.

In any case, I was back and it didn't look as though very much time
had elapsed since my sudden departure. It was still the same little convention, and no one seemed to have been aware of my brief absence.

Then I noticed something out the corner of my eye.

Something was different.

Russell Baldwin was no longer sitting alone at his table.

He was now sharing the table with another old man, apparently just
now arrived and settling in with some autographed pictures to sell. For a
second, I thought it might be the missing ventriloquist finally making a
late appearance, but I didn't see a dummy with him.

The man was past seventy and much thinner than he was in his hey-
day, but I recognized him at once.

A man who had been dead for 45 years.

Shocked, stunned, I stumbled towards him, unable to believe it. But
there he was.

Chubby Dale.

Alive. As he would have been towards the end of a lifetime he had never been allowed to have.

No eager young fans were crowding his table yet, and he looked up as I came staggering towards him. A puzzled look flashed across his face.

"Do I know you from somewhere?" he asked, his voice as gravelly as ever. "You look familiar somehow…"

I wasn't sure what to say. Instead, I reached for my wallet, pulled out my learner's permit, and showed it to him.

*Now* he remembered me. The memories came back from across the decades and he smiled. He stood up and stretched out a hand.

"Hello, Jack. It's been a while. By the way, you have some spaghetti sauce on your shirt."

I glanced down as we clasped hands. "Oops. I guess I got kind of sloppy there at Vito's…"

"You mean all that *just now* happened for you? It's been 45 years for me." He sat down again, shaking his head. "We'll have to get together sometime and talk about this. I have a few questions I've been wondering about all these years, like how a teenage boy from the future pops up out of nowhere to warn me about somebody wanting to kill me. And when you suddenly disappeared, right out of a moving car, I had a dickens of a time explaining to the police where one of the chief witnesses had gone. If it hadn't been for Dorothy turning on Ganton and singing like a canary, the case might have been dismissed for lack of evidence on that score alone."

"Sorry about that," I said, a little amazed by picking up a conversation nearly half a century after it left off, "but it wasn't like I had any choice."

"You look pretty normal," Chubby added, "not like how I'd imagine a guardian angel or a time traveler. Who *was* behind it all, and how did you manage it?"

"Maybe we can talk about it over a spaghetti dinner," I suggested. "Is Vito's still around?"

"Indeed it is, though it's in the Valley now. His grandson runs it. You don't even have to wear a suit and tie these days." He smiled, maybe thinking of the spaghetti.

Just then, Mel came up, carrying some purchases he had made at the dealers' tables. "Where the heck have you been, Jack? I've been looking all over for you and—" He realized Chubby and I had been talking and looked a little surprised. "You two know each other?"

Chubby's smile broadened into a wide grin. "Of course we do, Mel. You might say we're old friends."

The look on Mel's face was priceless. For once on this trip, for one delicious moment, I'd gotten one on him!

Then I happened to notice what he was holding, something he'd just bought. A small poster showing two men in suits and derbies, a fat man and a skinny man. I'd never seen them before, and I'd never heard the name emblazoned at the top of the poster. Without thinking, as though a weekend of letting my ignorance flap in the wind hadn't taught me anything, I made the mistake of opening my big fat mouth — right during a sudden random moment when conversation in the guest area and the dealers' room chanced to die away to near stillness and I could be heard all the way to the farthest corners —

"Who the heck are *Laurel and Hardy*? I've never heard of them!"

For a long moment, the only sound was a swish as about 50 heads swiveled on their necks to stare at me. Even the *Deuces Wilde* movie playing in the film room was in the middle of a rare quiet scene.

Then the whole place exploded in a storm of laughter.

Somehow Mel got me outside to escape the excruciating embarrassment that I still didn't understand, and we sat down on the steps in front of the women's club. "Are you kidding?" he demanded, the most exasperated I had ever seen him. "Nobody living on this planet for the past 40 years hasn't heard of Laurel & Hardy!"

Then what planet *had* I been living on? I was coming up so empty that I was at a complete loss for anything to say. Then Mel added, "And you even saw one of their shorts last night at the Silent Movie Theater!"

"I did? Are you sure? I'd think I'd remember it if I had…"

"Of *course* I'm sure! The guy who owns that place *always* runs a Laurel & Hardy short at one of his shows! He'd go bust in a month if he didn't — they're his biggest draw, even bigger than Chaplin, so he always shows at least one Laurel & Hardy and one Chaplin. If you've been to a Silent Movie Theater show, you've seen a Laurel & Hardy short, guaranteed!"

I tried to think. "Then what did we see last night? I remember the Snub Pollard short—"

"Right…"

"Then a Chaplin…"

"Yep."

"Then a Chase Brothers…"

Now it was Mel's turn to look blank. "A *what*…?"

I felt the earth quiver beneath my feet, and I don't think it was because of one of the famous southern California earthquakes. The same Mel Endicott who had told me the night before all about the Chase Brothers' career now couldn't remember them?

"No," he said with complete conviction, "they ran Laurel & Hardy's *Big Business* after the Chaplin. You were right there next to me laughing your head off along with the rest of the audience at how the Boys destroyed

James Finlayson's house."

Now I *really* felt queasy. "It sounds like I had a good time," I murmured. "I wish I'd been there…" But who *had* been there?

Mel stood up. "There's somebody I need to talk to about a fanzine article. I'll let you untangle this on your own. Catch you later—"

I just sat there, probably looking like I'd been hit with a Louisville Slugger across the snoot.

After a while, Chubby came out and sat down next to me.

"I think I've figured it out, Jack," he said, and proceeded to explain.

Chubby was never a star again after he left Ganton, but he did work for various studios as a bit player and an extra. Eventually he drifted into other fields, did well in real estate, married, and had a family. He still kept a hand in the business yet, doing occasional small roles and even cartoon voices where his gravelly voice worked to his advantage, though anymore it was mostly just to maintain his eligibility for health benefits as a performer. "I had a good life thanks to you, Jack," he said warmly.

Back in 1922, though, that rising young English star Ganton Lumiscope had hoped to hire with Chubby's insurance money must have been one Arthur Stanley Jefferson — better known as Stan Laurel. In that other world where Chubby died, going to work for Ganton may have been a bad career move, as the *Lord Limey* series never went anywhere, either. Laurel had his brief time on the stage and then was forgotten. Perhaps the experience soured him enough that he gave up on movies entirely and went back to England. Since the management at Ganton didn't treat their stars very well, it wouldn't have been surprising. In the world where Chubby lived, the bad publicity from having one of its chief officers in jail for the attempted murder of one of its own stars pushed the already shaky Ganton Lumiscope into immediate bankruptcy and dissolution. It was just a little hard to attract and retain talent with that kind of employee relations policy. Stan Laurel went elsewhere, finally landing at Hal Roach, and a few years later he teamed up with a rotund bit player named Oliver Norville Hardy. The rest was history, though history that was all news to me.

"Out of all us old-time comedians," Chubby wound up, "they were the ones who became legends. Fifty years from now, a century from now, we'll mostly all be forgotten, even Chaplin eventually — but Stan and Ollie will still be remembered."

"You knew them?" I asked, noticing his use of their first names.

"Of course I knew 'em," Chubby said. "I even worked with 'em a time or two. That was my pants they ran off in at the end of *You're Darn Tootin'*, I'll have you know. Oh, wait, I guess you wouldn't have seen it." He got to his feet, still pretty agile despite his age. "C'mon, I've got to get back to my table, and we can exchange addresses."

On the way inside, it finally hit me. What this had all been about. What the anomaly had been.

It hadn't been about Chubby Dale at all.

The anomaly was a world without Laurel & Hardy.

Just as Chubby was sitting down in back of the table again and I was writing my address down on a card so we could write to each other and compare notes — it didn't look like we'd be able to coordinate our schedules for that spaghetti dinner on this trip — the intense girl with the camera came by. "Can I get a picture of you, Mr. Dale?"

Chubby nudged Mr. Baldwin. "Let's get a picture of *all* us old-timers!" He waved to Polly Zinger and the formerly sweet and little Arlene. "You, too, ladies!"

Except for the TV horror host down at the other end, traffic was a little slow for everyone at the moment, so why not? The foursome stood together and the girl stepped back to get them all into the shot.

Mel turned up again about then, and even he seemed impressed by what he saw. "That's an awful lot of movie history you're getting into one picture, Lisa," he remarked. (*Of course* he knew her.)

"Ain't it the truth?" Mr. Baldwin said. "Maybe Hollywood didn't treat some of us very well, but we were there just the same and we've got our memories."

Polly Zinger nodded. "That's right. They can't take that away from us."

"After all," Arlene added, "you can't change history!"

When Chubby laughed, he could rattle the windows.

Mel still seemed a little irritated by my colossally ignorant goof earlier, but I couldn't tell him that while I may not have known who Laurel & Hardy were, I had been somewhat responsible for making sure that they came to be in the first place. He never would have believed me if I had tried to tell him what I had just been through, and I certainly couldn't prove it. I had to let him go on thinking they sure grew 'em dumb out in Ohio and he'd have to accept me as I was, and hopefully my other fine qualities outweighed my defects. By the time we were riding the bus back to his house, he seemed to have forgotten all about the incident and we were talking about movies and comics like nothing had happened. Or maybe he did remember and got me for it later...

I was looking forward to a quiet Sunday just relaxing. A little time to think about everything that had happened and come to terms with my now considerably enlarged view of the universe would have been nice. I had forgotten that the word "relaxing" wasn't in Mel's dictionary.

After breakfast, he asked, "When was it you said your parents were picking you up?"

"Around five," I replied.

"Oh good," Mel said. "I have a birthday party at one and you can help me."

When Mom and Dad showed up that afternoon, I was still trying to wash the clown make-up off.

# TV Comics

Prologue

The farm looked moderately prosperous. The barn had recently been painted a bright red and bore the date **1924** on the roof. The motto **CHEW MAIL POUCH TOBACCO** was emblazoned in big letters on the side facing passing traffic on the highway across the field of brown, harvested corn stalks.

It was a cool, clear fall day in northwestern Illinois — Friday, October 20, 1967, to be exact — and the trees around the farmhouse and in the woodlots scattered across the distant countryside were balls of orange, yellow, and brown. Patrick Collins, a stout, middle-aged insurance agent in a suit, and Billy Erwin, a lean farmer of about forty in a windbreaker and overalls, stood in the barnyard discussing the recent fire that had left one end of the barn roof a charred, blackened hole, now covered with a tarp.

"You were fortunate that it wasn't any worse than it was," Mr. Collins said, about to pick up his briefcase and head back to his car. The fire had been discovered early and quickly put out, damage was relatively minor, there were no signs of obvious negligence, and everything seemed to be in order as far as filing a claim went.

"That's for darn sure," Billy Erwin agreed. "If the whole barn'd gone up, it might've spread to the house, too." He glanced back at the white, two-story farmhouse across the barnyard, and added, just to make conversation, "That really would've been bad, with all that..." He trailed off, suddenly looking a little uneasy as he scratched the graying stubble under his chin.

Mr. Collins raised an eyebrow. Billy had clearly been about to say something he realized he shouldn't mention to an insurance agent. The Erwins didn't seem like the kind to have a still or some other illegal and dangerous operation in the basement, but you never knew. Mr. Collins had seen some things that made him shake his head even after a quarter-century in the business.

"Are you saying there's some sort of fire hazard in the house?" he asked.

Billy looked as though he was sorry he had ever opened his mouth. "Well, I dunno... I'm not sure it's even worth mentioning. Forget I said anything."

Mr. Collins tried to sound reassuring. "I'm your insurance agent, not the fire chief. I'm on your side. If there's anything I can help you with, give you some advice about, that's what I'm here for."

Billy seemed torn, then finally shrugged. "Yeah, there's something, all right. I think you better talk to my mom about it. C'mon inside."

Not much later, Mr. Collins was sitting in a comfortable chair with doilies on the armrests in the Erwins' cozy warm parlor and sipping a welcome cup of hot tea. Billy had gone back outside, leaving the insurance agent to talk with his elderly mother.

Mrs. Erwin sat in a chair across a low table from him. She was terribly thin, with a time-worn, wrinkled face and gray hair turned almost white, and wore an old-fashioned print dress with a shawl over her shoulders, as though she was perpetually cold no matter how warm the room around her was. She moved with some difficulty, perhaps due to arthritis, and her hand shook slightly as she held her teacup.

Seemingly grateful to have someone to talk to, she was telling Mr. Collins in a somewhat quavering voice about herself, her family, and the farm. Most of this he already knew, since he had been the family insurance agent for years, but all his dealings up to now had been with Billy.

"My husband, Carl, passed on about ten years ago, and left me and the boys to run the place. I don't get around as well as I used to and had to give up my butter and egg business, and nowadays I just keep my eye on things in the house while the boys do all the farming. Last winter I fell down the cellar steps and broke my hip, and I was all crippled up for months, so Billy's wife had to take over the housework. Oh yes, the boys all got married years ago and they live in their own houses, all except Billy. He and his wife live here with me and the others just help farm. Billy's wife is over to her sister's today."

In the soft comfort of the overstuffed chair and the warmth of the parlor, Mr. Collins was on the point of dozing off as Mrs. Erwin rambled, but the mention of the house reminded him of what he had come inside to find out.

"Excuse me, Mrs. Erwin, but that's what I wanted to talk to you about. Billy wasn't clear on the details, but it sounded as though you have some kind of fire hazard in the house. Since I'm your insurance agent, it may be something I should know about and maybe I can help you with it."

Mrs. Erwin looked startled. "Oh my… I don't know if he ought to've mentioned it, really. It's never been a problem before. Anyway, when I'm through living here, Billy will take over the whole house and he'll probably get rid of everything of Carl's that I've been saving. Such a pity, too. Carl loved to read so much, and to have everything thrown away just like that wouldn't be any good. I'd give it all away if I could find somebody who'd appreciate it the way Carl did, but I don't know anybody who'd have room for it all…" She drifted off again.

Mr. Collins wasn't a great deal wiser than before, but it did sound as though there was a sizeable mass of reading material in the house. Books? The Erwins didn't strike him as particularly intellectual, but perhaps the old man had needed something to do to while away the long evenings before television. The main thing was assessing the potential for a fire, so Mr. Collins pressed on.

"What exactly did your husband have?"

"I suppose I should explain how things were," Mrs. Erwin said, setting her teacup down on the tray on the table in front of her. "Carl liked to read, he did. I never saw man who was so hepped up on reading the way he was. He never cared for movies or radio. He just liked to read. He never threw anything away, either, because he liked to save everything so he could read it again. He always said that when you heard something on the radio, you only heard it once and that was the end of it. When you read something, you could read it again later and enjoy it just as much as you did the first time." The old woman leaned back, chuckling as she recalled fond memories. "Oh, land! How that man would read anything! Even the back of the cereal box at breakfast if that's all there was! He really loved his story magazines, especially if they had something to do with going to the Moon and things like that. But most of all, he liked to read those funny picture books of his! We must have thousands up in the attic!"

*Now* Mr. Collins understood. He almost spilled his teacup as he realized what the fire hazard actually was. Funny picture books… *comic books*! *Old* ones, none newer than ten years old. *Thousands* of them.

Mr. Collins was not completely unfamiliar with comic books. He had seen them around the barracks during his World War II service, and even read a few for casual entertainment himself when nothing else was available. Years later, his son had brought some home now and then, which was typical for boys of the time. What wasn't so typical was that his daughter had then picked up on them as well. In the last few months, at the age of fifteen, she had even turned comic books into something of a hobby. Mr. Collins had long half-humorously wondered if there were some boy repellant available on the market that he could spray on the front lawn when the young louts started noticing his little girl, but the two boys who had been hanging around the house lately were fellow comic book devotees and seemed pretty harmless. The one thing he had picked up from overhearing the kids talk and from his daughter's dinner-table conversation was that old comic books were worth money. That key point had been further corroborated by some sensational newspaper articles he had read, though he hadn't given them much thought at the time.

*Don't rush things*, he told himself as the possibilities began to take shape in his mind. *Let's see what she has first.*

"What kind of funny picture books?" he asked, as though merely making polite conversation.

"Oh, all kinds. He started buying them back in the '30s when they first started coming out, and I don't think there were very many he didn't buy!"

*Interesting... and it's the really old ones that the collectors are looking for.* He had learned that much from the random snippets of his daughter's conversations with her friends that he had accidentally listened to. "Could I see them, please? I just want to evaluate the risk of a fire."

"I guess we've been lucky. Those books have been sitting up in the attic all these years and we've never had any trouble. But I suppose there's such a thing as pushing your luck too far... All right, then, I'll show you what we have and you can see for yourself."

Mrs. Erwin stood up and hobbled slowly to the narrow staircase, and Mr. Collins followed her. Besides any arthritis, she had apparently never completely recovered from the broken hip. She led the way up the stairs and progress was maddeningly slow. On the second floor, she took him to an even narrower stairway, and at length Mr. Collins stood on the top step and looked around in the dusty gloom of the attic.

Cardboard boxes. Lots of them. Stacks of them. Filling the attic as far as the eye could see in the dim light. Partly covered with sheets, it was as though Mr. Collins was surrounded by a low mountain range, with only a few gaps left to keep the low, dirty windows from being blocked. Dust and spider-webs were everywhere.

"Nothing's been touched since Carl passed away ten years ago," Mrs. Erwin said, standing in an open area between boxes, "so things are a little dusty, I'm afraid. But everything's in boxes, and unless the mice got into them, the story magazines and funny picture books should be all right."

Such seemed to be the case. Mr. Collins pushed a covering sheet back and opened a random box. Inside, on top, was a large-sized magazine with a logo in odd block letters arching across the top of the cover and reading

*Amazing Stories*, with a painted scene below of people in fur coats ice skating under a looming planet Saturn. In the attic gloom, it was hard to make out the small type but Mr. Collins thought he saw the date as some-time in 1926. And the magazine looked as clean and new as though it had come straight from the newsstand the day before instead of more than forty years before.

A look in another box revealed comic books, with the top one bearing the title *Captain Marvel Adventures* over a scene of some vaguely familiar he-man character in red longjohns appearing amid a cloud of smoke and a silver lightning bolt. It, too, looked to be in newsstand-fresh condition although Mr. Collins' faint memory of Captain Marvel dated back to his Army days during the war. The comics beneath it seemed to be just as much ancient relics that had miraculously survived the ravages of time.

Mr. Collins was not only a practical man, he was an intelligent man. Everything was coming together — his daughter's casually overheard chatter, the newspaper articles he had read — and the conclusion seemed inescapable. By sheer luck, he had stumbled across a phenomenal hoard of rare old magazines and comic books of just the kind the collectors were paying large sums of money for. Who those collectors were or how to reach them, he didn't exactly know, but his daughter would.

"Mrs. Erwin, what do you plan to do with all these… er, books?"

"Well, if you think they're a fire hazard, I suppose we'll have to get rid of them. Hate to do it, though, because I'd get to thinking about how much they meant to Carl. But nobody I know would want them, except maybe my grandchildren, and they'd just tear them up. It seemed to me they weren't hurting anything up here and it was easiest just to keep them. I suppose Billy could just clear out the attic and burn everything…"

Mr. Collins decided to go with the notion taking shape in his mind. "*I* could take them off your hands, Mrs. Erwin."

"You mean you'd take them to the dump for us? That'd be awfully kind of you, but Billy could do that—"

"No, I mean I could *buy* them from you."

Mrs. Erwin seemed astonished. "You *want* all these old funny picture magazines? But why?"

"Uhm… for my daughter. She wants to be an artist. The ads and illus-trations in the magazines could give her ideas and she can study the tech-niques." He was improvising on the spot, but it might not be so far from the truth.

"But they're all so old. Wouldn't she rather have new magazines?"

"The old ones are the best, ma'am."

Some further back and forth followed, with Mrs. Erwin wavering on whether she was really honoring her late husband's memory or not, versus the need to clear out the attic. They finally settled on a down payment of $100 for the lot, with the promise of more later if Mr. Collins happened to sell some of the collection, and he wrote her a check on the spot.

If he'd been inclined to play the game that way, he probably could have had everything in the attic for nothing, since Mrs. Erwin seemed to have no idea what she had up there. He could have said he was taking all the worthless paper and potential fire hazard to the dump as a neighborly gesture, just one more service of their friendly neighborhood Midwestern Mutual agent, helping make their house safe... but the Erwins read the same newspapers he did, and if they hadn't seen the articles about old comic books being worth big money or connected them with the stash they had in their attic, there was no guarantee they'd miss the next such article. You couldn't play underhanded tricks like knowingly deceiving your own customers and expect to survive as a small-town businessman — everybody knew each other and people talked. No, this had to be on the up and up.

*Funny how problems can solve themselves...* he thought as he filled out the blanks on the check. The Erwins had a fire hazard they needed to get rid of. His little girl would be going off to college in a couple of years and there would be a lot of bills to pay. The answer to one problem solved the other.


Billy was drafted to help carry boxes down from the attic. He also provided the services of his pickup to take the books into town, an old and well-worn green Dodge flatbed truck with a framework of wooden slats enclosing the bed like a board fence.

Billy paused for a moment during the loading, and looked off in the direction of the barn.

"Something wrong?" Mr. Collins asked, breathing a little hard and grateful for the break from lifting and heaving heavy boxes.

"Nah... just had a funny feeling for a second. What's that fancy French term for when you feel like you've been someplace before?"

"*Déjà vu?*"

"That's it. For a moment there, I was half-expecting to see Dad come running up from the field, and mad as hell. This isn't the first time I've been here loading his books into a truck."

"Oh?"

"It was back during the war and I was a kid helping one of my teachers with a paper drive. Mom wanted to donate all of Dad's story magazines and comics on the Q.T., so we had to pick 'em up while he was out in the field. And wouldn't you know it, he came back to the house right then to get something, and boy, was he sore when he saw what was going on! He put a stop to it *real* quick. Nobody ever dared touch his books again after that."

"Your mother tried to get rid of his books without even asking him?"

"She *hated* the things," Billy replied, stooping to pick up another box of comics. "Don't tell anybody I said this but he read mostly to get some peace from Mom. She was never happy and always complaining about something."

"She seems like a nice lady to me," Mr. Collins said diplomatically, giving Billy a hand with loading the box in the back of the truck.

Billy sighed as he shoved the box in with the others. "You should have seen her ten years ago. Short fuse, bad temper. My wife thinks Mom went stir crazy out here on the farm miles from anywhere with nobody to talk to all day long, and then come evening, Dad would just ignore her and bury himself in a book. Oh, they loved each other, and they stayed married all their lives, but I think she was jealous of his books because he sometimes seemed to prefer them to her. But now, Mom has mellowed as she's gotten older, and she probably feels sorry they didn't get along better all those years."

Mr. Collins nodded thoughtfully. "And here we are, running off with his books when he isn't around to stop us. I hope it doesn't bother your conscience."

"Not a bit." Billy glanced up at the clear blue sky. "I can't explain it, but I've got a feeling we're doing the right thing. Dad's done with his books now, and if they're going to somebody who can appreciate them half as much as he did, I think that's how he'd want it."

Pam Collins got off the school bus near her house that afternoon mainly with thoughts of *Star Trek* on her mind. She was a pretty girl of 15, slim with long, light brown hair, large green eyes, and a perky, upturned nose set among some fading freckles. Besides her school clothes of skirt and low-heeled shoes, she wore a jacket against the autumn chill, and carried her books in her arms as she walked along the sidewalk.

The TV listings for tonight's episode had given its title as "The Doomsday Machine," which certainly sounded exciting and she hoped it would be a good one. She was also glad that her father had finally bought a second TV set for the den, since now she wouldn't have to miss the first half of *Star Trek* because he wanted to watch *Gomer Pyle*.

The Collins house was a bay-windowed split-level in a section of town with all-new houses and tiny trees, which the old-time residents somewhat disdainfully referred to as "New Shetland." With time, progress, and a few new industries, the sleepy little upstate Illinois town had found itself with no choice but to grow beyond the central neighborhood of old houses around the downtown area. Pam's house was at the corner of two streets, and not far away was open country with now barren fields and distant orange woods.

Pam came into the house to find her mother sitting in the living room and looking off into space. Mrs. Collins turned and looked at her daughter with a strange expression.

"What, Mom?"

"Either your father's had a brilliant inspiration or he's gone completely crazy, and either way you had something to do with it."

"Pardon?" Pam asked, setting her books down on an end table and starting to unbutton her jacket.

Mrs. Collins got up. "Leave your coat on and follow me. You *have* to see this."

They went out to the split-level's attached two-car garage. In the open space next to Mrs. Collins' Fairlane, where Mr. Collins' car was normally parked, were stacks of cardboard boxes.

"He went for another load and should be back soon," Mrs. Collins said. "I don't know how much more is out there."

"How much more what?"

"Take a look and see."

Pam opened a couple of boxes at random and her normally rather large green eyes went even wider. Old comic books and pulp magazines? She'd only heard about most of what she was seeing here — this was the first time she had ever seen the real thing.

"I guess he'd heard you and the boys talking about these old books," Mrs. Collins said, "so he jumped right on it when he found out one of his clients had a lot of comics in the attic. He figures he can sell them for a lot of money. First he wanted to take the boxes right up to my sewing room, but I insisted we leave them here for the time being until we can inspect them for things like mice and bugs. From what he said, they've been in an attic for ten years at least."

Just then, Pam heard the sound of an approaching motor outside.

"That must be him now," Mrs. Collins said.

Pam looked out the side door and saw a battered old pickup truck slowly backing up the driveway to the front of the garage. As soon as it stopped, Mr. Collins got out from the passenger side and came into the garage. His suit was very dusty.

"Oh good, you're home," he said to Pam. He gestured to the boxes already stacked up, noticing that a couple had been opened. "Just for my own peace of mind, can you tell me what this stuff is worth and where to sell it?"

Still astonished by what was happening, Pam nodded. "Uh, yeah, actually... I borrowed something from Bob Trent that might be able to help."

She dashed into the house, went up to her room, and returned with a thick magazine. Its black and white cover drawing showed a scene of what looked like Tarzan on the back of a jet plane with the Earth far below. The title of the publication defied ready comprehension: *The Rocket's Blast/ Comicollector*.

"It's the main place where people advertise old comics for sale," Pam explained, handing it to her father.

Mr. Collins leafed through it. He glimpsed enough of the ads with their lists of comics and prices being asked to get a good idea of how things worked. A slow smile crossed his face. "This is *exactly* what I want! It might take me a while to unload all these books by advertising them and selling them through the mail, but it looks doable."

"Can't we just sell everything all at once to one of those dealers and be done with it?" asked Mrs. Collins hopefully.

"Not a good idea," Mr. Collins said, giving the magazine back to Pam. "I've insured a few collections in my time, so I've seen how it goes. If old comics work like old stamps and coins, a big dealer will just pay you the lowest price he can for the lot because *he* has to make money selling them in turn. If we sell them ourselves, we can charge the going rate. It'll take longer but we have a couple of years before our little girl heads off to college."

Mr. Collins opened the garage door so he could start helping Billy bring in the boxes he had already unloaded from the truck and set down on the driveway pavement.

"Is that all of them?" Mrs. Collins asked, again hopefully.

"Nope, there's plenty more back at the farm," Mr. Collins replied. "I'd like to make at least one more trip before it gets dark. Want to come along, Pam? I could use some help in seeing just what's there and getting an idea of what it might be worth."

And so, on the next trip out to the farm, Pam went along, squeezed between Billy and her father on the seat. There wasn't much conversation, as Mr. Collins and Billy had probably already said everything they had to say to each other on the previous two round trips.

Quietly watching the rural autumn countryside slide by the truck windows in the oncoming evening, she could only wonder how she got there.

It had started with her older brother leaving his comic books lying around the house. She would read anything that had printing on it, and the colorful and exciting art piqued her interest all the more. She had always liked fantasy and science fiction, and the comics were a concentrated dose.

Of an artistic bent herself, she even tried to imitate the various artists' styles in her own drawings. After her brother left home for college, she had picked up occasional comic books on her own, and was fond of a few titles that she bought regularly, like *Fantastic Four*, *Thor*, and *Magnus, Robot Fighter*.

Things had advanced to a higher level that past spring when she stopped in the drugstore downtown to see if any new comics had come in, and happened to run into somebody she knew slightly from her art class the year before. That was Ernie Volney, crouched in front of the magazine rack to scope out the comics himself. A conversation ensued and Pam was delighted to discover that she wasn't the only fan of her age in town. She hadn't expected it to go any further than having somebody to talk with about the latest comics now and then, but a few days later, Ernie's friend Bob Trent suddenly needed a cover for his fanzine and Ernie remembered that there was another fan close by — and one, he knew from that art class they had been in together, who could draw. That brought Pam on board as to what fanzines were and she started sending for a few herself, then contributing art to them and even joining a fanzine-exchange club over the summer. It was an outlet for her creativity that she had always wanted but never knew where to find before.

And now *this*…

A little later, looking around the Erwin attic, she was astonished by what still remained after two truckloads. Then she had a sudden thought and spoke up. "What about Bob and Ernie, Dad? They're comics fans, too. Shouldn't we let them in on this?"

"Pam," her father said in a low voice, after making sure Billy was well down the stairs with another box and out of earshot. "I'm doing this for *you*. These books are your college fund. I found them, I bought them, and a couple of knuckleheads you barely know from school don't have anything to do with it. Let them find their own comics!"

She wondered how she was going to tell them…

Chapter One: HATCHING THE PLOT

"The *luck* some people have!" Ernie Volney fumed. The lanky blond teenager stopped pacing the carpet in Bob Trent's bedroom long enough to give vent to his frustration, then went back to wearing a path in the rug. "Those comics were just sittin' out at that farm only a few miles away all our lives an' we never knew a thing about it! Then somebody comes along an' grabs 'em before we can even get a sniff of the pulp paper!"

Trent looked up from his bed, where he lay reading a batch of assorted comic books that had come out that day. "Are you still going on about that?" he asked.

J. Robert Trent, Jr. was a somewhat heavy-set, dark-haired youth with black plastic-framed glasses under a mop of dark hair. That he wasn't entirely a comic-book fanatic was attested by the well-thumbed poetry books on the shelf built into his bed's headboard, but the rest of the room, dominated by a heavy wooden bookcase crammed with comic books and decorated with a few painted superhero models, as well as a six-foot poster of Spider-Man taped to the inside of his door, showed where his mind spent much of the day. A calendar on the wall was turned to November, 1967.

"It's been three weeks," Trent added. "You should be over it by now."

Ernie spun in mid-course to face Trent with an exasperated expression. "Are you kiddin'? You don't get over losin' out on the most humungous collection of old funnybooks in the history of the world that fast."

"Well, I don't know…" Trent said uncertainly. "It was kind of a lucky break for Pam's dad…"

"Lucky? Christ on roller skates, Junior! We're talkin' 'bout miracles! We're talkin' 'bout angels comin' down outta the sky an' practic'ly handing Pam's ol' man every comic ever published on a silver platter! It just ain't fair, Bobaroonie!"

"Oh, come on, Ernie!" Trent said with a hint of impatience in his voice. "You know as well as I do that we never had a chance at them. We didn't have any idea there was a collection like that anywhere around town until Mr. Collins made the deal, and then it was too late."

"Yeah, an' it would be the father of the only other fan in town. That means he knows exactly what the goodies are worth an' where to sell 'em. We can't even hope to buy some comics from him, at least if we don't wanna lose our shirts. Meanwhile, we sit here havin' to read today's Mavels while that girl sits on top of all those golden oldies, an' I don't think she knows what's she's got or even cares that much…"

"Speaking of 'that girl,'" Trent said, glancing at his watch, "it's time we went over there."

Ernie went to the window and looked bleakly out at the darkness. "You go on alone, Trentbob. I'll stay here. I can't stand it anymore. I can't go over to her house an' look at all those old comics I can't have."

Trent rolled off the bed and stood up. "Be serious for once, would you? She said we could borrow anything we wanted to read, remember? I'm going over tonight to pick up her set of Golden Age *Captain America* issues for that article I'm writing for *Shockwave*. You can wait downstairs in the living room if you want—"

"An' let Mr. Collins try an' sell me an insurance policy?" Ernie asked, turning away from the window to join Trent at the door. "I'll come along, but I'm warnin' you — the smell of all that pulp paper'll turn me green. With envy."

Some Shetlanders called the housing tract where Pam lived "Indian Village" because it had amused the developer to dub the streets with names like Mohawk Avenue, Apache Court, Navajo Lane, Miskatonic Road, and Narragansett Street. Pam's house was at the corner of Algonquin Way and Potawatomi Drive, and not far away was snow-covered open country.

Trent pulled his sadly deteriorating '57 Chevy up in front of the split-level house and he and Ernie clambered out into the chilly evening air. When Trent went up the front steps and rang the bell, the door was opened by Mrs. Collins, a rather portly middle-aged woman.

"Oh, Pam's where she usually is these days," she said. "Upstairs in the sewing room. Only now her father's spending his evenings up there, too. I may have to take up sewing again so I can join them. It's getting a little lonely down here by myself." Judging by what was on the TV in the living room, she was making up for her loneliness by watching *The Red Skelton Show*.

Ernie looked quizzically at Trent. *Her father?* he seemed to be wondering.

The answer to that question was forthcoming when they went upstairs. What Mrs. Collins called her sewing room had once been the bedroom of Pam's older brother before he went off to college, then had been used as a spare room with a sewing machine in one corner. Since

Mrs. Collins rarely sewed now and the room was largely unoccupied except by occasional visitors, Pam had taken it over as a workroom when she started getting serious about her artwork. First she had moved in her drawing table, art supplies, desk, radio, and record player. More recently, her father had moved in the boxes of old comic books and pulp magazines that he had bought from old Mrs. Erwin. While many of the boxes were still unopened and piled on top of each other, others had been emptied and stacks of comic books and pulp magazines awaited sorting and listing. The room was now filled with pulp paper, with only narrow paths winding between the perilously teetering piles of cheap thrills.

As Trent and Ernie came in, Pam was at her drawing board by the window, diligently working on some project and almost completely hidden by the surrounding mounds of old magazines. Mr. Collins sat at the desk along the wall with a small stack of comic books in front of him, apparently figuring their book value from a dealer's list in the latest issue of the *Rocket's Blast/Comicollector* and totaling them on a crank-operated adding machine. If Mrs. Collins was serious about returning to sewing, she would have to find the sewing machine again, and in that warren of comic books and pulps there was no telling where it was.

Hearing Trent and Ernie come in, Pam looked up. "Hi guys!" she called cheerily. "Be right there!"

Mr. Collins raised his balding head, nodded a distant welcome to the boys, though not quite successfully masking a fleeting grimace of annoyance, and went back to adding up figures.

Pam scooted her chair back from the drawing board, stepped over a low pile of *Doc Savage* pulps on the floor while pantomiming lifting non-existent petticoats as though gingerly avoiding a mud puddle, and emerged from the stacks. Her long, light brown hair was loosely tied in a ponytail to keep it out of her eyes while she worked, and she wore jeans, white socks, and a paint and ink-splattered old white shirt that was so baggy on her that it was probably a cast-off from her father. Trent had known her at all well for barely a few months, but he had been told by her former classmates at the Catholic school she had attended through Eighth Grade that in years past she had been skinny and gawky, with rather prominent front teeth, to the point some mean kids had called her "Bugs Bunny" behind her back — which she had overheard and apparently hadn't much minded, since she liked Bugs Bunny. Either discreet dental work or just growing up had largely solved that problem anyway. Puberty had wrought miracles for her. Trent it had mainly given the odd pimple and at 16 he wasn't even shaving regularly yet.

"Howdy, Pam!" Ernie greeted, bowing with mock formality.

To that the lady herself responded with a simulated curtsey, the fact that she was wearing jeans getting in the way of actually doing it. "Top o' the evening to ye!" she replied in an outrageous brogue.

Trent rolled his eyes. He could never match them when they went into routines. "Hi, Pam," he said quickly. "Do you have the comics I asked for?"

"Sure and I do." Pam turned and produced a pile of some 80-odd comic books she had previously set aside and put on top of a waist-high stack of prehistoric periodicals. "Here ye are and welcome. *Captain America* #1 through whatever." She dropped the Irish washerwoman and went back to Northern Illinois, though some affected Emma Peel from watching a few too many episodes of *The Avengers* came through now and then. "You know, when I first went through that stack, I thought Mr. Erwin had either misfiled some comics or some wrong comics had slipped into the Cap set when we were moving them — but no, the last Golden Age issue really is called *Captain America's Weird Tales*, and Cap isn't anywhere in it, just those really gruesome horror stories, and Marvel really did try to bring Cap back in the '50s, which is why those issues of *Young Men* and *Men's Adventures* are in there."

Trent's face glowed with wonder as he looked through some of the comic books, most in shockingly new-like condition for their age as the earliest ones dated back to 1941.

"Wow, Pam!" he exclaimed. "That's the best part about your collection — the research value! You've got practically everything, so all I have to do to write an article is come over here and—"

Mr. Collins overheard and spoke up, interrupting Trent. "Pam, I don't think it's a good idea for you to be lending comics out. I'm trying to sell them and raise money for college for you, so you should try to keep them in the best condition possible. No offense, Bob, but anything could happen to these rare and valuable comics if we let people come and take them out of the house."

Pam addressed her father. "Dad, he just wants to write an article, and I already promised him that he could borrow them. Bob is the most unbelievably responsible person I know, so the comics are safe with him."

Trent didn't care for the half-spin she gave the words "unbelievably responsible" — it reminded him a little too much of the taunting he'd had from other kids in years past for being a teacher's pet and getting good grades — but coming from Pam, he had to take it as a compliment.

Some back and forth between Pam and her father followed, with Mr. Collins offering to compromise by letting Trent come by to consult the comic books he needed when he wanted to write an article, provided the comics didn't leave the house and he made an appointment first, while

Pam held out for letting him take the comics home. Some of Pam's arguments Trent found more disheartening than anything else: she seemed to be thinking less of his convenience and more of keeping him away in the evenings when she wanted to work at her drawing board without distraction.

Meanwhile, Ernie had gotten bored and was wandering around the room, idly picking up some of the comic books that lay within easy reach and leafing through them, content to let others decide the future of comic-book scholarship. "*Keen Detective Funnies...*" he muttered, examining a random title from 1940. "Now there's a dumb name for a comic book!"

After a few minutes, Pam's arguments seemed to be gaining the upper hand, even if her debating style consisted mainly of quietly and firmly staking out a position and holding on to it until the other side caved in.

"All right," Mr. Collins said, sounding weary of the whole thing and sorry he had ever brought it up, "Bob can take the comics home this time, but not for more than a couple of weeks. We aren't running a lending library here, you know—"

Trent's feeling of relief suddenly went cold. Out of the corner of his eye, he spotted Ernie tugging at a comic book in the middle of a stack of paper periodicals piled on top of a box and almost as tall as he was. "Ernie — watch out!" he muttered urgently.

"Don't be such a worrywart, Junior!" Ernie replied between clenched teeth, pulling harder at the firmly lodged comic book with one hand and bracing his other against the stack for support. "Just... wanted... to... see... what... this... is..."

Without warning, the comic book came free. Ernie toppled over backwards into the stack behind him, which toppled in turn into the stack behind it. Fragile comic books and pulp magazines over two decades old spilled everywhere in a four-color cascade.

Trent never would have believed that a pot-bellied, middle-aged insurance agent could move so fast, but Mr. Collins sprang out of his chair like an Olympic-class jack-in-the-box, bellowing loudly enough to crack the plaster. "Out! Out! Get out, you vandals!"

It took Trent a moment to realize that Mr. Collins meant him, too, but Ernie, no stranger to situations in which he was in for stormy weather unless he cleared out fast, instantly scrambled to his feet and scampered out the door, propelled by sheer instinct.

Trent glanced at Pam. She shrugged tiredly and resignedly. While she might have been sympathetic, she clearly wasn't about to go through the whole appeals process all over again. Trent had no choice but to follow Mr. Collins' implacably pointing finger out of the room and downstairs.

Pam caught up with him at the front door. Ernie had already torn through the living room and was somewhere outside by this time, much to Mrs. Collins' perplexity when he raced past her without even saying good night.

"That Ernie!" Pam exclaimed to Trent. "Just when I had Dad agreeing to let you take the comics, he had to go and pull a stunt like that! Sometimes I wonder why you hang around him so much!"

"He's my friend," Trent replied, puzzled to think that anyone could question a fact of life so basic.

The answer seemed to bring Pam up a little short, as though it made her realize something she had never considered before. "Anyway," she went on quickly, "with Dad in the mood he's in now, you'll have to wait a while on the comics until I think of something else. Okay?"

"Okay, I guess..." Trent agreed reluctantly, seeing how few his options were.

Ernie was already sitting in the car and whistling some random tune or other when Trent opened the driver's side door and climbed in behind the wheel.

Trent was furious and needed the distraction of starting the car and moving out into the dark street to calm down enough to say anything. "Well, I hope you're happy," he groused after a minute or two of heavy silence hanging in the air had ticked by. "You really ruined things for me and *Shockwave* this time."

"Oh, come on, J. Robert!" Ernie exclaimed. "Mr. Collins'll cool down eventually. You can just write an article about something else while you're waiting to do the one on Cap an' Bucky!"

"Ernie," Trent said, forcing himself to be calm and rational even though he was still seething, "I don't think you quite understand what's at stake here. Do you know why Pam's collection is so important?"

"Sure," Ernie replied, sounding relieved that Trent was going to have a normal conversation instead of yell at him, "she's got a lot of old an' rare funnybooks that po' folks like you and me'll never get to read 'cause big-time dealers charge big wads of moolah for 'em."

"That's part of it, but — Lord, Ernie! Am I the only one who understands?" It had been building up inside of Trent for a long time, almost since that day in 1965 when, at the age of 14, he first got a fanzine in the mail, sent to him in response to a letter of comment he'd had printed in an issue of *The Fantastic Four*, but only now were his thoughts on the matter crystalizing. "Look, here we have this big area of literature that only the fans care about. Nobody's ever written a book on comic books except Dr.

Wertham and Jules Feiffer, and Wertham's book is just an attack on comics and Feiffer's is just one man's nostalgia."

"Great reprints, though," Ernie said.

"True. Those stories Feiffer reprinted are about the only way you're going to read some of them. And that's kind of my point. Comic books have been published for about 30 years now, but nobody's listed them all, and they cost too much for serious researchers to get at them very easily. But Pam has just about everything—"

"Not quite," Ernie put in. "She was tellin' me that Ol' Man Erwin musta started slackin' off in the late '40s, 'cause she's findin' an awful lot of holes in later runs. If you want love comics or spook comics or crook comics or stuff like that, forget it, 'cause he wasn't botherin' with 'em. Guy had *some* taste."

"I meant the early '40s comics, with the World War II superheroes. Pam has their entire early history in one room. But you know her as well as I do — she isn't that interested in it. When I asked her the other day to dig out her Golden Age *Captain America*s, she asked me perfectly seriously, 'What do you want that dreadful old stuff for when you can get brand new Captain America stories by Lee and Kirby that are a lot better written and drawn every month in *Tales of Suspense*?' And you know her father. He's going to try to sell most of that collection in bits and pieces to the highest bidders. When he gets done, that incredible collection of comic-book history will be split up among a hundred different collectors all over the country, and the chance to do research with it will be gone forever. So I've got to get in there and do as much as I can before Mr. Collins breaks it up, and publish the information in *Shockwave* so it'll at least be on record for other serious fans. Otherwise it'll be lost. That's why my Captain America article is so important. It would have been just the beginning. That's what you just spoiled."

"Oh," said Ernie, and fell silent for a moment. Then he added, "Sorry 'bout that, Chief!"

Ernie was quiet after that, lost in thought for the rest of the drive back to Trent's house. Which was fine with Trent, still too upset to want to talk about anything else.

Once back in Trent's bedroom, however, the dam broke on Ernie's inspiration. He picked up a copy of the *Rocket's Blast/Comicollector* from the top of Trent's desk and riffled through it. In that phase of its long existence, the *RBCC* was what was called in the trade an "adzine," consisting almost entirely of ads for fanzines and back issues of comic books, and its circulation of some 2000 souls was roughly coextensive with active comics fandom.

"Look at all these ads for old comics," Ernie said, holding the magazine open to a random two-page spread. Since the dealers prepared their own camera-ready ads that the editor pasted down with no more thought than to cram as many as he could in the available space, the pages were a layout-artist's nightmare, but somehow the sloppy format and densely printed, minusculely reproduced typewriter type never seemed to deter bargain-hunting fans.

"So?" asked Trent irritably from where he lolled on his bed.

Ernie stood in front of him. "Have you ever stopped to wonder where these big-time funnybook wheelers an' dealers got all their comics in the first place?"

Trent's irritation gave way to blankness. "Huh?"

"Think about it, Junior. Those greedheads weren't born with 'em, an' they sure as hell didn't buy 'em from other dealers. I mean, if New Low Prices Howard is charging $12.50 for *Fantastic Four* #1, he didn't buy it for ten bux from Fatcat Comics, Inc. — he prob'ly paid some neighborhood kid fifty cents for it, if that much."

"I guess," Trent conceded, "but what can you do about it? If you want some comic and only a dealer has it, you're stuck paying his price—"

"The hell you are!" Ernie snapped. "Sometimes you're so dense I wonder why you don't sink through the floor. I'm sayin' we should eliminate the middleman — line all the dealers up against the wall an' shoot 'em! We can get old comics from the same places *they* do! From the basements an' attics an' garages of the people who bought 'em 25 years ago an' put 'em away someplace. How many more stashes like Ol' Man Erwin's are there, just waitin' for us to turn 'em up?"

"But how do we find them?" Trent asked. "Pam's dad just sort of lucked on to hers..."

"Advertise, how else? We put an ad in the paper. If we offer people money for their old funnybooks — not much, but some — we'll smoke out all those piles of old comics that've been sittin' around for all these years in Grandpa's steamer trunk."

"I don't know..." Trent murmured doubtfully. "It sounds like it would still cost us a lot of money just to get started."

"That's the beauteous part of it! This scheme pays for itself! Once we get in the first batch of comics, we sell off the dupes and what we don't want for ourselves through *RBCC* ads, an' use the money to buy *more* comics! Or we trade for what we want. Whichever. You get all the old comics to write your book reports on, I get to read 'em, an' we both get rich to boot! It can't miss!"

"Ernie! Are you suggesting we become dealers? *Us?*" The thought all but shocked Trent.

Ernie nodded gravely. "Us little guys've been pushed around long enough. It's time we started pushin' back. If you want money for old comics, it's either this or get a *Grit* route."

Trent sat upright, stunned by the sheer enormity of the idea. The potential rewards and problems both seemed too vast to comprehend easily. "Good Lord. I mean, it's just something I never thought about. I suppose if we put an ad in the *Times*, we might get some response..." With that, a chilling implication occurred to him. "Wait a minute. If we advertise... people would find out I collect comic books."

"Look, Junior," Ernie said with no little asperity, "ain't that kinda like the basic idea?"

"Ernie, you know I've always kept quiet about my hobby. If my teachers found out, they might think I was feeble-minded and make it harder for me to get good grades or recommendations for college, and all the jocks would make fun of me. Those guys tease me enough for reading poetry and listening to classical music as it is." He thought of one lissome lovely in particular in his English class and felt his vertebrae turn to pudding. "And what would the *girls* think?"

"What was that high-falutin' line you were quotin' at me the other day?" Ernie replied evenly. "'Into each life a little rain must fall'? Well, if you wanna scare up some funnybooks, you're gonna have to put up with gettin' a little damp. 'Sides, you can get the teachers off your back by showin' 'em *Shockwave*. When they see how creative it is an' you're even puttin' out your own magazine, they'll ooh and aah and get all dewy-eyed. The jocks an' the chicks, well, I hate to say it, but they already think you're pretty weird just for bein' a good-grade-gettin' bookworm, so your reputation's shot anyway. You might as well forget 'em and do what you darn well please without worryin' what they're gonna say."

"I guess you're right, but... let me think about this for a while, all right?"

Ernie shrugged. "Sure, but don't take too long with your thinnin'. I'm hot to trot *now*."

Perhaps it was because of Ernie's powers of persuasion, or perhaps it was because of subconsciously gloating over all the old comics he might uncover, but by the next morning, without ever making a deliberate, waking-state decision, Trent was ready to go along with the scheme.

Over the next two days, he and Ernie hashed everything out at length, making plans, laying groundwork, hatching plots, and spinning webs. The result was a loose partnership dubbed Trent-Volney Comics, or TV Comics for short. Trent knew only too well that the quickest way to blow their friendship apart in a flurry of squabbling would be for them to attempt to function as a single business with assets held in common, so he cobbled together a framework in which they would operate as independent dealers, each responsible for his own wares and funds, while sharing advertising and other joint expenses. Any windfalls of unusually valuable old comics would be divided equally.

Operating capital was the next hurdle. Ernie was fairly well fixed in that on Saturdays he earned the odd dollar helping out his father, who was foreman at Shetland Sanitation Services, when the garbage crews were short on manpower. Also, he had a large stock of duplicate copies of numerous recent comics, the harvest of picking through garbage cans while dumping them, so he was all but ready to set up as a comic-book dealer right away. Only the newest of new fans wouldn't already have almost all of the extra comics he had, however, which meant he still needed older comics to have something that might actually sell.

As for Trent, getting started in serious comic-book dealing would require an initial investment of more money than he had in his pockets, especially since half the justification for the enterprise was buying people's presumed hoards of Golden Age comics. That meant tapping the Uncle Harry Fund.

More precisely, Uncle Harry had been Trent's great-uncle, an elderly bachelor of comfortable means who had expired the year before with few heirs. Trent wouldn't have had a car at all if Uncle Harry hadn't had a '57 Chevy sitting in his garage when he joined the angelic choir. In addition, Uncle Harry's estate had included some actual cash, and the amount that finally filtered down to Trent ran to several thousand dollars, which his parents had promptly put aside as college money.

Trent broached the subject to his father, who was surprised by the idea if only because he had once tried unsuccessfully to interest his son in Junior Achievement for the sake of soaking up practical business experience. A comic-book dealership was completely out of left field, but reasoning that if Bob, Jr. had enough expertise in *anything* to make money at it, it had to be comic books, Mr. Trent gave his blessing and opened the vaults for a loan of $200 to get started.

And so TV Comics lifted anchor and sailed out of port.

Chapter Two: GETTING THE WORD OUT

On Friday, Trent sat at his desk in third-period study hall and contemplated the blank sheet of paper in front of him. The task at hand was to compose a classified ad for the school newspaper.

Ernie had talked him into this one. An ad had already been placed in the *Times*, Shetland's foremost (and only) community newspaper, and was scheduled to appear in the Saturday edition. Trent privately nursed the hope that the ad there would be sufficiently conspicuous to attract some notice among the older adults most likely to have a heap of decades-old comic books in the attic, but small and obscure enough that jocks and pretty girls wouldn't see it. Ernie, however, wanted complete coverage of every possible source of back issues, and if Trent's academic and social dignity suffered a little as a result, then tough luck, Junior.

The empty expanse of paper stared back at Trent. Not an easy job, this. He felt like his French teacher's son, who according to her story wanted to tell a certain girl that he liked her, but asked his mother how to say it in French so the girl wouldn't understand him when he said it. (The rest of the story was that the boy was instructed to say "*Je t'adore*," but when he did tell the girl that, she replied, "Shut what door?") How could Trent announce to the world that he collected comic books without anyone finding out?

The teacher was out of the room just then, and what was going on around Trent might have been written up as a campus riot in some newspapers. But ignoring the paper airplanes and spitballs, and tuning out the insults and ribald remarks some of the guys were amusing each other with, Trent concentrated on the matter at hand. Then he sensed a presence at his side, asking in a high-pitched, nasal voice, "Nhee... c'n I borrow a quoddah?"

Without having to look up, Trent knew who it was and suppressed a groan.

When he had quoted that line to Ernie about a little rain falling into someone's life, it was in reference to this particular downpour. Comicbook artist Ogden Whitney would have been dumbfounded to meet

Mickey Gompers and discover that the character he drew, Herbie Pop-necker, a short, nearly spherical fat boy with glasses and black hair seemingly cut by trimming around the edge of a bowl on his head, had a real-life counterpart. Like Herbie, Mickey was something of a mystery in many ways, but whereas Herbie had strange powers and was smarter than he let on and usually underestimated by everyone around him, Mickey's mysteries were simply sad. Did he have an actual speech defect or just a perpetual bad cold? He was always shabbily dressed — did a poor home environment contribute to his seeming slowness on the uptake? He did have a slightly older brother who was enough like him to be a twin. On the other hand, he attended the public high school and took the same classes as everyone else, so he must have had some wits about him. In fact, Trent remembered once overhearing Mt. Schatten say that Mickey's grades were often as good or better than those of supposedly more capable students because "he did the work."

Whatever his story, Mickey knew he had a friend — or at least a soft touch — in J. Robert Trent, Jr., who never teased him or played mean tricks on him. Trent gave him the quarter he wanted in the hope he would go away, and that Mickey did after sniffling a quick "T'ank 'oo!"

Before he could get started on the ad, Trent happened to notice Mickey passing the desk of Bill Hunter, a brawny senior with social connections in both the Athlete and Hood castes, a couple of aisles over. It was hard to see exactly what happened with the intervening desks and the people sitting at them blocking a view of the floor, but just as he came abreast of Hunter, Mickey seemed to stumble and take a step back.

"Dgee, Bill," he said, gently admonishing and giving sincere advice as though Bill Hunter was his best friend on Earth, "you oughtta watch where you 'tick your foot out. Tumbuddy could twip over it!"

Evidently, Mickey had seen Hunter's nether member just in time or he would have gone sprawling.

"Yeah," Hunter growled. "I'll have to watch that!"

Then, as Mickey went on by, Hunter turned back to look at his snickering buddies behind him. With a rueful grin, he made a fist-pumping gesture as though to say, "Curses, foiled again!"

*Poor Mickey!* Trent thought and went back to his work.

And now, with Mickey Gompers out of the way, to work.

Trent worried and fidgeted with the ad for some time, finally settling on **"WANTED TO BUY: Old Comic Books"** to start it off. He spent the rest of the study hall trying to decide whether to leave it at that or specify how old, just to avoid being deluged with painfully recent comics people would be convinced were worth big bucks.

During his lunch period, Trent dropped by the Journalism classroom to turn in the copy for his ad. There he ran into Laurie Saunders, the editor of the Shetland High School *Express*, who was spending her lunch period working on a problem of her own.

Laurie was a rather dumpy senior with short, mouse-brown hair. One or two well-meaning friends, noting with sorrow Trent's lack of female companionship as he trudged his lonely way down Life's highway, had suggested that he take up with Laurie since her student journalism activities suggested that she had an intellectual side. Trent's idea of a romantic evening running to reading his Robert Frost while his one true love read her Emily Dickinson, he was more appalled than intrigued by the idea, as not only was she loud and brash, she could probably pin him to the floor three falls out of three.

While Trent stood by, Laurie sat at her desk and read the ad, then she looked up at him with her usual slightly sour expression. "Comic books, huh? Are you serious?"

"Er... yes," Trent replied, looking longingly at the door. He had just wanted to submit the ad, not justify his right to good air.

"Hmm," Laurie muttered, looking at the ad again. "I hear they're worth a lot of money these days."

"Uh... some of them are. The really old ones. A few are worth as much as a hundred dollars."

"You got a lot of 'em?" Laurie suddenly asked, zeroing in on his face with gimlet eyes. "You collect 'em?"

"Well, uh, yes," Trent stumbled, losing track of the lie he had prepared in advance about needing the comic books for a term paper on contemporary media, not that he really enjoyed them or would read them if some mean old teacher hadn't made him.

"Calm down, fella — I'm not going to bite you. I'm going to make you famous!"

"Huh?"

"It's like this, Bob. I've got a hole you could drive a truck through on page 2 and the deadline's coming up fast. So I was thinking... How would you like to be interviewed for 'Ponies You Should Know'?"

Trent could feel the blood drain out of his face. "Ponies You Should Know" was a semi-regular column that threw the full glare of the *Express* spotlight on Shetland High School students who had accomplished something notable, like the girl who had finished second in the statewide extemporaneous speaking competition, or who had remarkable interests or hobbies, like the farm boy who was raising a buffalo calf. Submit to being interviewed for that column and Trent could wave a sad and forlorn farewell to all hope of staying anonymous.

"Er... ah, I don't know — I mean, I'm not sure—"

Laurie exhaled impatiently. "Well, think about it, will you? I'll be in here last period, so if we can work something out, come back and see me then."

"No, ah — I just have to talk it over with my partner," Trent tried to explain, but Laurie was already waving him away;

Trent found Ernie in the cafeteria, reading a *Doc Savage* paperback while he munched on a sandwich, and told him what Laurie had said.

"Oh, come on, J. Robert!" Ernie exclaimed when Trent had finished. "Use your head for something besides a place to put your glasses! We'll get a hell of a lot more publicity out of an article than from a winky-dinky little classified ad!"

"That's kind of what I was afraid of..."

Ernie sputtered bread crumbs. "If you wanted a nice, safe, respectable, *boring* hobby, why didn't you take up *stamps*, for Chrissake?!"

That afternoon, Trent went to his English class in a gloomy frame of mind. English was the class where he shone brightest. It was where most of his interest lay and where he found most of his friends — as well as most of the girls he was ineffectually attracted to. He pondered the effect exposure of his vice in the *Express* would have, and he grew more depressed as he walked.

Not watching where he was going, he didn't notice a girl trying to go through the doorway into the English classroom at the same time he reached that point in space, and ran right into her. Her books spilled all over the floor.

"Fancy meeting you here," the girl said with icicle-dripping sarcasm, and bent down to pick up her books.

Trent could have died on the spot. He wanted to run to the nearest wall and bang his head against it. He hadn't bumped into just any girl, he had just sustained a collision with the single most desirable feminine specimen in the entire known universe. "Uh... sorry, Linda!" he blurted, scrambling to assist her in gathering up her books. "Let me help—"

"Don't bother," the girl said coldly. "I can manage."

Trent went on to his desk and sat down, now not only depressed but sick at heart. Romance was another comedy of errors that had somehow never been very funny for him. He had been through his share of futile crushes in earlier years, then having a car had gotten him only as far as a couple of movie dates with girls who seemed disinclined to repeat the experience. Even the all but unimaginable fantasy coming true of a pretty girl he had barely known turning out to be a comics and science-fiction fan who could even draw covers for his fanzine had mainly resulted in adding a third member to Shetland Fandom. Pam had no romantic interest in him or anyone else as far as he could tell, and over the past several months in which he had gotten to know her at all well, he had to admit that he had no romantic interest in her. Since they shared so many of the same interests, maybe he should have, but something in the chemistry didn't mix. Then one day in English, Trent had noticed that — in theory — a certain slender brunette's waist was just the right size for putting an arm around. That odd realization was chemistry's way of telling him something was cooking.

Her name, oddly enough, was that of a comic-book character: Linda Lee, though her last name was Jespersen. She reminded Trent of Stephen Vincent Benet's lines from *The Ballad of William Sycamore*: "*Till I lost my boyhood and won my wife, a girl like a Salem clipper! A woman straight as a hunting knife, with eyes bright as the Dipper!*" She was tallish and imperially slim, one of the few girls in the class who really had the legs to look splendid in a miniskirt. She had the body of a model and the face of an angel, if a somewhat cynical and worldly-wise one. Her father was plant manager at Dyna-Wave Radio Products where Trent's father worked, so her family was well off, and her intelligence was phenomenal. Top grades in English regularly alternated between her and Trent, and she was much his superior in math and science where he seemed to have a built-in blind spot. She was also a free-thinker: she had shocked the advanced English class a while back by choosing *Catcher in the Rye* for an oral book report and tearing it apart because she thought the main character was a creep, and she had eviscerated some other favorites of the class intelligentsia as well. Strand *her* on an island with a bunch of other kids, and she'd have things organized and humming without any descent into savagery like in *Lord of the Flies*. Linda Lee Jespersen's combination of brains, beauty, wealth, status, and independence took Trent's breath away.

Unfortunately, his attempts to talk to her had usually dissolved into stammering and stuttering, and he had reason to believe that she had not been much impressed with the J. Robert Trent, Jr. brand of wit and charm. So he could only look miserably on while she consorted with the handsome, athletic, well-favored chaps, mostly seniors, whom Ernie had once pegged with his usual crude but devastating accuracy as "blondie studs," and hope that one day the wind might change direction.

Now, however… Trent glanced across the room and saw Linda drop her books on her desk in obvious annoyance. The wind hadn't changed direction, and it had gotten a lot colder.

At that point, the teacher stopped by Trent's desk, handing back some papers. Mr. Gillespie was a tall, bespectacled scarecrow of a man with a beak-like nose and a thatch of uncombed, pure white hair, who always wore a suit jacket with a bowtie. Childhood memories of reading *Donald Duck* comics and seeing the character Gyro Gearloose always came to Trent's mind when he encountered this particular teacher.

"That was a very good essay you wrote on Dickenson's *I Died for Beauty*, Bob," he said in a raspy, somewhat high-pitched voice that reminded him of the character actor Sterling Holloway. "It was quite perceptive."

Trent beamed, suddenly cheered. Mr. Gillespie was the one teacher in the whole school he loved like a kindly uncle, the one bright mind in all of Shetland with whom he could discuss the beauty of formal verse structures and language made lyrical. Winning Mr. Gillespie's approval was extremely high on Trent's list of priorities.

"The only thing is," Mr. Gillespie went on, picking up Trent's essay to read from it, "I don't quite see the point you were trying to make with your comment that '*In lesser hands, the theme and setting of the poem would have been no more than a gruesome horror story in some trashy comic book such as infested the newsstands of the early 1950s.*' Really, Bob! Comparing Emily Dickenson to horror comic books! Even to show how much better she is... well, that's hardly necessary. I think you might be best advised to leave irrelevant comparisons with vile forms of popular subculture out of your writing for class. But it was a very good essay otherwise."

Mr. Gillespie left, leaving Trent suddenly depressed again. The reference to horror comics had been a little off the wall, and he had realized it at the time he wrote the essay, but the superficial resemblance of Dickenson's poem, which described two corpses in adjacent tombs chatting until the moss covered their lips, to what he knew of EC horror comics from fanzine articles and Dr. Wertham's book had been too tempting to let pass without comment.

Losing Linda's esteem was bad enough — he'd never had it to begin with. But what would Mr. Gillespie think when he read the article in the *Express*? Trent felt the beginnings of a stomachache coming on.

In the end, Ernie's bullying triumphed over Trent's queasiness. However reluctant he might have been at heart, Trent reported to Laurie Saunders that afternoon that he was ready to be interviewed. Ernie's bullying might not have worked if Trent had known beforehand what Laurie was going to spring on him once he agreed. The interview, she told him, would be conducted at his house the next day, and the staff photographer from the *Express* would be along to take pictures of him and his collection.

Trent swallowed hard, wondering where it would all end.

Laurie was nothing if not efficient. She rang the doorbell at Trent's house at precisely 10:00 on Saturday morning with the *Express* photographer, a thin and pimply senior named Daryl Knudsen, in tow. Trent felt mounting irritation with the whole business: he'd had to get up early to put his bedroom in order, and between that and the interview, he'd had to miss the few Saturday morning cartoon shows of any interest to him, in particular the Hanna-Barbera *Fantastic Four* and the Grantray-Lawrence *Spider-Man* programs. Sue, his 14-year-old sister, took full advantage of the situation to watch a movie on the independent station that didn't show cartoons, chortling over the fact that her big brother was for once out of the way and unable to monopolize the tube.

While Laurie set up her portable tape recorder on Trent's desk, threading the small reels and testing the microphone, Daryl took pictures: Trent standing by his comic-stuffed bookcase, Trent standing by the six-foot Spider-Man poster on the door, the poster and the bookcase without Trent, Trent pretending to read a recent Marvel comic — he had to refuse point-blank to be photographed reading an issue of *Batman* and posing as though chewing his knuckles in suspense. "Aw, it'd be cute!" Laurie insisted, but she let it drop. Then Laurie was ready to interview him and he sat down at the desk in front of her.

Trent was nervous at first, as well as uncomfortable with the idea of having a girl in his bedroom, but the door was ajar and Daryl was wandering around and poking into things, so it all seemed very proper. Besides, Laurie was about the last girl he'd want to be improper with.

It was a long interview. Trent went on the offensive at every opportunity, employing a strategy he had worked out the night before. The only way he could forestall the derision of his peers, he had reasoned, would be to convince them that comic books were no longer the kid stuff they remembered. Trent showed Laurie how Stan Lee, the writer of most Marvel comics, used big words that wee tykes couldn't hope to understand in his stories, argued that the Incredible Hulk was deeply symbolic of the human condition, and claimed that Marvel Comics were so literate that even college students were reading them now.

"After all," he pointed out, "the Marvel fan club, the Merry Marvel Marching Society, has chapters at a lot of universities, and *Esquire* Magazine took a poll that showed Spider-Man and the Hulk were two of the 28 people who count most on college campuses!"

Trent went on to show her copies of his fanzine *Shockwave* as well as other fanzines produced by fans around the country, then pointed to the unbelievably deep articles in them written by intellectual fans, fans who went so far as to declare that the very term *comic book* ought to be replaced by the far more impressive *graphic novel*. Finally, just when he was gearing up for a windy dissertation comparing the existential plight of Stan Lee's Spider-Man with that of Franz Kafka's Gregor Samsa, the only difference being that Samsa didn't put on a skintight costume and fight crime as Captain Cockroach, Laurie ran out of tape and called a halt.

"I think I've got enough here to write the article," she said, seemingly amazed by it all.

Trent settled back in his chair and let out a long breath. The interview had been exhausting as well as long.

Hardly had he cleared Laurie and Daryl out of the house and gone into the kitchen to ask his mother about lunch, the thump of something hitting the front door announced the arrival of the *Times*. Trent spun on his heel and headed out to retrieve the paper from the porch.

He unfolded the *Times* on the living room carpet, passing over the headlines (**NORTH VIETS SHELL YANKS NEAR DAK TO: VIET CONG ENVOY SEIZED IN SAIGON**) as unimportant. He turned to the classified section and ran his finger down the **Wanted to Buy** column. And there, third from the bottom—

### CASH PAID FOR OLD COMIC BOOKS
by collector. Call J. R. Trent, Jr. between
5 and 10 weekdays, all day Saturday and
Sunday. Will pick up. SHetland 3-5299

When composing the ad, he had hoped that the slightly unfamiliar version of his name would decrease the chances of recognition by any of his compeers who might happen to see it. Of course, anonymity would be pretty much a dead issue next Friday, when the *Express* was distributed to the masses of Shetland High School, but he hadn't figured on that when the *Times* ad was in production.

Now he only had to sit tight and wait for all the calls in response to his ad to start ringing the phone off the hook.

But when the afternoon had dragged past three o'clock and the only call had been Ernie asking how the interview had gone, Trent began to feel somewhat discouraged.

He pulled a paperback book at random off the shelf and idly reread it: Ace Books' reprint of Ralph Milne Farley's *The Radio Beasts*. In recent years, he had been collecting Ace's editions of the works of Edgar Rice Burroughs, and he had expanded his reach into ERB's imitators as well. Ace had begun Farley's Venus series with the second book, and Trent had no idea where to find a copy of the first volume. Having missed what in comic-book terms would be considered the "origin," Trent felt all the frustrations of coming in late on a series as he ran across references to events he'd never read about and characters he'd never heard of. The introduction to *The Radio Beasts* told him the first book had been called *The Radio Man* and he could guess from *Beasts'* publication details that *Man* had probably appeared before 1925 in a magazine called *Argosy*, but he wasn't sure if even Pam's collection went back that far. Unless he got very lucky, it looked as though Trent would never find out how the Earthman hero got to Venus in the first place.

His frustration was hardly alleviated by reading the book for a second time, so he finally gave up on it and turned to a book of poetry instead. About 3:30, he was contemplating a line in one of William Blake's poems: "*Tiger, tiger, burning bright.*" Apart from its metaphysical underpinnings, it reminded Trent of the tigers he had seen the previous summer at the Brookfield Zoo on a family outing to Chicago, and now that he thought about it, tigers did seem to burn from within with a baleful orange and yellow glow.

Then the extension phone on the lamp table by his bed rang.

*Not Ernie again!* he thought and picked up the receiver. "Hello?"

The answering voice wasn't Ernie's. It was that of a mature woman, and not one that Trent recognized. "Mr. Trent? This is Mrs. Stanley Martin, and I saw your ad in the paper today…" She trailed off uncertainly.

*We got results!* "Yes?" Trent prompted.

"Well, we have some comic books. They belonged to our son, Frank, but he's… gone now, and we thought we might sell them. If you're interested, I mean."

Frank Martin? The name sounded vaguely familiar, but Trent couldn't match a face to it immediately. "Sure, I'm interested. I'll be right over if it's convenient."

It was, and Mrs. Martin gave him an address on the east side of town, out where local industry had concentrated.

On the way downstairs, Trent's mind suddenly made the connection about Frank Martin. He would have realized who Frank Martin was right away if he had followed Shetland High School football at all. Martin had been a star player for SHS in years past, of such renown that even Trent had heard of him, although he had no idea what position he played or what he had done that was so notable. When Frank Martin graduated, probably in the Class of 1965, he was promptly drafted and sent to Vietnam. He did not come back.

*Oh,* Trent thought, sobered. *No wonder they're selling his comics.* He told his mother where he was going and went out to his car.

The Martin home was a modest bungalow hardly to be distinguished from the several one-story houses built on the identical plan around it. The working-class neighborhood wasn't far from the Dyna-Wave Radio Products factory where Trent's father worked as manager of the technical publications department and knew Mr. Martin slightly as a shop foreman out in the plant.

Mrs. Martin, a small, sad, graying woman in her 40s, answered the door. She looked tired, not just physically, but as a reflection of an exhaustion that went much deeper. Trent recalled Blake's lines about tigers burning bright and wondered what the poet would have said about a gray woman whose grayness hinted at the cold ashes of a fire that had long since burned out.

Mrs. Martin's dull eyes flickered a little in surprise when she saw Trent. "I thought you'd be older... I guess I was looking for your father. Well, come on in and I'll show you what we have."

Trent followed her through the neat living room to a dark bedroom at the rear of the house. She pulled the dusty curtains open and in the sudden burst of daylight Trent could see that the room had once been Frank's and had not changed much since. Not because the Martins were preserving it as some sort of memorial, but due to simple disuse. Some boxes of household goods were stacked in a corner and a worn easy chair from the living room blocked access to the closet, but otherwise the room was still the same as it was on the day Frank left home to report for duty. His model cars and airplanes still stood on the wall shelves, though filmed over with the dust of two or three years of casual neglect, and a brown pennant was still tacked on the wall just above the head of the bed, bearing a yellow stylized horse's head and a yellow-lettered motto, "**GO SHS PONIES!**" A framed diploma from Shetland High School, Class of 1965, hung on the wall next to a framed photograph of the Ponies posing for the camera in their helmets and uniforms. The room was an unintentional museum — no, more than a museum. It was a bubble in the stream of reality where time had stopped at 1965 and Frank Martin could be expected to walk in the door at any moment, still 18 years old and just out of school.

"I'll get the comics for you," Mrs. Martin said, pushing past the easy chair and opening the closet door. Frank's clothes still hung inside and Trent had a glimpse of tennis shoes on the floor, model kit boxes, a catcher's mitt, and a baseball bat.

Mrs. Martin dragged out a large cardboard box filled with comic books, and left the room to allow Trent to inspect them at his leisure. He sat down on the floor by the box and began to sort through the comics.

The room was quiet, a touch stuffy from lack of use and ventilation, and even uncomfortably warm from the late afternoon sunlight pouring through the windows. No one came in to distract Trent and he could devote his full attention to seeing what he had here.

Golden Age comics would have been too much to expect, of course, but Trent was nonetheless pleasantly surprised by what he did find. Frank Martin's active years of comic-book buying spanned roughly 1957 to 1963, and along with a mass of largely unmarketable titles few serious fans would want (Archie comics mostly, seasoned with a sprinkling of war comics like *Star-Spangled War Stories* with strange stories about American GIs fighting dinosaurs in the Pacific during World War II), he had managed to pick up a number of eminently worthwhile issues, like most of the early Marvels from when the company had reinvented itself with superheroes around 1961 and 1962. Now that Trent thought about it, even the Archie stuff might be worth going through. Pam was inordinately fond of the extra-thick *Little Archie* comics from the early '60s, and a trade deal might be worked out if she didn't already have some of the issues in the Frank Martin collection.

But as Trent worked his way through the comic books in the stillness of the warm, stuffy room, an oppressive feeling crept slowly over him — on little cat feet, as an Illinois poet might have expressed it.

A boy's room is to a boy as a body is to a soul, an extension of himself, shaped by his personality. Without the boy, Frank Martin's room was no more than a corpse, retaining the form it had held in life but without its vital animating principle. Trent had the uneasy feeling that he was trespassing on someone else's life, poking in somewhere he didn't belong, even grave robbing. He consoled himself by reasoning that he was doing at least a little good since the money he paid for the comic books would help Frank's parents.

Mrs. Martin came back into the room a little later and asked Trent if he had found anything he could use. He surprised her by offering to buy the lot, and was surprised in turn when she accepted his initial offer of $25 without argument. Merely clearing the comics out of the closet seemed more important to her than any money she might squeeze out of them.

As Mrs. Martin opened the front door so Trent could struggle out with the heavy, unwieldy box of comic books, she murmured tonelessly, "You know, he was just a boy…"

To that, Trent had no answer at all.

## Chapter Three: FUNNYBOOK BOB

Over the next several days, life proceeded in fits and spurts. On Sunday, two more calls came in about the *Times* ad. One was from a Mrs. Carney, who had obviously been reading a few too many articles about the high prices collectors were paying for old comic books. She was convinced that a mouse-stained, coverless copy of a 1964 issue of *Superboy*, which she had just brought to light from under the freezer where her little Stevie had lost it some time back, must be worth at least $50 because it *looked* so old. The other call came from a 13-year-old boy wanting to sell his small accumulation of mostly last year's comics to raise money to buy a slot-car racing set. Trent had to explain the facts of life to both parties, and neither went away very happy. For his own part, he was beginning to despair of ever blasting open the fabled vaults where wartime superhero comics were stashed.

Meanwhile, he stayed abreast of TV shows of interest. Besides *Get Smart* on Saturday, *Voyage to the Bottom of the Sea* turned up on Sunday night, and Monday offered *The Monkees* (although Trent was indifferent to the music, he rather liked the surreal comedy), while Tuesday offered *The Invaders*.

So far, no one he knew at school seemed to have noticed the *Times* ad.

Ernie was hardly sitting on his hands in his own quest for salable old comic books. He just had other ways of going about it. As Trent understood his explanation over lunch one day, he made quiet inquiries among his circle of acquaintances in the lower depths of high school society, and flushed out someone in his American History class who had some old issues of *Mad* from when it was still a color comic book. Ernie had vaguely known from fanzine articles that *Mad* hadn't started out as a black and white magazine, but he had never seen the early comic-book version and thought it was worth following up. His contact brought five issues of it into class on Wednesday, all in acceptably good shape for being about 14 years old even if a little musty smelling from spending most of those years in somebody's basement. Ernie took one look at the Wally Wood art in them, in particular Wood's "Superduperman" parody in issue #4, and wasted no time in forking over a dollar for the lot.

"I'd like to see those comics myself," Trent remarked as Ernie told his story. "I've read fanzine articles raving about the Harvey Kurtzman work in the early ones—"

"Sorry," Ernie said mournfully. "Don't got 'em no mo'. I done a baaad thing!"

"You didn't sell them already, did you? Ernie! We're supposed to be partners!"

"Nahh, I didn't sell 'em! Dummy here couldn't wait to look at 'em, so—"

Ernie had tucked the comics inside his notebook and the American History teacher caught him sneaking peeks at them during class. Following a drumhead court martial, the teacher slowly and methodically tore each issue of *Mad* in half and then in quarters, and dropped the shreds in a nearby wastebasket. Then he sent Ernie back to his seat with the warning that any further reading comic books during class time would be met with even sterner measures, perhaps even an unpleasant quarter of an hour with Mr. Wickersham, the school's dreaded assistant principal.

"Christ!" Ernie snorted to Trent. "You'd a thought I was sellin' funny cigarettes to little girls or somethin'!"

"It just goes to show that we'll have to be extra careful if we get into any extensive comic-book dealing here at school," Trent said, ready to weep over the loss of the vintage *Mad* issues and swallowing hard at the thought of Mr. Gillespie catching him at something similar. That would be almost worse than being sent to face Mr. Wickersham.

In one of Shetland High School's dank, ill-lit corridors, Pam spotted Trent in the press of students changing classes about the middle of Thursday morning and hailed him. They found a clear area along the wall between the end of a bank of lockers and a drinking fountain, and stopped to talk while people streamed past.

"I haven't seen much of you lately," Trent said.

"I've been kind of busy," Pam told him. "Besides schoolwork, I've been sketching on a new project, sort of an illustrated novel with myth and magic."

Any other time, Trent might have been interested in hearing all about it, but he had his priorities. "How are things over at your house? With *Captain America*, I mean?"

Pam's thin shoulders rolled in an eloquent shrug. "About the same. Ernie's little stunt put the kibosh on that idea for the time being. Maybe I can sneak the comics out of the house for you eventually, I don't know. I do know how you feel about comic-book scholarship and I tend to agree, and better you should plow through all those dreary old World War II comics than me. Oh, Ernie's been telling me how you guys are setting up shop as comic-book dealers. You're welcome to all the bother as far as I'm concerned. Dad may be a pest at times when I'm trying to work, but I'm glad he's taking care of peddling the merchandise and I don't have to worry about it."

On that note, they had to part to go to their respective classes.

From a distance, Trent saw Linda go by in the crowded hall, walking with one of her gentlemen-admirers from the senior class and laughing and talking as though she enjoyed his company more than anything else in the world. To Trent, she had been barely up to the level of civil, seemingly resenting having to acknowledge his presence when he said "Hi" to her in passing. Miserably, Trent decided that it would be unseasonably chilly in the infernal regions when he and Linda became more than distant acquaintances.

Thursday was a long, bleak school day like any other. Trent came home with only the prospect of *Batman* on TV that evening, and even that was less of a joy and more of a chore. As a comics fan, he felt obligated to keep up on the show, if only because it was the major exposure comics-oriented culture was getting these days out in the great wide world.

No exposure might have been better, he sometimes thought. He still remembered all too clearly January 12, 1966 — Black Wednesday, the fateful day when the *Batman* TV show premiered as a mid-season replacement for some other show. He had been 14 then, just shy of turning 15, still a touch naïve as a comics fan, and he had looked forward to it as a triumph for his hobby, a vindication of his interests, proof that comic books were more than mental chewing gum for infantile minds. Why, even adults would be watching this show, and they would see that comic books were something for them, too. He went so far as to badger some of his friends at school until they agreed to watch it. Then he actually saw it.

He tried to rationalize it, tried to put the best possible face on it, but he still had to face his friends the next day. In the end, he only felt betrayal. Somebody out there in Hollywood was making a pile of money by throwing mud at everything Bob Trent held holy, laughing and sneering at it with this "camp" business, and soon the whole country was laughing and sneering at *Batman*... and, he felt, at Bob Trent.

Tonight's episode was "The Bloody Tower" with Rudy Vallee and Glynis Johns as guest stars. The only approval it dragged out of Trent was a grudging admission that Yvonne Craig filled her Batgirl costume rather well.

After *Batman* was over, Trent went back upstairs and called Ernie to discuss it as well as make plans to get together to assemble their first joint *RBCC* ad. Finally, Trent had to break it off, saying, "Well, I've got home-work to do—"

"You've *always* got homework to do!"

"—So I'd ought to get to it. And I'd better brace myself. The *Express* with my interview is coming out tomorrow. I just hope Laurie put every-thing I told her in it."

The story broke the next morning when copies of the December 8, 1967 edition of the *Express* first hit the halls and the home rooms. With trembling hands, Trent opened his copy to page 2. Since football season was over, news during the stretch between Thanksgiving and Christmas was a little slack, and the page was filled with minor items such as "Pony Tales" (the gossip column Laurie ghosted under the name of the school mascot, Edgar Allan Pony), an appeal for everyone to donate toys and canned goods to the Bureau County Forgotten Family Christmas Fund, and a story about the debate team not doing very well at the match in Peoria the week before written in terms of "hey, they tried really hard" and "we're laying the foundation for next year." And "Ponies You Should Know."

Glaringly conspicuous was a large, grainy picture of Trent stiffly posed holding several comic books while standing in front of the six-foot Spider-Man poster on his door. Then he read the article itself — and it was like being hit across the nose with a two-by-four.

## *Ponies You Should Know*

# Zap! Pow! SHS Student Collects Comic Books

by Laurie Saunders

Holy bank account! Did you know that old comic books which once cost a dime are now worth a lot of money? Pow! Bob Trent ('69) knows. Zap! Bob is quite a fanatical collector. He has a whole room

full of comic books and is looking for
more. His favorite comics are all about
super-detectives in brightly colored long
johns who fight crime and save the universe from super-baddies. Biff! They
really turn Bob on. He has teamed up
with his friend Ernie Volney, who is also
a comic freak, to buy old comic books.
They call themselves Television Comics.
There are many other comic book collectors all across the country, too, Bob says,
and he prints his very own homemade
magazine called *Shortwave* with articles
and stories about all the different comics
to keep in touch with his fellow comics
nuts. Bob says the funnies are really very
interesting and some are not as childish
as you may think. Wham!

Trent was beyond horror or anger. He was completely numb. *She
didn't listen to a single word I said!* he thought once his mental gears
engaged again.

He looked fearfully around his home room and saw half the students
reading the *Express* — and most seemed to be staring intently at page 2.
He wanted to get up and snatch every last copy out of their hands before
they had a chance to read that humiliating article, but it was too late. Much
too late.

The class funnyman, Steve Sheldon, put his paper down and pointed
at Trent for the benefit of his buddies. "Hey, guys!" he exclaimed. "We
got us a real celebrity in here!"

Now Trent only wanted to find a deep hole and pull it in after him.

For two periods it went like that, with people pointing at Trent as he
went by, or coming up to him and telling him they had seen him in the
paper. Some even seemed to think he didn't already know about it. It was
always the same: "I don't read comic books anymore myself, Bob, but I've
seen *Batman* on the tube and it's real dumb, so what do you see in the
things, anyway?"

Each time he saw someone reading the *Express*, Trent felt a new
tingle of horror rappelling down his spinal column. By the time he reached
third-period study hall, his nerves were shot — and there was Mr. Schatten, the teacher assigned to monitor the classroom, sitting placidly at the

front desk and leafing through the *Express*. Then Bill Hunter came in with his pals, saw Trent, and snickered, "Hoo hoo! Funnybook Bob! Hoo hoo!"

If Trent had only been slightly more prone to violence, Laurie Saunders would have found an early grave. Or at least backed into a corner and yelled at.

"Hey, Funnybook Bob!" Hunter called. "Whaddya do with your funnybooks when you've read 'em? Trade 'em to Mickey for new ones? Hyuk hyuk!"

*If I go to the nurse and pretend I'm sick,* Trent thought miserably, *would she let me go home? Then I wouldn't have to face anyone until Monday.*

"Nhee…"

And certainly of all the people he didn't want to face, Mickey Gompers ranked high on the list, but there he was, a squat, dwarfish humanoid in the shape of a deflated snowman, standing in front of Trent's desk and looking like he wanted something.

"Yes, Mickey?" Trent asked, wondering only what a malevolent universe was going to hit him with now.

"Nhee… you gib munney for cummic books?"

"Well, yes, for old ones," Trent replied. What kind of cummic books would Mickey read? *Little Dot*? *Richie Rich*?

"We god lods ob cummic books in our batement," Mickey said, "an' dey're real old, doo."

Trent sighed. Well, it was at least possible that the kid had something worthwhile, and in this business even the unlikeliest leads should be followed up. It was just that the prospect of having more to do with Mickey Gompers than he absolutely had to was dispiriting. "I'll have to take a look at what you have first," Trent told him cautiously.

"Okee, I'll bring tum in on Munday," Mickey promised, and went off happily to his desk.

"Oh, great…" Trent muttered, wondering if a day like today was the reason why, in the Edwin Arlington Robinson poem, Richard Cory "*one calm summer night, went home and put a bullet through his head.*"

At lunch, Trent sought out Ernie. "I can't take much more of this!" he exclaimed. "If I hear somebody call me 'Funnybook Bob' one more time, I think I'll start tearing my hair out!"

"Take it easy, Junior," Ernie soothed, chewing calmly on a sandwich. "Me, I'm doin' fine. Thanks to that mention of me in the article, I made a coupla contacts already that might pay off. Nothin' big, but one guy's got what sounds like a pretty complete collection of old Marvels, *Fantastic Four* #1 on up."

"That's great — for you!" Trent said peevishly. "But Laurie Saunders didn't make you look like a complete idiot, either!"

"Ahh, it'll all blow over by Monday."

"Sure and between now and Monday is my English class. What will they say about me *there*, for heaven's sake?"

He found out early. Going into the classroom, he encountered Mr. Gillespie coming out. "Oh, Robert," the teacher said sadly, as though his heart were breaking, "I wish you had told me about this... er, comic-book thing before."

"Well, uh, it never seemed to come up..."

"I had such hope for you!" Mr. Gillespie went on, growing even more mournful. "The first student to come along in my classes who was acquainted with Keats and Shelley as old friends, who knew poets and their works the way other boys know baseball players and batting averages, who didn't snigger and wink when I discussed *The Rape of the Lock*... and I find he reads comic books! '*How arrives it joy lies slain, and why unblooms the best hope ever sown?*'"

"Thomas Hardy, *Hap*," Trent said automatically, then remembered where he was. "I mean, I'm sorry, sir, but—"

"We'll speak more of this later, Robert," Mr. Gillespie interrupted, and went on his way down the hall to run some pre-class errand or other.

Trent walked on in to the classroom with a heart going down for the last time. His favorite teacher had reacted to the *Express* article as though Trent had just run over his dog. How could he explain to him that "*I could not love thee, Comics, so much, loved I not poetry more*"?

He sat down at his desk and looked out the window at the gloomy, cloudy December day. The bleakness outside matched that in his soul. Perhaps it was time to get out of this comic-book thing before it ruined his life completely...

He was so low in spirit that he barely noticed Linda Lee Jespersen come into the room, books in her arms. Then, to his mounting amazement, he saw her walking purposefully towards him instead of to her desk in the far corner. His attention snapped away from his other problems and his lungs sagged when she stopped in front of his desk. "Uh... hi... Linda," he croaked.

"I just saw your write-up in the paper," she announced. Even when it was so abrupt, that husky contralto voice by itself reminded Trent of moonlight and roses.

"Er... I can explain that," he said quickly.

"Never mind," she broke in. "I know how Laurie Saunders' mind works and I can guess that whatever you told her was pure drivel by the time she finished with it. She did it to me a while back with the Latin Club's Roman Banquet — I gave her a straight story and she made a bunch of jokes about eating while lying down on couches. But you know something, Bob? You've got more guts than I gave you credit for." Then she turned and strode off to her own desk.

Trent rolled that around in his mind for a while, trying to decide if it meant she liked him after all, but finally came to the conclusion that it was too left-handed a compliment to give him much cause for cheer.

With Mr. Gillespie still out of the room the class couldn't begin, and the students talked quietly among themselves. Several of the boys drifted over to Trent's desk to tell him that they had seen the *Express* article, too.

Here, in his favorite class, surrounded by generally sympathetic intellectuals, Trent realized that this was his last chance to salvage anything of his reputation. To his assembled friends, he quickly explained that Laurie hadn't really understood him, then summarized what he had actually said.

"So you see," he wound up, "comic books today deal extensively with mature, adult themes."

The group seemed to be buying it — until someone at the fringe suddenly sputtered, "Bob, you're nuts! What you're saying is pure bull!"

"Come again?" Bob said blankly, startled by the vehemence.

Speaking was Warren Cooper, who was new at Shetland High that year. Warren's father, like Trent's, worked at Dyna-Wave Radio Products and had recently transferred to the Shetland plant from out of state. Warren was a quiet, deliberate sort who seldom said anything unless a national emergency had been declared.

"So comics are adult literature, huh?" Warren challenged. "Let me tell you a little story. When my family and I moved to Shetland, our new house wasn't ready yet, so we lived for a month in the other half of that old dump on North Main Street where the Gompers live—" There were gasps from the listeners. "Yeah, Mickey Gompers' family! The walls were pretty thin and sometimes you could hear what they were saying on the other side. Especially in the bathroom, since the Gompers bathroom and ours were directly opposite. One night I was taking a bath and over on the other side of the wall, I could hear Mickey and his brother Dicky, who's just like him, taking a bath together — and they were playing *Batman*!"

Warren shook his head as though he still couldn't quite believe what he had heard with his own ears, waiting for the laughter to die down a little, then he continued. "God, just the thought of those two naked little butterballs sitting in the bathtub together with their Soaky toys and playing Batman…! It was incredible! You haven't lived until you've heard how the Joker and the Riddler joined Thrush, so Batman had to team up with James Bond, Napoleon Solo, and J. Edgar Hoover to go after them!" He launched into singing the Neal Hefti *Batman* TV theme song, using a dead-on imitation of Mickey's all-purpose conversation opener, his nasal *nhee*, for the notes, and more laughter exploded from everyone listening — except from Trent, who was suddenly very conscious of the red blood in his cheeks. Then Warren switched to Mickey and Dicky voices: "'Bedder watch out, Doker! I'm comin' t'getchoo!' 'Nhee... nhat's what *choo* t'ink, Batman! Not even *Tuperman* c'n 'top me now!'" Against the gales of hilarity from all sides, Warren finished by pointing a finger at Trent and demanding, "And so, Bob, you're trying to tell me comic books are for *adults*?!"

Red-faced and stung by the hooting from every corridor, Trent protested: "But that's the *TV* Batman! They got it all wrong! The comic book's different! And besides, *Batman* is a DC comic — it's *Marvels* that are mature and literate!"

But it was no use. No one was really listening. The other boys went back to their seats, making jokes in Mickey voices, and leaving Trent alone and discouraged. Then Mr. Gillespie returned and the class started in earnest, and Trent had to forget about his problems for a while and concentrate on the meanings and implications of *The Old Man and the Sea*.

When class was over, Mr. Gillespie caught Trent as he was getting up from his desk and indicated that he wanted to talk to him. Trent sat down in the chair by the teacher's desk, dreading what was surely coming.

"I simply don't understand it, Robert," Mr. Gillespie said sadly, shaking his head and looking afresh at the new *Express*. "After all the exposure I've given you to the great masterworks of Western culture, you still read these frightful things in your spare moments. Where have I gone wrong?"

"Nowhere, really," Trent tried to explain. "It's just for fun, you see, and comic books aren't quite as bad some people think..." He trailed off. That wouldn't work, either. Mr. Gillespie just wasn't listening.

"And it's not due to any congenital flaw in your reasoning faculties, either," Mr. Gillespie mused half to himself, picking up a file folder and leafing through it. In the sheath of reports and listings was the record of Trent's entire academic career. "You've had excellent grades all the way through and your teachers have uniformly praised you — well, your gym teachers haven't, but always being chosen last for volleyball games is certainly no crime, or I would be in the cell next to yours." He picked out a sheet bearing a column of names and numbers. "I hope you will forgive me, but I took the liberty of looking up your standardized achievement test scores just to make sure my perception of your intellectual potential was not mistaken."

Trent gave a start. The teacher was referring to a battery of tests — called "the Nebraska Test" or something along that line — that he and everybody else in school had taken every year since earliest grade school. While it wasn't exactly an IQ test, it seemed to track overall intelligence much the same way and was used like an IQ test for purposes like assigning students to advanced classes. Like the very same English class Mr. Gillespie taught in which Trent was one of the students, which might explain why he had access to the scores.

"In fact," Mr. Gillespie continued, "you have one of the highest scores in the entire junior class. And yet you read subliterate trash intended for brainless imbeciles. What can you possibly find worthwhile in comic books?"

Mr. Gillespie put the Nebraska Test results down on the desktop and regarded Trent with a mournful expression that would have left a basset hound depressed. Rather than face that heartbreakingly sad countenance, Trent dropped his eyes and suddenly found himself looking at the test scores. Although the sheet was upside down relative to him, he could read the top names well enough. He immediately spotted TRENT, J. R. in fourth place. First place was JAEGER, F. W., which was no surprise — that was the kid who could do cube roots in his head and was taking the senior-level physics and trigonometry courses. But the two names between him and the boy Einstein were what caught Trent's stunned notice. Third place was JESPERSEN, L. L., which was no surprise, either, since he already had a strong suspicion that she was smarter than he was. It was the name that topped even Linda's with a higher score yet that left him fighting to keep from gasping out loud in front of Mr. Gillespie, who sat waiting expectantly for him to answer his question.

The second highest Nebraska Test score in the entire Shetland High School Junior Class belonged to COLLINS, P. J.

*Pam?!* Trent knew she wasn't exactly deficient in brainpower, but *that* smart? And yet there she was. With only the math prodigy ahead of her, like Abou ben Adhem's her name led all the rest.

"Well?" said Mr. Gillespie.

For a long, bad moment, Trent couldn't say anything. He couldn't focus his mind on the comic-book question when the discovery of Pam's astonishing intelligence was rearranging a large part of his mental landscape.

"Uh... well, they're fun and entertaining," Trent was able to get out at length, "and they, uh, create their own worlds with their own laws where anything might happen, and Stan Lee uses a lot of Latin in *Sub-Mariner*, and *Thor*'s sort of written like Shakespeare, so they aren't just bubblegum for the brain..." He couldn't collect his thoughts well enough to invoke the comparison with Franz Kafka, and his defense of comic books went precipitously downhill from there. The Nebraska Test scores lay in plain sight on Mr. Gillespie's desk, riveting his attention and sabotaging coherent thought about anything else.

"Oh, never mind," Mr. Gillespie interrupted after a while, tired of Trent's stumbling. "You young people just need a world of your own where adults can't go. Some of you find it in your acid rock and roll music or drugs, and you happen to find it in comic books. So there's probably no way you can explain it to me. I am over 30, after all, and for you young groovy people, that's the Enemy nowadays." He forced a weak smile. "But please, in your idealistic rebellion against the outmoded mores of an older generation, don't forsake the beauty of poetry!"

"I don't plan to, Mr. Gillespie!" Trent exclaimed. "I'm not rebelling against anybody!"

But Mr. Gillespie had made it clear that the interview was over, and Trent had to go to his next class.

After fretting and stewing all day, Trent finally had no choice but to seek out the author of his misery and beg to know the reason why. He found Laurie Saunders at her locker after school, slipping into her heavy winter coat.

"Laurie!" he exclaimed. "That article you wrote about me — you left out all the important parts!"

Laurie shrugged, calmly buttoning her coat with no sign of being moved by his complaint. "Look, I've thrown the bull enough times myself to know when Ferdinand's going flying. Comic books are comic books, and a lot of fancy words and bogus philosophy won't change that. Besides, nobody would've been interested in all that guff anyway, so I boiled it down to the basics."

"But you made me look like an idiot!"

Laurie eyed him coldly as she closed her locker door. "I'm not much to look at, either, but at least I don't blame the mirror for it. Now if you'll excuse me, I've got a bus to catch—"

It was beginning to snow in the fading afternoon as Trent walked despondently out to his car in the school parking lot. That was when Pam caught up with him.

"Hi, Bob," she called, a little out of breath, clutching her notebook and textbooks to her chest and looking remarkably like a snowbunny in her long, hooded coat. "You couldn't take a poor beggar girl home, could you?"

"Sure, okay." It was considerably out of his way to make a side trip out to Indian Village, but this was Pam, after all. He decided not to say anything about the Nebraska Test revelation. It was really none of his business, and Pam might not appreciate knowing he had even accidentally found about something so personal.

"I could have taken the bus like I usually do," she went on once they were in the car and moving down the street, "but I wanted to talk to you." She let out a long sigh. "Whew! Another long week behind us! At least *Star Trek* is on tonight. It makes holding out until Friday sort of worthwhile. Did you see it last week — 'Friday's Child' with Julie Newmar? Boy, is she tall! I remember her on *My Living Doll* when she played a robot. I also remember that leering article some sci-fi writer who should have known better wrote for *TV Guide* about it — really rubbed me the wrong way. Anyway, the paper says tonight's *Star Trek* is called 'The Deadly Years.' I hope it's as exciting as it sounds!" She paused, then smiled a little self-consciously. "Sorry. I'm just running off at the vocal cords again. Actually, the reason I wanted to talk to you was that *Express* article."

"I'm afraid it didn't do much for fandom's reputation," Trent admitted sadly, staring ahead out the windshield as the houses passed by on either side of the street.

"Look at it this way," Pam said. "We fans knew this job was dangerous when we took it. If we want to teach other people to appreciate comics for the art and imagination the way we do, we'll have to learn to expect this kind of thing at first. It's just too bad Laurie pulled such a dirty trick on you."

They talked about it at some length on the way out to Pam's house. By the time he dropped her off, Trent was feeling a little better about the whole thing, if only because he'd finally had a chance to unload all his woes on a sympathetic listener.

"Maybe we should just forget about being dealers?" Trent suggested to Ernie as he sat on his bed contemplating his Coke in his bedroom the next afternoon.

Ernie glanced idly through the comic books heaped on Trent's desk: the Frank Martin Memorial Collection, which still awaited detailed listing and appraisal of condition. "Give up?" he snorted. "Hey, we haven't done too bad so far. You got a good haul here, an' I should get somethin' like it Monday if the deal I got cookin' goes through. Instead of givin' up, what we should be doin' is startin' to think about more ads in the paper. Your secret's out, so you don't hafta be shy about it anymore, an' we can run some ads that might get more attention. You can't expect miracles the first time out, you know. We gotta stick with it!"

"I guess," Trent agreed a little tiredly. "But... well, the reason I got into this was to find Golden Age comics. And nothing's turned up. They'd be only about twenty, twenty-five years old now, and a lot of people should still have some in their drawers or in a box somewhere. What could have happened to them all? Without the Golden Agers, I'm not all that interested in just buying and selling recent comics. I'm a student, a scholar. I wasn't cut out to be a comic-book peddler. And now my reputation at school's down the drain, too. Lord, what a world!"

Chapter Four: UNCLE DIMMY'S CUMMIC BOOKS

On Monday, December 11, Trent got through his first two periods with no more damage than a few basically good-natured calls of "Hiya, Funnybook Bob!" By third period, he was beginning to dare hope that the passage of a weekend had allowed the embarrassment to die down somewhat.

But just as he was settling into his desk in study hall, he saw Mickey Gompers approaching with something in a paper bag. "Hi, Bub," Mickey greeted cheerfully, so much through his nose that he hardly needed to open his mouth to talk. "I got tumpin' for you! It's a cummic book, an' it's preddy old, doo!"

Trent groaned silently. What was preddy old for Mickey — a Charlton hot-rod comic from 1965? He glanced around the room to make sure the teacher hadn't come in yet. Mr. Schatten was remarkably lenient in some ways, but Trent wasn't about to challenge the authorities with his comic books no matter who they were.

"Okay," he told Mickey, "let's have a look at it." His lack of enthusiasm was so obvious that even Mickey could probably sense it. The preddy old cummic book was doubtless something like *Casper, the Friendly Ghost…*

Mickey pulled the comic book out of the sack — and it was anything but what Trent could have expected. To his amazement, it really was preddy old, from about 1950 and in surprisingly good condition. It was something called *Campus Loves* #2, with a cover drawing of a cute blonde girl unable to decide between a football player in an old-fashioned leather helmet, a fraternity man with a pipe, a scholar wearing a mortarboard, and a regular Joe College in what looked like a polo hat. One blurb promised *"Pulsating tales of the care-free lives and intimate loves of enchanting co-eds!"* and another bemoaned the fact that *"They said I was fast — I was free with my kisses because I could not be denied the excitement I craved!"* Trent had to think for a moment to realize that slang had changed in 17 years and a girl who was "fast" was not necessarily a female track star.

"Nhee…" Mickey said. "Whaddya tink, Bub? It's real old, just like I taid!"

"Uh… Mickey, it isn't *quite* what I had in mind," Trent began. *Captain America* #1 it wasn't — did anybody even collect stuff like this? But it *was* old and there might be more where this came from, perhaps more worthwhile comic books. "I'll tell you what," he added quickly, seeing Mickey's crestfallen face. "I'll buy this one for a quarter and you don't have to pay back what you owe me, all right?"

"Nhee… okee!" Mickey agreed, suddenly brightening.

"And do you have any more old comic books?"

"Oh, ture, we god lods of old cummic books in our batement! I'll bring tum more in toon, okee?"

"Okay." Trent wanted to be more specific about what he was looking for, but Mr. Schatten had come into the room and the bargaining session had to close. He just hoped he could sell *Campus Loves* for what he had paid for it.

At lunch, Trent and Ernie compared notes.

"That guy had a fairly decent collection of old Marvels," Ernie reported. "All the Ditko Spideys, like that there. Even *Amazing Fantasy* #15, which is probably tough to find since nobody saw Spidey comin'. I gave 'im a few bucks an' now he's happy, an' I got my locker crammed full of funnybooks. They're gonna be lotsa fun to cart home on the bus…" He finished on an expectant note.

"Oh, all right," Trent said, resigned to the inevitable. Having a car meant he had to do an awful lot of favors for people. Besides, it was for the benefit of the firm. "I'll drive you home. Anyway, I didn't do quite as well as you did today. I just bought one comic book from Mickey Gompers." He showed Ernie the copy of *Campus Loves* #2.

"Not exactly prime goods," Ernie judged, leafing through the pages, "but some of the art ain't bad. An' it is kinda old. Wonder where Laughing-boy got it?"

"Mickey isn't one for meaningful dialogue," Trent said, "but he told me had some old comic books in his basement besides this one. Maybe somebody who used to live in the house before left them behind. If that's the case, there may be something better in the lot. So my thought is to go along with Mickey until I get some idea of what he has."

"Prob'ly more junk like this," Ernie said, "butcha never know. I s'pose we'll find out, though, now that he knows he can sell his comics to you."

Ernie needed only a crystal ball to put any carnival fortune teller out of business. That afternoon, as he and Trent walked out in to the school parking lot, carrying the stacks he had bought that day in their arms, they found Mickey waiting for them in the cold.

"Nhee… I went home at lunchtime t'ged anudder cumic book," he explained, holding out a sack. "C'n I hab anudder quoddah?"

"Christ!" Ernie muttered under his breath. "I can see it now! Any time he needs some extra money, 'Nhee… time t'tell anudder cummic book!'"

Trent let out an exasperated sigh. "Just a moment, Mickey. Let me and Ernie get these comics stowed in my car first."

Mickey hovered around them impatiently while Trent unlocked the car door with one hand and nearly dropped the cumbersome load of comic books with the other. When Trent and Ernie had piled the comics in the Chevy's already cluttered rear seat, they turned their attention back to Mickey and he triumphantly pulled his comic book out of the sack for them to see.

"Oh Lord!" Trent gasped.

"Oh boy!" Ernie leered.

It was *Reform School Girl* from 1951. According to the blurb above the title, the comic book was "*The graphic story of boys and girls running wild in the violence-ridden slums of today!*" Below the title, a large text box blared that, "*They succumbed to temptation! This is the story of youth gone wrong… and of the penalty hundreds of pretty girls have to pay when they allow themselves to fall victim to unscrupulous men, their own wayward emotions, and other hidden pitfalls of a sensation-crazed society!*" The real prize was the cover illustration itself, a photograph of an attractive if hard-looking girl — she reminded Trent of Linda in a way — with a cigarette dangling from her lip, glaring defiantly out at the viewer as she adjusted the garter holding up one of her black nylon stockings. She wore only a frilly black slip, so short that stocking tops and garters showed below it. The problems of the cover girl for *Campus Loves* who was free with her kisses seemed awfully innocent compared to this…

"Uh… no, Mickey… no…" Trent managed to say while thinking, *What if Mom saw this, for heaven's sake?!* "Uh, it's a little pornographic for us, you see…"

"Huh?" Mickey blurted, puzzled. "Whad's wrong wid a preddy lady?"

"My sentiments exactly, Mickey old bean!" Ernie exclaimed. "Here's a quoddah outta my own pocket! *I'll* take it!"

If Mickey was bewildered by the flip-flopping between Trent and Ernie, a quoddah was a quoddah and he ambled away in satisfaction.

"What did you buy that for?" Trent asked as soon as they were in his car and rolling out of the parking lot. "It'll never be worth anything — there aren't any superheroes in it!"

Ernie leafed through the comic book. "Yeah, the insides are crap, but I figure that cover alone's worth what I paid the little lunk for it. Hell, I'm in good company! I mean, ol' Doc Freddy musta liked it — he put it in his book!"

"As a bad example," Trent reminded him, remembering Dr. Wertham's sarcastic caption in *Seduction of the Innocent* for his reproduction of *Reform School Girl*'s cover: "*Comic books are supposed to be like fairy tales.*"

"Ahh, who cares?" Ernie demanded, holding up the comic and looking at the cover with a pleased grin on his face. "Hubba hubba. They just don't make funnybooks like this no more!"

"Thank God!" Trent exclaimed.

In third-period study hall the next day, Mickey approached Trent at his desk once again. "Nhee... I god anudder cummic book. You god anudder quoddah?"

*Not more junk?!* Trent thought, annoyed beyond endurance. "Oh, all right. Let's see it." He braced himself for more outrageous strangeness from the deservedly forgotten backfiles of the comic-book industry, wondering if it would be worth even a quarter.

He still wasn't ready for what Mickey produced from his sack.

Bold block letters proclaimed the title: *An Earthman on Venus*. In the cover scene, a girl with antennae cowered before an attacking ant the size of a horse while the eponymous Earthman hastened to the rescue. Small lettering under the logo added that it was by "Ralph Milne Farley."

Trent's delight grew as he realized what it was: a comic-book adaptation of Farley's unavailable first Venus-series novel, *The Radio Man*. If he couldn't find a copy of the book itself, this was certainly the next best thing, since it would give him the bare-bones plot and explain all the things that had mystified him when he read the second novel in the cycle. Besides, it featured 26 solid pages of Wally Wood artwork. It was definitely worth a quoddah.

Relieved and pleased at once, Trent gave Mickey the money and asked, "How did you get all these old comic books, anyway?"

"Dey were my Uncle Dimmy's," Mickey replied. "He lef' 'em in da batement when he moobed years 'n' years ago, toe it's okee if I tell 'em to you!"

*Hmm...* That being the case, Trent had an idea. "Say, instead of buying your comics from you one at a time like this, why don't I come over to your house and buy the whole collection? That way, you'll get a lot of money all at once instead of just a quarter now and then."

"Oh, ture," Mickey said, and thought. "Okee, how 'bout t'morrah after school? I godda go away t'night."

"Fine," Trent said, suddenly realizing what he had let himself in for.

At lunch, Trent showed Ernie *An Earthman on Venus.*

Ernie examined it approvingly. "Well, whaddya know? The little maroon actually came up with somethin' halfway decent! Not bad for a quoddah, Trentbob. I see it's from '51 — all the comics you've gotten from Mickerooni so far've been from right around then."

"I guess that just happened to be when his uncle was reading comic books. 'Uncle Dimmy,' he calls him. I'm not sure if the man's name was James or Timothy."

"'Uncle Dimmy,' huh? Boy, that says it all!"

"Anyway, I'm going over to Mickey's house tomorrow to take a look at what he has and maybe buy the whole works. Anything to put an end to his daily routine of bringing me one comic book at a time."

Ernie's jaw dropped. "Gawd, J. Robert! You're goin' into *that* house? It must be like the Bizarro World in there!"

"Oh, come on, Ernie. It can't be that bad. I don't expect to enjoy the experience, though. So how have you been doing in your own pursuit of the elusive comic book?"

Ernie suddenly looked say. "Not so good. We got a problem."

"*We* do?"

"Remember that kid I bought all those Marvels from?"

"Yes?"

"He wants 'em back. Says he changed his mind."

"So? This is Ernie 'a deal's a deal so get lost' Volney talking?"

"Yeah, well, I gotta live with the guy for the rest of the school year. He's givin' me a coupla bucks for my trouble, so I'm doin' all right on the deal. Jeeze! I never expected people backin' outta deals right after they make 'em when I got into this racket!"

"Ernie, there are a lot of things I never expected when I got into this. But why do *we* have a problem and not just you?"

"I gotta take the comics back to the guy an' *I* don't have a car. So..."

Trent went to his English class wondering why he always let Ernie talk him into these things.

Down in Hell, they must have wondered who turned the air conditioning on, but up in Mr. Gillespie's English classroom, Linda Lee Jespersen dropped by Trent's desk before class started and of her own free will initiated a brief but quite pleasant conversation about the current assignment. Baffled but feeling warm all over, Trent could only go along.

Not that he could quite believe this sudden reversal of fortune was genuine. *Why is she talking to me?* he asked himself. *Does she need to copy my notes or something?*

Then, almost as an afterthought, Linda added, "Oh, by the way, my brother left a box full of comic books behind when he went off to college. I don't know if they're exactly what you have in mind, but he told me when he called home last night that he'd be willing to sell them. Maybe you'd like to drop by my house some evening and at least take a look at them?"

Down in Hell, they were ice-skating on the burning lake. An invitation to Linda's house?! Trent's ears roared, his breath choked — and his heart sang. "Well, uh, oh — sure!" he fought to say. "When?"

Linda shrugged. "Whenever. Tonight would be fine, say around eight?"

"Okay, sure." *Wow!*

The arrival of Mr. Gillespie put an end to any further discussion of the matter, but Trent spent the rest of the period in a warm, happy fog — while damned souls in the fiery pits below built snowmen and threw snowballs.

After class, Trent stopped at Mr. Gillespie's desk to talk about "the comic-book thing" but the old English teacher had errands to run and places to go — with no doubt *"promises to keep and miles before I sleep"* — and couldn't stay any longer just then. Trent left it at pressing copies of *Shockwave* on him to examine at his leisure as a shining example of what a healthy interest in comics could inspire. Trent was much more comfortable writing than talking, and perhaps the written word would be more convincing than him stumbling through another desperate statement of his position.

The first order of business after school was driving to Ernie's house out in the country to pick up the comic books delivered there just the night before and returning them to their once and future owner. During the trip, Ernie noticed that Trent was obviously excited about something.

"What's up, Junior? You're practic'ly bouncin' up an' down in the seat!"

"It's a cold day in Hell, Ernie!" Trent burbled. "Linda invited me over to her house later tonight to look at some comic books!"

For once, Ernie was struck dumb with amazement. "Well, kick my teeth out an' call me Gummy!" he finally blurted. "I'd heard she an' one of the senior blondie-studs broke up 'cause she didn't think he was smart enough for her, but… zowie, Trentbob! Holy jackpot! Unless…" he added as he thought about it a little more, "she's in the same boat Mickey is an' she's just sellin' off the funnybooks to get a little extra money."

Appalled that Ernie could even think of Linda and Mickey in the same breath, Trent protested. "Come on, Ernie! This is *Linda Lee Jespersen!* She's *rich!* She doesn't *need* the money!"

Ernie shrugged. "Y'never know. I've heard rich poppas can be as stingy as poor ones. If they got rich by bein' tight with a buck, they ain't gonna change once they get their loot socked away. So maybe Linda *is* hard up for spendin' money. Just her lipstick bill must be sky-high!"

"I would prefer to think her motives are friendlier than that."

"Okay, Junior, have it your way. An' good luck. But don't getcher hopes up too high just yet. There's no tellin' what she might pull on you."

Dwight R. Decker

Chapter Five: A COLD DAY IN HELL

After dinner, Trent's excitement had wound up even more tightly, and he raced out of the house and into the night with an anticipation that was almost feverish.

When he had told them where he was going, Trent's sister teased him unmercifully and his parents were nothing short of flabbergasted. Linda was the daughter of Mr. Trent's boss's boss, after all. Mr. Trent muttered something about a PFC he had known in the Army who started dating the base commander's daughter — and was shortly thereafter transferred to Alaska. He saw his son off with the cryptic comment, "Whatever you do, don't forget where your allowance ultimately comes from!"

The Jespersens lived in the country some distance south of Shetland. Trent had to drive through the darkness down River Road along the Little Bureau River a mile or two past the city dump, then turn east for another mile out on Galena Road. The large ranch-style house, ablaze in the coruscating, multi-colored lights of an elaborate outdoor Christmas display, was set on a rise some distance back from the road along a long, curving driveway, and surrounded by broad expanses of snow-covered lawn and shrubbery.

As Trent pulled up in front of the house, his headlight beams caught Mr. Jespersen's luxurious black '68 Thunderbird and Mrs. Jespersen's practical but little less luxurious Mercury Colony Park station wagon with simulated wood trim on the sides, parked side by side in front of the two-car garage. Looking at the cars, the huge lawn, and the big, warmly lighted house, Trent felt daunted even though the Jespersens couldn't have been colossally wealthy. As a plant manager for Dyna-Wave Radio Products, Mr. Jespersen was hired help and not ownership, however exalted and high up the corporate escalator he might be. Even so, if the Jespersens weren't really rich, they might as well have been from where Trent sat in his rusting ten-year-old Chevy.

By the time he had parked and walked up the long sidewalk to the front door, Trent's nervousness had increased to the maximum. Only a supreme act of will kept his entire body from collapsing into a puddle of

120

quivering Jell-O on the steps. Even his right index finger shook too much to make a very good stab at pressing the doorbell on the first attempt.

Some darkly muttering gossips at Shetland High would have suspected a maid or perhaps even a high-toned British butler to answer the door, but the Jespersens were hardly in that tax bracket. Linda opened it herself, her slim form fetching even in jeans, tennis shoes, and an old sweater.

"You're right on time!" she greeted, sounding more impressed by his punctuality than expressing delight in seeing him. "Come on in — I've got the comics ready for you."

"Uh… hi," Trent said, his voice barely above a cracked whisper. His slightly plump figure may have presented a placid exterior to the world, but deep within, ferocious energies were being directed to override his paralyzing nervousness and unlock the muscles controlling his legs so he could step forward into the foyer.

Linda seemed unaware that the mind of her guest was so overwhelmed by the sheer magnificence of her presence that he was almost unable to function. "This way," she said, and turned to lead him through the house. Trent could only follow dumbly along the hall after her.

Passing an open doorway, he caught a glimpse of an enormous living room, with a carpet so thick that if it had been the Trents' front lawn, his father would have him out mowing it. The furniture looked new and expensive and somehow unused, as though no one actually lived in the living room and it was used at most for occasional entertaining. Given the size of the fireplace, the Jespersens could have easily put on an ox-roast. Trent also had a quick look at an elegant, wood-paneled dining room with a table large enough to seat most of King Arthur's knights around it.

They encountered Mrs. Jespersen in the hall. She was fortyish, in many respects an older edition of her daughter, though more worn around the edges. She was fully made up and wore her tarnished blonde hair in an elaborate coif that would have broken if she fell down. Linda introduced Trent to her, but Mrs. Jespersen's interest in him was conspicuously slight, and after some minimally polite amenities, she hurried on into the dining room.

Linda led Trent down some stairs into a basement recreation room — but it was nothing like the rec rooms common in Trent's neighborhood, where the common practice was putting linoleum down on the cellar floor, covering the concrete block walls with wood paneling or just painting them, putting up a dart board, and furnishing the place with worn-out chairs and a sofa retired from upstairs. This was a recreation room where a family of four could have lived comfortably, with wall-to-wall carpeting and better furniture than the Trents had in their living room, with oak-paneled walls, a pool table, and a fully equipped bar at one end. The walls sported an outdoors motif: wooden duck decoys perched on shelves, guns hung on racks, and the framed pictures were all hunting scenes. Along one wall was a bookcase filled with old books that looked as though they hadn't been opened in generations and a home entertainment complex with a radio/hi-fi system and a color TV set. The shabby necessities of a furnace, a hot-water heater, and a washer and dryer were evidently hidden discreetly away in another room,

The comic books were neatly stacked in several piles on a table and Linda had Trent sit down facing them after draping his coat on the back of the chair.

"Oh, do you like music?" she asked.

"Sure," Trent replied, thinking of Bach, Beethoven, and Mozart.

"Okay, then let there be music," Linda said and turned on the radio.

From the speaker burst a jingle chorus singing "W-R-O-K, Rockforddddd!" with the help of an echo chamber, and a frenetic disk jockey by the name of "Madman Mike" announced the next song, something called *Itchycoo Park* by some group called "The Small Faces." Trent had certainly heard the song before — it was next to impossible for anyone young and alive in 1967 to be completely unfamiliar with what the radio stations were playing — but it was hardly one of his favorites.

Besides improving his acquaintance with Linda, he had come here for a reason. Sighing softly to himself, he began looking through the comic books.

As *Itchycoo Park* throbbed out of the speaker, Linda threw her whole lithe body into the rhythm. Singing along, she undulated over to where Trent sat. "It's all too be-yoo-ti-ful!" She stopped when the song went off on some undanceable tangent and asked a little plaintively, "Don't you like it?"

"Er... I'm not sure," Trent said cautiously. Recalling that one of the song's key lines, in answer to the question of what the lead singer really did at Itchycoo Park, was "I got high!," he added, "But it's about drugs, isn't it?"

Linda shrugged. "I just like the way it sounds. I don't pay too much attention to song lyrics. They're a lot like poetry — they're just meant to rhyme, not make any sense."

Outrage flashed briefly through Trent's cerebrum. She may have been the single most desirable girl in this end of the galaxy, but that slam against poetry was almost too much for him to bear. *Careful!* he told himself. He clamped down on a suitable hot retort and directed his attention to the comics. Unfortunately, a quick glance made it all too clear that this would not be one of the better hauls. Linda's brother had evidently been an ardent fan of Superman and little else: the collection consisted almost entirely of issues of *Action, Superman, Jimmy Olsen, Lois Lane, Adventure,* and *World's Finest* from roughly 1959 through 1963. While Superman may have been the very first superhero and was still potentially the greatest adventure character of all, Trent had to admit that Supes had fallen on some hard times during that period. The comics were deliberately aimed at children and now struck mature fans like him as silly and juvenile. Someone consciously trying to assemble a collection of kiddie fodder couldn't have done much better than Linda's brother had.

*How can I tell her it's all pretty much kid stuff fans wouldn't buy?* Trent wondered with a sick feeling. It would hardly improve his standing with her if he told her the dismal truth about her brother's collection.

Meanwhile, Linda sat down at the table across from him and idly leafed through a random comic book. "I don't read comics myself," she said without preamble, "but I think I respect them. At least they're about *heroes* doing great things. Too much modern literature is about creeps and jerks, and I don't like it."

Trent thought Linda was overstating the case but held his peace. It occurred to him that Pam and Linda were alike in that they both had older brothers who had read comics and had since gone off to college, but while seeing the brightly colored periodicals around the house had inspired Pam to take an interest in comics herself, Linda had been immune or at least indifferent. The comic-book bug apparently didn't bite everybody.

On the radio, *Itchycoo Park* wound up and was replaced by Spanky & Our Gang singing *Lazy Day*. To Trent's mind, it was not much of an improvement.

A minute or so passed with neither of them saying anything while Trent continued to go through the stack of endless hoaxes, dreams, and imaginary stories. Then Linda suddenly asked, "Bob, do you think I'm stuck up?"

Trent looked up, startled. "Huh? What?"

Linda leaned back in her chair. "Look, I have ears. I hear things. Like people saying I'm a snob because Dad makes a good buck. I'm sick of being called a 'rich bitch' behind my back. Because Dad has a little money, that's supposed to be why I don't bother with the creeps and jerks around here. Hah! They don't really know me — not the *real* me!"

"I'm sure they don't, but..." *Why is she telling me all this?*

"I just want out of this boondocks little town," Linda went on, looking somewhere past Trent. "I'd like to go to New York where things are bright and exciting. There aren't any opportunities around here in Shetland, Ill-an*noy*, for God's sake" The amount of contempt she infused into the name of the place was astonishing.

"Oh, I don't know," Trent said, trying to be diplomatic. "I kind of like Shetland. It's home."

Linda curled one corner of her mouth in disgust. "This dump? Where's your spirit of adventure? I go to the movies and see New York City on the screen, and I want so much to be there, right in the middle of all those lights and excitement and glamor, but then the movie's over and I come out and it's just blah little Shetland and I'm with some dumb football player who's mainly interested in me because he wants to get in a little necking so he can brag about it to all his buddies in the locker room the next day — well, it makes *me* want to throw up! It bugs me that day after day I have to put up with all these hick-town losers. I'd feel a lot better if I could just talk now and then to somebody who's halfway intelligent. You're smart, Bob, what do you think?"

"About what?"

Linda waved her hand vaguely. "About anything. Everything." She brought her hand down and looked directly across the table at Trent. "Am I coming on too strong for you?"

"Well, no, not exactly—"

"People tell me I do that, but I just don't like to waste my time or anybody else's. I like to get right to the point."

An awkward silence followed with Trent unsure what to say next, and it may have begun to dawn on Linda that the point wasn't being gotten to at all. For his part, Trent quite failed to understand what was going on, and his earlier nervousness had given way to growing bafflement. Linda clearly had something on her mind, and as nearly as he could reason things out, it didn't have so much to do with him personally as him being handy to talk to.

Then Linda tried a different tack. "I've seen you talking to Pam Collins a lot. Is she your girlfriend?"

Stunned by the impression Linda had of affairs and her blunt, almost accusing question, Trent rushed to explain. "Oh no, not at all. Pam and I are just friends."

"Hmm. I didn't know she had any. I don't know how you can even stand to be around her for very long. She drives *me* up the wall. Look, I admire guts and independence, but I'm afraid your little Pammy is just plain *weird*. She draws all this cutesie stuff about fairies and flying horses and knights in armor with flaming swords — she has talent but not the brains to use it. She's *silly*, when you come right down to it. Or maybe even half-cracked, who can tell. I don't know what you see in her."

"She's not half-cracked!" Trent protested, stung, and flabbergasted that an appointment to buy comic books had turned into having to defend

Pam's honor. "Pam's really very smart — she just has her own way of doing things."

"Do smart people get drippy over fairies and flying horses? *I* don't."

"But Linda!" Trent exclaimed. "Pam's even smarter than *you* are!"

"Oh?" said Linda, her voice sounding like an icicle freezing over. "Would you care to explain that?"

Realizing too late that he had blurted precisely the wrong thing to say in the heat of the moment, Trent stumbled helplessly on, wondering if trying to elaborate would only make things worse. "I saw the Nebraska Test scores on Mr. Gillespie's desk the other day. You're third in the Junior Class, Pam's second, and that Jaeger kid who gets all the top grades in his math classes is somewhere way out ahead. I'm fourth," he added weakly.

Linda's eyes narrowed. "Mr. Gillespie just *happened* to have the Nebraska Test scores lying on his desk out where you could see them? And he just *happened* to look the other way so you could read them? You'll have to do better than that if you want to lie to me about your... *friend*, Bob."

"But it's the *truth*, Linda—!"

"I think you'd better leave. *Now*."

When his mind was functioning properly again, Trent was at the wheel of his decomposing Chevy and the Christmas lights of the Jespersen house were receding into the night behind him, and he still wasn't any too sure how he had landed there. He had only a blurry memory of Linda peremptorily hustling him out of the house without even a comic book for his trouble. All he knew was that he had been given a test of some kind, and he had just flunked.

In the aftershock, he felt terrible. His insides were tied up in square knots and run through a blender. Whatever his hopes and dreams about Linda Lee Jespersen had been in the past, he could forget about them as of tonight. After this, he would most likely never be able to talk to her again. And it was all because of—

In his black misery, he didn't go home. Instead, he headed towards Indian Village. He had to talk to someone, and in this particular crisis there was only one person who might understand.

Trent sat on the desk chair in the comic-book jammed spare room at the Collins house, his head bowed and hands folded across his lap, and told Pam in a thick, halting voice what had happened. Sitting at her drawing board, Pam listened in amazement.

"And that's the story," Trent finished bleakly. "She kicked me out of her house and she'll probably never speak to me again."

Shaking her head sympathetically, Pam stood up and walked over to Trent, stepping over some smaller piles of comic books as she went, and put her hand on his shoulder. "I never realized you felt that way about Linda. I guess we don't exchange confidences much. I'm sorry it came to this and I somehow helped cause it." She paused, then added quietly, "I already knew about those Nebraska Test scores. They just got me yanked into the guidance counselor's office where Mrs. Krauss tried to convince me I ought to be more active in school stuff like clubs so I could live up to my potential or something. She couldn't believe it when I tried to tell her that what I really want to do is tell stories the best way I know how. At least it was a little better than last year, when she was trying to tell me that because of my art talent there was a bright future for me in designing department-store window displays. My thought was, 'Look, people, I already know what I want to do, so just stand out of way and let me do it already!'"

Then, seeing that a forthright statement of her principles wasn't helping Trent very much, she changed the subject back to his problems. "Oh yeah, that's Linda, all right. She sought me out, too, when I started at the public school. I guess she's lonely because she's so smart and self-sufficient, and she wanted to be my Friend because she thought I was a kindred spirit. But I wanted to practice my art and read and dream and tell stories, and she just wanted to grow up as fast as she could and get out of Shetland. As you found out the hard way, we didn't get on too well. So don't feel too bad. She has her own private set of demons jabbing at her from behind with pitchforks, and there isn't much you or I can do about it. But Bob—" her voice went low "—you stood up for me. I want you to know that I really appreciate it."

She bent down and kissed his cheek. "Thank you," she whispered.

It was the first time Pam had ever shown Trent any particular affection. The sad part was that he was too sick at heart to be cheered by it.

Chapter Six: TO DA DUMP!

Matters were hardly any better the next day. If Linda's attitude towards Trent had been arctic before he had briefly seemed to her an independent thinker who relished tales of heroes, now it would have had a native of Pluto banging on the pipes for more heat. When Ernie met up with him later and casually asked how things had gone over at Linda's the night before, clearly with intent to get in a ribald dig or two, Trent cut him off with such a frosty "*Don't ask!*" that he got the general idea at once and backed away. He would hear the whole story sooner or later, but Trent was in no mood at the moment to tell it. Besides, while Ernie was a good friend in many ways, being a shoulder wasn't one of them.

Then Mr. Gillespie returned the copies of *Shockwave* that Trent had lent him, saying only, "I just wish such an outpouring of creative energy were devoted to a worthier cause." And finally, Trent had to go over to Mickey Gompers's house that afternoon to appraise Uncle Dimmy's comic-book collection.

That last may have been the worst of it. First there was the indignity of being seen walking through the hall on the way out of the school building in Mickey's company. "Hey, Funnybook Bob!" Bill Hunter had called after him. "Looks like you got yourself a buddy! Gonna trade funnybooks?" What really hurt was how close to the truth Hunter was. Then there was Mickey's endless stream of nasal conversation, which he kept up in the car all the way to his house. Fortunately, it was only a matter of a few blocks, but even a short trip was much too long for Trent's liking and patience.

"Nhee... I don't really read cummic books much. I jus' like to t'look at da pikshures, 'specially da ones wit' preddy ladies."

Trent found the prospect of listening to Mickey discuss his romantic fantasies nothing less than horrifying, so he almost fell over himself trying to think of something else to talk about. "Uhm... What are you going to do with the money I give you for the old comic books?"

"Oh... prob'ly buy tigarettes. I nebber hab enough munney f'r tigarettes."

Now Trent was helping support somebody's bad habit. Oh well, there was probably very little he could do to make Mickey any worse off than he already was. Mickey rambled on about tigarettes and cummic books, and Trent unconsciously sped up as he drove, trying to make the horrible ride come to an end all the faster before his slipping fingers lost their precarious hold on sanity.

Then they were there, and Trent pulled up along the sidewalk in front of the Gompers house on North Main Street. He paused for a moment, looking dubiously at the decaying, shabby old two-story frame house that long before had been divided into a two-family dwelling. The white paint was peeling badly, some of the windows were cracked and mended with masking tape, the front porch was missing some floorboards and sagging in other places...

"C'mon!" Mickey urged. "Less go look at my cummic books!"

*Might as well get this over with*, Trent thought and reluctantly got out of the car.

"It must be like the Bizarro World in there," Ernie had said. Not quite, but the interior of the Gompers side of the duplex was bad enough: old, broken, worn-out furniture, cluttered rooms, an all-pervading stale smell hinting of last week's boiled cabbage and an ancient grandfather's cigars, garbage left in the wastebasket too long, and the close-quarters living of maybe half a dozen people.

Then there was Mickey's mother, who got up from her chair in the living room where she was watching TV to meet Trent. She was middle-aged and must have been well over 300 pounds, with unkempt gray hair and several missing teeth, wearing a ragged housedress and pink bedroom slippers. She smiled warmly at Trent and said, "Oh, I'm so glad Mickey's finally bringing some of his friends home from school."

Feeling a little sick, Trent mumbled something that seemed to fit and seemed to satisfy her, and she went back to her afternoon soap opera.

Then Mickey wanted to show Trent his room. "The comics, Mickey, the comics!" Trent muttered urgently, but Mickey was so very proud of the room he shared with his brother Dicky that he wanted to show it off before they did anything else.

It was just a second-floor room with two unmade beds in it, reeking to Asgard from piles of dirty laundry in the corners and one of the brothers' problems with bedwetting. Mickey showed Trent his model-car collection, an unpainted white plastic fleet of the most ineptly assembled model kits he had ever seen. Mickey had never quite grasped the fine art of not spilling glue on exposed surfaces. He had, however, tried to hone his painting skills on some Aurora movie-monster kits like Frankenstein and Godzilla, but the results were worse. Far worse. And the kid was *proud* of them, Trent realized in dismay.

Mickey thereupon produced a board game. "Wanna pway a game? It's real easy, doo. I lost some o' da pieces, but dat's okee, we c'n play it anyway."

Trent shook his head — a little desperately. "No, no. I have to be going home soon. Let's see your comic books, all right?"

"Nhee... okee. C'mon."

Mickey led him back downstairs and into the kitchen where the door leading to the basement was. First, though, trying to play the thoughtful and considerate host, Mickey offered Trent a drink. "Wouldjoo like a Fizzie? We only god one lef', but we could drink outta da same glass."

"Uh, thanks, but no, Mickey. I'm not really thirsty right now. The *comics*...!"

"Okee-dokee." Mickey opened the basement door and went down the narrow, rickety wooden steps, and Trent came after him.

The basement was little better than a cave, lit by a single dim, bare, cobwebbed bulb. A mine scene in a low-budget Western could have been filmed there and no one would have known the difference. In the gloom, through the dust, the spiderwebs, and the musty tomb-like air, Mickey led the way into an unfinished room next to the coal bin. Here the basement had not been completely excavated and the outer walls were earthen mounds supporting the foundations of the house, and the floor was just a few boards on hard-packed dirt. The junk of generations of renters had been stashed in this room, including an old dress form, a wheelless bicycle frame, a crank-operated phonograph with a smashed speaker horn, and a couple of broken metal lawn chairs, all covered with dust and spiderwebs.

But in the corner to which Mickey so confidently guided Trent was... nothing.

Mickey was staggered. "Tumbuddy 'tole our cummic books!" he screeched, then spun around, barged past Trent out of the room, and thumped frantically up the basement stairs. "Mummy! Mummy! Where's da trunk wit' Uncle Dimmy's cummic books?"

Faintly, Trent heard Mrs. Gompers' reply from upstairs. "I didn't think you and Dicky ought to be looking at such bad books! Ever since you two got into them the other day, you've been looking at those bad picture books! I looked at a couple myself, and such goings-on I found in them! So I decided you shouldn't ought to look at them because they'd give you bad ideas! I called the garbagemen this afternoon and had them take the trunk away."

"But Bub was gonna buy da cummic books! He was gonna gib me munney for 'em!" Then Mickey started crying, a heaving, wracking sob that threatened to shake the house.

"Good Lord..." Trent murmured. "What I get myself into..." Resigning himself to the fact that his quest for old comics had drilled another dry hole, he stepped out of the room and started up the stairs.

That was when his temporarily stymied brain slipped into gear. Since his best friend was a garbageman's son, he had overheard enough about the ins and outs of local trash collection to know something about how these things worked. The garbagemen Mrs. Gompers had called would have come out in the dump truck the Shetland Sanitation Service used on special calls outside the regular weekly collection schedule, so the trunk would have reached the dump intact without being crushed to kindling by one of the big garbage trucks that compressed its load as it went along. Whether the trunk had been buried later by the bulldozer out at the landfill was another matter, but if it was picked up in the afternoon, perhaps not. Ernie's father was foreman of the garbage crew and had a key to the gate at the dump. And Ernie should be home from school by now...

When Trent emerged into the kitchen, Mrs. Gompers was telling her wailing son that he shouldn't have been looking at books with bad pictures in them anyway, but Mickey was evidently thinking more of the money he could have gotten for them and howling all the louder. Trying to make himself heard over the uproar, Trent asked, "Can I use your phone?"

The gray winter afternoon was already fading into evening and it was snowing lightly as Trent drove along the narrow River Road south of town. Most of the topography around Shetland was dead flat prairie, but here the Little Bureau River, barely more than 40 feet wide, had carved out a respectable gorge for itself over the ages. River Road followed the winding riverbed and at several sharpturns only a thin metal guardrail separated the berm from empty space and a ten-foot drop. Trent took one turn too fast and nearly skidded into the railing.

"Hey, take it easy, Junior!" Ernie yelped from the passenger's seat next to him.

"I just want to get there before it's completely dark!" Trent snapped, angrier at himself for the near-accident than at Ernie for mentioning it.

"Well, let's get there *alive*, huh?"

It also pained Trent to remember that the last time he had come this way, it had been for a rendezvous with Linda Lee Jespersen. Now he was just with Ernie. And Mickey.

From the back seat, Mickey whined, "Why did I godda come wid you guys?"

"Because," Trent said through clenched teeth for about the fifth time, "you know what that trunk looks like and you can point it out to us!"

"Oh. Okee." He went back to looking out the window at the darkening scenery and idly playing with the pompom on top of his knit cap.

As was his habit, Ernie began singing, this time something to the tune of what he would have thought of as the *Lone Ranger* theme and what Trent recognized as the *William Tell Overture*. "To da dump, to da dump, to da dump dump dump!"

"Never mind that!" Trent exclaimed exasperatedly. "Did you bring the key?"

Ernie held it up, a single key on a tagged ring. "Yep. Ain't left my hot little mitts since we pulled outta my place. Pop wasn't home yet when we left so I had to take his spare key — he'd *kill* me if I lost this!"

A little further down, River Road veered away from the Little Bureau itself but ran along the edge of several acres of low-lying, rough-terrained bottomland, perhaps the remains of a lake that had dried up long before even the Indians moved into the area. Now it was the site of the Shetland city dump, a landfill in the process of being filled with the town's garbage. If the archaeologists of hundreds or thousands of years hence knew where to dig, they would find a rich harvest of ancient artifacts waiting for them. As Trent saw it, his job now was to make sure they didn't find a rotted trunk filled with the dust of what had once been Uncle Dimmy's comic books.

Trent pulled up in front of the chain-link fence by the gate and parked at the side of the road, and everyone climbed out. Scattered white snowflakes continued to drift down lazily in the glare of the flashlights that Trent and Ernie both had thought to take along now that the twilight was well into its last gleaming.

Ernie unlocked the padlock on the gate and the threesome trooped into the grounds. Just inside stood a weather-beaten tarpaper shack, a set of rusty bedsprings propped up against one side, where the dump supervisor spent his day, but he had gone home and the shack was dark and empty. A little past that, the level ground dropped off in a steep slope, and out in the misty gray of falling snow, down on the floor of the ancient lakebed, a bulldozer sat cold and untended in front of the mounds of garbage. A layer of snow thinly covered everything, but the bright colors of empty cans and boxes still showed through in a lot of places. Garbage, garbage, everywhere, but not a trunk in sight.

Behind him, Trent heard the motor of a vehicle coming up the road and stopping at the gate. He turned and saw the dim figure of a man jump out of a pickup truck and approach them, silhouetted in the headlights that he had left on. He wore a beat-up old jacket but no hat. "Hey!" the man yelled. "What th'hell are you kids doin' in there?"

Trent froze. "Uh oh! We're in for it now!" he blurted to Ernie. Dire forebodings of merciless authority coming down hard on him flooded his imagination.

"Not hardly!" Ernie exclaimed, looking back. "That's just Ol' Squirrelly! He's the guy that runs this joint! Dunno what he's doin' back here — shoulda gone home by now, but..." He trotted back towards the gate, a big grin on his face. "Hey, Squirrelly! How ya doin'?"

"Ernie?" Squirrelly replied, suddenly puzzled. He was a grizzled, middle-aged man with a day's worth of gray stubble on his weather-worn face. "Is that you, Ernie?"

"Yeah," Ernie said as they met and paused to talk, "my ol' man left somethin' behind when he brought in his last load today an' he wanted me to pick it up for 'im, so I got a buddy of mine to drive me over."

"Oh, okay," Squirrelly said. "I left somethin' here myself an' I was drivin' back this way to get it an' saw the car here, didn't know it was you or what was goin' on. Long as it's you, that's all right."

"By the way," Ernie added casually, "you didn't happen to notice if the guys on the dump truck brought in an old trunk, did you?"

"Nah, I don't pay attention to that stuff. They dump it, I doze it. But I'll show ya somethin' I did find in one of the loads that came in today." Squirrelly went into the little shack and came out a moment later with his hat, along with a small slip of paper. "Ever seen anything like this? Must be a dollar bill that gone through the wash!"

Trent had followed Ernie once he realized the crisis was defused, and he saw the master of the dump show him a white piece of paper with dollar-bill markings on it. But only on one side: the other side was blank.

"Hate to tell ya," Ernie said, "but it ain't real — somebody just made a photocopy of a dollar bill."

Trent had already guessed as much. It looked as though it had come off the photocopier in his father's office: only outlines reproduced very clearly and the interiors of any black areas faded to a fuzzed-out gray. He had seen fanzines that had been produced that way, and the results were not good.

"You mean I can't spend it?" Squirrelly asked sadly.

"I hear they got laws about that kinda thing," Ernie told him. "Counterfeitin', I think they call it."

Worried, Squirrelly crumped up the bogus bill and tossed it on the ground. "Thanks for tellin' me! — I mighta got in trouble! I thought I really had something there! Well, don't be too long in the dump. Gettin' dark, ya might trip an' fall or somethin'. G'night!"

As Squirrelly went back to his truck, Trent turned to Ernie. "Why would anybody make a photocopy of a dollar bill? No store would take it!"

"No," Ernie agreed, "but the change machine down at the laundrymat just might."

"Ernie! Don't tell me you've tried it!"

"You kiddin'? My uncle *owns* the laundrymat an' you don't try an' pull stuff like that on family. For one thing, they know where you live. Let's jus' say whoever made that copy ain't the first clown in the circus to think of it, an' I've heard Uncle Pete complain about things like this. Now, they got change machines rigged so they won't take photocopies very handy. Hell, they're so touchy that half the time they won't even take real dollars! Anyhoo, as long as we're here, let's get excavatin'!"

Behind them, Squirrelly started his truck and drove off. As the three-some headed back towards the yawning landfill, Mickey suddenly stopped.

"I wanna go home!" he whimpered. "It's cold an' it's dark an' I'm 'keered an' I wanna go home!"

"Mickey!" Trent barked harshly, fighting down the temptation to grab the kid by the shoulders and shake him until he saw things differently. "Do you want that money for your comics or don't you?"

"Oh... okee." Thus encouraged, Mickey fell in step with Trent and Ernie.

By this time, the gathering darkness was almost total and the snow seemed to be coming down more heavily. Trent and Ernie stopped at the lip of the long-dry lakebed and played their flashlight beams down among the piles of snow-dusted garbage in the crater below.

"All right, Ernie," Trent said. "You know how they do things around this place. Where would the trunk be?"

Ernie scratched his head under the earflaps of his hat. "Hell, they coulda dumped it anywhere! We'll hafta go down in there an' jus' look around for a pile of tree limbs or anythin' else that don't look like mashed-up regular garbidge the packers woulda dumped."

They went down a graded slope scarred by tire tracks and ruts from the heavy garbage trucks that had gone into the landfill to empty their loads. Unbidden, lines from Henley's *Invictus* came to Trent's mind: "*Out of the night that covers me, Black as the Pit from pole to pole...*"

They looked high and they looked low. With their flashlight beams, Trent and Ernie probed in every corner, in every nook and cranny, in every last spot large enough to hold a trunk, and turned up nothing useful. Ernie then picked up a metal pole and poked it into several heaps of freshly dumped garbage, but didn't strike any hollow-sounding objects large enough to be a trunk.

Meanwhile, Mickey's attention span hit its limit and he roamed the dump aimlessly, picking up things at random but forgetting what he was supposed to be looking for. Trent lost sight of him for a while, then suddenly heard him shout—

"Vwoom, vwoom!"

Startled, Trent turned his flashlight on him. Mickey was sitting in a go-cart frame that lacked wheels and a motor, and making engine noises.

"Kah-rist," Ernie muttered. "If his house ever caught on fire, he wouldn't try putting it out, he'd roast weenies!"

After something like ten more minutes of searching, during which time they had exhausted every possible place for the trunk to be as well as any number of places where it couldn't possibly be but they looked anyway just to be sure, and were taking second looks at places they had already checked, Trent was forced to conclude that the trunk had never made it to the dump at all. He asked Ernie about the garbage crew's standard operating procedure.

"It's *gotta* be here someplace!" Ernie insisted. "They don't take the dump truck back to the garage without unloadin' it first. Unless it fell off the back of the truck before they got to the dump, which I kinda doubt, the trunk's here. All we hafta do is find it."

With that in mind, they looked some more. Even so, after several more minutes of searching, the trunk still failed to materialize.

"Maybe there's somethin' under here," Ernie suddenly said, and tugged on a tree limb protruding from the bottom of a steep pile of garbage some ten feet high.

Trent saw the pile shimmy and shake, and realized that it was about to fall over on top of Ernie. He remembered only too well what had happened when Ernie tried much the same thing with the stack of comic books at Pam's house. "Ernie — wait!" her yelled and rushed forward.

Just as the garbage pile toppled.

Ernie jumped nimbly back and avoided it, but Trent caught the brunt of the falling detergent boxes, grocery bags, banana peels, newspaper, tin cans, cereal boxes, coffee grounds, and a whole lot of other household discards. When everything finally stopped coming down on him, Trent found himself buried in a mass of largely paper goods. He seemed unhurt; at worse he was only surprised. Then the unmistakable stench of overripe kitty litter rose into his nostrils from somewhere uncomfortably nearby, bringing home the fact that he was lying under a mound of garbage, pure and simple, and he really ought to see about getting out of it.

Then Ernie was at work, clearing some of the fallen debris away from Trent. "Hey, you okay?" he asked anxiously as soon as he had uncovered a head to talk to.

A little unsteadily, Trent pulled himself the rest of the way out of the garbage. He sat up on a relatively dry sheet of cardboard on the bare ground and brushed some broken eggshells out of his lap. Thoughtfully, Ernie reached over and pulled a potato peeling out of Trent's hair.

Trent looked slowly around the dump, mostly shrouded in darkness now. Ernie and Mickey looked down at him uncertainly. Finally, Trent hit his gloved palm with his fist. "*Darn* it!" he exclaimed, all of his mounting frustration and disappointment coming out at once. "The trunk just isn't here! We've looked everywhere and it isn't anywhere! We might as well give up and go home!"

"Yeah, I guess you're right," Ernie agreed reluctantly. "I know this dump about as well as anybody, an' if I can't find it, it just ain't here. But it's *gotta* be here! The only thing I can figure is that Squirrelly musta already buried it with the bulldozer whether he noticed or not."

"Aw, dgee!" said Mickey mournfully. "No cummic books!"

Dispiritedly, Trent got to his feet and led the others back to the car. His pants and coat were a mess, he noticed — snow, mud, tomato sauce from the remnants of somebody's spaghetti dinner — but the physical damage didn't seem permanent.

The damage to his psyche was another matter. *No matter what I do*, he thought tiredly, *it turns out wrong*. And after all this, he didn't even have a comic book to show for it.

Down the road, he saw the headlights of an oncoming car, gauzy in the falling snow. The car seemed to be moving at a speed in excess of what Trent would have considered safe in this kind of weather and he waited by the front of his own car for it to go by. Instead, however, it began to slow down, skidding a little in the slushy snow on the road as the driver braked, and finally stopped alongside the Chevy. With a sinking feeling, Trent recognized the black '68 Thunderbird.

The door on the driver's side opened and Linda stepped out, leaving the motor running and the lights on. It was difficult to see through the windows very well, but Trent thought he could identify her passenger as an athletic senior named Roger Something-or-other, who fit Ernie's "blondie-stud" classification just about perfectly. After discharging one blondie-stud, she apparently hadn't wasted any time recruiting another one.

"What's going on?" Linda asked. "You didn't have a breakdown, did you?"

Before Trent could answer, Mickey stepped into the light. "Hi, Winda!" he called cheerfully. "No, Bub's car's okee — we're just here lookin' for cummic books!"

Linda looked at Mickey and shuddered, then glanced back at Trent, taking due note of his dirty, mud-smeared and food-stained coat and pants. "I should have known. You certainly do have some strange taste in friends, Bob. And I suppose *he's* smarter than me, too?" With that, she slid back into the Thunderbird, slammed the door, and roared off in a spray of snow and gravel.

"You certainly do have a way with wimmin, Bobby ol' buddy," Ernie said. "Now I guess she's gonna have fun, fun, fun 'til her daddy takes the T-bird away."

"Let's just go!" Trent exclaimed, feeling worse about everything than ever.

With the expedition a complete bust, the only thing to do now was go home. Trent drove back towards Shetland to drop Mickey off first, and on the way and at Ernie's insistence he explained what happened the night before with Linda.

Sitting in the back seat, Mickey couldn't help but overhear it, and when Trent had finished his story, he leaned forward. "Nhee… why dint-cha jus' tell Winda you wiked her? Dat's what *I* did!"

No wonder Linda had shuddered when she saw him. But much as Trent detested the idea of letting Mickey give him romantic advice, curiosity won out over resentment. "Er… what did Linda say to that?"

"Oh, she was real nice! She jus' taid she alreddy had a boyfrien' but I'm a nice guy an' tumwhere out dere's a gurl who's jus' right for me! Boy, dat made me feel real dood!"

Ernie snickered. "How 'bout that! She gave 'im the old 'Let-'Em-Down-Easy' line! There must be a summer camp somewhere where girls go to learn all the tricks of the trade like that! I've heard that one a dozen times! But no matter how nice they are about it an' how easy they letcha down, it all comes out to the same thing — it's time to renew your subscription to *TV Guide* an' get out the Solitaire deck, 'cause you ain't goin' nowhere on Friday night!"

"Well, dgee," Mickey said. "It made *me* feel dood!"

"That's 'cause you're the only one who'd believe it," Ernie replied.

"At least she let *him* down easy," Trent said to Ernie, thinking that it spoke rather well of Linda that she had tried to be kind to Mickey in discouraging his clumsy attempt to improve their acquaintance. "Me, she kicked out of her house."

"Don't worry about it," Ernie told him. "You couldn't have afforded her anyway."

That was very little consolation.

Trent drove on into Shetland and after passing through the downtown area, he came to a stop in front of Mickey's house to let him out. And Mickey started crying.

"Now what?" Trent demanded.

"We didn't find da cummic books!" Mickey sobbed. "Now I'm not gonna get any munney!"

Trent glanced at Ernie for a suggestion as to what to do. Ernie just shrugged, as though to say, *This one's your problem, Junior.*

After a few moments of Mickey's gratingly loud whimpering, Trent finally gave in. "Oh, all right. I guess you couldn't help it if your mother had them taken away. How about if I gave you ten dollars?" It was a lot of money for non-existent comic books, and on his own dime Trent never would have offered so much. But making Mickey go away happy or at least quietly would be well worth a tenner, and besides, Uncle Harry was paying for it.

"Nhee… t'anks!" Mickey stopped crying and cheered up with almost suspicious alacrity.

Trent pulled out his wallet and gave Mickey a ten-dollar bill. Ernie opened the door on his side and let Mickey out of the back seat. Mickey pushed eagerly past him and waddled quickly up the sidewalk to the porch.

Ernie jumped back into the car and Trent drove off, relieved beyond measure to be rid of Mickey for… oh, hopefully the rest of his life. At least what had become a daily ritual of Mickey coming up to him in study hall one comic book at a time seemed to be over.

"I dunno, Trentbob," Ernie said, "but is payin' ten bux for cummic books we *didn't* get exactly a way to get ahead in this racket?"

"So where were you with any better ideas when I needed one?"

"Just askin', J. Robert, just askin'!"

After that, conversation died away to almost nothing. What with everything that had happened that evening, Trent hardly felt like talking. At the edge of town, he turned east on Rogersville Road and proceeded another mile or so out into the country, then turned off on the dirt road that led through some woods to the Volney house. As Trent brought his car to a stop in front of the small cottage, his headlights were reflected back in the taillights of a dirty white '60 Falcon that looked as though it had seen combat. If anything, it was even more rust-eaten than his Chevy.

"Pop's home," Ernie said. "Hope he didn't get too bent outta shape 'bout me runnin' off with his spare dump key."

"Thanks for coming along on this wild goose chase anyway," Trent said with a long, weary sigh. "I'm sorry things didn't turn out any better."

"Hey, you don't hafta apologize. You're the guy who got garbage dumped on him, not me. An' cheer up — mebbe we'll find some old funnybooks tomorrow! Good ones!"

"I'm not even sure I really care anymore. But... thanks, Ernie."

"Any time, Junior!" Ernie said, getting out of the car. "Welp, keep 'em flyin'!"

While Ernie bounded on into the house, Trent turned the car around in the driveway and slowly headed back up the lane towards Rogersville Road. *Oh, what's the use?* he wondered as he drove. He was out ten dollars with nothing gained, his reputation at school had gone down in flames, he wasn't sure if Linda actually hated him or if she only had utmost contempt for him... *If there are any gods out there, give me a sign that it's all worth it!*

Suddenly, from somewhere outside the car, he heard an approaching yelling. "Woo-*hoo*! Woo-*hoo*!" Puzzled, Trent stopped at the intersection with the highway, just as Ernie caught up with him, thumping on the car windows and beating on the hood. If anything, Trent was reminded of some cartoon he had seen in which Daffy Duck had gone berserk. He rolled the window down.

"What's wrong, Ernie? I didn't run over your foot, did I?"

"Hell, no, Junior!" Dancing up and down first on one leg and then on the other, Ernie grabbed Trent's coat sleeve through the window. "Get a load o' *this* — we didn't find Mickey's cummic books at the dump 'cause they never got there! One of the guys on the dump truck wanted the trunk for somethin', so they opened it after they picked it up an' they found the funnybooks. They all know I collect comics, so they saved 'em for me! Pop brought 'em home an' all those funnybooks we've been chasin' after to hell an' gone — they're sittin' in our kitchen right now!"

"Good Lord...!" Trent choked.

The gods had answered.

A few minutes later, after making a stop in the bathroom to clean up a bit, Trent was sitting at the table in the tiny, crowded Volney kitchen, going through a cardboard box of comic books with Ernie.

Ernie's father, a lean, middle-aged man with an unshaven, weathered face and wearing a grimy, worn, gray work suit, sat at one end of the table eating a bowl of beef stew. "Dunno what you boys see in those things," he muttered.

Ernie's mother, an exceedingly plump little woman with gray hair, bustled about at the sink, pausing to lean over and tweak her husband's ear with soapy fingers. "At least Ernie's reading something. I can't get you to read more than the sports section."

Mr. Volney brushed the suds off his ear, then slipped an arm around his wife's ample waist and squeezed. "Ain't got the time to read." He then pointed a hopelessly dirty finger at Ernie. "But you — you got the time. Keep on readin' — maybe you can get a job workin' inside somewhere, not outside like me."

Trent's concentration on the comic books was broken by a large collie sitting down next to his chair and putting her chin on his thigh. She looked up at him with huge, soulful brown eyes and her tail thumped loudly on the bare linoleum floor.

"Er... hello, pooch," Trent said warily, extending a hand to pet her on the head. He had never been entirely at ease with dogs of this size, since they seemed to have an alarming number of teeth.

"Hey, I think Heidi likes you!" Ernie exclaimed.

"I'm glad *something* female does," Trent said under his breath and went back to the comic books. Sensing that she wouldn't get much attention here, Heidi moved over to Ernie for some better petting.

He was too busy now to pay her any mind, however, and she curled up on the floor at his feet. Ernie had pulled a recent issue of the *RBCC* out of his back bedroom and was checking titles in the box against a dealer's list. "Lemme see... there's a *Crime SuspenStories* #2 here... almost said *Crime Suppositories*..."

"Ernie!" exclaimed his mother from the sink.

"I said I *almost* said it, so it doesn't count. Anyway, that's eight bux. *Crime Can't Win* #8... well, ya can't win 'em all. Seventy-five Lincolns, an' I don't mean the paper kind. *Weird Science* #12... whoa, Nellie Belle! Fifteen smackeroonies! 'We're in the mun-nee...!'"

Mr. Volney stopped eating for a moment and stared at Trent and Ernie, astonished. "Maybe you boys've really got something there!"

One of Ernie's little sisters, age about ten, wandered in from the living room where she had been watching TV. "Ooo! Look at the comic books!" She reached into the box to pick one up.

"You leave that alone!" Mr. Volney roared, scaring her halfway across the kitchen. "It's valuable!"

The girl was more startled than genuinely frightened, however, since he had managed the difficult trick of roaring with a twinkle in his eye. She just rolled her eyes and said, "Oh, Daddy!" and drifted back into the living room.

But valuable the comic book was. Uncle Dimmy had been buying his comic books during the long dry spell between the expiration of most superheroes in the mid-'40s and their resurrection in the late '50s, and almost none of them were anything Trent would have wanted to read, let alone have around. Well, he could make an exception for the EC science-fiction titles, say, but the rest were crime comics, jungle comics, horror comics, love comics, war comics — representatives of genres that were now either extinct or on the ropes. But they were all in good shape and worth a fair amount of money on the collectors' market. For ten dollars, Trent had done rather well for himself after all.

Of course, there was a minor hitch about exactly who their owner was. Trent had bought them but they had ended up at Ernie's house. The only reasonable solution seemed to be sharing the proceeds from their eventual sale equally, as had been agreed at the start for any windfalls.

Ernie went through the box and while he might borrow some to read, particularly the EC science-fiction, he couldn't find any comic books that he particularly wanted to keep.

"I don't mind a good horror comic now an' then," he said, "but they get kinda old after a while, so you can take the rest of the crook and spook junk. When you sell off the first batch, you can deduct five bux of my share to cover half of what you paid Mickey."

A little later, Trent went out to his car carrying a heavy box of comic books, his mood almost mellow. The comics hadn't been quite what he was looking for, but they were money in the bank and certainly a good base for further dealing and trading.

Another line from Henley's *Invictus* came to Trent as he drove home through the snow-shrouded night: "*Under the bludgeonings of chance, my head is bloody, but unbowed.*"

Epilogue

As Trent clumped through his front door, grappling clumsily with the big box of comic books, mellowness turned to horror. Pam and his mother sat on the living room couch together, paging through a frighteningly familiar-looking photo album. When she saw Trent come in, Pam hastily clapped her hand to her mouth to stifle the giggles.

"Mom!" Trent blurted, aghast, nearly dropping the box. "You aren't showing Pam *those* pictures, are you?"

Mrs. Trent looked up from pointing out a particularly juicy shot. "Why not?" she asked mildly. "You told me Pam likes comics, too, so I thought she might be interested in seeing pictures of the Halloween when you and Sue went trick or treating as comic-book characters…"

Halloween, 1958: Susan Trent was five and J. Robert Trent, Jr. was seven. That was the year Mrs. Trent dressed them as Little Lulu and Tubby. Even now, Pam was looking at snapshots of little Bobby Trent, lingering baby fat and all, wearing shorts and a child-sized sailor's cap. She was trying desperately to hold her giggles down and still be ladylike about it, but she wasn't having any better luck than Trent was in fighting back a groan of dismay.

"I'm sorry!" Pam exclaimed. "It's just that you looked so much more like Pugsley from *The Addams Family* than like Tubby!" Then, realizing from the look of mortification on Trent's face that Pugsley wasn't exactly an improvement over Tubby, she apparently decided that the only way to spare everyone further embarrassment was to talk about something else fast. "Oh, I see you bought the comics your mom told me you went out after. Can I look at them?"

Trent put the box down in the middle of the living-room floor and Pam slipped off the couch to her bluejeanned knees on the carpet to give the comics a once-over.

Seeing that the session of rattling the skeletons in the family closet was over, Mrs. Trent packed up the photo album to leave the young folks to some amount of privacy in the living room. However, she couldn't help but notice the mud and spaghetti sauce stains on her son's coat and pants. "What on Earth did you have to do to get those comics?" she wondered.

Trent sighed. "It's a long story. I'll explain later."

Shrugging, Mrs. Trent left the room, quite failing to notice the daggers her first-born glared at her and the photo album.

"You say you got this lot from Mickey Gompers?" Pam asked in amazement, putting down *Film Star Romances* and picking up *Weird Science-Fantasy Annual*. She glanced at some of the other titles — *Shock SuspenStories, Crime Detective, Crime Must Pay the Penalty, Vault of Horror, Tomb of Terror*, and dozens more — and shook her head. "It wasn't a very good period for comics, I have to admit. That was when they were at their coldest, cruelest, and most heartless, all death and gore and violence and crummy contemporary 'realism' muck. Barf!"

"I agree," Trent said. "If I'd been a fan back then... well, I wouldn't have been a fan. That stuff would have turned me right off. And maybe I wouldn't have gotten tangled up in this business."

"Bob, what is it? I've never seen you look so... so haggard."

"Does it show?" Trent collapsed heavily in the easy chair and gave Pam a brief account of the evening's events. "But what really did me in," he finished, "was after being in that run-down, dirty, smelly house with Mickey, his mother told me she was glad he was finally bringing his friends home from school. I was almost sick — with pity, I guess."

"The point being," Pam said, "that Mickey doesn't have *any* friends?"

"None that I know of," Trent replied. "Some people pretend to be friendly just so they can tease him better, but as far as an honest-to-goodness friend he can really talk to and who won't play mean tricks on him... no. And it's no wonder. I mean, I'm decent to him and I don't make fun of him, but I couldn't be a real friend to him if I wanted to. It's not just different interests, we don't even think the same way. I just don't have anything to say to him, at least not that he would understand. And how did we get off on this? Does it really matter?"

Pam nodded. "It does matter. Something you said that night you and Ernie came over and my dad kicked you out... it made me think. I asked you how you could put up with Ernie's goofiness and you explained it by saying he's your friend. I realized, I think, that I don't have all that many friends myself—"

"But there's Ernie and the people you know in fandom and, well, me—"

"Yes, but... it isn't what I mean. And then you told me last night how you stood up for me in front of Linda even though it probably killed whatever hope you might have had of being *her* friend. After you left, I realized maybe I do have a friend and I ought to be holding up my end of the deal. So I had a talk with Dad and…" She stood up, pulled out a heavy grocery bag that had been standing inconspicuously next to the couch, and carried it over to Trent.

It was filled with comic books: on top was a 1954 issue of *Captain America* with the headline "Captain America… Commie Smasher!" Gasping for breath, Trent gently lifted out a few comics and saw that they were all the old *Captain America* issues he needed for the article he had wanted to write in the first place, from the brief 1950s revival all the way back to the first one in 1941.

"Mom had to go into town to do something for one of her clubs," Pam went on, "so I had her drop me off here with the comics. And if you want to do other research projects, talk to me and maybe we can work something out."

"I… I don't know what to say," Trent stammered in surprise.

"'Thank you' would be nice. Dad wasn't all that easy to talk into letting me take these out of the house. Anyway, Mom should be coming by in a few minutes to pick me up—"

Something occurred to Trent. "Wait a minute. I think I know just how to say 'thank you' at that." He left Pam in the living room and went upstairs. A minute or two later, he came back down with a small pile of comic books extracted from the Frank Martin collection — copies of the *Little Archie*s Pam liked so much.

Pam's eyes went wide as she looked through them. "I've got this one… I *don't* have this one, or… good grief! I didn't know this one even existed!" She held up a copy of something called *Little Ambrose* #1, evidently a spin-off of one of the *Little Archie* characters into his own book. "Uhm… Bob, old chum, you say you're giving them to me?" Outside, a car horn sounded. "Uh oh, that's Mom now—"

"In return for the loan of the *Captain Americas*, yes, I'm giving them to you. Compliments of the management," Trent added, thinking of something he'd seen printed on one of his father's matchbooks. Then something else occurred to him, an idea so breathtaking that he hardly dared even breathe it out loud. But if he didn't get it out now, he might never have the courage and be in the right place at the right time to do anything about it again. "By the way," he went on as he politely helped Pam put on her coat, trying to sound casual, "*Thoroughly Modern Millie* is playing at the Prairie. Maybe you and I could, uh, see it, say Friday night?"

Pam smiled — a little wryly, it seemed. "Sure, okay. It sounds like fun. Well, thanks for the comics and I'll see you at school!" Then she picked up the *Little Archie*s and went out the door.

*I just made a date with Pam!* Trent realized in amazement as he closed the door behind her. He knew her too well to have any thoughts of it going anywhere, but still… It was something.

After Pam had left, Trent went to his room and called Ernie to tell him about getting the loan of Pam's comics after all. He didn't mention the movie date with her, however. Even though it would be just a Friends sort of thing, he didn't want to subject it to Ernie's jokes just yet. Some things were sacred.

"Hey, TV Comics is movin' right along!" Ernie enthused. "With our Uncle Dimmy haul, we can start wheelin' an' dealin' for real in the *RBCC!*"

"I don't know…" Trent said a little tiredly. "I got into this thing mainly for the sake of Golden Age comics for research, and if I can borrow Pam's now, there isn't any *need* for me to be a dealer anymore. Besides, we haven't turned up *one* Golden Age comic book since we started. I don't know where they all went, but there just don't seem to be any out there. Not around here, anyway."

"Aw, c'mon!" Ernie wheedled. "Stick with it! We're just getting' started! Ol' Man Erwin didn't buy all the Golden Agers in Bureau County! I bet if we keep on sniffin' around for old comics, we'd find out what happened to 'em all!"

"I suppose you're right," Trent agreed without much conviction.

He had no idea *how* right Ernie was… but that's another tale for another time.

# What the Jokes Are

In which some of the more obscure references in the story "TV Comics" are explained:

"I'm going over tonight to pick up her set of Golden Age *Captain America* issues." As terminology evolved, the first flowering of superheroes during the World War II era became referred to as the "Golden Age." Logically, then, when superheroes returned to the newsstands in the late '50s and early '60s, that must be the Silver Age, though that term hadn't emerged yet in 1967. The terms "Golden Age" and "Silver Age" applied originally only to superheroes: early '60s comics fans were superhero buffs first and foremost and hardly cared about other genres. There has since been considerable confusion on what the terms refer to as newer fans have forgotten or never knew the original definitions. "Golden Age" has now come to loosely refer to just the '40s and "Silver Age" the '60s irrespective of genre, and who knows what to call the '50s.

"You can just write an article about something else while you're waiting to do the one on Cap an' Bucky!" Child endangerment laws apparently weren't in effect in the 1940s as numerous superheroes fought crime in the company of juvenile partners, most famously the duo of Batman and Robin. In the real world, this was supposed to give the juvenile reader a character to identify with, but the common complaint of many old-time fans was that they had hated the kid and just wanted to read about the grown-up hero. In *The Great Comic Book Heroes*, Jules Feiffer explained it as Batman being somebody you had some hope you could be like in a few years if you worked out, took your vitamins, and studied hard, but Robin was just depressing because he was your age and had *already* achieved the perfection you were clearly lacking. In any case, Captain America had Bucky (who was also called Bucky in his civilian identity but nobody ever made the connection) as his youthful partner in peril.

"New Low Prices Howard." A back-issue dealer of the time was notorious for prices considerably above the average. Since he advertised extensively, he was often the first dealer new collectors encountered, who paid his prices without knowing that the goods could be had more cheaply elsewhere. When the newbies got a better sense of the lay of the land, their chagrin was considerable upon realizing how much they had overpaid. Adding insult to injury, the dealer advertised with the motto "New Low Prices," though with what justification was unclear.

"Get a *Grit* route." *Grit* was a nationally distributed weekly newspaper that was less news and more upbeat general-interest features. Comics fans were familiar with it because *Grit* ran ads in comic books showing coarsely half-toned photos of teenage bumpkins holding up fistfuls of green-colored cash allegedly earned by selling the paper in their home towns. The catch was that there weren't any established routes like there were for the local newspaper: you had to build up your own business by badgering your relatives and neighbors into taking this odd weekly thing nobody had ever heard of. Some fans who had actually seen copies of *Grit* spoke highly of its selection of comic strips, however.

"…a gruesome horror story in some trashy comic book such as infested the newsstands of the early 1950s…" Tastes differ, of course, and this is simply Trent's own opinion of horror comics. While most fans of the time were primarily superhero fans, horror comics, particularly those published by EC before the mid-Fifties Trouble, had their devotees. EC's horror and science-fiction comics were a cut above most such comics, but didn't survive the controversy; the publisher got out of color comics entirely and concentrated on a single humor magazine called *Mad* that endures to this day.

*The Radio Man*. The author's name, Ralph Milne Farley, was a pseudonym for someone actually named Roger Sherman Hoar — which certainly sounds like a good argument for a pseudonym in this case. Ace Books probably published only the second and third books in the series because the rights to the first were held by another company. A paperback edition of *The Radio Man* had been published by Avon Books in 1950, although Trent was unaware of it. The comics adaptation of *The Radio Man* was in fact published by Avon's comic-book division under the title *An Earthman on Venus*.

"He still remembered all too clearly January 12, 1966 — Black Wednesday, the fateful day when the *Batman* TV show premiered as a mid-season replacement for some other show." Time has smoothed some of the edges. The *Batman* TV show that caused serious comics fans so much grief or at least mixed feelings has come to be regarded with nostalgic affection. Some of us old-timers have even come to prefer a Batman like that — a heroic crusader for justice — as opposed to the grim avenger we thought we wanted and then actually got.

"Even *Amazing Fantasy* #15, which is probably tough to find, since nobody saw Spidey comin'." Spider-Man's first appearance was in a story run as an experiment in the last issue of a comic book otherwise devoted to one-shot fantasy and science-fiction stories. The first issue of Spider-Man's own comic book was technically his second appearance.

"From the speaker burst a jingle chorus singing 'W-R-O-K, Rockforddddd!'" At the time this story was first written, long before the Internet, there was no easy way to look up radio stations and their call letters. That Rockford, Illinois might have a station called "WROK" was a pure guess on my part. When this book went into production, I checked and discovered that not only does a station WROK exist in Rockford now, it was there in the '60s and actually was Top 40 then.

"Trent had to admit that Supes had fallen on some hard times during that period." Another case of time softening perceptions. Fans nervous about their seeming maturity had grown up on the *Superman* comics of the period, then realized that the comics were pitched to a juvenile audience they had grown out of. Later, the *Superman* comics of the late '50s and '60s would be appreciated in retrospect as perhaps silly but in an endearing sort of way.

"He had seen fanzines that had been produced that way, and the results were not good." While a few fans had tried printing fanzines on office copiers, usually teenagers getting their fathers to do it for them at work, the inability of '60s-era copiers to reproduce black areas led to poor results. Eventually, Xerox-type copiers would improve to the point of printing quality equal to photo-offset, but that was years away yet.

# THE OLD ABANDONED WAREHOUSE

## 1944

"Hey! What the hell you doin' with my story magazines?!"

Seventeen-year-old Billy Erwin froze in mid-motion when his father's outraged voice boomed across the farmyard that warm spring afternoon, and the stack of comic books and pulp magazines he had been loading into the bed of the dusty old Model T pickup truck fell to the bare, hard-packed dirt.

Carl Erwin, a grizzled, sun-dried farmer in his late 50s, loped around the corner of the big red barn and broke into a trot towards the truck. His denim coveralls flapped as he ran and his straw hat was caught by the breeze and blown off his head.

"Uh oh!" Billy exclaimed, terrified, "Now I'm gonna catch it!"

Mr. Wickersham, Billy's dapper young science teacher, was just then stepping off the porch of the house with an armload of pulp magazines and humming *As Time Goes By* to himself. Even when he was at work out in the country, he was wearing his best suit and fedora. "Let me handle it, Billy," he said, stooping to set the magazines down on the truck's running board. He noticed once again the lurid painted cover of the topmost issue — *G-8 and His Battle Aces*, with swooping biplanes and blazing machine guns in stormy skies — and shook his head. As he stood up, he glanced at the truck bed, already piled high with bales of newspapers and magazines. "When your father sees how his friends and neighbors have contributed to the paper drive, I'm sure he'll be only too happy to do his patriotic duty."

"You don't know my Pop!" Billy warned. "He likes to read his story magazines an awful lot!"

Carl Erwin's anger only mounted as he approached the truck. For a moment, he looked as though he was about to kick Billy around the barnyard, but then he saw Mr. Wickersham. Fists clenched and breathing heavily, he confronted the smiling teacher. "You put my boy up t'this?" he demanded.

"Now, Mr. Erwin," Mr. Wickersham said smoothly, politely taking his hat off, "he was just trying to help our boys overseas. Everybody on the home front here in Bureau County has to do his part for the war effort, and supporting the paper drive is as important as buying a bond. We at Shetland High School even have a slogan: 'Help Hang the Paperhanger with Paper!' Surely you want to help us foil the *Führer*, don't you?"

"Not with my story magazines, you don't!" Carl Erwin snapped. "You can start takin' 'em right back in the house!"

Mr. Wickersham bristled with righteous indignation, his oily smile draining away from his mouth. "Well, if you don't want to help us defeat Hitler and Tojo very much, then I guess all our boys died in vain at Pearl Harbor—"

Carl Erwin turned purple, and for a moment only supreme self-control kept him from grabbing the wide lapels of Mr. Wickersham's double-breasted suit coat and trying to throttle him. He took a few deep breaths to calm down, then stood with arms akimbo, glaring at the teacher. "I got a boy in the Navy, I got another boy in the Air Corps, I gave my old cook-stove to the scrap drive, I gave my old tires an' kitchen grease to those drives, I got a Victory Garden out back of the house, I bought bonds 'til I was blue and broke, I done everything but join the Commandos — but one thing I ain't done is waste gas an' tire coupons tootlin' around the county actin' important and accusin' *other* folks of bein' unpatriotic!"

That last remark hit Mr. Wickersham like a Bronx cheer in the face, but just as he was about to bring up the verbal ack-ack guns for a hot retort about how even more sacrifice was demanded, he looked at Carl Erwin in the bright sunlight and saw only grit and steel glaring back. "Oh, all right," he said after a moment. "I guess you have done more than your share already…"

"Damn right, bud!" Carl Erwin declared, then turned to his son. "Say, whose idea was it anyway to take all my story magazines without askin' me first?"

"Aw, gee whiz, Pop!" Billy exclaimed. "All the fellows at school have been givin' their comic books an' stuff, an' Mom said you wouldn't mind once you heard it was for the war effort…!"

"I shoulda known your Ma was behind this…" Carl Erwin muttered half to himself. "Okay," he said to Billy, "there's a stack of newspapers in the barn. You want paper for your paper drive, you can take them — but the story magazines go back in the house *right now!*"

"Yes *sir!*" Billy agreed, relieved that the heat seemed to be off him for the time being, and dropped to his knees to begin gathering up the fallen comic books and pulp magazines.

Then, curious, Carl Erwin looked in the back of the truck. "Whaddyuh got in there, anyhow?" He saw only bales of loosely tied newspapers and various issues of *Life*, *Liberty*, *Colliers*, and other magazines — until something brightly colored caught his eye. He reached in and pulled out an issue of *Marvel Mystery Comics* with a high-octane cover of flying, flaming characters battling Japanese soldiers about to load a presumably American woman in a cannon. "Hey!" he cried. "Here's one I ain't seen yet! Musta missed it somehow!" He dropped it on the stack Billy was assembling.

"Mr. Erwin!" Mr. Wickersham gasped indignantly. "Taking your own funny papers back is one thing, but that was donated to the paper drive by someone else!"

Carl Erwin hitched up his overalls. "Look, bud, when a fellow I don't even know comes up to me on my own property an' practically calls me a Quisling for no good reason I can see, I deserve some satisfaction! You're just damn lucky I don't decide to blitz your teeth instead!"

A little later, with Billy on the seat beside him, Mr. Wickersham drove the truck down the short dirt lane to the highway and turned east on Illinois Rt. 92. The neat little farmhouse and the red barn with 1924 on the roof shrank in the distance behind them, lost in a flat, empty green sea of cornfields stretching endlessly in all directions.

"Your father certainly likes that blood and thunder tripe," Mr. Wickersham said suddenly.

"Oh yeah," Billy replied, "he reads it all the time. Mom says it's a waste of money an' yells at him a lot for it, but he just doesn't pay any attention to her an' goes on readin'. Y'know, I bet that's why she told us to take that stuff in the first place."

*Caught in the middle of a domestic squabble*, Mr. Wickersham thought. Evidently Mrs. Erwin had been trying to get rid of the magazines for some time and saw him as merely a convenient scapegoat for the blame when her husband inevitably found out and made a scene. But then Mr. Erwin had come in unexpectedly from the fields and caught him and Billy in the act of lifting what must amount to the family jewels in the old boy's eyes. Everything was copacetic now, but still… "Your father seems to be an intelligent man," Mr. Wickersham remarked after a moment's thought. "What can he possibly find interesting in such semiliterate sensationalism?

How can a grown man enjoy such childish nonsense as *Superman* and *Captain Marvel*?"

Billy shrugged. "Well, I guess some of it's just for fun. He has all those copies of *G-8* because he was in France himself back in the first war an' he likes to laugh at all the crazy stuff the writer came up with. Then he reads mags like *Amazing* and *Astounding* because he thinks all that stuff about going to the Moon might come true someday."

"Not in either of our lifetimes, I'm sure," Mr. Wickersham said drily.

"But mostly he just reads because it relaxes him after working outside all day, an' he doesn't have to listen to Mom complainin'. He also hangs on to everything because he likes to read it again if he doesn't have anything new in the house to look at."

*Poor kid*, thought Mr. Wickersham. A nagging mother and a father addicted to moronic fantasies. Perhaps it *is* up to the schools to make up for deficient homelives and instill progressive values in the students. "Anyway, Billy," he said with slightly forced heartiness, "I'm glad you could help me out with the paper drive. After we stop at a couple more places, we can take this load to the collection center at Camp Douglas."

"Say, that's swell!" Billy exclaimed. "This is just like Little Orphan Annie and her Junior Commandos!"

*Good Lord!* Mr. Wickersham thought, appalled. *The creeping mental rot has infected the kid, too!*

# 1967

After borrowing a large stack of fabulously rare and valuable comic books like a complete run of Golden Age *Captain America* comics, the only proper thing to do was to bring them back within a decent interval. And that Bob Trent did, though not without prodding. To him, the interval had been anything but decent.

"Look, I'm sorry," Pam Collins said again for about the fifth time from where she sat at her drawing board by the window, "but Dad found a buyer for the comics and he wants to send them out right away." Pam was a slender, green-eyed brunette about a month shy of turning sixteen; she tied her long hair back in a loose ponytail to keep it from dangling in her work at the drawing board, and she was wearing one of her father's old shirts as a protective smock although it was almost comically too baggy for her since Mr. Collins had a rather more ample figure to cover. Numerous paint and ink stains showed that it had already come in for some hard use. She smiled — it was a dazzling display of brilliant white teeth that could light up a dark room when she really worked at it, but now it came off a little weak and apologetic. "So what can I do?" she finished.

"Yes, I know," replied Trent, a slightly pudgy, dark-haired teenager with black plastic-framed glasses. "I'm not blaming you — it's just that the week I had them wasn't nearly long enough to get them all even read, let alone write the article about them. I've been planning that article for *Shockwave* for a long time and I was hoping to at least have the comics read over Christmas…" He trailed off, sounding forlorn and pathetic.

They were in Pam's workroom, actually a spare bedroom. The last sign that it had once been her older brother's room was a faded pennant reading **GO PONIES!** with a snarling horse's head on one of the walls. Mrs. Collins still hopefully called it her "sewing room," but "the comic-book room" would have been more apt now. Mr. Collins' discovery and purchase of a huge treasure-trove of old comic books out at the Erwin farm in October had ended up with the entire hoard stacked in enormous piles in the room and he had appointed himself business manager to list and sell them. Everywhere Trent turned in the room, a perilously teetering pile of cheap thrills was in the way, and navigation was difficult and even treacherous through the narrow path winding between the stacks of pulp magazines and comic books. Somewhere in the maze, shoved against the wall and forgotten, was Mrs. Collins' sewing machine.

In the pause that followed, Trent wondered if he should think of something else to say, just to fill the emptiness hanging in the air. It had been like that when he and Pam had gone to see *Thoroughly Modern Millie*, their first and so far only date. They didn't have much to say to each other outside of comics, and when it got to the point that Trent found himself wishing his friend Ernie had come along on the date just to keep things moving, he knew the relationship had some problems. Sometimes it seemed as though Pam went places where he couldn't follow...

Pam was trying to work on a pen and ink drawing, but she was distracted by both Trent and the view out the window past the house across the street and out on scattered woodlots and open cornfields beyond, vague and misty through a gauze of falling December snow. Trent hadn't been there very long, but already his decrepit '57 Chevy was covered by a thin layer of white.

"Snow is such an artistic medium!" Pam suddenly exclaimed.

"Er... huh?" Trent blurted, startled by the sudden change of subject.

"Just look at what it's doing to your car," she pointed out. "Snow is a discreet white blanket that covers your car's cancerous rust with virgin purity."

"Pam, if anything, the snow will just make the rust worse when it melts!"

"Hmm..." Pam reflected. "You know, I think there's a meaning in there someplace."

Trent sat close by a large wooden desk, carefully trying not to disturb Mr. Collins' paperwork. A large crank-type adding machine, a copy of the latest *Rocket's Blast/Comicollector* opened to a comic-book dealer's multi-paged ad for Golden Age superhero comics, sheet after sheet of notebook paper filled with listings of the Erwin Farm inventory with condition and approximate market value noted for each item... even if Pam herself had so overdosed on Golden Age comics that she had largely lost interest in them, Mr. Collins was more gung-ho than ever about selling the collection. This would go a long way towards putting his little girl through college, after all.

Mr. Collins wasn't home at the moment, which was the main reason why Trent could even be in the room. After his friend Ernie had knocked a stack of precious and fragile comic books over, Mr. Collins had ruled that henceforth the room was off-limits to unauthorized personnel, particularly Pam's less-coordinated friends. Actually, though, if Mr. Collins had come in unexpectedly just then, he probably wouldn't have complained very much about Trent, who was almost obsessively responsible and conscientious. Ernie he would have shot on sight.

"Anyway," Trent went on, trying to turn the conversation away from Pam's metaphysical musings and back to the original topic, "maybe Ernie did have the right idea the other week. I can't keep borrowing comics from you forever, and if I want to do research on Golden Age comics for articles for my fanzine, I should get a collection of my own. But I can't afford the big dealers' prices, and when Ernie and I advertised for old comics in the paper, we didn't have a whole lot of luck."

"I thought you did pretty well," Pam said, resuming her inking work with brush in hand. "Those *Little Archie*s you gave me were just plain wonderful."

"But what we did get was mainly recent stuff. The only old comics we found were in that trunk of '50s horror and crime junk that Mickey Gompers had. What I really wanted was 1940s superhero comics, and we didn't find a single one of those. I keep wondering — where did they all go? Carl Erwin can't have been the only one buying comic books in Bureau County during World War II. What happened to all the rest of the comics sold around here?"

"They aren't very durable, you know," Pam said. "They're just cheap paper, and if more than one or two kids read a comic, it'd go to pieces pretty fast — and it has been 25 or so years now. It's no wonder there aren't very many left. The only ones that would survive would be the ones kept on purpose in collections like Mr. Erwin's, or by accident, like being put in a box someplace and forgotten about like those at Mickey's house. But as for what must have happened to a lot of them, well, I ran across this the other day." She put her brush down and pulled a comic book from a nearby pile to show it to Trent.

It was DC's *Comic Cavalcade* #6 (Spring, 1944). The cover featured Wonder Woman and the Golden Age Flash and Green Lantern hard at work collecting bales of paper. A sign on a building wall read:

# *War Production Urgently Needs*
# *WASTE PAPER!*

"Good grief!" Trent choked. "This is a comic book that practically urges its own destruction!" He thought of something he'd once seen while driving through the country: a farm woman sitting on the steps of her house and plucking a dead chicken while other chickens in the flock wandered aimlessly around her, blithely uncomprehending of what she was doing to one of their number. Well, the analogy wasn't quite exact, but the same obliviousness to the looming threat of one's own extinction was there.

"And I've read in fanzines that a lot of old comics did get destroyed that way," Pam added. "That's part of the reason why they're so rare and valuable now: they were eaten up in the paper drives. Of course, it was all very patriotic and maybe helped us win the war, but it doesn't do the fans now much good."

"I can't even imagine what the paper would have been used for other than beating Hitler over the head with a rolled-up copy of *Captain America*," Trent said, suddenly depressed by the sheer magnitude of the waste of priceless collectors' items in the wartime drives. He shook his head to clear the gruesome nightmare vision out of his mind and turned his attention to something else. "By the way, what have you been working on so diligently over there ever since I came in?"

"A little project of mine," Pam replied picking up the sheet of drawing paper to scrutinize the work in progress more closely. Then, from almost out of nowhere, she produced a stack of notebook paper and leaned over to hand it to Trent at the desk. The top sheet bore the title:

# MARJOLAINE

A sketch underneath showed a blonde girl in glowing armor holding her helmet against her side with one hand and raising a flaming sword high with the other.

"Er… what do you want me to do with it?" Trent wondered.

"Read it! I want to print up some copies as an illustrated novelette, but before I type it up on ditto masters and draw spot illos for it, I'd like to have somebody go over it for grammar and spelling."

Who that somebody was going to be was obvious. Trent leafed through the manuscript, noting from how Pam's normally artistic handwriting had collapsed into all but illegible scrawl in places, like a deafening screech overloading an oscilloscope trace, that she must have written it in the heat of inspiration. Just trying to decipher it would be a job, but…

"Well, okay," he said, "but what's it about?"

"It's sort of Joan of Arc with magic," Pam explained. "You see, I was doing my French homework just before Thanksgiving, and I was looking up some word or other in the dictionary, and then I came across the word *marjoram*…"

"Margarine? Like for bread?"

"No, o most foolish and silly one, *marjoram*. It's a plant used for seasoning. I think they make oregano from it. Anyway, the French word for it is *marjolaine*, and I thought, 'Hey, what a great name for a character!' And so I created the character to match. Marjolaine lives in the Duchy of Arvergne, which is like Middle Ages France except magic works there. She has a flaming sword called *Flamberge*, a gorgeous prancing white stallion named *Bolide*, a faithful troll companion and squire named *Karl* who talks in a really thick Sveedish accent, by yingo, — oh, I have it all worked out! You'll see what I mean when you read it. What I've been working on today is a cover for Richard Caldwell's fanzine, *The Arkham Advertiser*. He wrote me a while back asking for one, so…"

Richard Caldwell was a twenty-ish college student and science-fiction fan who lived in St. Louis. His irregularly published fanzine was his means of venting his spleen on any subject he chose as well as answering his mail in public and feuding hilariously with some opponents who were badly outclassed when it came to slinging invective. Of late, Caldwell had parlayed the fact that the house he shared with several other fans was infested with cockroaches into a series of wild and woolly stretchers about "Iron Mountain Roaches," according to him the hardiest and toughest living creatures on the planet, able to invade a hot oven and strip a baking pizza without even working up a sweat. Caldwell spun his yarns in a dry, laconic style that made them almost believable, and some readers were convinced that he was about to make a permanent contribution to American folklore much in the same vein as Paul Bunyan's herd of cattle with legs shorter on one side than on the other so they could graze on hillsides.

Pam's cover for *The Arkham Advertiser* showed a grinning Marjolaine in full armor, her helmet off so her long hair could flow freely, riding a giant roach with her flaming sword held aloft in one hand while she waved a frothy tankard of ale in the other. Troll Karl and Bolide the horse stood in the background and looked on in bemusement.

"What do you think?" Pam asked eagerly.

"It's… well, good, really good," was all Trent could say, amazed that anyone could make a cockroach look so cute and adorable. "But about *Marjolaine* overall… I was wondering, don't you think a flaming sword might be a bit much along with everything else?"

"Give the poor girl a chance!" Pam exclaimed. "I figure she'll be up against big hairy guys who weigh about 200 pounds more than she does, and she certainly doesn't have the muscle power of your average ogre, so she needs something to even the odds. Besides, ever carve a turkey? Dad let me do the honors this past Thanksgiving, and trying to saw through that hunk of meat convinced me that Marjolaine needs *something* with some cutting power. I could have used a flaming *knife!*"

And that settled that. Trent left shortly thereafter, while it was still light out and before the snow got to be too heavy. He was a little glum at having to give up the *Captain America*s so precipitously and prematurely, and somehow not at all enthusiastic about wading through at least fifty pages of Pam's handwriting.

Getting home was another matter. First Trent had to brush the virgin purity off his windshield just to be able to see out, then start the car. And the '57 Chevy, which had definitely seen better days, was perfectly happy to stay where it was. When Trent turned the ignition key, even the grinding of the starter seemed to protest. *"I don't wanna! I don't wanna!"* Eventually, though, and after several attempts, Trent persuaded it otherwise and could move off down Potawatomi Drive and out of the semi-rural subdivision.

Among other things wrong with the Chevy, the heater knob had long since broken off the stem, and Trent could turn the heater on only by inserting a key in the slot and manipulating the remnant stub inside. But whatever good effect the heater might have had was counteracted by the wind whipping up through a gaping, rust-eaten hole in the floor by the gas pedal. When Trent looked down, he could see snow-covered pavement passing by underneath. The Chevy, it seemed, was not far from the great highway in the sky, where it would doubtless join its previous owner, Trent's late great-uncle Harry, upon whose passing from this plane of existence he had inherited it. With no other elderly great-uncles with cars to bequeath on the horizon, Trent couldn't soon replace the Chevy, and he had to get every last remaining mile out of it he could while it still ran.

Homework being rather on the heavy side, Trent still hadn't even begun reading *Marjolaine* by the time he reached school the next morning. Or at least that was the alibi he planned to give Pam if she asked about it. Having to do homework was a wonderful excuse for not doing other things, and he used it a lot.

When Trent was stowing his coat in his locker, Daryl Knudsen emerged from the crowds of teenagers streaming through the hall and came up to him. Knudsen was a thin, pimply senior who occupied his spare time as photographer for the Shetland High School *Express*. In fact, he had taken the pictures when the editor of the paper interviewed Trent not long before about his comic-book hobby.

"Hey, I've been trying to find you for a couple of days," Knudsen said. "I was going through the *Express* files the other day looking for something, and I found an old issue you might be interested in, since you're really into comic books and stuff like that."

Trent found himself ducking involuntarily as he had been doing ever since that interview came out and people started calling "Hey, Funnybook Bob!" after him. "Er... oh, thanks. What's in it?"

"An article about comics," Knudsen told him. "Goes all the way back to the '50s. I don't know if it's important or not, but I thought you might like to see it just in case." He gave Trent an old newspaper and added, "Give it back to me when you're done with it."

Trent took the paper with mumbled thanks, but it wasn't until he was sitting at his desk in his third period study hall that he had a chance to look at it.

The issue was dated Friday, February 25, 1955, and it was filled with the news of another epoch, of a time when the student population wasn't as large, when Eisenhower was President, and when the girls wore much longer dresses and didn't look as pretty as they did now. *Maybe it's the dowdy hair-dos*, Trent reflected. Otherwise, Shetland High School hadn't changed much in nearly thirteen years. The old brick building dated back to the 1930s and looked about the same in pictures taken two decades later, and many of the same teachers had been there then.

Trent quickly found what had caught Knudsen's eye: a picture of a man pushing forty, with a receding hairline and a growing paunch, smiling with the satisfaction of a job well done as he watched a pile of burning… comic books. Horrified, Trent read the accompanying article.

# LOCAL DRIVE ON COMIC BOOKS A SUCCESS
## Students Rush to Trade 10 for a Classic

The Shetland Committee for Better Juvenile Literature carried out a "highly successful" two-hour drive on Saturday, February 19, to rid Bureau County of objectionable comic books, according to committee chairman Grover C. Wickersham, who teaches science at Shetland High School.

A total of four hundred boys and girls from area elementary schools and students from SHS traded 5000 comic books for five hundred good books bought by the committee. The comic books were then hauled to the city dump where they were burned under the supervision of the Shetland Municipal Fire Department.

"We burned them so they would not get back into circulation," Mr. Wickersham explained. "Comic books have been implicated in causing juvenile delinquency and many other social problems."

However, a dissenting note was sounded by Mr. Howard Phillips, who teaches American History at SHS. Said Mr. Phillips: "While I think comic books are loathsome, detestable bilge, the symbolism inherent in burning them disturbs me. Didn't we fight a war ten years ago against people who also burned books they didn't like?"

Mr. Wickersham replied that burning comic books is not the same thing. "We had to dispose of them somehow," he stated. "Besides, no one objects when batches of poisoned food are destroyed. What is wrong with destroying poison for the mind?"

To collect the comic books, the committee offered a classic for every ten comic books turned in, then put in a stock of twenty-five books and opened the doors of the Lincoln Elementary School lunchroom for business. They were swamped. More than one hundred boys and girls showed up during the first half hour and committee members had to make several hurried trips to Sanderson's Book Store to purchase more good books.

The books included some dealing with magic, inventions, doll dress making, Indians, Kit Carson, Buffalo Bill, trains, boats, Betsy Ross, American history, and the police. There were volumes

in the Hardy Boys and Tom Corbett series
as well as *Pinocchio, Robinson Crusoe,*
and *King Arthur and his Knights.*

*Good Lord!* Trent thought, choking on a vision of some little girl trading copies of *Action #1, Superman #1, Detective #27, Batman #1, Whiz #2, Captain Marvel Adventures #1, Pep #1, Captain America #1, Marvel Comics #1,* and *Human Torch #1* for a book on doll dress making.

*Wait a minute.* The comic-book conflagration took place in 1955, some 15 years or more after those comics came out. It wasn't any more likely that a little girl had comics that old than a little girl of today had comics from 1952. Well, Pam did, but that was a special case. Trent's grasp of comic-book history was shaky for the decade following World War II, when most superheroes had faded into limbo, and what he did know came mainly out of Dr. Fredric Wertham's anti-comic-book screed *Seduction of the Innocent,* but he suspected Mr. Wickersham's haul had consisted almost entirely of material that would make any self-respecting collector turn up his nose in disgust: horror comics, crime comics, love comics, jungle comics, funny animal comics, that sort of thing.

It was just galling that Mr. Wickersham had done so much better than he had in assembling a big pile of comic books from the local citizenry, and for all the wrong reasons.

For that matter, Mr. Wickersham was still around the hallowed halls, having been promoted into management over the years, and he now held the office of assistant principal. He mainly handled the school's day-to-day operational matters that Mr. Buchholz, the principal, was too busy to attend to. Like discipline. If Trent happened to be caught wheeling and dealing in comic books in class, Mr. Wickersham would be the one he'd be sent to, and from the sound of things, the assistant principal would not be the most sympathetic of judges when such charges were read. Trent swallowed and made a mental note to be extremely careful if he ever bought any more comic books from fellow students… when an idea occurred to him. A perfectly preposterous idea, yes, but also perfectly feasible.

At lunch, he sought out his friend and fellow comic-book collector, Ernie Volney. Ernie, a blond youth with a build rather like a healthy beanpole, was sitting at a table in the cafeteria and munching placidly on a sandwich while reading a paperback reprint of a 1930s *Operator 5* pulp novel when Trent came up.

"'Lo, Junior — whaddya got there?"

Trent sat down next to him and showed him the *Express* article. Ernie took one look at the date and the picture of Mr. Wickersham overseeing the comic-book burning, and muttered through his sandwich, "It figgers!"

"But it gave me an idea," Trent said. "I'm going to try to interview him for *Shockwave*."

Ernie sputtered, spraying bits of bread, ham, and cheese everywhere. "*What?!* Have you gone clean tootsie-frootsie, Trentbob? That guy's the assistant warden! He doesn't meet you halfway trying to teach you somethin' like the teachers, all he's here for is to keep a lid on the brats! He hates us, we hate him, and that's all there is to it. He looks at you like you've just gotta be guilty of somethin', an' it's his job to find out what! He's just the kinda jerk who'd get his kicks torchin' a whole lot of innocent funnybooks, too! Why mess with the clown when you don't have to, f'r Chrissakes?"

"Well, in the first place, I'm not guilty of anything, so I don't have to worry if I talk to him. In the second place, you read so much about comic books in the '50s in fanzines, about how Dr. Wertham singlehandedly put EC out of business and all that, but nobody seems to have a clear idea about what *actually* happened. It's all speculation and paranoia, not history. But Mr. Wickersham was *there*. He was part of it even if he was one of the villains at the time. I just thought it might make an interesting article for *Shockwave*, especially since the *Captain America* article just had the rug pulled out from under it."

Ernie shook his head. "It's your party, Junior, an' I'm just glad I ain't invited! Ol' Wickerwham an' me've been duellin' it out ever since I kinda accidentally-like put that baseball through the music-room window — I wouldn't go near 'im now for all the funnybooks in China!"

Under normal circumstances, Trent wouldn't have been any more enthusiastic about improving his acquaintance with Mr. Wickersham than Ernie was. But when it came to getting an article for his fanzine, Trent had astonished himself several times in the past with what he would go through for the sake of *Shockwave*. It may have been only typed stencils, crudely traced line artwork, and spotty mimeography on the ancient hand-cranked machine in the basement at home, all stapled together in his bedroom, but it was *his*. He stopped in the school office and made an appointment to see Mr. Wickersham during his third-period study hall the next day.

That evening at home, he settled in at his desk to start on his homework, but Pam's manuscript caught his eye. He had been putting that off long enough, and Pam would only get antsier the longer he delayed. American History could wait, he decided, and picked up *Marjolaine* instead.

161

"*A Novel in Words and Pictures by Pamela Jean Collins,*" read the subtitle. At first, Trent thought he had never read anything like it. Then, as he read further, he began to identify Pam's source material. She had stolen from Joan of Arc, borrowed from Tolkien, pillaged King Arthur, plundered Grimm's Fairy Tales, looted Norse myth, and ransacked half a dozen other places. Her character and place names were about what might be expected from someone with a couple of years of French classes under her belt. And she was not a trained writer. She wrote with passion and energy, but she also had a disconcerting habit of piling adjectives on top of each noun to squeeze it dry of every last drop of emotional and sensory nuance.

And yet, she had a smooth, natural style that occasionally broke through the clouds when she was too occupied with something like clashing swordplay to strain for literary or artistic effects. In spite of everything, reading *Marjolaine* was like riding a roller coaster: it had its ups and downs as well as hairpin turns, but once Trent started on it, he couldn't stop until the bumpy ride was over.

When he had finished, still stunned by it all, he had to wonder, *Pam wants me to correct this?! I wouldn't dare change a word!* He left it at marking a few places where Pam had spelled the possessive of the word "it" with an apostrophe, and moved on to American History.

As soon as he arrived at school the next morning, Trent stopped by Pam's locker. Before he could say anything, Pam beat him to the draw by asking, "Oh, hi — have you read *Marjolaine* yet?"

"Er... yes, but I left it at home," Trent replied, struggling desperately to think of an excuse to explain why that was more honorable than simple lapse of memory.

"No problem," Pam assured him. "I won't be able to get started typing it up on ditto masters until Christmas vacation anyway." To emphasize her point, she glanced down at the books she was pulling out of her locker, indicating a sketchpad and a large notebook along with her regular schoolbooks. "It seems like I have everything to do and no time to do it in. How did you like the story, by the way? Did you have to mark it up much?"

"No, it's pretty clean," Trent said, uncertain how to deal with her eagerness to hear his reaction to her story. Most of the authors he usually had to critique were either dead, as in his English class, or remote and inaccessible, as in his fanzine articles. Doing an on-the-spot review with the author herself standing live and in person in front of him was distinctly intimidating. "It's a good story," he added, "and I really liked it. But why did you want me to look through it instead of an English teacher?"

"You know how *they* are," Pam said, then slipped into a sarcastic voice impersonation. "Elves and fairies? Yucch! Why aren't you reading something *good*, like *Silas Marner*, instead of that Tolkien nut?"

Trent thought she was being a little hard on English teachers, who were some of his favorite people, but it was time to head off to their respective homerooms and they had to leave it at that.

"Ah, so you're Bob Trent," Mr. Wickersham said, glancing up from the papers on his desk as Trent came into the inner office for the interview. "I've seen you around but I don't think we've done business before. Take a seat, son." His voice and manner were probably about as affable as they ever got, but still ponderous and forced: a hangman seldom has an opportunity to practice social graces with his clients. Middle age had been hard on the man. Not only was he heavy and almost bald now, but his once handsome features had collapsed into fleshy, hanging jowls, and his expression usually had the look of a man sucking on a lemon.

Trent sat down in a chair facing the desk. Since he didn't have a portable tape recorder, he had brought along a pad of paper to take notes. Around him he noticed the memorabilia of the decades Mr. Wickersham had spent in educational service: framed diplomas and certificates of merit for this or that, group pictures of science clubs for which he had been an advisor in years long gone, bowling league trophies, stand-up photos on his desk of wife, kids, and even dog...

"You know how it is," Mr. Wickersham added. "You kids come and go. Old ones leave and new ones come in every year. There's a complete turnover every four years, and you never really get to know any of them except for maybe the ones you deal with professionally. Like your partner, Ernie Volney." He smiled suddenly, reminding Trent of a shark about to tell a joke. "We're *very* well acquainted!"

"Er... you know Ernie and I are in business together?"

Mr. Wickersham picked up a recent issue of the *Express* — an all too familiar issue as far as Trent was concerned. "Yeah, after you told me yesterday what you wanted to see me for, I remembered this article about you and looked it up. So you and Ernie have gone into the comic-book business, eh? Comic books... sometimes I think I've been fighting them all my life."

"All your life, sir?"

"Sure." Mr. Wickersham smiled nastily again. "You'd have to run home and change your underwear if I told you many comic books I've burned or torn up in my time, ever since World War II. It started when I was in charge of the local paper drive during the war, and when comic books turned filthy rotten in the '50s, I burned a bunch then."

"I saw the article about that in the *Express*," Trent said.

"Been doing your research, I see. I remember that article — best picture of me the paper's ever run. Of course, old Phillips — he was a history teacher who retired before your time — didn't like it, but he was always something of a reactionary anyway. He said I looked like a Klansman at a cross-burning in it."

Not sure how to respond to *that*, Trent happened to think of the cover of *Comic Cavalcade* #6 he had seen at Pam's, with DC's second-string superheroes promoting their own annihilation. "You were in charge of the paper drive here?"

"Yeah, I had some health problems, so I was 4-F, but people were looking at me funny because I didn't seem particularly sick, like maybe I had an uncle on the draft board instead of a heart murmur. So I figured I'd better help out on the home front and I volunteered for the paper drive. Got a lot of comic books before that was done, too. I bet they would've been worth a lot of money these days, judging by what I've been reading in the papers lately."

Trent felt as though he were turning green. "When was this, exactly?"

"Oh, the big one was in the spring of '44. One of the local boys — who, I've since forgotten — and I went around the county in an old truck I borrowed, and we collected a lot of paper. Got a nice write-up in the *Express* about that, too, as I recall."

"Why do you hate comic books so much, Mr. Wickersham?" Trent asked, deciding it was time to get down to the basics.

Mr. Wickersham looked surprised, as though he wasn't quite prepared for Trent's bluntness. "It's not so much *hate* as — well, look, my own generation had its share of cowboy and Indian hair-raisers to read, but comic books are even less like real literature than those were. Comic books are just badly printed little pamphlets with a lot of badly drawn pictures in them, with no educational or redeeming social value whatsoever. I've never understood what kids found in them that was so interesting — they just waste the time they should be spending on their schoolbooks."

And on and on like that.

Coming out of Mr. Wickersham's office at the end of the interview, Trent looked over his notes and sadly concluded that he had very little new information that was remotely useful. In fact, towards the end of the interview, Mr. Wickersham had been grilling *him* about why *he* liked comic books so much. Trent had an uncomfortable feeling that his stammering and stuttering hadn't impressed the assistant principal very favorably.

One thing was certain: Mr. Wickersham had been on the spot at critical moments in comic-book history, much like that story the American

History teacher liked to tell about Abraham Lincoln's son, who, through the machinations of an inscrutable Fate, was in the immediate neighborhood of the assassinations of not only his father, but of Presidents Garfield and McKinley as well. A comic-book burning in the '50s, a paper drive in the '40s…

*Wait a minute!* Trent thought, remembering something Mr. Wickersham had said. There might be a short article for *Shockwave* about this paper drive matter, since such things were apparently part of the reason why Golden Age comics were so rare today. On a hunch, Trent went to the Journalism classroom and as he had hoped, he found Daryl Knudsen.

Handing back the 1955 issue of the *Express*, he asked, "How far back do the files go?"

Knudsen thought for a moment. "To the '30s, I guess, all the way to the first issue."

"Could you find an issue for me? I'm not sure of the exact date, but it's sometime in the spring of 1944. There should be an article about Mr. Wickersham and a paper drive."

"Mr. Wickersham?" Knudsen echoed. "Was he here back then? God, the good ones go first and the rotten apples stick around forever! It shouldn't be too hard to find. The *Express* was monthly during the War, so I only have about three issues to go through. I'll check the files tonight, Bob, and I should have it for you tomorrow."

The next day was Friday, December 22, the last day of school before Christmas vacation. The general consensus of opinion overheard in the halls of Shetland High was that with only Christmas week and New Year's Day off, everyone was being badly cheated in terms of vacation time, unlike some years that offered nearly two weeks of glorious freedom…but just see how much good griping about it would do.

Pam found Trent at his locker first thing. "Did you bring *Marjolaine* with you? I want to get started tonight on typing it up…"

"That I did," Trent replied, and gave her a bulging manila folder.

"Thanks! Now I can really get going on it! 'Bye!" And off she scampered.

Hardly had Pam disappeared into the crowded hall, Daryl Knudsen came by. "Found it," he said, and presented Trent with a copy of the May, 1944 issue of the *Express*.

Trent waited until study hall to look at it, and the drop through time was even more drastic than it had been with the 1955 edition. Smaller page size, more cramped type style, fewer grainy half-toned pictures, news of an almost alien era… and there it was:

# PUPILS TO BE CITED FOR PAPER SALVAGE

## MONTHLY AWARDS TO BE GIVEN TO SCHOOLS BY MAYOR FOR MEETING COLLECTION QUOTAS

Shetland area school children and students who have painstakingly rummaged through cellars, attics, and buildings to collect waste paper will be rewarded for their efforts, it was made known last week.

Through a plan of the Bureau County Waste Paper Salvage Committee, approved by Dr. Ward B. Schroeder, city Superintendent of Schools, and Mayor Emmett D. Kinswood, each school meeting a monthly quota of eight pounds per pupil will receive a "citation for service on the home front," signed by the mayor.

According to Mr. Grover C. Wickersham, chairman of Shetland High School's paper drive and a science teacher, the "collection of waste paper by SHS students not only helps the war effort, but also gives students a sense of responsibility and initiative." Mr. Wickersham also pointed out how important waste paper is to the war effort when it is salvaged and used to make new products. One example he gave is that an aviator's vest is 75% waste paper.

Mr. Wickersham has been very active in the paper drive campaign. On one day alone (Saturday, April 22), he and a student volunteer, Billy Erwin ('45), collected 327 pounds of newspapers, magazines, and other periodicals from local farmers. He encourages all patriotic SHSers to take part in the drive so that the eight-pound quota may be met and SHS will win the citation.

*Billy Erwin?* Trent thought. Pam's father had bought her comics from a farmer named Erwin. Idly he wondered if they were any relation.

The next day was one of those occasional Saturdays when Ernie didn't have to work on a garbage truck helping his father, who was fore-man at Shetland Sanitation Service, although the week following Christ-mas when people threw out their wrappings and boxes would be a different story. He was over at Trent's house early to watch cartoons on the color TV set and discuss plans for the future of TV Comics, the collective comic-book dealership they had begun with such high hopes not long before.

After watching the few worthwhile cartoons, they went upstairs to Trent's room. Amid the bookshelves crammed with paperback science-fiction novels, comic books, a few dusty superhero models, and even a stray volume of poetry here and there, Trent paced the carpet while Ernie lounged on the bed.

"I was giving it some thought last night," Trent said. "Lord knows I wasn't meant to be a businessman, but if I want comics for research, I've got to get my own so I don't have to depend on Pam… or her father."

"So we're back to bein' funnybook tycoons," Ernie concluded, pick-ing up a copy of *Castle of Frankenstein* from Trent's nightstand to leaf through. "Great. That's what I've been sayin' we should do all the time."

"I wish you wouldn't call them 'funnybooks,'" Trent complained. "It isn't respectful. Anyway, our ad in the *Times* didn't get much in the way of results at all. It might be worth running again in case some people didn't notice it the first time, but there's probably a limit on how much response we *can* get. We've been forgetting about a certain major bottleneck in buy-ing and selling comic books."

"A bottleneck?" Ernie repeated blankly, looking up from the monster magazine. "Whaddya mean, Trentbob?"

"I mean *distribution*," Trent replied, taking the chair at his desk. "We live in a small town, there are only a few places where people can buy comics, and each of those places only gets a few copies of each comic. Even then, a lot aren't sold and end up tossed in the dumpster after having their covers stripped. So there can't be very many comics out there to begin with."

Ernie thought about that for a moment. "Hey, there useta be a lot more stores around here that sold 'em," he pointed out. "Like about ten years ago, when I was first noticin' the things, you could buy funnybooks at just about every Mom & Pop grocery, drug store, and dime store in town. I can still remember Mom ploppin' me down at the funnybook rack at the supermarket just to keep me outta her hair 'til she was done loadin' up on eats, an' I couldna been more'n six. I can still remember one comic that really made me mad. It was called *Super Duck*, an' I wuz expectin' to read about a duck with super-powers, but it was a *Donald Duck* swipe an' Supe didn't have any powers at all, so why'd they call it that? Anyhoo, even Kresge's sold comics, f'r Chrissake! But that was way back when."

"I know about Kresge's," Trent said. "Our next door neighbor used to work there when I was little, and every so often she'd bring me comic books with the top third of the covers torn off. They did that with unsold comics: they could send the top strip back to the distributor and get credit for the whole comic, and throw away the rest, which was how she got them. And now Kresge's and the grocery stores don't bother with comics at all, and it's just down to Brinker's Drugs, the Ridgeland Café, and one or two other places. But you see what I'm getting at, don't you? Even when a lot more stores carried comics, there were never very many sold around here. Things like the comic-book burnings during the uproar in the '50s and the wartime paper drives probably destroyed a good portion of what was sold, and natural wear and tear took care of the rest. Our idea may have been hopeless from the start. How many collections like the one Pam's dad lucked onto at the Erwin farm can there *be?*"

"Yeah…" Ernie considered. "Paper drives, funnybook barbecues… an' I know real good how many comics get tossed in the garbage 'cause that's where half my collection comes from. Well, if we keep at it, maybe we can squeeze every copy of *Fantastic Four* #1 an' other recent comics worth messin' with outta this burg, an' use 'em to trade up for *real* old comics in ads in the *RBCC*."

"That's one approach," Trent said, "but I had another idea. Why don't we attack the problem at the source? Both Brinker's Drugs and the Ridgeland Café have been in business for decades, so the owners probably know who their regular customers are. Mr. Brinker certainly knows *me*, since he's told me often enough that he keeps a drugstore and not a reading room. Why not go to both places and ask who was buying comic books 20 and 25 years ago? We might be able to track down somebody's forgotten collection that way."

Ernie pondered, then nodded. "It's what I call a desperation move, but… yeah, okay. Couldn't hoit. But will Pops Brinker or anybody else remember that far back? They'll prob'ly just tell you it's been 25 years' worth of kids an' let it go at that. What do they care as long as we fork over our twelve centses?"

By then it was time for lunch, and with Ernie there and not going anywhere for a while, it was only natural to invite him to join in. An extra grilled ham and cheese sandwich or two probably didn't make a lot of difference in the long run. After that, they had the whole afternoon free to put Trent's idea into practice.

Once he and Ernie had boarded the salt-encrusted Chevy out in the driveway, Trent tried starting it. For a long moment, he was afraid it wouldn't start at all, but after some pumping of the gas pedal and fiddling with the choke, the engine finally turned over.

"Don't sound good," Ernie observed.

"I think it's just cold weather. It's been a little slow to start lately, but it runs fine once it's warmed up."

"Maybe you should take it into the shop?"

"One of these days," Trent said vaguely. "Dad has a 'drive it until it drops' philosophy, so it's hard to get him to pay for maintaining my car as well as his, and I can't afford to do anything with it right now. I'm a comic-book baron, remember? The car will have to wait until I can sell some of my surplus comics."

Trent parked in a municipal lot just off Main Street and he and Ernie walked from there to Brinker's Drugs. On a bright, crisp, and clear Saturday afternoon two days before Christmas, downtown Shetland was crowded with shoppers despite the snow and the cold. Above the storefronts, plastic Santas, candy canes, and bells were hung from every lamppost and from green garlands strung across the street.

Brinker's Drugs was a maze of narrow aisles between high, overstocked shelves. Magazines and paperback books were jammed into some heavy wall-mounted shelves in a corner in the back, sandwiched between an old-fashioned cabinet-type wooden phone booth in which Clark Kent might have changed in perfect privacy, and a doorway leading to a side room filled with greeting card racks, Christmas decorations, gift-wrapped candy boxes, and home hospital supplies like bedpans, enema tubes, and crutches.

Here was the fountainhead of comic books in Shetland. Brinker's got in almost everything sooner or later. Trent had haunted the place for years, hanging around on Tuesdays and Thursdays like a dog waiting to be fed when the distributor dropped off the wire-wrapped bundles of comic books, hovering nearby while the clerks opened them and stocked the shelves. Once Trent had even tried to follow the advice given him in a comic-book house ad to "reserve" a copy of some particularly attractive upcoming issue, but all that got him were some strange looks from teenage girl clerks who couldn't tell one comic book from another.

White-haired Mr. Brinker, still an impressive figure in his white pharmacist's jacket and with his bushy mustache though he must have been past 70, stood behind the prescription counter and thought for a moment.

"I can't really say," he told Trent and Ernie after their mission had been explained to him. "I've always stuck to the prescriptions and hired high-school girls to run the cash register, so I've never really gotten to know many of the customers who didn't bring me pieces of paper with atrociously scrawled Latin on them… but it runs in my mind that there was one old fellow who was in here quite a bit, once or twice a week for something like twenty years running, buying magazines and comic books to beat the band. He was a farmer, I think, but he died about ten years ago."

Trent groaned. "Carl Erwin. Thanks, Mr. Brinker, but we know where *those* comics ended up. Let's go, Ernie."

That left the Ridgeland Café, out on Ridgeland Street near the Farmers' Exchange and the Illinois Central freight station. Trent didn't go there for comics as often as he went to Brinker's Drugs, but sometimes the Ridgeland Café got in titles the drugstore missed or put them out on the racks sooner. It had even happened on occasion that something Trent particularly wanted was sold out at Brinker's by the time he had accumulated the wherewithal, but was still available at the Café.

"Are you sure it's worth the trouble?" Ernie asked in the car on the way over. "If the ol' farmboy bought comics an' stuf' at Brinker's, it's a safe bet he musta bought even more at the Café. It's where all the farmers hang out when they come into town. Betcha ol' Carl Erwin's the only guy they remember, too. You know they don't pay any 'tention to the kids 'cept to yell, 'Hey, you! Put that *Playboy* back!'"

"I don't know," Trent admitted a little tiredly. "I just don't want to leave any stones unturned. Who knows… we might find out something anyway."

They left the Chevy on a side street in the shadow of the towering grain elevators of the Farmers' Exchange, and went into the shabby restaurant nearby, across from the railroad tracks and next to a farm equipment dealer's lot filled with green tractors and combines. The Ridgeland Café was little more than a dimly lit lunch counter and bar, with some booths and tables and chairs to one side, three pinball machines, and racks of newspapers, magazines, and candy near the end of the counter with the cash register.

Ernie gravitated at once to a pinball machine while Trent went up to the counter and spoke to the ancient proprietor, known to everyone in the world as "Chet" with no man alive aware of any last name to go with it. He was a skeletally thin, bald old man with an awesomely hooked nose, and Ernie liked to claim that Chet was really Spider-Man's archenemy, the Vulture, after retiring from a life of crime and putting on a dirty apron. Chet had been in the process of tacking up some cheap red paper bells and silvery garland behind the bar, but the effect in such a place was less festive and more dreary. The only other people in the Café were a wizened old farmer nursing a beer at the counter a little way down and a couple of young boys looking at the comic books — perhaps the next generation's Trent and Ernie.

"Regular customers who bought comic books, huh?" Chet said when Trent put the question to him. In the background, bells rang and flippers smacked steel balls as Ernie became one with the pinball machine. "Oh, Jesus, kids come in all the time and buy 'em, but hell, they grow up and stop comin' in, so there's always new kids, never the same ones for more'n a coupla years except for you and the pinball ace over there. 'Course, there was that one guy, an old farmer, but he died years ago—"

"Carl Erwin?" Trent asked with a sigh.

"Yeah, that was him. You heard about 'im already, I see. His boys come in for lunch or a beer pretty often, but none of 'em read comic books the way their old man did. Funnybooks are for kids, really."

Trent didn't feel like trying to argue the point. But even though he had been told more or less what he had expected to hear and was ready to leave, Chet was just warming up to the subject.

"Christ, funnybooks!" Chet exclaimed, laying the Christmas decorations aside and taking up washing glasses in a pan of soapy water behind the counter. "What a pain those things are! Like about fifteen years ago, there were hundreds and hundreds of 'em comin' out all the time. We went nuts tryin' to stock 'em all and keep 'em neat on the racks after the kids came through an' messed 'em up. There were so many funnybooks comin' out that they were killin' each other. Nobody could possibly read all of 'em.

"And," he added, "there was all different kinds of comics. Blood 'n' guts comics, mushy love comics, creepy spook comics… but not too many about guys in costumes like Batman, which is what I guess you kids are after these days. Then, back in the '50s, there was all that trouble about 'em bein' bad for kids. I even had to throw that one bird from the high school, whatever his name was — Dickerdamm or somethin', I think he's assistant principal over there now — outta my place because he came in tryin' to tell me what I could and couldn't sell.

"Can you beat that?" Chet suddenly demanded, as though it was still fresh and sore in his memory. "And I wasn't even sellin' skin mags then, not even under the counter like some places. I can sell skin mags now, though, and nobody raises a stink as long as I keep 'em outta the kids' reach. And just between you and me, you'd be surprised who from the high school buys 'em — and what *kinds* of mags!" He leered evilly and Trent flinched.

"Well," Chet went on, "all that trouble was nationwide, and not just around here, and a lot of outfits that put out funnybooks musta just plain went outta business. That was okay by me, since it cut down on how many we had to mess with by a lot, and they sold a little better without so many of 'em. There was something about a 'code' of some kind to make sure they were decent for the kiddies, but I never paid much attention to it. Far as I could tell, the really good comics with the cartoon characters like Donald Duck never even had a code, and they sold better'n anything. The main thing was probably that TV was comin' in big around then, and that cut into things. Nobody was readin' much of anything after that, and a lot of the story magazines died then, too."

Chet paused in his reminiscing and wiping glasses to reflect for a moment, then shrugged and smiled crookedly at Trent. "These days... well, we sell quite a few comics at 12¢ apiece and a quarter for the big ones, but I dunno... the profit on 'em ain't much and they're as big a pain as ever to bother with. It takes me just as long to ring up a *Playboy* as it does a *Superboy*, and I make a hell of a lot more per copy off the skin mags than I do the funnybooks. So don't be surprised if you walk in here someday and see I've cleared out the comics entirely."

"Thanks for your time, sir," Trent said, trying to be polite even in the midst of disappointment, and turned to get Ernie. If he wanted old comic books for research for fanzine articles, it looked as though he really did have to depend on Mr. Collins' good will.

Ernie was just then pounding on the pinball machine in frustration. "Damn!" he cried. "Tilted *again!*"

"I'm not surprised," Trent said. "I've seen how you play pinball — you practically turn the machine upside down to get the ball where you want it to go."

"That's the only way to play this man's game, son," Ernie said, looking helplessly at the relentlessly flashing *TILT* sign with no replay. "Body English. 'Bout time to hit the road, ain't it?"

"I guess," Trent replied. "I didn't turn up any leads here, either."

That was because they had arrived a few minutes too soon. Their lead was only just now coming in through the door, a wiry man of about 40 with a case of perpetual gray stubble. He wore overalls, a red-checked coat, and a cap with a "DeKalb" logo embroidered on it, advertising a brand of hybrid corn.

Chet recognized him at once as a regular customer. "Hey, Billy! You came just at the right time! These boys were just askin' about your old man and his funnybooks!"

*Carl Erwin's son?* Trent thought. *Billy Erwin? The paper drive—!*

Billy Erwin took his coat and cap off and hung them on a rack by the door, then turned to Trent. "Well, if you're hopin' to buy any comic books, you're out of luck. We sold 'em all to our insurance agent! He'll probably sell 'em for more than we could ever get out of 'em, but it's just a relief to have 'em out of the house. I can give you the guy's name, if you want."

"Thanks," Trent said quickly, "but we know him already. I was wondering, though... back during the war, did you help Mr. Wickersham with a paper drive?"

Billy was flat out astonished. "How do you know about that? That was more than twenty years ago!"

"I was looking at an old issue of the school paper and saw an article about it," Trent explained. "Do you mind if I ask you a couple of questions?"

Billy seemed in the mood to talk and invited Trent and Ernie to sit with him in a booth, even buying them Cokes to keep Chet from being annoyed by their lingering.

"Yeah, that was me, all right," Billy said after Chet had taken their orders. "Jesus, that was a long time ago — back when I was your age! But I still remember it pretty well. Pop practically strangled Mr. Wickersham right then and there when he saw him and me trying to run off with all his comic books!"

"Too bad he didn't finish the job," Ernie muttered. "Saved me a lot of trouble with ol' Wicky if he had!"

"Christ!" Billy exclaimed. "Is Wickersham still there? That must make 25 years now that he's been at that school! What a way to spend your life! Of course, I'm working my dad's farm now, where I've lived ever since I was born, but it's different when it's a place of your own and you're adding to it over the years."

"Can you tell me a little more about the paper drive?" Trent asked. He might get an article out of this yet.

Chet brought Cokes for the boys and a beer for Billy just then, and Billy pondered the foam in his mug before answering. "Ain't much to tell, really. Sounds like the article you read pretty much covered all the bases. Only thing is... oh, Jesus! I'm not even sure I should be tellin' you this, but... well, the hell of it all was, that whole damn paper drive was a waste of time!"

"How's that?" Trent wondered, startled by Billy's sudden vehemence.

"It's like this," Billy explained. "In anything as big as a war, there's a lot of wasted effort. It's so big that nobody has a handle on all of it and the right hand never knows what the left hand is doing. Things fall through the cracks. The whole point is to win the war no matter what, so the people in charge of things will put up with unbelievable amounts of waste and inefficiency that wouldn't be tolerated in peacetime. My brother told me that when he went to an Army camp in Louisiana for training in motor repair, every new class got a brand new set of tools even though the tools left over from the class before were still perfectly good, so they ended up burying the old ones just to get rid of 'em. That's just one example, and it's nothing new! My wife's church group had a speaker in talking about Biblical archaeology, and he said they dug up a *ton* of iron nails at an old Roman army camp somewhere. Seems the Roman soldiers didn't have anything else to do there, and somebody's bright idea was to put 'em to work making nails. But when they pulled out, they had all these nails and there wasn't time or transportation to get 'em where they were supposed to go, so the Romans buried the nails — just to get rid of 'em. It was going on 2000 years ago, and I wouldn't be surprised if somebody found out the Babylonians were doing it, too."

"That's interesting," Trent said, "but how does all that tie in with the paper drive?"

"To boil it down," Billy said, "*all that paper we collected was never used!* We turned it in at the collection center at Camp Douglas and it was piled in a big warehouse there, but it never got moved anywhere else. When I was in the National Guard after the war, about '47, we had a training exercise at Camp Douglas, and I found out then that the warehouse was *still* full of all those magazines and newspapers. Maybe the War Production Board forgot about it during the war, or maybe the war just ended too soon before they could get around to picking the paper up, but as far as I know, all that paper hasn't been touched to this day."

Trent and Ernie both almost spilled their Cokes as the implications sank in. Billy went on to chat a little more about his father and how much the old man's "story magazines" meant to him, but neither of the boys was in a state to pay very much attention. They left with profuse thanks for the Cokes as soon as they politely could.

Once they were in the car and driving away, Ernie started singing: "Comics an' magazines an' pulps — oh my! Comics an' magazines an' pulps — oh my!"

"My God!" Trent burst out. "That old warehouse must be full of old comic books! *Every* superhero comic published before the summer of 1944 must be in there! *Dozens* of copies of each!"

"We could give copies of *Action* #1 away as a free bonus to customers!" Ernie exclaimed gleefully. "We could run 'New Low Prices Howard' an' every other dealer outta business an' then jack up prices 'til they squeaked! Hot diggetty-damn, Trentbob! We've discovered buried treasure! It's the chance of a lifetime! Zowie! Yee-*hah!*"

"Wait a minute," Trent said, his mind racing and suddenly running into a brick wall. "All those comics are government property in a government warehouse on government land. We can't just walk in there and take what we want — it'd be breaking and entering, theft, burglary, and God only knows what all, and it'd probably be a *federal* crime to boot!"

Ernie whirled in his seat to face him, incensed and outraged, probably restrained from grabbing Trent's shoulders and trying to shake some sense into his pudgy form only by the fact that Trent was driving. "What are you — *chicken*?!" he demanded, more furious than Trent had ever seen him before. "Are you gonna let an opportunity like this go by just 'cause you're scared of the cops?"

"Seems like a pretty good reason to me," Trent answered meekly.

Ernie willed himself back into a state of relative self-control. "Well, listen to me, Junior. I know Camp Douglas like I know my backyard! I even think I know which buildin' Billy was talkin' about an' where it is! Dad's taken me huntin' there lotsa times! You can call it trespassin' if you want, but the place ain't guarded. Most of the buildin's are empty an' boarded up, so I s'pose they don't think it's worth havin' guards there. The only time they ever open the place up's in the summer when they have shootin' matches. We could sneak in there every night 'til spring and they'd never know! An' who the hell's it gonna hurt? If the government hasn't touched that paper in over twenty years, it ain't like they really need it — they sure as hell wouldn't miss a few funnybooks!"

"Uh... ah... I don't know..." Trent said, torn between the opposing forces of caution and greed.

"For God's sake, J. Robert!" Ernie pleaded. "Don't chicken out on me now! We can't let a chance like this go by! We could have every last damn funnybook in the world if we jump on this!"

"Well..." Trent wavered miserably, "maybe we could drive over and at least take a look at the place..."

"Swell! Pick me up at my house tonight right after it gets dark!"

"*Tonight!?*" Trent demanded. "What's the rush?" Having found himself agreeing to the scheme in principle, he had hoped to at least put it off for as long as possible.

"Why waste any more time? We've got Christmas right around the corner an' after that we don't get a whole lotta vacation this year. If we have a bunch of comics to start listin' an' advertisin', the sooner we get started, the better."

"Er... okay, I guess... Should we tell Pam about this?"

"Nahh, we can tell her later. She's got plenty of her own comics anyway, an' we should keep this little project just between ourselves."

Trent nodded, though it seemed to him that Pam was just the sort of girl who would have enjoyed an evening of midnight skulking.

Posterity accords few laurels to people who lose. The honorable Stephen Arnold Douglas, who served the Great State of Illinois with distinction in the United States Senate and won the nomination of the Democratic Party for President in 1860, lost the election to a country lawyer from downstate, and with his death the following year, his shade shuffled off into obscurity. His memory was freshened in 1917 with the inauguration of an army camp in north central Illinois, christened Camp Douglas. Barely a year and a half later, however, the Armistice ended the World War and the camp's services were no longer required. It was largely mothballed until the next time a war broke out in Europe. After another frenetic few years of activity, Camp Douglas reverted to its ghost-town status at the end of World War II. It was used occasionally thereafter for National Guard exercises and marksmanship competitions, but in the main it was isolated, ignored, and eventually all but forgotten. Senator Douglas may have deserved better, but this was what he got to perpetuate his name.

Some ten miles out of Shetland, Trent parked his car — actually a rolling icebox that for some reason sported chrome *Chevrolet* lettering instead of a logo for *Frigidaire* — at the berm of a deserted back road and he and Ernie clambered out into the arctic night.

The temperature had plummeted when the sun went down, probably not even stopping at zero. Both Trent and Ernie were stuffed into heavy coats, scarves, gloves, and hats, but the cold seemed to penetrate to the bone just the same. The inky black sky overhead was about as clear as it would have been without any atmosphere at all, and the stars glittered icily.

Just across the snow-filled ditch was a chain-link fence topped by several lines of barbed wire, emblazoned with a dauntingly official-looking red, white, and blue U.S. Government **NO TRESPASSING** sign. On the other side of the fence began the forest primeval, dense woods of barren, snow-draped trees fading into the darkness,

"Here we be," Ernie said, producing a flashlight and snapping it on. His breath congealed thickly in the bitter cold. "Camp Douglas. C'mon — I know how to get in."

"But Ernie!" Trent protested. "There's a fence there! And we'll leave tracks in the snow leading right from the car! How can we—?"

Ernie pointed the flashlight to a place where a section of the fence had fallen inwards, and Trent followed his lead with his own flashlight. Tracks showed that any number of people had gone inside the perimeter by that route since the last snowfall.

176

"Hunters," Ernie said. "A few more tracks won't make no diff'rence a'tall. As for the car, nobody ever much comes down this road, an' I'm sure the sheriff's got better things to do on a night as cold as a funnybook dealer's heart. Let's get movin'."

Stepping gingerly over the fallen barbed wire as he followed his partner into the woods, Trent had to wonder, despite Ernie's reassurances, how his father would take having to come down to the jail in the middle of the night to bail him out.

They made their way through the snow-buried woods without saying anything for a while, the only sound the swish as they plowed through drifts and the crunch of compressed snow beneath their boots. Somewhere on another vibratory plane, a legion of long-dead Indians was doubtless giving their lack of woodsmanship a hearty horselaugh.

Ernie went ahead, surveying the ground with his flashlight and following the main hunters' trail. He seemed to know exactly where they were going, and before long they emerged from the woods onto the open grounds of Camp Douglas proper.

The rows of dark, deserted barracks were silhouettes against the starlight, shadows of a past fifty years gone when the old wooden buildings were first built. Other than for the scattered pawprints of what may have been a loping rabbit, the snow was as it had fallen, undisturbed, and there were no signs of any recent human activity. Only brooding silence lay over the camp as Ernie stood still for a moment, getting his bearings.

"Ah ha!" he said suddenly. "Now I know where I'm at. This away." He started off straight across the vast, empty parade ground, unconcerned about the tracks he was leaving behind in the snow, and Trent fell in after him.

In a few minutes, they had reached the fabled warehouse, a huge, windowless wooden building the size of an aircraft hangar, off by itself well away from the main part of the camp.

"Now how do we get in?" Trent demanded, huddled in his coat and his hands jammed into his pockets against the cold. "It's probably locked and there aren't any windows."

"Leave that to your ol' Uncle Ernie." Ernie trained his flashlight on a small door in the front end wall. Perhaps it had once been padlocked, but the latch had long been torn off and the door stood slightly ajar. "Yep, thought so. Tolja I'd been here before."

They pushed the door open with a creak of rusty hinges unnervingly loud in the overhanging silence and stepped inside what may have been a small office. Trent tried the light switch but nothing happened, so Ernie gave the office a once-over with his flashlight. It was now just an empty room stripped of everything but an old potbellied stove. The interior walls were no more than thin plywood partitions about eight feet high, dwarfed by what appeared to be dirty white, flat-sided columns towering high overhead towards the distant rafters lost in the yawning gulfs of the warehouse. By the stove, the floor was littered with old newspapers, food wrappers, and beer bottles and cans.

"Y'see," Ernie pointed out, "some passin' bum who needed a roof over his head on a cold night like this did our breakin'-in work for us."

An open doorway in the opposite wall led into the main part of the warehouse and they went on through, then stopped and Ernie played the flashlight beam from the floor to the rafters. Something small, brown, and furry squeaked in alarm when the light fell on it and it scurried out of sight under a pallet.

"Je-*sus*!" Ernie exclaimed.

Everywhere, stacked twenty feet high and more on wooden pallets, covered with dust and spider webs — bales on top of bales of old newspapers in endless rows along narrow aisles. The enormous gloomy interior of the warehouse must have been close to being a solid mass of newsprint.

"Good Lord!" Trent breathed. "This must be all the paper they collected from at least half the state!" Then he sneezed as his nostrils inhaled the musty, dusty smell of decades-old paper, mildew, vermin, and rotting wood.

"Dammit!" Ernie choked. "I shoulda known! I was thinkin' of a whole warehouse chock full of funnybooks an' not much else — I forgot it'd be mostly newspapers! They didn't even bother to sort 'em! All the comics are prob'ly scattered all through that glom, an' we'll hafta root through three cubic acres of newspapers to *find* 'em!"

Trent shivered. If it was any warmer inside the warehouse than out, it wasn't by much. "I guess this was just a collection center," he said, trying to articulate clearly through teeth doing their best to chatter. "The sorting would've been done wherever they took the paper from here. Well, as long as we've come this far, we might as well see what we've got."

"My thoughts exactikkelly, old bean," Ernie replied and pulled a jackknife out of his pocket.

He cut the twine securing a bale of paper that lay by chance on top of a waist-high stack nearest at hand, and he and Trent looked through it. It was mostly old newspapers, with headlines reporting the battle news of the first years of World War II, interspersed with issues of magazines like *Life*, *McCall's*, and *Time*, many with black and white covers. The state of preservation was generally good, especially for copies buried well within the stack that hadn't been exposed to open air.

Trent reflected that the magazines alone would be a lucky find for a history buff, but as far as he knew, they weren't particularly rare and were probably available to researchers in any well-stocked library, either physically or at least as microfilmed copies. The matter at hand here was comic books, which few people bothered to save and which no library worthy of its dignified intellectual standing would have subscribed to or even dreamed of saving. Then, suddenly, unexpectedly—

"Holy moley, Trentbob!" Ernie gasped in wonder. "Lookit *this! Whiz* #10! Sha-*zy*-am, Sgt. Carter! This joint does have comics! We've done it, J. Robert! We've discovered the comic books' graveyard — where old funnybooks go to die!"

He held up the ancient relic of Fawcett Publications, dated November, 1940, a comic book featuring the adventures of a long-gone hero called Captain Marvel, shown on the cover in his red-longjohnned glory catching a flying torpedo about to crash into a small boat while a pretty lady cowered on the deck behind him. The condition was nowhere close to mint, evidently because it had passed through numerous hands before being donated to the paper drive.

Like dogs suddenly catching the scent of the rabbit they had been trailing, Trent and Ernie started tearing into the lower, more accessible stacks to see what else they might turn up, scattering the newspapers and magazines in a flurry to the floor around them.

By the time they had unearthed the next prize, a much-worn and soiled copy of *Action* #22 from March, 1940, with a tattered and nearly detached cover showing Superman pushing back a steam shovel, the cold was almost too much for them to continue. Even in his gloves, Trent's fingers had grown stiff and numb. He wondered if his ears were still attached under the flaps of his hat, and Ernie seemed to have developed a bad case of unstoppable nasal drip.

"Trentbob," Ernie said after a minute, "we can't keep this up much longer, or they'll find us still here after the spring thaw. We gotta get ourselves warm!"

"But how? Go back to the car for a while?"

"It's a mile the other way! We'd be cold again by the time we got back here. Nah, we'll use the stove in the office. There's some scrap wood around here from a busted pallet, an' we can get it goin' with some newspaper. There's sure as hell plenty of *that* around here!"

"What if somebody sees the smoke?"

"Don't worry 'bout it! Ain't nobody for miles! C'mon, or we'll be fansicles in a few minutes!"

Ernie gathered up the broken pieces of wood and an armful of newspapers, and carried them into the office. He stuffed them into the old stove, produced a cigarette lighter from his pocket — smoking was something of an occasional thing for Ernie that he indulged in mainly when he was with his other friends who weren't disapproving spoilsports like the overly fussy J. Robert Trent, Jr. — and lit the newspaper. Before long, a cheerful fire was crackling and the office had warmed up noticeably.

"Ah, now we're in business!" Ernie exclaimed. "Hey, we oughtta camp out here some night an' really do the job right!"

"Er... not tonight," Trent said a little dubiously. "I told Mom and Dad I was going to your place and I'd be home before midnight."

"Funny, I told my folks I was goin' to *your* place. Oh well... let's get back to work an' scrounge up some more funnybooks. We can duck back in here every few minutes an' warm up."

Trent was reluctant to leave the warmth of the stove, but it did seem as though duty called. With a sigh, he went back out into the deepfreeze to look through another bale of newspapers.

To maximize the results of their effort, he and Ernie split up, working on different bales. Soon, Trent began to understand those gee-whiz stories he'd been told in science class about gold being present in seawater, but in such diluted form that extracting it was uneconomical. Compared with all the other paper — newspapers, magazines, etc., etc. — comic books were there but few and far between. One entire bale turned up only a poor condition *Animal Comics* #2 from early 1943 with Uncle Wiggily and what looked like an extremely early and primitive version of Pogo, and a late '30s reprint of *Dick Tracy* newspaper comic strips was in even worse shape.

"Hotcha!" Ernie suddenly yelled from his bale, and shone the flashlight on his find for Trent's admiration: Quality Comics' *Crack Comics* #6 from October, 1940, featuring the Black Condor with art by Lou Fine, and the condition wasn't bad at all. "It can be done, Junior! They're here — we just gotta look for 'em!"

Trent wearily glanced around the unending rows of stacks of baled newspapers reaching into the darkness overhead and wondered how many years they would be at this before they had gone through even a significant fraction of the warehouse. The place was a comic-book fan's dream come true, but like so many dreams, the reality had a catch to it.

Then, just when he was at his most discouraged, he pulled some newspapers off the bale he had just opened and uncovered a lode of comic books. At first he thought the topmost comic was *Crack Comics* #4, but the title lettering didn't look like that on the issue Ernie had found. Trent looked more closely and realized that his myopia had been getting in the way. Instead of Quality's *Crack Comics*, it was actually another company's *Crash Comics* from September, 1940, and this particular issue featured the first appearance of a hero called Cat-Man. In fact, further inspection revealed not just *Crash* #5 but several issues of *Cat-Man* as well. Only

Cat-Man didn't have a teenage boy companion like Batman did — he had a teenage *girl* companion called Kitten. If Dr. Wertham could find questionable implications in the relationship of Batman and Robin, Trent had to wonder what he would have said about Cat-Man and Kitten.

By this time, the cold was having its way with Trent again and he retired to the office to defrost his fingers over the stove.

Ernie came out a couple of minutes later, bringing more newspapers and chunks of wood to stuff down the stove's gullet to keep the fire going. He had been less fastidious than Trent about opening up the dusty bales of newspapers: his face was smudged with dirt, his coat was smeared with dust, and his gloves were almost black with ink rubbed off the pages.

"Makes ya feel like arkyologists bustin' into King Tut's tomb, don't it, Trentbob?" he asked happily as he fed the fire.

"I don't know," Trent said, having recently read a book about the discovery of King Tutankhamen's tomb and able to discourse at length about it. "I have a feeling most professional archaeologists would disapprove of our methods of excavation. We're more like the tomb *robbers* who came before the archaeologists and made a mess of so many tombs, which was why King Tut's tomb was so special — the robbers had missed it." Then, seeing that he was losing Ernie with his technical explanation, he asked, "How are you doing?"

"I found some sci-fi pulps in pretty bad shape, but I'm kinda runnin' dry on funnybooks. Just for the hell of it, I think when I go in again I'll climb up an' open one of the bales on top of the high stacks, just to see if there's anythin' different up that way."

"Be careful," Trent urged him. "It's a long way to fall from up there."

"No prob, Bob! Remember, I'm the guy who could climb up the rope better'n anybody in gym class! Mr. Beckert said I must be part mountain goat!"

Ernie's self-confidence wasn't misplaced, either. Trent shone his flashlight on him as he scaled the sheer face of a cliff of newsprint, using the wooden bracing that supported the walls of the office from the warehouse side of the partitions to get started. With exemplary nimbleness, Ernie made the climb and disappeared over the top into the gloom near the ceiling far overhead. A click and a sudden glow showed he had turned his flashlight on.

Ernie's face appeared at the edge of the stacks, a tiny, pale, distant oval. "You wouldn't believe what a mess it is up here! Spider-webs an' just plain dirt an' dust... But that's only on top. The stuff under the first newspaper or two oughtta be okay. I'm gonna try diggin' into a bale up here. See you in a bit!"

Ernie's face disappeared again. Shrugging, Trent went to work on a bale much closer to the floor. After a few minutes of silent effort, he again uncovered an ore-bearing vein — this time it was several old comics from the Timely company, what Marvel Comics had been in the 1940s, include-ing *Captain America* #8 (November, 1941) and #11 (February, 1942).

Nothing short of sheer delight flooded Trent's whole being. This was what the whole struggle had been all about: finding Golden Age superhero comic books, preferably the forerunners of today's Marvel Comics heroes, so he could do research on them and write up his findings for *Shockwave*. And now, he held the first fruits of his success in that endeavor in his own gloved hands. After all the work and all the heartaches, after braving the cold and possible federal criminal charges, he had won the battle. Tri-umph, glorious triumph almost beyond imagining was finally his.

He glanced through the comics and was struck once more by the dif-ference between the 1940s and his own era. The old comic books had more pages and fewer ads, a slightly larger page size and more stories, with pri-mitive plots and characterization, and their dialogue wasn't much more than "Take *that*, you Jap-a-Nazi rat!" But it was more than that. Modern comics just seemed uncertain about how to treat the war in Vietnam, but the World War II comics were definitely "All out for Victory!" with their exhortations to buy bonds and keep 'em flying.

*The past is a different country*, Trent had read somewhere, *and they do things differently there.*

His reverie was suddenly broken by Ernie's screech from far above, the howl echoing throughout the building. Startled, Trent looked up. In his flashlight's beam, he saw the row of newsprint columns in front of him tilt and slowly topple past him towards the open space of the office. The thin walls cracked, splintered, and finally collapsed, and the ponderous flood of heavy bales of newspapers hit the floor in a thunderous roar. A thick, choking cloud of dust rose from the avalanche, threatening to engulf the entire warehouse.

"Ernie!" Trent yelled, frantic. "Ernie! Are you all right?" Where are you?" If Ernie was unconscious, buried in the middle of the landslide, finding him and then digging him out might be next to impossible.

"Keep yer shorts on, Junior! I ain't *that* easy to kill."

Trent whirled around with his flashlight and to his all but tearful relief, he saw Ernie in the light, clambering down a stack of newspaper bales behind him. "Ernie — for God's sake, what happened up there?"

Ernie continued his calm, unhurried descent, then jumped lightly to the floor as soon as he was low enough. "Oh, nothin' — just lost my bal-ance an' the stack I was standin' on started to slide, but I jumped in time. I'm okay now. Nothin' to worry 'bout."

"Oh yeah?" Trent demanded. "How are we going to get out of here? I think we've got about a ton of newspapers between us and the door, and you demolished the office—" He broke off, suddenly realizing something. "Oh, Lord…!" he choked. "What did all that paper do to the *stove?*"

Ernie knew at once what he meant and managed a blurted "Uh oh!"

They both turned and leaped down the aisle to the colossal mound of paper that marked where the office had been. The individual bales were far too large and far too heavy for even the two of them to lift or move very far. And it was soon clear that deep down in the pile of bales, the stove had been knocked over and its flaming contents spilled. Smoke began to curl lazily through the crevices between the bales and a faint crackling could be heard. A cascade of loose newspapers might have smothered the fire before it had a chance to catch, but the block-like bales let in enough air between them for the fire to get a good start.

"*Now* what do we do?" Trent exclaimed desperately.

Ernie thought fast, "We can't put the fire out — no water, an' we can't even get *at* it. Let's get the hell outta here first, then worry about everything else!"

"But *how?* The door's blocked!" Cold, gnawing fear was beginning to set in on Trent's stomach.

Ernie, however, remained unperturbed. Perhaps he had realized that the fire would be slow to spread, at least at first, and they had a little time to look for a way out. Then he had it. "Ah ha. Follow me."

They sprinted down the narrow aisle to the other end of the building. Large, garage-type doors were set in the outer wall for moving bulk freight in and out of the warehouse.

"Let's see if we can get these open," Ernie said.

They had to work together at lifting the heavy iron bar that secured the doors on the inside, and at first Trent had the agonizing fear that its hinge was rusted solid and would never move. Then, with a loud shriek of outraged metal, the bar rose out of its holder and the door swung open into the night.

"If we can get to a phone real quick," Trent said, relieved to have escaped doom for the moment and somehow not even minding being back out in the raw cold, "we can call the fire department and maybe they can save most of the warehouse. Is there a camp office somewhere around here?"

Ernie thought. "The main part of the camp is way over that way an' mebbe there's a phone in one of the barracks, but I wouldn't bet the farm on it. This place has been stripped of everything over the years an' all the buildin's are boarded up or locked. Best thing to do now is get to your car and drive until we find a house we can call from. Now let's run for it!"

Before they were even halfway across the grounds to the woods, it was obvious that the fire was gaining rapidly. They could see enormous tongues of flame licking the sky at the front of the warehouse now, and they could hear the snap, crackle, and pop of burning wood.

"Gawd!" Ernie exclaimed between gasps for breath when they paused for a moment to look back. "That fire'll burn for ages! It'll burn off one layer of newspaper at a time an' take forever! I know 'cause that's what happened when Mom caught me with my *Playboy* collection under my mattress an' made me go out an' burn 'em." Shaking his head, he turned and started towards the edge of the woods some distance ahead across the snow.

Trent trotted along heavily, trailing the more athletic Ernie, and his breath came in short, painful gulps as he swallowed the frigid air. His mind was working again and he soon realized that he was missing something. "Oh my God!" he burst out.

Ernie lurched to an instant halt ahead of him and spun around in his tracks. "What th—?"

"Ernie! We forgot to take any comic books out of there with us!"

"Christ on crutches!" Ernie exclaimed, slapping his forehead. "We were in such a rush gettin' outta there that... Well, it's too late now! C'mon, let's *move* it!"

Sometime later, they had come through the woods and climbed over the fallen fence, and were legging it along the road towards Trent's car, still parked where they had left it.

"Maybe we should call the police, too, and tell them what we did...?" Trent started to say.

Ernie choked. "Oh, Lord love a duck! Don't pull a goody two-shoes on me! I'm sure as hell not takin' the rap for somethin' like this! Or do you *like* the idea of tryin' to explain it to your old man, then to the judge?"

The prospect of facing his father convinced Trent more effectively than that of being tried in juvenile court for arson. "Okay, okay, we don't know anything about any fires at any warehouses." He still felt painfully guilty about it, even if the fire was, strictly speaking, Ernie's doing. Ernie seemed to have had an awful lot of bad luck with falling stacks of things lately...

They climbed in the car, much to Trent's relief as he was about 30 seconds from freezing solid. He turned the ignition key and—

*I-don't-wanna!*

"Holy hell!" Ernie sputtered. "Not *now!* Not *here!* We've gotta get as far away from here as fast as we can if we want our alibis to hold up! Try it again!"

184

Frantically, desperately, Trent struggled to force the Chevy into life, but each time he turned the key, the starter only groaned away without effect. It was a nightmare made real — particularly the one about standing unable to move in the middle of a railroad track with the glaring headlight and the screaming whistle of the Midnight Special coming up fast.

"That's just running the batt'ry down," Ernie said after a few tries. "Lemme think... there's gotta be a way outta this! Your Uncle Harry shoulda left you a book on how to take care of your car along with the Chevy..."

"Blaming me isn't going to help anything!" Trent snapped peevishly. "Besides, the only thing Uncle Harry left me with the car was that can of spray gunk under the seat, whatever it is."

"Spray gunk? What's it called?"

"Oh, something like 'Cold Start'—"

"Sufferin' succotash! Lemme at it!" Ernie immediately bent down to reach under the seat and extracted an aerosol can. A moment later, he was outside and lifting the hood. He did something Trent couldn't see, then yelled, "Now try it!"

Trent tried it — and the engine nearly fell over itself starting up. Ernie slammed the hood down and hopped back into the car.

"What did you do?" Trent asked, nonplussed by the now purring engine.

"That stuff's ether," Ernie told him. "Just sprayed it into the carbure- tor. Hoo-wee! Sprayed a little too much — 'bout burned my eyebrows off when it flamed up. A little more an' I'd been the Human Torch. Now let's peel out!"

And Trent peeled out, though for a moment he was almost convinced that to add to his woes, the car was going to be stuck in the snow. Then it was free and moving down the plowed road at a respectable clip.

Some two miles later, just when Trent was beginning to breathe a little easier, the car died on him and refused to start again. Ernie went out with the Cold Start once more, but that kept the car going for no more than another couple of miles. After the third round of it, they were out of Cold Start and nowhere close to civilization.

They left the Chevy where it had gasped its last and began hiking across a vast, barren, windswept cornfield towards the lights of a farm- house at least a mile away. From there, Trent hoped to call his father and arrange for a pick-up. How he would explain the dirty messes he and Ernie had become was a problem he hadn't even begun to think about.

Off in the distance, somewhere miles beyond the treetops at the edge of the field, the erratic orange glow of the burning warehouse shimmered like malevolent Northern Lights, and a thick column of smoke blotted out the stars. Something told Trent that by the time the fire department reached Camp Douglas, assuming the trucks could even get close to the warehouse across the camp's mile or so of snow-covered, unplowed roads, the building and everything in it would be a total loss. Even if the trucks did make it through, water damage would certainly account for every last one of the comic books that the fire didn't burn outright.

"One thing," Trent said after several minutes of silent walking, each of them sunk in his own private misery. "Not a word of this to Pam. Not one word!"

"Right, Chief." Then, thoughtfully, Ernie added, "Y'know, I think we burned more funnybooks tonight than ol' Wickersham ever managed in his whole life!"

Trent's only reply was a soft groan.

# LETTERS TO THE FUTURE

In the spring of 1934, a widow with three children to support mailed the manuscript of a novel called *Love Against the Gods* to her publisher in London. As she rode her bicycle away from the Chipping Norton post office, she reflected that writing a book was like sending a letter to the future. She had poured her soul into that book, as the saying went, given it everything she had about love, honor, freedom, imagination, and courage, and she could only hope that eventually, perhaps years later, it would find its way to someone she had never met, perhaps someone not even born yet, but the kindred spirit she was writing for.

In the summer of 1965, a scrawny teenage girl rode her bicycle to the Shetland, Illinois Public Library in the hope of finding something interesting to read to pass the time on a long, hot day with nothing else to do. While poking through the shelves in the adult section, she came across a faded old book that had last been checked out in 1953: *Love Against the Gods* by Madeleine Tyndale. Leafing through it, she realized that it wasn't the sort of book she had been hoping to find — it was a sort of book she hadn't known even existed. She checked it out and took it home, and that night, utterly enthralled, she stayed up very late reading it.

It had taken more than thirty years, but the letter had been delivered.

Over Labor Day weekend in September, 1972, the World Science-Fiction Convention was held in Los Angeles. To be more specific, at the International Hotel in Anaheim.

As a last summer fling before starting her senior year in college, Pam Collins was there, hoping she could sell enough of her work in the convention art show to pay for the trip. It was the middle of the afternoon in the large ballroom filled with tables and stand-up displays where dozens of artists were exhibiting their paintings, drawings, sculptures, and *objets d'art* too esoteric for easy description, and she had just checked the bid-sheets on the table next to her array of paintings and drawings to see if there had been any new bids for her pieces. Nothing had changed since she had last looked, however.

At the age of 20, Pam was still a little thin, but had filled out since her scrawny days. She was just a little over medium height with green eyes and long, light brown hair loosely pulled back over her ears in a bushy pony tail, casually dressed in jeans with a few paint spots that no amount of washing had been able to remove. She wouldn't have attracted any particular attention on a college campus. On the other hand, one of the stranger advances she had fended off recently seemed to have been based on the reasoning, "I really want Diana Rigg to satisfy my fantasies but she's over in England and too old for me anyway while you're right here and you'll have to do as a second choice." Looking in a mirror later, she could see where that had come from though the resemblance was superficial at best.

Not that a little romance hadn't touched her life. She had resisted the earnest entreaties of any number of lonely male fans in the years she had been in fandom, the regrettable drawback of being active in a milieu where the male-female ratio was so drastically tilted to one side, but when she fell, she fell hard. She had met her match, which had been both exhilarating and maddening.

It was over for now, but she had a feeling that the last word hadn't been said. If he were to show up at the convention, the whole thing would probably start all over again.

No, best to let it rest.

At present, then, she was enjoying the single life, unencumbered and fancy-free, and preferring to keep it that way until further notice. Epic love affairs were all right in novels, but exhausting in real life, and she had other things to do with her life at the moment. Like sell her art at science-fiction conventions.

More to her weary amusement than her chagrin, the naked sea nymph whose charms were only barely covered by sprays of multicolored bubbles, which she had hacked out almost overnight as a coldly calculated money-maker, was still fetching double the far more technically challenging illustration of an intellectual dragon with spectacles consulting a learned tome in his vast library. *As if I didn't already know what sells...* she thought. Not that the dragon was exactly conceived with the highest principles of art for art's sake in mind, either, and it would bring a fair sum in its own right before the convention was over. Between those two pieces alone, Pam was well on her way to covering her travel and hotel expenses.

With no clear idea of where to go next, she cut through the Hucksters' Room, where dealers hawked books and other artifacts along aisles of tables and booths. It was that low point of a convention when she had already seen everything there was to see and had encountered everyone she knew who was likely to be at the convention at all, nothing looked terribly inviting on the schedule of panels or movies in the movie room, and dinner wasn't for a couple of hours yet.

She idly wandered along an aisle and for lack of anything better to do, decided to take a closer look at the wares of an old-book dealer conducting his trade under the sign of Rivendell Books to see if she had missed anything when she gave the booth a quick scan the day before. She wasn't even looking for anything in particular.

And there it was. A small, faded red book without a dust jacket, the title on its spine nearly worn to illegibility — *Challenge and Honour* by Madeleine Tyndale. It was a jolt just to see it and realize what it had to be.

Since reading *Love Against the Gods* at 13, Pam had gone to considerable effort to track down Tyndale's other books. Not that there were very many, but as British imports they were vanishingly scarce in the United States and she had turned up only a very few others. *Challenge and Honour* was one that had so far eluded her, and to find it at all for just a few dollars was a miracle on the scale of parting seas.

"Do you have any more books by her?" Pam asked the dealer, trying not to sound too bouncing-off-the-walls overjoyed. "Do you know anything about her? I've been trying to find her books for years but I don't think they've ever been reprinted."

The dealer, a middle-aged man with a gray beard, scratched his balding head. "I know my way around fantasy well enough to sell the stuff, but there you're getting into some pretty obscure territory. I got that book in an estate sale years ago and I thought it was an old historical novel — I almost pitched it until I happened to glance through it and saw it had some fantasy content. And in all these years I've been lugging it from con to con, you're the first person who's ever shown the slightest bit of interest in it and asked for more by the same author. Tell you what — I'll knock a bit off the price just to get rid of it, but I can't help you much beyond that. The guy you should talk to is Linc Arthur. He knows more about fantasy than anybody human."

"Great! Where do I find him?"

"Your best bet is to catch him at some panel — I know he's on several this year." The dealer picked up the program book and thumbed through it. "Ah, here we go. You're in luck, kiddo. He's got some kind of presentation in half an hour." Suddenly his eyes went wide and his breath caught in his throat. "Damn! And look what it's about! I wish I could get away from my table for this one!"

Half an hour later, Pam was sitting on a chair in a large, crowded conference room. She hadn't been able to talk to Linc Arthur before the presentation began, so she would have to sit through the whole thing and try to buttonhole him afterwards. She didn't even mind; the brief summary in the program book had made the presentation sound like something she would be interested in for its own sake.

While someone fiddled with a slide projector on top of a high metal cart in the middle of the room, a tallish, rather thin 40-something man with a mustache and goatee stood at a lectern to one side of a screen at the front. Next to him was a stand displaying a large book with an ornate cover.

Conversation among the fans in the room, mostly earnest young men with various degrees of hair length, died down as the man signaled that he was about to start.

"Greetings, gentlefen," he began. "I'm sure most of you know me already, but for the sake of formality, let it be recorded that I am Lincoln Arthur, editor of Bannister Books' Mature Fantasy Classics line. I am here today to present the results of my research into one of the most remarkable fantasy novels of all time. Lights, please."

The room lights dimmed, and a slide showing the cover of the book on the stand appeared on the screen.

"Before you is one of the very few known copies of what may be the fantasy collector's ultimate holy grail, *Enquestador* by Jeremy Hatchfield. But let me warn you. Even if you do manage to find a copy — and decide it's worth mortgaging your house for — it won't do you any good.

*"The book cannot be read.*

"Here's the story, as much of it as we know. In 1904, Jeremy Hatchfield was 47 years old and living in New York City, where he worked as the editor of a couple of trade magazines dealing with electrical equipment and manufacturing. Next slide, please."

The image on the screen changed to the cover of *Electrical Engineering Magazine* for Spring, 1903, merely a plain text listing in an antique type style of the contents, which were mostly grimly technical-sounding articles about impedance and transformers. At the bottom was the legend, "Jeremy Hatchfield, Editor."

"So far he gives the appearance of a perfectly mundane individual, if perhaps good with words, living a perfectly mundane life. But then he came into a great deal of money — the sort of rich uncle the rest of us can only dream of had departed from the Fields We Know. Suddenly, Jeremy Hatchfield could do anything he pleased, and what he did was something no one would have expected. He quit his job in New York and retired to a family home in Wisconsin where he spent the next two years writing the most remarkable fantasy novel ever penned, and then another two years seeing it through the press."

A slide showing a close-up of the book's title appeared, in flowing, almost unreadable script:

# ℰNQUEST𝒜DOℛ

"That was *Enquestador*. Only two hundred copies were printed, entirely at the author's expense, and he sent them to various of his friends and relatives as gifts for Christmas, 1908. The book was a sumptuous production, and I rather suspect his uncle's fortune was considerably diminished thereby. For one thing, the book is lavishly illustrated by an uncredited artist, and speculation as to who it was has ranged from Charles Dana Gibson to Maxfield Parrish."

The slides then showed several illustrations from the book, depicting scenes of high adventure and fantastic beasts in a world of fantasy — in the slightly antique, not quite what we're used to manner of how someone in 1908 would have conceived of fantasy. To Pam, who had made a casual hobby of studying illustration through the decades, they seemed like ghosts from a vanished age. The black and white illustrations were heavily inked, shapes and forms virtually sculpted by intricate line work, perhaps a stylistic holdover from the era of copperplate engraving. *Just the shading doubled his working time on that one!* she thought.

"While I personally tend to the idea that the artist would be someone forgotten today, most likely a technical illustrator who had already worked for Hatchfield on the trade magazines he edited, some people whose opinions I respect are convinced that the illustrations were a private commission executed by James Montgomery Flagg, famous for the 'I Want You' Uncle Sam poster of World War I."

A slide of the poster appeared.

"Whatever the case may be, the tipped-in color plates and the numerous black and white illustrations did not come cheap. Nor did the gilt-edged pages, the tooled leather binding, or the colored inlaid cover."

The next slide showed the book in a manner demonstrating the attributes he had just described.

"Now, most of us would be pleased to be presented with such a book as a gift. But there was just one small problem.

"*Enquestador* was not written in English.

"In fact, it was not written in any known language at all.

"It would appear that Jeremy Hatchfield was also an amateur linguist, and he wrote the novel in a language completely of his own invention."

The following slide showed a page of text from the book, seemingly random gibberish.

"I can assure you that it is *not* random gibberish. I have examined the text closely and can report that it shows every indication of being internally consistent and based on a systematic grammar. Further analysis suggests that it uses English word order, and if we only had a bilingual Enquestadorian/English dictionary, a simple word-for-word substitution would produce intelligible sentences.

"The one favor granted to anyone presented with the book is that the text is conventionally typeset in the Roman alphabet. The rather florid typeface is perhaps a little excessive for easy legibility, but it wasn't as though anyone was expected to actually *read* the book. Instead, the text exists merely as a stage prop, to give the *effect* of a book.

"Why didn't Hatchfield take that last step and invent his own alphabet as well? Perhaps he did. Some sort of non-Roman lettering is seen in the illustrations, as shown in the next slide — shopkeepers' signs, inscriptions on monuments, titles on books, that sort of thing. The letters resemble runes, but they are not the conventional *futhark* or any other known runic alphabet. It is possible the artist simply made up the lettering himself as a purely decorative element, but it also has a certain internal consistency that makes me suspect there's a system to it. My surmise is that Hatchfield did have some idea of using his invented alphabet for the book's text, but the expense of cutting an entire typeface for printing just one book was too much even for him.

"What we have, then, is an author's ultimate self-indulgence. Not only a created world but a created language long before the celebrated Professor Tolkien essayed such an endeavor. No expense was spared in the book's production, but no quarter was given to the reader, either. Precisely why he went to such extreme length to publish an elaborately illustrated, extravagantly produced volume that ultimately defeats the very purpose for which books are published in the first place, that is to say, to be read, is a riddle whose answer now lies irretrievably buried beneath the sands of time. Perhaps it was merely a very expensive literary joke, perhaps he was torn between a desire to tell a story and fear that no one who read it would like it, or perhaps he was simply a few marbles shy — we shall likely never know.

"Most of the book's recipients were doubtless completely baffled by the gift. Since there is little incentive to save a book you can't read, copies probably disappeared one by one over the years, quietly tossed out in the trash or given away to the first person to ring the bell soliciting for charity. I know of one copy that was used by a previous owner's children as a coloring book, which was probably the most good anyone ever got out of it."

The accompanying slide showed an illustration from the book badly colored with crayons, apparently by an inept four-year-old unclear on the concept of staying within the lines. "That knocks a couple hundred bucks off the price," someone near Pam muttered in the darkness.

"Nonetheless, a few copies eventually found their way into the second-hand book trade, where they came to the attention of collectors who prized them for the illustrations if nothing else, and the book's legend — and price — slowly grew.

"Unfortunately, serious interest in the book did not develop until after World War II. Jeremy Hatchfield had died fairly young in 1915, by his own hand for reasons that remain obscure, and over thirty years later, whatever private papers and notes he might have left behind were long lost. There had been some hope among fantasy fans that Hatchfield had first written *Enquestador* in English and then translated it into his invented language, and that the original English manuscript might turn up in the proverbial trunk in the attic. Failing that, copies of correspondence with the artist explaining what had to be illustrated would have shed a great deal of light on the story itself. Even the Enquestadorian dictionary Hatchfield must certainly have compiled for his own use would have been precious beyond measure, since the novel could then at least be translated. The sad fact of the matter, however, was that the surviving members of his family knew nothing about any manuscripts or other papers. Perhaps the same inner demons that drove Hatchfield to self-extinction also compelled him to burn his papers himself before bringing down the curtain, not only ending his existence but attempting to destroy any evidence that he had ever existed at all.

"No, Jeremy Hatchfield was probably not of sound mind in certain respects. But sometimes the boundary between madness and greatness is a thin and porous one. That unsound mind also gave us *Enquestador*, and just to leaf through the book is to sense something very great indeed, if only we could understand it.

"You are doubtless wondering, 'Well, then, if this story is so great, what is it *about*?' After many nights of studying the illustrations and trying to analyze the text for possible clues, I have come to a few tentative conclusions. A cursory glance at the pictures might make you think it's a standard pseudo-medieval romance, with a gallant young hero wielding a fiery sword almost as big as he is, a fair maid to be won, aged wizards weaving their enchantments, a quest of some sort through strange and exotic landscapes, and battles against dragon-like monsters. It does have that Middle Ages look so beloved of fantasy authors through the decades. But a closer scrutiny shows that it's a little different. Some ancient Rome and Greece got into that 14th Century England, and even the merrie olde England bits don't look quite right. Based on this and other literary detective work, I believe that the answer to the question of what the book is about is as follows:

"Hatchfield reasoned that if the lost continent of Atlantis had in fact existed, it would not have sprung up fully formed as an advanced civilization overnight. It would have had not only a long history but an even longer pre-history that after thousands of years even the Atlanteans themselves would remember only as myths and legends. My belief is that Hatchfield sat down and wrote the story of one of those legends of old Atlantis.

"Robert E. Howard's *King Kull* stories are perhaps the closest approach any subsequent author has made to this particular territory, but if my supposition is correct, Hatchfield took it much further. The *Kull* stories were the actual if imagined history of a non-existent continent, but Hatchfield wrote instead of that continent's gods and legendary heroes. It is as though Babylon were a legend to us, and someone wrote the epic of Gilgamesh.

"The concept of a myth having myths of its own is head-splitting enough, but it gets worse — one of the illustrations shows a character apparently telling a tale of a legendary hero from an even *earlier* day! (Slide, please.) *How far back does it go?* But to ponder this question too much perhaps leads only to madness, and we have Jeremy Hatchfield's own lamentable example to demonstrate that.

"Now, I would love to reprint the book as an inexpensive paperback under the Sign of the Griffin in the Bannister Mature Fantasy Classics collection, and make it available to a modern audience of fans and collectors. 'But Linc,' you say, 'how many copies would a book written in no known language likely sell?' Probably not very many. Ghu knows that John and Betsy Bannister have already taken a bath with some of the little-known fantasy books they've published in the series at my insistence. For most modern readers, Hodgson's *The Night Land* is probably not very much more readable than *Enquestador*. But I think John and Betsy would draw the line at something *completely* unreadable.

"So I have proposed a solution. While the narrative itself is written in an unknown language, character and place names can be identified. Further, the book is so heavily illustrated that it is possible to follow the story to a great extent. And because the pictures illustrate the story, it has been possible to decipher the likely meanings of many of Hatchfield's invented words. I think I have worked out the main outline of the story, and if given the go-ahead, I can add flesh to the bones by filling in details. The final result may not be precisely the story Jeremy Hatchfield originally wrote, but it will hopefully be in the same spirit. The main thing for most readers will be that there is a coherent and entertaining story that matches the illustrations. So at long last, after many years, *Enquestador* will finally reach the hands of enthusiastic fantasy fans who have hungered for it for so long!"

All through Linc Arthur's presentation, excitement had been mounting in the audience. Perhaps everyone was hoping for a surprise announcement that the original English draft of *Enquestador* had been found after all and Bannister Books would shortly publish it with the matching illustrations. Instead, the actual pronouncement that Linc Arthur was going to write his best guess as to what the story *might* be about only seemed to let most of the air out of the room.

There was some desultory applause when Arthur finished and the room lights came on, though not the enthusiastic cheers and huzzahs he had clearly expected, and several people in the audience asked some dispirited questions ("Are you *sure* there's no chance of ever finding the original manuscript?"), but mostly the atmosphere was one of crashing disappointment. Then fans began getting up and filing out, interested mainly in moving on to another conference room where a panel on the New Wave promised fireworks among some fiercely contentious authors.

As far as Pam was concerned, that had been an interesting presentation, telling her quite a bit about something she hadn't known anything about before — but it really had nothing to do with the reason she was here in the first place. She promptly tucked the matter of *Enquestador* away in that corner of her mind where she kept odd scraps of information that she had no immediate use for and made her way to the front of the room to catch Linc Arthur before he disappeared into the depths of the hotel. Along the way, what little discussion of the *Enquestador* presentation itself she caught in passing was mainly grumbling.

"It's maybe the greatest fantasy novel ever written," one fan muttered to another. "So who gets to rewrite it? A hack like Linc Arthur! Why can't they get J. Spriggs du Champ?"

Linc Arthur overheard it, too. "Because Spriggs didn't spend three years of his life trying to figure the book out, that's why!" he exclaimed a little testily.

Pam approached Linc, introduced herself, and showed him the book she had just bought. He was still clearly out of sorts from the disappointing reception to his presentation, but when he looked at the title, his eyes widened. "*Challenge and Honour* by Madeleine Tyndale? And I thought *Enquestador* was obscure!"

"Have you read it?" Pam asked eagerly. "I was just wondering if you knew anything about the author."

"My dear, there aren't many fantasy authors I don't know anything about," Linc said, apparently forgetting his chagrin of moments before. "But with Madeleine Tyndale, you're getting out to the far fringes of what's known by anyone. What I do know is that she was a British author with only a very few books to her credit, all late '20s and early '30s as I recall. They apparently didn't sell well since there weren't any American editions, or even any postwar paperback reprints in Britain. She gets listed in a few places but otherwise she seems to be utterly forgotten. I've never read any of her books myself and no one I know has ever mentioned having read them. So I may not be the one to ask. Now, it so happens that Derek Foster is standing over there. He's English and a walking authority on everything to do with British fantasy. If you catch him before he goes out the door, he might be able to tell you something. Oh, and here's my card. Drop me a note if you find out anything interesting or just to tell me about any of Tyndale's books you've read. If I don't bankrupt Bannister Books first by bringing out other fantasy books by authors nobody's ever heard of, I'm always looking for more."

Derek Foster was about thirty and distinguished by a magnificent curly black beard. If anything, he resembled a Santa Claus who had taken to using hair dye, wearing a t-shirt with the legend, "INTELLECT VAST AND COOL AND UNSYMPATHETIC," over a silhouette of a Martian war machine from Wells' *The War of the Worlds*. The obvious vast thing about him was the lower expanse covered by his t-shirt, but he turned out to be anything but unsympathetic when Pam caught up with him and showed him the book.

"Madeleine Tyndale..." Foster murmured, then said, "Even we don't know much about her. Her books are long out of print and forgotten, and hardly anybody has read them in decades. About all I can tell you is that we think 'Madeleine Tyndale' was a pseudonym."

"Really?" This was exciting — even that scrap of knowledge more than doubled what Pam had known about her before.

"The information is second or third-hand, but when we were compiling the Directory of British Fantasy & Science-Fiction Authors several years ago, somebody who knew somebody at a publisher's told us that Madeleine Tyndale wrote under more than one name. Mostly dire commercial rubbish not worth ferreting out now, but apparently she reserved the Tyndale name for the books she cared about. It makes sense, actually. She had to serve her apprenticeship somewhere, and hone her skills. Authors don't usually write in top form straight out of the gate."

"Which would make finding her all the harder, if she's even still alive."

"Well, she may not have written anything in nearly forty years, but we don't think she's dead, either. We tried to get in touch with her when we were doing the Directory, and she replied through some rather convoluted channels that she'd rather not be contacted, thank you. So she sounded pretty lively at least as of then. Why do you want to find her?"

"I'd just like to send her a fan letter and some drawings I did of her characters."

"Sounds harmless enough. Give me your address and when I get back home I'll see if anyone can nose around and turn up her real name and present whereabouts. When a fantasy fan is on the scent, no author can hide out for long."

As Pam reached into her bag to grab a piece of paper and a pen, she happened to glance at the front of the now almost empty room. Linc Arthur was sitting by himself on one of the chairs in the front row and arranging the papers in a briefcase. No eager fans crowded around him to pepper him with questions, and it was actually a little sad to see him so alone.

"Why don't fans seem to like him?" she asked.

"He has the reputation of being a hack," Derek replied. "He's certainly an expert on fantasy, and nobody can fault him for his editing of the Bannister fantasy line, but when he tries to write a book of his own... I've always rather enjoyed his books myself, but at times they do feel like imitations of books instead of real ones. Perhaps he's read so many books that all he can do is blend the ideas and styles of other writers instead of cook up something new of his own devising. A shame, really..."

Pam gave Derek the piece of paper with her address and they went their separate ways. In Pam's case, it was straight to her room to start reading *Challenge and Honour*.

She wasn't 14 any more with a whole hot summer day and the following evening free to do nothing but read — there were friends to meet for dinner and several matters relating to the art show to deal with — so she couldn't read the book all in one sitting. It wasn't until she was on a Chicago-bound plane after the convention that she finished it. She closed the book and looked out at the clouds and sky with a vague feeling of melancholy. As far as she knew, it had been the only Madeleine Tyndale novel she hadn't read yet, and finishing it was the closing of a chapter in her life that had begun seven years before.

But sometimes the ending of one chapter is the beginning of another.

With the convention behind her, Pam went back to college to start her senior year. Not only was her course load heavy over the weeks that followed, four private commissions for naked sea nymphs came in from the losing bidders on the one she'd sold at Worldcon. After the second commission, the character had acquired a name, as in "Oh no! I have to paint another 'Bubbles'!" In any event, she scarcely had time to give Madeleine Tyndale any thought. Then, somewhere about November, a letter with a

London postmark appeared in her off-campus apartment building's mailbox. She opened it and read:

*Dear Pam,*

*Success at last! The FBI (Fan Bureau of Investigation) always gets its man! Or woman, in this case. Our Madeleine turns out to be Maddie Smythe, a retired schoolteacher and village librarian living in Charlbury in Oxfordshire. The nearest town of any size is Chipping Norton and Oxford is not too far away, if that helps. Her address is appended below, so the next step is up to you.*

*Cheers,*
*Derek*

As if the next step wasn't obvious. Now that she had Madeleine Tyndale's address, she'd write to her, of course. She had a lot to say, things that she had wanted to say since that hot summer day some seven years before.

Freshly graduated in the summer of 1973, Pam took off for Europe with a couple of college friends to see the world before settling down in whatever phase of life came next.

It quickly developed that the three young women with backpacks were taking three separate tours and traveling together only in loose formation for mutual protection. Pam spent her time wandering the streets with sketchbook in hand looking for interesting scenes or haunting art museums and second-hand bookstores, and then in post offices sending a lot of odd books home to herself. If she wasn't dragging her friends to the Rijksmuseum in Amsterdam to see the Rembrandts, it was to the Louvre in Paris for the Mona Lisa and everything else. Beverly, on the other hand, was more interested in ordinary sightseeing and organized tours, while Anita seemed to be intent on sampling the delights of various local varieties of fermented beverages and the places where they were readily available. Then, in Paris, Anita "met some guy in a bar," as Beverly phrased it not so elegantly, and abruptly dropped out of the party entirely.

At the moment, Pam was in England on her own. Beverly had gone somewhere in the south of France to rescue Anita from the horrible jam that had resulted from meeting that guy in a bar. Pam had offered to go along on the extraction mission, but Beverly had rather nobly said, "No, there's no point in both our trips being ruined. Besides, you've had this visit with that lady author planned for months and my French is better than yours. I think I can manage to post Anita's bail or whatever by myself."

And Pam had in fact managed to make contact with the reclusive Miss Tyndale. Using the address Derek Foster had supplied, she had sent an introductory letter telling how she had she discovered a copy of *Love Against the Gods* in a library in the American Midwest and how much it had meant to her, and enclosed copies of pen and ink drawings illustrating her conceptions of the main characters. There was a somewhat stiff and formal reply from Miss Tyndale saying that she had left all that behind her long ago, but it was not unfriendly, and she seemed to appreciate Pam's interest. Pam responded with a follow-up letter, a correspondence ensued, and soon came an invitation to drop by if she were ever in the neighbourhood. It just so happened Pam was going to Europe that summer, and Paris and Amsterdam were surely close enough to England to be "in the neighbourhood."

So far, Pam's impression of England, at least once she got out of London, was that *it looks exactly like it does on TV!* If one watched a lot of syndicated British adventure shows or public television programs, that is. From the train window she had seen lush, green countryside with hedgerows and scattered villages under a hazy blue sky, and it wasn't hard to imagine herself sitting next to Steed in the Bentley racing down a narrow rural lane on the way to some new adventure.

She wondered what Madeleine Tyndale would be like. She hadn't gotten a very clear impression from her brief letters. A cranky old harridan who ate American girls for tea if they dared disturb her peace? Well, she wouldn't have invited Pam to visit her in the first place if she was that. More likely — an eccentric recluse? That was Pam's best guess and she prepared herself for it, though she found it hard to really believe if this had been the woman who wrote *Love Against the Gods*.

One passing thought intrigued Pam. Even if that had been Madeleine Tyndale's last published novel, could she have written others after it that weren't published? Maybe, if the visit turned out well, she would even let Pam read the manuscript of one of them. An unpublished novel by Madeleine Tyndale written at the height of her powers, when Pam had thought she had read everything the lady had ever put on paper under that name... *This is the real world*, Pam warned herself before her imagination ran completely away with her. *Don't get your hopes up!*

She got off the train at the small village of Charlbury, and following the directions she had been sent, it was only a short walk from the station to the house on the outskirts.

It was a well-kept little cottage with a small fenced yard that showed considerable gardening effort. A weather-worn sign on the fence post by the gate announced that the house even had a name: BRAMBLEMARSH, though neither brambles nor marshes were in evidence. Pam smiled: that had been the name of England's creepiest girls' boarding school in the only book that Madeleine Tyndale had obviously written for a juvenile audience — and since it was more darkly whimsical than her usual output, it had probably given more than a few little girls nightmares around 1930, explaining why there hadn't been any sequels. So the lady hadn't completely turned her back on the books she had once written, or at least she still had a sense of humor about it all. Things were starting to look promising.

Pam went up to the front door and knocked. After a moment, the door opened from within, and an elderly woman stood in the doorway.

Whatever Pam had expected, Madeleine Tyndale was something else. She was tall, rather thin, wore glasses, and had gray, almost white hair. The years had perhaps worn her down, but she still had an elegance about her, and her face showed something of the beauty she had once been. She had apparently put on her best dress, a little old and out of style though it was, having remembered that company was coming today.

There was an awkward pause, with Miss Tyndale looking at Pam as though she hadn't quite expected *her*, either. Pam wondered if she looked a little *too* American in jeans and tennis shoes, her sunglasses perched on her ponytailed head, and carrying a shoulderbag.

"I'm Pam Collins," she quickly said. "From America. We exchanged a few letters — you were expecting me today...?"

Miss Tyndale suddenly nodded, as though she had finished sizing her visitor up, and smiled. "So you're the one who answered *my* letter."

"Pardon?"

"Never mind. Just a game I once played with myself, thinking the books I wrote were like letters to the future, and you never knew who might receive them. But please, do come in."

Inside, the cottage was neat enough, but there were books everywhere, seemingly stuffed in every available nook and cranny. There was hardly room left for the two or three dozing cats on the chairs. Then Pam's attention was caught by several small, framed photographs on the mantel over the fireplace. Most were probably children and grandchildren, but one was a very faded sepia portrait of a handsome young man.

Madeleine cleared some books from the seat of an overstuffed chair and shooed a sleepy cat away so Pam could sit down. "Some tea, dear?"

"Sure." Pam glanced around as she took a seat. "You, er, seem to have a lot of books," she said a little lamely, trying to fill the sudden pause in the conversation.

"Yes, I know. It looks as though the Charlbury library lost its building and I'm just keeping the books until they can find a new one, but they're all mine. The children hereabouts call me the 'book-lady,' and I don't even mind. I've earned the title."

"I accumulate books, too," Pam said quickly, hoping she hadn't made it sound as though she thought book-collecting was a peculiar hobby. "You should see my room at home. It's getting hard to find my bed."

"Well, books first and furniture second, I always say," Madeleine said breezily. "The cats seem to find me on their own. Let me get the tea."

Soon she came out of the kitchen with a tray. By this time, a curious black and white kitten was curling up in Pam's lap for an afternoon snooze as she idly stroked it.

"I must say," Miss Tyndale said, setting the tray with its teapot and two cups and saucers down on a small table, "your first letter was quite a surprise after all these years." She sat in an armchair in front of the table and poured the tea. "I thought I was forgotten, and to be honest, I rather preferred it that way, having come to enjoy the peaceful life. Your letter interested me, though. In all these years, you seemed to be the first one to ever really *understand* my books, which was an even greater surprise. Still, I used to get a bit of fan mail when I was writing. Some of it came from young chaps, even the odd offer of marriage. I fancy they thought I must be as free-spirited in person as my heroines were."

"Weren't you?" Pam asked with a slight grin.

"Oh goodness, no," Miss Tyndale replied. "I was a respectable widow and mother." She winked. "I just had a very vivid imagination."

There was another pause and she sat back and contemplated her tea. "So, tell me about your journey here."

Pam shrugged. "Nothing to tell, really, I took the train from London, changed at Oxford without any problem..."

"I don't mean *that*. I mean there are millions of people in America, but you're the only one who ever found her way to my front step. That's the journey I want to hear about."

Pam had come here to meet Madeleine Tyndale, not talk about herself — she could have just as easily stayed home and done that. But under Miss Tyndale's gentle prodding, and the old lady actually did seem interested, she found herself opening up more than she ever had to anyone before. She had grown up in a small town in northern Illinois, closer to the Mississippi River than to Chicago, as a child almost too bright and curious for people around her to stand very patiently. Art particularly spoke to her, but with few outlets for her talents and no one to even talk to about the things that were on her mind, she felt close to suffocating by her teenage years. Her discovery of Madeleine Tyndale's books had been like coming across an oasis in the desert.

201

"You don't know how much *Love Against the Gods* meant to me at the time," she said. "Both for the feeling that real life could be like the story — and that it was possible to *tell* stories like that."

Then a couple of boys she knew from school introduced her to something called fandom. It centered on comic books, of all things, but the fans' amateur publications had given her the place she needed to express herself and introduced her to a network of other bright and creative people all over the country. Although she was still entranced by the idea of telling stories with pictures, in the end she had found comics fandom too limited by the dreary commercial reality of the comic-book industry to stay with it for more than a couple of years.

By college, she had moved on to the wider field of science-fiction and fantasy fandom — though sometimes she wondered if naked sea nymphs were really that much of an improvement — with an eye on a career in illustration. In a deal with her father, who was footing the bill and wanted her to get an education instead of just vocational training, she had gotten a regular four-year degree first, with a major in English and a minor in history, and would start at a commercial art school this fall. She was already selling her art on the convention circuit, but she was largely self-taught and needed formal training to get that last bit of professional polish she still lacked to break into bigger markets.

"That's pretty much it," Pam finished.

"I see..." Miss Tyndale said, nodding. "Lonely, bookish girl, too clever for her own good... it's an oft-told tale. Twice in this very room, it appears. Despite half a century and several thousands of miles, we weren't so far apart. But as for me..." She sighed, seemingly looking across the years. "I married when I was twenty. A little young, perhaps, but I was in love with a hero who might have been straight out of my books. David cut quite a dashing figure when he came home after the war, and half the girls in the town were keen on him. He had been an officer in France, won no end of medals... and I was the one who won *him*. But... it was after I had married a hero that I truly began to understand what it meant to *be* one, and I had to bid farewell to some of my romantic illusions. He was a brave and decent man, but he had seen some terrible things in the trenches when he was over there and he would wake up with nightmares. Being a hero isn't all brass bands and parades and having medals pinned on one. I think seeing an actual hero close to and the price he paid for it gave my writing later more depth than the usual sort of romance."

Madeleine paused to reflect and Pam wondered if she should say something. *No*, she thought. *Let her talk. This is already worth the trip — so much more than I could have expected.*

After a moment, Madeleine picked up from where she had left off.

"Then the babies came and not long after that there was a railway accident... My hero was gone but to carry on I had to find the same sort of strength within me that he had.

"When I lost my husband, times were hard and I had three children to raise. Since I could do it at home, writing for money seemed a congenial way to earn the odd extra pound, so I sent a few things out to see what would happen. Mostly they came right back and I was fairly discouraged and thinking I should perhaps take in laundry instead, but then one day a cheque showed up in the post. There is no greater inspiration than a pound sign, so I wrote more and before long the hits were outnumbering the misses. Most of what I wrote was non-fiction, such as helpful hints articles for the women's magazines, new recipes using Marmite, that sort of thing, but I also tried my hand at romantic fiction, the kind of stories that in those days gave the not very well educated shop girl something to dream about. I could be as good a Grub Street hack as any, even all the way out here. I had so many pen-names I could barely keep track of them after a while. Was Enid Gayley the specialist in new uses for common household utensils or was that Prudence Bailey and Enid was the queen of tear-stained tragedy and heartfelt happy endings? I didn't want to use my own name because it's a small village and it wouldn't do for the local school teacher and librarian to be found out writing torrid romances — which, of course, by today's standards were about as spicy as dishwater.

"Over time, I did well enough at it that I had put a bit of money by and the immediate emergency was past. I had also gotten a little tired of the same old trite fiction and endlessly rehashed articles. I think I invented 'recycling' before anyone ever thought the world needed a word for it. When I wrote for myself, that's when Madeleine Tyndale came out of the cupboard. Which is, by the way, my maiden name. 'Smythe' is my married name. I had some idea that I was calling up the shade of the girl I used to be. Someday you'll look back at your adolescent self and wonder what happened to the dreams that girl had before she grew up and adult responsibilities closed in on her. As Madeleine Tyndale, I wrote the books I would have wanted to read when I was 15 or 16, books expressing that spirit of independence and the feeling of the whole world opening up before me."

"I first read one of your books when I was 13," Pam said, "and that was exactly how I felt. I hadn't been able to express it before, but your book put it into words."

"I remember I received a number of letters from teenagers saying that very thing," Madeleine said, "both girls and boys, oddly enough. Perhaps I touched something very basically human that's in all of us. I once tried to explain it to a psychologist bloke I met at a meeting with my publisher

— he wrote some dreadful series of utterly useless self-help books back in the '30s, *Think Your Way to Success in Ten Easy Steps*, or something of the sort, best-sellers at the time but thankfully forgotten now — and he immediately popped out with the term 'arrested development.' I wanted to hit him with my bag. He seemed to think I was trying to extend an immature state indefinitely, staying a dewy-eyed adolescent forever, if you will. No, I wanted to scream, just the opposite. The kind of growing up we were expected to do was the real arrested development, killing your dreams, limiting your horizons, settling for the low and mean, basically giving up and resigning yourself to mediocrity. What I wanted was *continued* development, not only aiming for the stars but eventually reaching them.

"Well, as Madeleine, I gave it my best shot, but in the end, the times were against me. When life is hard and you're not sure you'll have a job next week, probably the last thing you want to read is a novel of delicately nuanced tragedy and triumph counterpointed with often hopeless but always heroic defiance of overwhelming odds in a world far, far away. My moment, if I ever really had one, had passed. I felt I was writing better than ever, but each of my books sold fewer copies than the previous one and finally my publisher said we couldn't go on like this. I thought I would put my serious writing aside until things improved, but they never really did. Then there was another war, and after that the world was a much different place."

"But there was a science-fiction and fantasy boom in the '50s—" Pam started to point out.

"By then, *I* was in my 50s. The spirit I was striving to express in my 30s just wasn't there anymore. I had gotten older, and perhaps I had finally made my peace with the world after all, if a little later than most. I didn't regret anything. I'd had a good long run as a writer and said about all I had to say, and put a roof over my children's heads besides, so I had no real cause to complain."

Finally, Pam saw an opportunity to ask the question she had been wondering about. "Did you write any more novels after *Love Against the Gods*, even if they weren't published?"

Madeleine shook her head. "I know what you're thinking. You're thinking I have a trunk full of orphan manuscripts languishing somewhere. No, *Love Against the Gods* truly was my last novel. Oh, I continued to write commercial articles under my pen-names for the income and I scribbled a few notes for possible new stories, out of force of habit most likely, but truth be told the writer known as Madeleine Tyndale had already given everything she had and she wrote no more. I'm afraid life isn't like a story. There isn't some long-lost manuscript of an undiscovered masterpiece mouldering just a few feet above your head. Everything I ever wrote that was of any consequence was published at the time, though it may be a little hard to find nowadays."

*What a shame*, Pam thought a little sadly.

Now that Madeleine seemed to have finished the story of her life and career, Pam decided to show her the illustrations she had drawn and brought with her. That meant dislodging the thoroughly comfortable and now thoroughly unhappy kitten in her lap and digging into her bag.

"These were inspired by *'Neath the Raven Banner*," Pam said, spreading the sheets on the table in front of her. "I always had a feeling that one was a little more personal than some of your others. It's supposed to be about Vikings and adventure, but it's really about the wife left behind with the kids on the farm, and she doesn't know if her husband's ever coming back..."

"You're marvelously perceptive to have picked up on that," Madeleine said as she looked over the drawings. "A couple of the reviewers at the time could guess that I was doing the *Odyssey* with Norse mythology — one review was even titled, 'Homer in a Horned Helmet' — but no one looked any more deeply. Yes, I'll admit Ragnhild's situation was much like mine at the time. I took my inspiration where I found it, and clearing the household expenses each month with the children to be fed was on my mind rather a lot. At least Ragnhild had the hope that her husband *might* return..." She trailed off. Pam could see that the painful memory had not yet healed even after so many years. Then she took a closer look at the drawings, and after a few moments, laid them down and shook her head. "It's not at all how I envisioned the characters, not at all..."

Pam's face fell.

Madeleine smiled. "...but it's probably how I'll envision them from now on!"

Pam wanted to hug her.

"You remind me a bit of my uncle..." Madeleine added. "Well, not in all respects. He had a moustache and smelt of pipe tobacco. No, I mean he was an artist, too, and there's something in your art that expresses a quality he had as well. He had gone off to America to seek his fortune before I was even born, and did well enough, I suppose, but he missed England too much and came back when I was nine or ten. I remember there was a novel he had illustrated and let me read... I thought it was the most marvelous thing I had ever read, filled with romance and adventure. I wanted to be able to tell stories like that, too. I truly think that novel inspired me to be a writer myself. You might say it was the letter to the future that *I* received."

"What was the name of the book? If it's the book that inspired *you*, I'd like to read it."

"Oh, I don't think it was ever even published. Not properly, anyway, Uncle Bert only had a copy of the manuscript that he used as a reference for his illustrations, and I had to read that. It was all some sort of private commission for a rather daft writer nobody's ever heard of. Pity, too, because the book was brilliant."

The wheels spun in Pam's mind. This couldn't be happening. It would be too much of a coincidence. But she had to know, she had to ask. It took a moment to recall the details from the convention nearly a year before, then struggling to keep her voice steady, she said:

"This novel... it wasn't *Enquestador* by Jeremy Hatchfield, was it?"

Madeleine was taking a sip of tea just then and nearly spilled it on her blouse. "Good heavens!" she exclaimed, shocked. "How could you know? That was it exactly! So it was published after all. I should have you find a copy when you get back to the States and send it to me — the old manuscript's fairly well worn after all these years and it would be nice to have a permanent copy on my shelf."

Pam nearly screamed. *"You still have the manuscript?"*

"Certainly I do," Madeleine replied, startled by Pam's astonished reaction. "After about the third or fourth time I asked Uncle Bert to lend it to me so I could I could read it again, he let me keep it. It was an important part of my childhood and you don't pitch something like that like yesterday's newspaper. It's in a trunk with the rest of my childhood things. Er... why are you staring at me?"

After Pam had explained the circumstances and Madeleine realized that threads of destiny stretching back nearly seventy years had just now come together in her living room, there was nothing else to do but dig the manuscript out of the trunk and read it. Pam didn't even suggest borrowing it and taking it back to London with her to read overnight in her hotel room. There was a definite feeling in the air of "Kindred spirits we may be, but I just met you and something so important to me does not leave my house."

Enough years had passed since Madeleine had last read the novel that she felt she would like to read it again, and they read it together over the kitchen table. Pam passed each page on as she finished it, more amused than annoyed by how Madeleine read some of her favorite lines aloud.

Although the yellowing pages showed every sign of being decades old, the manuscript had been neatly typed and was still easily readable. Since there were no strike-outs or corrections, Pam had the feeling it had been professionally typed by a secretary from Jeremy Hatchfield's original and probably far messier original manuscript in an era before photocopying machines so the artist could have something to work from. They probably had carbon paper in 1906 or whenever, but since it had been Hatchfield's intention to make sure there *were* no other copies, probably only this one typescript had ever existed. It had, however, been considerably marked up, apparently by Uncle Bert, with penciled notes in the margins and sections of underlined text indicating scenes to be illustrated; there were even occasional doodles and sketches of the characters, which more added to the flavor of the reading experience than detracted from it.

The long, hot, drowsy summer afternoon wore on and the shadows lengthened as they read one page after another. Pam wasn't even aware of the passing time, caught up as she was in the story's epic adventure and the inevitable clash of characters who were destined from birth to meet in final battle. *Enquestador* really was everything Linc Arthur had thought it was, a lost classic no one had ever heard of, a mad author's one shot at expressing what he had within him and pulling it off magnificently. But if it had been his perverse intention to write a masterpiece and then hide it in plain sight and forever out of reach, in that one respect he had failed — he had not reckoned with the one extant copy that was long out of his hands by the time he despairingly burned all his papers.

It was almost too dark in the kitchen to read by daylight any longer when Pam laid the last page down, leaned back in the chair, and let out a long breath. "Wow," she said, still feeling dazed by the impact of what she had read. Then she straightened up a little and, pointing at the stack of manuscript pages, looked at Madeleine and said flatly, "This has *got* to be published!"

"And I suppose you have a publisher up your sleeve?"

"Actually, I do." Quickly figuring the time difference and deciding it would be early afternoon in New York, Pam added, "Let me use your phone. I'll give you some money for the bill and if it's more than that I'll send you the rest. But there's somebody I need to call."

Madeleine was starting to seem a little dubious — perhaps events were moving too fast for her to keep up. And she had just met Pam, after all, a perfect stranger from across the ocean who despite her seeming kindred spiritude could turn out to be some brazen American adventuress perpetrating who knew what confidence trick on respectable old ladies. But before Madeleine could collect her thoughts or muster her objections and misgivings, Pam had fished Linc Arthur's card from her billfold and found the telephone, and with a local operator's help she was putting a transatlantic call through to somewhere on Long Island.

A woman answered — accompanied by barking in the background. "Hello? Arthur residence... down, Frodo! I said *sit*, Bilbo! Er... sorry. Can I help you? Gollum, *no!*"

"I'd like to speak with Mr. Arthur. I met him at Worldcon last year and—"

"I'm Holly, his wife," the woman interrupted, her voice turning distinctly chilly. Perhaps she was suspicious of young-sounding women who had met her husband at conventions. "I can't disturb him now (Frodo, *stop* that!) — he just got to bed after staying up all night finishing a novel and I wouldn't wake him for anything."

"You might want to for this," Pam said. "I'm calling from England because I found the original manuscript for the novel *Enquestador*."

There was a moment of stunned silence, followed by, "Just a minute. I'll go get him."

Several more moments ticked by as Madeleine's phone bill mounted. Pam heard the sounds of dogs yapping, then finally a distant, "*What?*"

Probably, if Holly had told Linc that the radio had announced that Russian missiles were on the way and one would hit New York City in fifteen minutes, he was so beat that he would have just rolled over and gone back to sleep. But *this* bit of news got him to the telephone in short order. When he picked up the receiver, he sounded barely awake, yawning, dead tired — operating on some last few dregs of energy and mainly force of will. "Is it true? You found the MS for *Enquestador*? Who are you?"

"It's true, all right. My name is Pam Collins. You might not remember me, but we met at Worldcon last year when I asked you about Madeleine Tyndale. You gave me your card and told me to let you know if I found out anything interesting. Well, call it serendipity or whatever, but while I was tracking down Madeleine Tyndale in England, the *Enquestador* manuscript turned up."

As soon as he realized what she was getting at, he cried out in horrified dismay, "*Why didn't you tell me six months ago?!*"

Having expected nothing but joy and jubilation, Pam was a little taken aback. "Uhm... because I only now found it by accident? Is there something wrong?"

"Just that I spent the last 32 hours straight slaving over a hot typewriter and finishing my reconstruction of the novel after months of work on it. If you really have found the original, there won't be any need for *my* version!"

"Er... sorry?"

"Never mind that," Linc said quickly, sounding as though he was waking up fast. "You remember my presentation at Worldcon, right? How close was I in guessing what the novel was about?"

"Pretty close, actually," Pam assured him. "It really is supposed to be a myth from ancient Atlantis."

"I'm glad to hear that... not that anybody will care how right I was.

What bothered me, though, was that I got the impression from the illustrations that it had a downbeat ending. It looked like the villain defeated the hero in the final battle, and while it's a little different for a fantasy epic, I was worried that it would be so counter to fans' expectations that it would just kill the whole thing for the modern reader. I figured it was perhaps understandable considering Jeremy Hatchfield's mindset, since he did commit suicide later, so he was probably darkly pessimistic and convinced that in the real world, evil would inevitably win out, which was reflected in his novel... er, why are you laughing?"

"Because you've got it so *wrong!*" Pam managed to say when she could choke back her laughter. "Look... it starts out with two boys, cousins, one's good but the other seems doomed to go bad. The good cousin is destined for the throne, he's the chosen one of the gods, he's good and kind, everyone loves him, only he is deemed worthy of wielding the flaming sword *Enquestador*, while everything seems stacked against the bad cousin..."

"I could figure that much," Linc said a little defensively, "and it was obvious that Enquestador was the name of the sword... a little too much like Excalibur, if you ask me, but if he's going to do the magic sword thing, he might as well go the whole way. But where did I go wrong? Doesn't the villain win in the end?"

"That's just it!" Pam exclaimed in a bright cascade of laughter. "By the end of the novel, the hero and the villain have *changed places!* The good cousin is weak and eventually corrupted by having everything too easy, while the bad cousin learns courage and honor — by the end of the book, the bad cousin *is* the hero!"

"But what about the being worthy of wielding the sword bit...?"

"That's the inspired part! As the wizard who made Enquestador said, how can a *sword* know who's worthy and who isn't? It's a flaming sword, and it'll burn the hands off *anyone* who tries to use it, worthy or not. So the test of worthiness is using the sword anyway, *knowing* what it will do to you, but using it because you must. In the story, the Duke of Shadows has to fight to save his wife and unborn child, but he's unarmed and Enquestador is the only weapon in reach. Wow, what a scene!" In fact, it had made enough of an impression on her that she still remembered the passage more or less word for word. "'...*And he changed the sword to his left hand only when too little remained of his right to hold it...*' Chills down my back, I'm telling you! Or the end of it... '*He may not have been worthy when he picked up the sword, but when the sword finally fell from the blackened, smoking stumps of his hands, there had never been one worthier.*'"

"Oh... great... Cthulhu..." Linc murmured. "Sounds a little gruesome,

209

though... The main character's hands are burned off?'"

"Don't worry. This is a world with magic in it. His hands grow back later... though it takes a while and it's pretty painful."

"Well, we'll have to work something out," Linc said, his tone turning brisk. "Since you were at my presentation, you know what a colossal discovery you've made, so don't let that manuscript out of your sight! There'll be something in it for you if we can arrange the details, a generous finder's fee or as much of one as I can talk out of the Bannisters. But now that I think about it... you asked me at the con about Madeleine Tyndale, an author I'd just barely heard of... and that got me interested in finding a copy of one of her books. I made some inquiries and it turned out that somebody I knew knew somebody who had a copy of *Love Against the Gods*. I borrowed it, read it — and I loved it! Maybe it was too much ahead of its time to be successful in the '30s, but today's readers would eat it up. I'd love to republish it in the Mature Classics line if I could find out something about Madeleine Tyndale, like where she is, to arrange the rights. Did you have any luck in locating her?"

"I sure did. I'm calling from her house and she's standing right here staring daggers at me because I'm running up her phone bill."

There was an audible gulp. "Put her on... please!"

Madeleine Tyndale lived into her 80s. Her books were reprinted and sold well, finding a new generation of readers. Once her newfound recognition enticed her out of her isolation, she became a great favorite at fantasy and science-fiction conventions where she delighted audiences with her wit and good humor in panel discussions. She also had the satisfaction of giving that ponytailed girl from America who had done so much for her a little boost by suggesting her as the perfect artist to illustrate the new printings of her books when the publisher decided the old 30's style Art Nouveau illustrations in the original editions were too outdated. "I never liked them anyway," she once admitted on a panel. (She remained puzzled, however, by Pam's cryptic remark: "Thank goodness you never wrote about naked sea nymphs!") Even Hollywood took an interest, though no movies ever actually resulted; still, the option money assured her of a comfortable old age.

She is gone now, but her books are still out there. Sooner or later, someone who wasn't even born when Madeleine was alive is going to find a copy of *Love Against the Gods* or *Challenge and Honour* and stay up all night reading it, and the oft-repeated and perhaps somewhat worn metaphor about letters to the future being delivered will be given new life once more.

Meanwhile, *Enquestador* became an instant classic as soon as it was published, and it remains in print to this day as one of the most remarkable fantasy novels ever written. Not only that, a forgotten artist named Bertram Tyndale finally got proper credit for his work some 65 years after the fact, thanks both to Linc Arthur's introduction recounting the book's long and strange path to publication and to the charming afterword Madeleine contributed in which she reminisced about her uncle as well as told of what the book had meant to her as a child.

Linc Arthur is gone now, too, and the one mystery remaining is what became of his reconstruction of *Enquestador*. The manuscript has been missing since the real novel turned up. In the fullness of time, the generation of fans that dismissed Linc Arthur as an unoriginal hack has been largely replaced by younger fans who simply appreciate a well-wrought tale, especially one that evokes the imagination and traditions of older works but is told in a lighter and more modern style with a wink or two between the lines. Now that the original version of *Enquestador* has long established itself as a modern classic every fantasy fan knows well, curiosity has grown about Linc Arthur's lost reconstruction, to see how another writer might have handled its themes and premises, and any of several publishers would be glad to take it on.

In what old trunk in what dusty attic is *that* manuscript mouldering?

There was one other far-reaching effect of all this. It started during that summer afternoon when Pam sat at a kitchen table reading *Enquestador*, and Madeleine read one of her favorite passages aloud—

*"I cannot give you a storybook wedding," Valdrick said. "We shall be married in the forest, not in the marble hall of a great temple. There will not be any musicians, nor will there be singers and dancers, no flower petals will be strewn along our path as we approach the high priest at the flaming altar, the sacred toast will not be drunk with consecrated wine in silver chalices, nor will your friends and family be in attendance in all their silken finery. We shall have to make do with just an old country priest to conduct the rite and with my men as our guests. I am sorry."*

*Rhishalla laughed gaily. "I think for the task at hand, one priest is all we need. Everything else is just unnecessary extravagance."*

*The wedding ceremony was held under the stars in a forest clearing lit by a hundred torches, witnessed by the small band of desperate fugitives who had joined the Duke's cause. Valdrick had said it would not be a storybook wedding — but it became one. For ten thousand years, for as long as the jeweled towers of old Atlantis still reared above the foaming waves, the wedding of Valdrick the Duke of Shadows and Rhishalla the Raven-Haired was the one told of in storybooks.*

"Is there something amiss?" Madeleine suddenly asked, noticing Pam was staring absently out the window.

"Oh no," Pam said, shaking her head. "I was just thinking of some-body I haven't seen in a while. Maybe it's about time to find out what he's up to..."

# THE GREATEST OF THEM ALL

From the story "Viper's Vengeance" in *Tales of Torment* #5 (1964). The competition between two downtown second-hand bookstores escalates into an outright riot. Art by John Stockman.

# THE GREATEST OF THEM ALL

**"Mule"**
(Possible Self-Caricature)

In the tiny, hopelessly obscure world of writers who have turned their attention to writing about fans, one forgotten man who was little known even in his own time stands out as the King of us all.

His name was John E. Stockman, nick-named "Mule," and he lived in Cincinnati, Ohio. Over a span of about 17 years, from approximately 1962 to 1979, he wrote a series of some two dozen astonishing and blisteringly funny stories about doomed fans, greedy collectors, and crooked dealers that are like nothing the world has seen before or since. Concentrating on his own little corner of collector-dom, isolated from the mainstream of science-fiction and comics fandoms, he created a consistent if somewhat dark and grimly humorous world in his tales.

The first few stories appeared in *Norb's Notes,* a fanzine devoted to the work of the author Edgar Rice Burroughs (*Tarzan, John Carter*), and published by one Charles Norbert Reinsel. Then Stockman came by a used mimeograph machine and published his stories himself in 16 issues of his own fanzine called *Tales of Torment* (and never was a fanzine more aptly named), with issue #1 dated Fall, 1963. In addition were four bonus sup-plements and an issue #3$^2$/$_3$ reprinting the continued story in issues #2 and #3.

For nearly two decades, John Stockman followed his unique vision, little changed at the end from what it was at the beginning. It was a remark-able achievement.

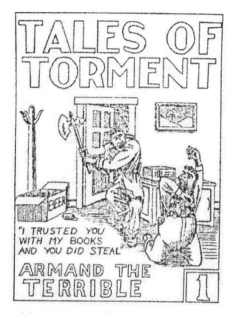

As much as anyone knows about him, Stockman was born in 1924 and died in 2008. He was a World War II veteran, referring to himself once as "the lard bucket who went through Germany squatting on his backside, in a halftrack" (*Tales of Torment* #10, 1969), and in his 40s when he was writing in the 1960s. Evidently a bachelor and living in a mobile home (his street address included "Lot 64"), he made a living at jobs like stock clerk and security guard, with a number of different collecting interests not untypical for a blue-collar man of his era who had grown up in the 1930s. In his stories, his ill-starred characters are variously shown to be interested in fantasy novels, comic books, guns, 78-rpm jazz records, Big Little Books, pulp magazines, and model railroading. Stockman himself was the product of an intersection of those collecting interests, with an emphasis on the works of Edgar Rice Burroughs.

For the Burroughs collector, the early '60s were an exciting time, with a new burst of interest in the grand old author's work and many of his old and out-of-print books being republished. Few other writers have inspired such a devoted following and his work continued to be in demand, giving rise to a collectors' market for his books. The fan and collector had plenty to work with, since Burroughs had a thirty-odd year career as a writer spanning the period from 1911 to the early 1940s, writing dozens of fantasy and adventure novels featuring Tarzan as well as adventures on other planets. There had also been any number of Tarzan movies, making the character well-known to the public and spawning a great amount of licensed merchandise, such as children's books, comic books, Sunday newspaper comic strips, toys, and much more.

Somewhat apart from the much larger and more comprehensive science-fiction fandom, Burroughs fans formed their own small fandom with organizations, dealers in collectibles, and fanzines like *Norb's Notes*. Somewhere in the mix we find a middle-aged fan named John Stockman shrewdly, cynically, and yet humorously observing the foibles of his fellow collectors. Burroughs inspired a number of imitators, and even more writers freely admitted to being influenced by his work, from Leigh Brackett to Ray Bradbury. None were quite like John Stockman, who didn't write fantasy novels like Burroughs', but instead wrote stories about people who *collected* Burroughs' fantasy novels. "Actually, it was during my collecting years that I dreamed up these ideas," he wrote in a 1975 letter to fan-publisher Rick Spanier, "(thanks to) my association with Norb and his zine and the (Burroughs collectors)."

Exactly how Stockman found his way to Burroughs and related fandoms is a little unclear, but there had been a large regional science-fiction convention (Midwescon) in Cincinnati in 1961, and the leading Burroughs fan group's annual meeting had been held in conjunction with it. Charles Reinsel of *Norb's Notes* was even one of the dinner speakers. Stockman's career in fandom began around that time, so it isn't hard to guess that he must have attended the convention since it was in town, and that it had impressed him enough to give him inspiration and material for years of stories. The scene in a 1964 story in which the main character is visited by a fan from out of town, with its odd capitalization and emphasis on *the* convention, suggesting that the author considered a certain specific convention to have been a major and memorable event, may have been based on that experience:

> *"Why, Buster, you old coot," Victor exclaimed on seeing a fan he'd met at the Science Fiction convention the year before.*

("The Crank," *Tales of Torment* #4, 1964)

One of Stockman's earliest stories was "The Meeting at Whartown," which appeared in *Norb's Notes* #15 (1962). The plot concerns dirty dealings at a small convention of Burroughs collectors, centering on the schemes of three collectors who are none of them exactly ethical, and leading to a climactic fistfight in the street in front of a second-hand bookstore. Only the quiet, reclusive little guy nobody pays much attention to comes out on top.

While the story stands up perfectly well on its own, it's evident that Stockman was ribbing *somebody* specific. In particular, the scene depicting the business meeting of the Burroughs collectors' club seems to be based on internal Burroughs fandom politics now lost on the modern reader. That Stockman was sending up real people and situations in the story was confirmed in another letter he wrote Spanier. After the story was published in *Norb's Notes*, one of the masters of Burroughs fandom "sent me a copy, he had received from Norb, back in shreds, so upset was this merchant over the profanities of 'Meeting at Whartown.'"

The story is immersed in the Burroughs collecting subculture, with some knowledge assumed of book titles, publishers, and editions, particularly what was rare and in demand by collectors and what was common and of little value. In a tour de force of inside Burroughs baseball, Stockman tells of one collector starting with some valuable books and through bad judgment trading steadily downward until he winds up with just cheap junk, documented every step of the way with examples that probably made old Burroughs collectors cringe.

Comic books are mentioned in "The Meeting at Whartown," but Stockman was enough older than most of the comics fans in 1962 that his interest in comic books was for the very early titles in the 1930s that reprinted Sunday newspaper comic strips, probably what he was reading in his own youth. He seemed to regard superheroes of the Superman type that first appeared in the late '30s as some sort of recent aberration the kids liked but too new and juvenile for him. Or for his characters, half of whom would kill for a copy of *Tarzan* (Single Series) #20, a 1940 comic book reprinting Sunday newspaper comic strips drawn by artist Hal Foster (who would be better known later for *Prince Valiant*). A turning point in "Whartown" comes when the victimized collector tries to console himself with the fact that he at least came out of the disaster with a copy of the much prized *Tarzan* #20 — only to look at it more closely and discover that it has pages missing.

Even when his characters are younger than Stockman would have been and are said to be collecting Golden Age superhero comic books of the 1940s or pre-Code EC comics of the 1950s like the more typical

"Got it"

comics fans of the day, as in the case of "The Return of Harry Orland," the older comic-strip reprint titles are still what they end up going after. The back cover drawing of *Tales of Torment* #8 (1967) shows Harry smiling and pointing triumphantly with one hand to a copy of *Tarzan* #20 in the other with the caption "Got it."

Old Man Teeverburg's sentiments are no doubt Stockman's own:

*The old man passed the time during these days of leisure by reading comic books. He was seen daily at the corner drugstore buying each issue he had not seen before. He remembered a long time ago, when he was much younger, when he bought comic books which were much different than the ones he was buying now. The old comics had reprints of Sunday comic pages in their contents. Oh, how he wished he could get those type of comic books now instead of the fabulous super hero epics he had to be content with at the newsstands.*

("Old Man Teeverburg," *Victor's Views* #1, 1964)

Adding to Stockman's uniqueness was his *style*. He was evidently self-taught and his writing had its technical lapses, particularly in punctuation, but the sheer force of his narrative was a tank shoving all grammatical obstacles aside. As he wrote in the editorial for *Tales of Torment* #7 (1966), "There is a story to be told and it is told by whatever means available." He learned as he went along, however, and his later stories show more polish.

And the *way* he wrote! It was a cheerfully mean-spirited Omniscient Narrator freely expressing his own opinions about the people and events he was describing, with a kind of gleeful sarcasm. Some readers have theorized that Stockman learned his writing technique from all those pulp magazines he must have read, but most pulp writers tended to get out of the way of the story they were telling. Stockman was right in there swinging. In "The Punk Commands" (*Tales of Torment* #6, 1965), for example, he variously referred to the story's fifteen-year-old protagonist as a punk and even a jerk. "There was never a thought in his putrid brain of helping his parents around the house, or of performing anything in the way of physical activity."

Or take his description of the mad fanzine editor:

*Victor was always something of a nut, but as time wore on he became even nuttier. He was slowly but surely driving his wife goofey too. She had all she could do to keep her wits. If Victor wasn't in their living room running off his fanzine he was darting about the house like a maniac hunting for some item he had put away but didn't know where.*

("The Crank," *Tales of Torment* #4, 1964)

As a sample of Stockman's prose at its peak, here is an excerpt from 1974, following a dozen years of practice and with some two dozen stories under his belt. Victor had returned after a decade, but he hadn't changed much—

*It was a pleasant day in early Spring. There was a slight chill in the air, and the night before a soft rain had fallen to give (the town of) Greyvine a fresh invigorating smell. Ah! It was good to be alive in Greyvine that day. However, at the house of Victor Karl Vackie,*

*problems had reared their ugly head to give the mighty editor a seri-*
*ous setback. His faithful ditto machine had broken down.*

*Victor snarled as he stepped back from the drum type duplicator.*
*How many thousands of pages had he run off on the machine? He did*
*not know. Surely the fanatical fan editor had run off over two hundred*
*editions of his fanzine. Day and night he had cranked away. Now,*
*after a long night, in the wee hours of the morning, the shaft had*
*broken in two, and all further activities had to be curtailed until*
*repairs were made.*

*"Gnnnnaaagggg!" Victor cried as he held his head in two*
*sweaty hands. "Am I to be forever victimized by worthless tools? Will*
*the incompetent swine ever put decent equipment on the market*
*again? God of Gods! Will you strike down the dogs who plotted*
*against me this night!"*

*There was no doubt about it. The mighty Victor was mad. He*
*whirled about, in his tracks, while retaining his hold on his head with*
*those two sweaty hands. He spun like a top for some moments,*
*uttering incoherent sounds, until finally he toppled over and fell to*
*the litter strewn carpet of the living room. There the great fan editor*
*lay for a period of some fifteen to twenty minutes before dragging*
*himself to his feet. He staggered much in the manner of a drunken*
*sot, while his body shook from a crazy giggling laugh. The laugh*
*increased until it became a madman's howl. Then Victor pulled him-*
*self to a second floor bedroom where he plopped exhausted across an*
*unkempt bed and fell asleep.*

("The Crackpot," *Tales of Torment* #14, 1974)

Over time, fans new to the zine may have complained in letters of
comment about Stockman's idiosyncratic punctuation and unique writing
style. *Tales of Torment* #13 (1973) includes a testy sounding note on the
contents page:

*Once again let me remind the readers that we are not engaged in*
*a spelling bee, nor are we entered in any contests on prose. Like the*
*grumpy old umpire at the ball game who calls 'em as he sees 'em — I*
*writes 'em as I sees 'em. J.E.S.*

Compounding the somewhat surreal effect, his characters had bizarre
names not quite resembling any you might find sported by real people in
mid-20th Century America. After Victor Vackie, Dirty Kyndt, Armand
Tooner, Dinky Belchinky, and Hinkus Gambol, a name like Gottlieb Snaplanger sounds almost normal. Some may be the burlesqued names of real
people he was lampooning, with their referents lost in the half-century
since. Many names seem distinctly Germanic, which may be only natural
for a German-settled town like Cincinnati and perhaps reflected his own

heritage (according to his funeral announcement, his mother's maiden name was Boehmer).

In the editorial portions of his fanzines, Stockman adopts a probably somewhat fictitious persona under his nickname "Mule," writing in the same mock-imperious tone as in his stories, and keeping his distance from the reader. He often refers to his band of oddly-named local cronies, and while some of them were likely flesh and blood, others may have been just pseudonyms for himself to keep the fanzine from looking too much like a one-man show. How many real people are covered by the term "Mule and his men" is difficult to say. The letter column in #12½ (1971) is supposedly administered by "Alf Clinghound," with Mule's doings and opinions described in third person, but it sounds like Stockman himself stepping out of character as Mule for a moment and for once speaking to the reader in something like his normal voice.

In that letter column, a reader commented:

*I can't help but think that all the loyal members of the band are fictitious. Nobody could have some of the names some of the guys have. Names like Alf Clinghound, Chats Gringle, and Checker Byhorn. Nobody could have names like that, could they? And noticing the characters in your stories have equally ridiculous names...*

To this, "Alf Clinghound" responded:

*And what about the names we use? What about the goofy names of all the staff members? Naturally these are real people. What did you think they were? Huh? Did you think they were a bunch of flakey collectors? Bah!*

Stockman was also his own artist. The illustrations in *Tales of Torment* are sometimes credited to "Tub Peevy," who was said to work for a free lunch, but Tub's alleged drawings are in the same style as Stockman's own. The covers and interior illustrations show that Mule was a capable cartoonist despite the limitations of the mimeograph format. The story "Viper's Vengeance" in *Tales of Torment* #5 (1964) featured several illustrations with Stockman at the top of his game, particularly a full-page scene of a riot at a downtown bookstore with scads of figures. An altercation in the serving line of a cafeteria is more subdued, but impressive just for the accurate perspective of things like railings. While Stockman's human figures are often grotesque caricatures, they *match* the stories in their own way, and are as competently rendered as they need to be. Stockman's drawings add to the fun rather than detract from it, and it's hard to imagine his publications without his artistic stylings.

For *Tales of Torment* #6 (1965), Stockman tried his hand at a comic strip, called "Big Nasty." In six pages and 23 panels, he told a simple story of an unpleasant book-collecting businessman who chances to discover

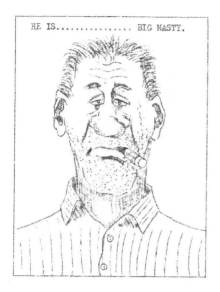

HE IS.............. BIG NASTY.

that two of his employees (named Nick Kidby and Kid Nickby) are also collectors (notably of Robert E. Howard of *Conan* fame in this case, rather than the usual Burroughs — a rare volume of *King Kull* is the object of desire in the story). He invites them to visit him at home and bring their most cherished collectibles to show him, but once there he tells them they will *give* those collectors' items to him outright or face immediate dismissal from their jobs. Since Nick Kidby and Kid Nickby were shown driving to Big Nasty's house with an idea of somehow cheating *him* in a trade deal, the reader's sympathies are a little torn, but surely there were laws against bosses extorting their own employees even then. It's one more story in which virtue not only doesn't triumph, it doesn't even seem to be anywhere in sight. In any event, the comic-strip idea wasn't repeated:

> *BIG NASTY has finally put in his appearance and I only hope none of my readers has to work for similar characters. Mighty as he is dirty, Nasty will get his way regardless. However, the tracing of the drawings on stencil... was something of an arduous task. It is quite possible we have seen the last of his ugly pan on these pages.*

As it was Big Nasty's only appearance, Stockman was right about that.

The circulation of *Tales of Torment* was probably not very large, perhaps never more than a hundred or so copies of a given issue if even that many. At one point, a first edition of fifty copies of an issue with the possibility of going back to press for more is spoken of; in later issues, the editorial sections talk about destroying stencils just to make room rather than bother with reprinting older issues. By issue #14, the only back issues listed as available are #1 ("Expand your storehouse of crap by adding this valuable edition before the stock dwindles and vanishes") and #13. Stockman even stated that he preferred to keep the operation small in "Alf Clinghound's" answer to a reader's letter:

> *Usually we do not advertise in other zines simply because we're not looking for more subscribers in bulk form. That is, if someone wants to subscribe to our zine, we will naturally accept his money*

*and mail him the issues he has contracted for, but we are not inter-
ested in having large lots of subscribers. It is hard enough for Mule
to get out the editions he does in the quantities needed. It is too much
trouble running off mountainous stacks of back copies and big piles
of current editions. Mule does not want to do this... We do not have
the storage space nor the time to fool around with mailing lists much
larger than the one we are using.*
(*Tales of Torment* 12½, 1971)

Instead, Stockman was probably publishing for his own amusement
and that of a few friends who would get the jokes, and judging by the tone
of the comment above, he was surprised when a few fans outside his circle
began to notice his publications and take a puzzled but appreciative interest in them.

Today, copies of *Tales of Torment* are rare and command high prices
on eBay when they turn up. They may even be worth more than some of
the Burroughs books, pulp magazines, comics, and other collectibles so
many of Stockman's characters committed mayhem to get their hands on,
which is irony of a sort.

## The Works

In discussing Stockman's stories, I will give away the endings of
some of them. This is unavoidable with Stockman's intricate plotting and
his "you can't win" philosophy carried out to its inevitable conclusion.
Since the stories are hidden away in publications forty to fifty years old,
never had much circulation to begin with, and are probably unobtainable
for most readers of this book, the chances are slim that you will ever be
able to read them anyway, so spoiling the endings hardly matters. Besides,
even if the stories are eventually reprinted, you will have forgotten what
you read here by then.

Stockman's world is a milieu of medium-sized Midwestern American
cities, downtown cafeterias, and seedy side-street second-hand bookstores.
It was all probably a reflection of Cincinnati where he lived and he was
writing what he knew, but the settings resonated with me when I spent my
college years near Toledo and hung out with the local fans.

For that matter, college doesn't figure in Stockman's world. His characters seem lucky to have gotten out of high school alive, they apparently
still live in the same towns where they grew up, and when employed at all
they work at marginal blue-collar jobs or in low-level retail positions:

*Victor Vackie, a rug salesman in a local department store, was
also a widely known fan of comics, fantasy fiction, and monster
motion pictures.*
("The Crank," *Tales of Torment* #4, 1964)

For all the pulp magazines Stockman must have read in his youth, the one standard pulp plot he didn't use was boy meets girl. There are no hints of romance in his stories. The only acknowledgement biology even exists appears in the story "Viper's Vengeance" (*Tales of Torment* #5, 1964), in the description of what a character named Dinky Belchinky buys on his regular visits to a bookstore and newsstand:

*It was also the custom of Belchinky to buy up a supply of Purney's "Girlie" magazines to gloat over while he wasn't occupied with comic books or pulp magazines.*

Young male characters tend to be single, while older characters have either never married at all (Old Man Teeverburg was said to have been still living with his parents at the age of 45) or they have long since been married but seldom happily. Women are few in Stockman's stories, mostly seen as the wives of the main characters, ranging from simply uncomprehending of their husbands' hobbies to downright disapproving. "My old lady just ain't sympathetic to the cause," complains a model railroader in "The Schemer" (*Tales of Torment* #11, 1969). "She thinks it's silly for grown men to be playing with kids' toys."

Perhaps the oddest marriage was that of the main character in "Today I Steal," an early story from about 1962: his wife was described as a "smart young hide" ("hide" = Stockmanese for "wife") with a career of her own and their relationship that of roommates who mostly went their separate ways. It's such a contrast to the more typical 1962-era stereotype of bickering blue-collar spouses in Stockman's stories — and so unnecessary, as the wife is only briefly seen on stage and the protagonist might as well not be married at all — that one wonders if Stockman had some real-life example in mind.

Then there was "The Tragic Case of Harry Orland" (originally published in 1962 in *Norb's Notes* and reprinted in *Tales of Torment* #12½ in 1971). Harry was 27, a stock clerk in a local store, married, and the father of two. He also had overbearing in-laws to contend with.

*(His wife Erma) had a hard time of it, trying to make ends meet. Feeding the two house apes, clothing them, putting food on the table was enough. Then she had to watch her own needs plus those of Harry. This was doubly hard when Harry only made $35.00 a week and $25.00 of this sum went for comic books.*

*You may ask how the rent was paid? How could a family possibly live on $35.00 a week when $25.00 went for comic books. As a matter of fact they could not do it. Erma had to run home to mama more often than not and beg for money.*

*"Why don't you leave that louse!" her dad, Heinrich, would howl.*

But Erma sticks with Harry despite his shabby treatment of her as his collecting mania consumes him. She even waits for his return during the four long years he spends in an insane asylum. That four-year period seems to be Stockman accounting for the real-time gap between the first story that appeared in 1962 and its sequel, "The Return of Harry Orland," published in *Tales of Torment* #8 (1967). Four *months* in the "home" might have been more credible, as Erma hasn't long since divorced him under pressure from her father while his brother-in-law has arranged for him to get his old job at the department store back. Now that he's out of the asylum and declared cured, Harry just has to stay off the comic books. But like a recovering alcoholic who falls off the wagon, his fever to collect old comic books sets in again and the game is once more afoot. Even after a new round of complications, however, Erma is still with him at the end.

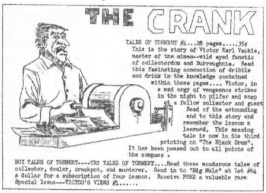

First appearing in the story "The Crank," (*Tales of Torment* #4, 1964), Stockman had a running character in Victor Vackie, a crazed fanzine publisher who turned out endless issues of a near-worthless publication called *Victor's Views*. The name's similarity to *Norb's Notes* seems hardly coincidental, but whether this is the visible tip of an actual fan feud, a hint of something else that is now forgotten, or just Stockman's whimsy, is lost to the ages. Stockman describes *Victor's Views* as an erratic, almost unreadable, badly printed, bleary purple mess printing amateurish art and whatever else the readers contributed for free at the publisher's begging. Without too much exaggeration, the description could fit copies of *Norb's Notes* I've seen. Stockman even published two simulated issues of *Victor's Views* as free bonuses for the readers, but they are far more readable than the genuine article supposedly was.

As the madness of publishing fanzines takes over his life, Victor Vackie treats his wife ever more badly. One scene stops just short of outright spousal abuse and is difficult to read now. When the story's crisis comes to a head, Victor literally trades Mrs. Vackie to another collector for a stack of pulp magazines. As the story is told, the outcome is a little more plausibly developed than it might sound stated so bluntly, and Mrs. Vackie was willing and even glad to leave Victor for someone who was kind and appreciated her. Still, even with the elaborations, Victor's ill-repute as the man who traded his wife for pulp magazines was fixed for all time.

A typical issue of *Tales of Torment* ran about thirty pages, sometimes more, with a single story as the main feature and several pages given over to editorial and other features. With #10 (1969), Stockman pulled out all stops and published a 100+-page issue described as a "weighty volume of sacred collector's lore," most of it taken up by what amounts to a short novel called "The Path of Greed." This may be Stockman's magnum opus, both for length and for including so many of his favorite themes in one story. It begins with a young collector named Herman Slanter visiting dealer Jacob Greedon, who is also the master of Burroughs fandom and related interests. In fact, Greedon publishes a fanzine called *Master's Memos*. During his visit, Slanter arranges a trade deal for some vintage *Flash Gordon* Sunday newspaper comic pages in exchange for his relatively valuable books and comics, then waits at home for weeks before Greedon finally mails the goods to him. Slanter excitedly opens the package at long last and finds—

*THE UGLIEST MESS HE HAD EVER HAD THE MISFORTUNE TO GAZE UPON!*

*The very first Flash Gordon page, which Herman pulled off the top of the stack, was so full of holes that it gave the appearance that someone had blasted it with both barrels of a ten gauge shotgun. The worst was yet to come.*

Slanter realizes he has traded his valuable books and comics for outright junk, but the mighty dealer refuses to make good, saying a deal's a deal and besides, he's already sold what Slanter traded him. Greedon doesn't realize it, but he has just signed his own death warrant with those words, as Slanter embarks on a fiendish revenge that will indirectly leave the dealer "under the sod," as Stockman put it.

The story also features one of Stockman's few prominent and well-defined female personages, Maggie Greedon, the crooked dealer's wife and partner in his dubious doings. She is definitely not a nice person: Herman Slanter first meets her on the occasion of his visit to the Greedon house, and she is described as "hard looking," with "glaring eyes" when she answers the door. "'What do you want?' she snapped. 'We're busy around here! Can't be fooling with peddlers!'"

Soon after that, she is shown ordering one of the Toylet boys around. (That is, Jacob Greedon has two brothers named Tommy and Danny Toylet working as virtual slaves for him. It seems like an uncharacteristically unseemly joke for Stockman, who had avoided overt crudeness in his stories up to this point.)

*She was snapping orders at him so fast that Herman wondered
if he understood what was being asked.*

*"Get that stuff ready for mailing!" she cracked. "Let's get some
of these orders ready today. People will be wondering where the
goods are. We're behind now. Come on — move!"*

Maggie, however, has no particular interest in what her husband sells.
For her, it's just a way to make a living. At the end of the story, with Jacob
dead, the Toylet brothers hope Maggie will take over the business and
things will go on as before, but instead she coldly tells them to move out
and get "man's jobs" because they're "finished here!"

*"Listen, you boobs! I'm fed up to here with this dump! What I'm
going to do is sell this whole mess, house and all. The whole collection of magazines, precious collector crap, books, the printing press,
and every lousy, phony piece of garbage Jake accumulated through
the years — all goes! Then with the dough I'm going to take a trip to
Florida and squat there on my backside! Now! What do you two bloggon heads think of that?"*

I'll tell you what those two bloggon heads thought of that. Jacob
Greedon treated them like slaves, exploiting them as all but free labor for
the price of a little space for their cots and what little food they could grab
at dinner time before Jake snatched it all, but they loved serving the great
master of fandom and have nowhere else to go and no marketable skills
for getting real jobs. The argument goes on for several more pages, with
Maggie growing ever more sneering and insulting, and it ends with the
outraged Toylet brothers going berserk and beating her to death — just as
the cops walk in to follow up their investigation of the recent robbery by
Herman Slanter. The problem of where the Toylet boys are going to go is
subsequently solved by a judge and jury.

As usual, no one comes out of the story at all well, least of all Herman
Slanter, except for a rival dealer who buys the Greedon collection from
Maggie's next of kin. That dealer is even now cataloguing the vast col-
lection before putting it on the market, so fans are advised to be patient.
"But, brother, you can be sure there will be no patience with the prices he
intends charging."

About the only story in the known works with anything like a heroic
main character was "Gunfight at Hambol's Junkyard" (*Tales of Torment*
#7, 1966), which centers on a gun club that rents a farmer's land for a day
of target shooting in the country. The competition turns deadly serious as
long-simmering conflicts among the various members boil to the surface
and everything ends in a bloody massacre. Nearly the lone survivor, the
hero realizes it's time to be moving on to the next town before the authorities arrive and ask difficult questions, and even he isn't so noble that he

doesn't stoop to emptying the wallets of some of the dead club members for a stake before lighting out.

As a change of pace from the usual woes of cheated collectors, "Death at Weaselville" (*Tales of Torment* #12, 1970) starts out pleasantly enough. When old Gottlieb Snaplanger reaches retirement age, he is finally able to do what he always wanted but never could before: be a writer of wonderful fantasy stories in the Tolkien vein. Settling in a little house in a small town, Snaplanger proceeds to spend his evenings writing about elves and fairies. Soon, harsh reality sets in. He probably started too late as a writer, and his books are flops. Worse, the townspeople, formerly so friendly to him when he first moved there, are now cold or actually hostile for no apparent reason. Between mounting frustration over his failure as a writer and the townspeople being outright vicious to him, Snaplanger finally, er, snaps, and lashes out in a Rambo-like revenge that ends with himself and many of his tormentors dead and the town pretty much burned down.

Only then it comes out that when the townsfolk learned he was writing novels, they automatically assumed that he must be writing a *Peyton Place* type of exposé about them and the town's seamy underside that would reveal everyone's dirty laundry to the entire country if published, so they were trying to run him out before any beans were spilled. (How they thought a stranger new to the town who keeps to himself would even find out about the local closeted skeletons is explained rather weakly by the professed fear that he would maliciously write outright lies to defame the good citizens.) That Snaplanger might be writing silly and harmless elf and fairy fantasies instead never occurred to anyone.

Fortunately, most of Stockman's stories didn't end in mass slaughter like these last two (though some fatalities were not unknown in others), but happy endings were still rare, if any of his stories even had one. The only example may be "Old Man Teeverburg," which isn't so much a story as a vignette describing the title character's retirement made blissful by reacquiring the old comic books he had loved in years past. More typically, the cheating dealer got the better of the honest collector, or taking it to the next level of plot permutation, a not so honest collector trying to stiff a cheating dealer came out on the short end anyway.

> *So this story ends. Harry Orland, the comic book collector, went to his reward in the booby hatch while Jakturpott, the sneaky dealer, reaped the rewards of the poor sap's collection. So it shall end. A dealer richer by all our efforts.*

("The Tragic Case of Harry Orland")

One such story told of a club of model railroaders who need a place in which to build the miniature empire of their dreams ("The Schemer," *Tales of Torment* #11, 1969). A certain shady character with the odd but fitting name of Dirty Kyndt offers them the empty attic in his house at no charge, the answer to their prayers, and even supplies free coffee and sandwiches over the next year as they build the greatest and most magnificent model railroad layout ever. But when it's completed and they can finally run their trains on it, they find the room empty and the layout gone. It turns out that Dirty wasn't so altruistic with the free room and the free snacks after all, and uses them as justification to claim ownership of the model layout and sell it, pocketing the money, with, of course, the club members out the year of their time spent building it and all the money they spent on modeling supplies and equipment. Dirty gets his comeuppance in the end and the honest model railroaders get some satisfaction, but no one finishes out the story very happily.

Issue #14 was published in 1974 and featured the return of Victor Vackie. Time had moved on, however, and the story seemed to reflect the *Norb's Notes* era of fandom of some ten or more years before. Issue #14 also had an announcement of #15 to follow in due course:

> *Working in virtual bondage, a flunky to the Spedler family, operators of a clothing store, is the Monster mag and film fan, Belter Haskett. Here he plays a lone hand in attempting to even scores with his employers while fighting off his obnoxious and domineering father, Bolter Haskett, and parrying off the none too bright intrusions to his domain by his brother, Bilker Haskett. Here is a story relating to the woeful life of another collector who drives on in a never ending search for additional trash to add to already bulging chests of junk. Do not forget to order, read, and treasure the forthcoming edition...*
> THE FLUNKY, *coming soon in* Tales of Torment #15.

"Soon," however, turned out to be three years, as #15 was not published until 1977. By then, much had changed. Stockman had moved out of the trailer at Lot 64 and into a house (dubbed "Mulewood"), and had apparently taken on some debt to do it. He speaks in the editorial of having to hold two jobs to increase the flow of shekels into the fold, cutting down on the time he could devote to the fanzine. Stockman's moonlighting as a security guard did pay off in other ways than just additional income, as one of the plot points of "The Flunky" involves a deception anyone who has ever been a security guard having to make regular rounds with a certain clock-like device in hand will appreciate.

If Stockman had largely avoided crudity in his stories up to this point, he lost all his inhibitions in "The Flunky" when the main character gets his revenge on his employers by spiking their food with a violent purgative, and the spectacular results are described in detail. Whether it was a new direction in Stockman's evolution as a writer or simply a sign of a growing weariness with recounting the trials and tribulations of collectors is hard to say, but the story was mostly concerned with the protagonist's mundane job-related problems and its connection with more fannish pursuits was secondary at best.

The 16th and final issue, featuring a story called "Foul Play" and dealing with the theft of a collection of Big Little Books, was another two years after that, reaching whatever remained of the mailing list in the spring of 1979. The long gaps between issues suggest that Stockman's interest was fading. He would have been about 55 in 1979 and had been writing stories for 17 years. Simple weariness of the whole thing would have been understandable. Stockman had told Rick Spanier in a letter as far back as 1975 that "I don't write as much as I used to. I suppose this is because I'm not as interested as when I first started to collect various objects of interest."

Even so, announcements in the zine indicate that he had plans for further issues through at least #18, with a possible third Victor Vackie story beyond even that. But whether due to lack of time or loss of interest, issue #16 was when he hung up his spurs.

In the last letter Spanier received from him, dated June, 1981, Stockman said: "I doubt if I run off any more editions of *Tales of Torment*." After that, the rest is silence, although Stockman lived another 27 years.

Stockman never had a chance of publishing his fan-oriented stories professionally. Innocent of formal writing technique, he invented his own literary style, which would have left most English teachers aghast. He wrote for the tiniest of audiences, perhaps a few friends at most, and probably mainly to amuse himself. His stories were limited to the minuscule world of fans and collectors, and beyond that to the even smaller corner of it he was most familiar with. Almost all of the general public would find his stories incomprehensible, and perhaps that was what he was getting at with the townspeople in "Death at Weaselville" being so ignorant of genre fiction that they automatically assumed a writer must be writing some tawdry mass-market would-be best-seller. And yet...

In the realm of amateur and aspiring writers, it's hard enough for many wannabe authors just to finish one story, but Mule polished off at least two dozen complete and intricately plotted tales of torment. In their own unique way and in their own unique world, not a few of those stories are comic masterpieces. What kept him going year after year, writing story after story that few people would ever read? An irresistible urge to express himself? A cockeyed sense of humor inspiring him to satirize his specialized collecting hobbies? Whatever it was, there was never anyone like John Stockman and never any stories like his. In the little world of fanfiction writers who wrote stories about fans, no one has ever matched him for volume, persistence, consistency, and faithfulness to his personal vision. For that achievement, little noticed by the larger world and now almost forgotten, I honor him here as the greatest of us all.

So what became of John Stockman, anyway?

Even in his forties, Stockman must have had eventual old age and retirement on his mind, as he presents two different idyllic visions of old men happily whiling away their golden years. The evening routine of Gottlieb Snaplanger in his country cottage is described in loving detail as he takes a break from writing wonderful stories to sit down for a snack of hot chocolate and cookies. If it weren't for the fact that it all goes terribly wrong and the story ends in fire and slaughter, it sounds like the retirement I would like to have.

Then there's the vision of Old Man Teeverburg:

*Now the old man sits in his favorite leather chair with a stack of old funnybooks by his side, as he sips his hot chocolate and reads away the time. Such is the retirement of "Old Man" Teeverburg.*

It's how I would like to think John Stockman ended his days.

# Acknowledgements

Rick Spanier for invaluable research assistance and permission to quote from his correspondence with John Stockman.

Bill Schelly for a copy of *Tales of Torment* #15 and general encouragement. Schelly's reprint of Stockman's story "Armand the Terrible" from *Tales of Torment* #1 (1963) in the now out-of-print anthology *The Comic Fandom Reader* (Hamster Press, 2002) may be the most readily obtainable of any of Mule's tales at present.

# A SHORT HISTORY OF COMIC BOOKS AND COMICS FANDOM

RBCC #54 (late 1967).
Art by Wallace Wood.

**W**hat exactly *is* a "fandom," anyway?

In its broadest sense, it might be the collectivity of all the fans of something, from people with just a casual interest in whatever it is to the fanatical devotees whose entire life revolves around their object of adoration. But as the term evolved, a fandom became a more or less organized community of people with a common interest, who by and large knew each other and did something more with their interest than just privately and anonymously collecting or otherwise appreciating it.

With science fiction and comic books, the distinguishing characteristic of their fandoms in the 20th Century was the fanzine: an amateur magazine published by fans to exchange news and information about their interests not covered in the commercial press, and often just to communicate with like-minded friends and acquaintances. The most concise definition of a fan active in fandom might be someone who got fanzines, since you had to be at least somewhat in the loop to even hear about them.

Science-fiction fandom dates back at least to the early '30s, emerging from letters printed in the letter columns of professional magazines and efforts to start fan clubs. Fans got in touch with each other, which led to fanzines circulated among the growing community, then conventions, and a whole subculture with its own traditions and jargon bloomed.

Comics fandom derived in part from science-fiction fandom, but it had a long gestation. The creators of Superman, Jerry Siegel and Joe Shuster, got their start as teenagers publishing a mimeographed science-fiction fanzine. The appearance of Superman as a comic-book character in 1938 led to a swarm of imitators from various publishers. There were many other genres of titles and characters published as well, but the novelty of the superhero concept along with the fervor of the World War II era helped put comic books on the map as a form of mass entertainment. After the war, times changed and most of the superheroes died away as the 40s wore on, and comic books moved on to other genres, with funny animal, teenage humor, western, romance, horror, and crime comics popular into the '50s.

Comics fandom came together in the early '60s, just as a new generation of superheroes was starting to appear in comic books. On the one hand were collectors who had never been part of science-fiction fandom and were solely interested in comic books, mostly young men who had been boys during World War II and remembered the wartime superheroes with nostalgic fondness. On the other hand were science-fiction fans with experience in the older and more evolved science-fiction fandom, dabbling in comic books as a side interest.

The science-fiction fans brought with them their traditions and terminology, particularly with fanzine publishing, to the point that comics fandom was often perceived as an offshoot of science-fiction fandom, even serving as a sort of junior auxiliary to it. There was in fact considerable overlap, as comics fans usually had some interest in science fiction, but over time the older comics fans with roots in science-fiction fandom were vastly outnumbered by new comics fans coming in as teenagers, and the two fandoms pretty much went their own ways.

Way back when, comic books had an utterly terrible public image, which persists to some extent even yet. There was prejudice against the very *idea* of telling a story through pictures, which supposedly contributed to illiteracy. (These days, I've run into English teachers who've experimented with using comics as a way to get their students to read *something — anything*.) In the popular mind, comic books were cheap, shoddy, and anonymous, the dregs of the publishing industry, produced by sleazy, fly-by-night publishers barely above the level of racketeers and con-men. If they could be justified at all, comic books were cheap entertainment for children, and anyone who still read them after about age 12 was probably a mental defective who didn't like to read real books because his lips got tired.

Those first few fans and collectors who founded comics fandom, however, included a college professor, an English teacher, and a newspaper reporter. They had grown up with comic books and regarded them with fond memories, not as a threat or menace. Then, as the '60s wore on, Marvel Comics found a formula that appealed to somewhat older readers, perhaps because editor/writer Stan Lee was just tired of the old lead up to a twist ending in six pages straitjacket sort of story that had always been done before and decided to have some fun with the thing. His humor and enthusiasm were infectious, and brought in teenaged readers who realized that something was *happening* at Marvel. Something in the combination of fantasy and imagination, art and story, had an appeal beyond just the mind-rotting cheap thrills assumed by disapproving parents and teachers. The literacy level of '60s fanzines was surprisingly high even when they were produced by kids barely into their teens, and impressed even as biased a critic as Dr. Wertham (who seemed to have forgotten about that astonishing and thoroughly unjustified slur in his 1966 book *A Sign for Cain* claiming that the readers of comic books of yore had turned into child-abusing parents). The Marvel fans of my own generation pretty much turned out all right, with an inordinate number of lawyers (among them a couple of judges), newspaper reporters and editors, and creative types like writers and artists.

The history of comic-book collecting has been one of expanding horizons, as collectors have moved out of the strictly superhero-centric preferences of fandom's founders. A look at 1967-era fanzines will in fact show ads offering non-superhero comics, though the heroes were still the main interest for most fans back then. Almost anything ever published will eventually be of some interest to somebody, given enough time.

As fans and collectors realized, comic books had been produced by artists and writers who usually had a craftsmanship ethic despite the often low pay and poor working conditions. Real people with names had made comic books, people who could be identified and appreciated. There was mediocrity, to be sure, even downright sleaze, but there were also gems to be found. Even the run of the mill comics had their charms, whether as often quirky artifacts of their times or simply interesting collectibles.

The mythical little old lady with piles of old comic books in her attic (and unaware of how much they were worth) was already something of a cliché in the mid-'60s, but there was considerable truth to it. Comic books were not seriously collected by very many people until the early '60s, and were mostly considered disposable by most of their readers and not worth saving. Second-hand bookstores that sold old comics at some cheap price like two for a nickel were not unknown, but the customers were probably just casual readers looking for something more to read without much thought of keeping it for a collection's sake. Comic-book publishers even sold advertising with rates based on the assumed "pass along" readership, the idea being that a single comic book could be read by as many as eight or so individuals as kids traded them. In his 1954 book *Seduction of the Innocent*, the ferocious comic-book critic Dr. Wertham mocked even the thought that anyone would even think to save old comic books as cherished mementoes of childhood.

Some people actually did, though. Perhaps not as systematic collections but simply as accumulations of comics casually bought and read over the years, tucked away somewhere along with other favorite childhood memorabilia, and never sold or given away. As newspaper articles appeared about how much old comic books were worth to collectors, a number of accumulations came out of the attics where they had been for twenty or more years. Probably just about all of the hidden hoards of old comic books were found long ago, if only because the newspaper articles made it too well known that people were sitting on top of gold mines if they did have a stash of vintage comic books in an old trunk, but there have been some surprise discoveries in relatively recent years. In 1967, the Golden Age of comic books had been less than thirty years before, and the hunt was still on for the fabulous hoards of treasure that just had to be out there in who knew what attics.

Once you started collecting, you didn't have to go looking for fandom — it found you. It was fairly easy to have a letter published in a comic-book letter column, and many letter columns printed the writers' complete addresses. Have a letter published and it wouldn't be long before you started receiving back-issue comic-book dealers' lists and sample fanzines.

Besides allowing fans to contact each other for buying and selling old comic books, passing along news, or just plain friendship, fanzines published information that no one had bothered to put into print before. In the world at large, comic books had never been taken seriously. Fans and collectors had a major task in the early days of comics fandom just determining what had been published over the previous quarter-century that hardly anyone had ever paid attention to. Unlike today, there were no books about the history of comic books, no reprint volumes. Jules Feiffer's *The Great Comic Book Heroes* in 1965 was a major breakthrough since it had been written by an industry insider and included reprints of actual vintage stories. Otherwise, the history of comic books had to be compiled by a legion of collectors working from their own collections and laboriously listing titles, publishers, and artists, then publishing their findings in fanzines.

Fanzines also presented fans' more creative efforts like opinion columns, amateur artwork, comic strips, and fiction. More than a few amateur artists and writers got their start in fanzines and went on to professional careers in comics or other fields, Stephen King being one famous example.

For a lot of new fans, you didn't have to be in fandom and reading other people's fanzines very long before you wanted to get in on the fun of publishing a fanzine yourself. In the days before cheap photocopying, there were only two economical home or office printing methods for producing a fanzine: ditto and mimeograph.

"Ditto" was a brand name that had become generic for a duplication process that involved typing on carbon-backed masters, which were then used to print with an alcohol-based solvent called ditto fluid that lent the freshly printed pages a distinctive odor. People of a certain age will remember that tests in school were often printed that way, and it was almost a ritual to give a test paper a good sniff when it was handed out.

Ditto masters came in several colors, but purple was most often used for typing text because it was the strongest color and produced the most copies; black masters faded to faint gray in short order. Since it was easy to draw on ditto masters, ditto printing was often used for artwork, and interesting color effects were possible by combining masters of various shades. Drawbacks were the sheer messiness of the process, bleary and washed-out printing, and an upper copy limit of maybe 300 for purple and often much less for other colors. Making corrections to typewriter text was another headache: you had to scrape the mistake off the back of the master with a razor blade, which inevitably scattered crumbs of colored carbon that stained everything they touched a livid purple. I ruined a couple of desktops that way... Ditto printing could also fade over time, though ditto fanzines that were well printed to begin with forty or more years ago are often still readable today (unfortunately for some of us).

The competing printing method was mimeograph, which worked by squeezing ink through typed stencils. Mimeo was rated better for text and a stencil could print as many copies as anyone would likely want, but it was troublesome for art, as lines had to be carved into the stencil with a stylus.

More upscale fanzines went to photo-offset, professional printing offered by your friendly neighborhood quick-print shop, with pages shot directly from your camera-ready copy. The expense of photo-offset printing for entire fanzines was relatively enormous, though many fanzines compromised by having photo-offset covers so that better-quality artwork could be reproduced well, with the interior pages produced by the usual mimeo or ditto.

The real problem in all this was illustrating articles about old comic books, with direct reproduction of the printed pages next to impossible for the usual home printing methods and bad tracings often the only recourse. Many fanzines relied on cartoons and "spot illos," random drawings of superheroes or fantasy motifs contributed by aspiring artists wanting to showcase their work, not related to the written content on a given page but there to add a little visual relief to the columns of typewriter text.

With the passage of time, photocopying has come to equal the quality of photo-offset printing, memories have faded, and people have forgotten or never knew about now virtually extinct ditto and mimeograph. I have actually seen those aromatic school tests referred to as "purple mimeo," which is badly confused. Fanzines are still being published even yet, produced on computers rather than typewriters and technically better than ever with professional-looking type and justified margins, and gray tones and even color possible for illustrations and photographs, but the Internet has largely taken their place for communication between fans.

There was a very strange sequel to the Fanzine Era. In 1954, an era when juvenile delinquency was a hot topic, the aforementioned psychiatrist Dr. Wertham attempted to show in his sensationalistic book *Seduction of the Innocent* that crime and horror comics led to bad behavior by young readers. As one of the very few books ever written about comic books at the time, *Seduction* was well known to fans of the '60s and Dr. Wertham was everyone's favorite bogeyman, the mean ol' man who wanted to take your comic books away. When Dr. Wertham came into contact with comics fans in the late '60s (among them your humble servant), he was enough charmed by fans and their fanzines that he wrote a puzzled but approving book about them called *The World of Fanzines* (1973). He didn't seem to understand that comics fanzines were basically an internal hobby press for comic-book collectors, and thought they were a spontaneously generated peaceful and non-violent communication medium for gifted teenagers who for some unaccountable reason talked about comic books a lot. Few books have more hopelessly misunderstood the subject they were supposed to be about.

Three of the stories in this book take place in 1967. At the time, comics fandom was thought to number about 2000 active fans, more or less identical with the subscription list for the leading fanzine, the *Rocket's Blast/Comicollector*, or the *RBCC* for short. (The odd name was the result of the merger of two earlier fanzines.) The *RBCC* was a thick, professsionally printed and bound bimonthly magazine that mostly ran advertising. The ads were composed and typed by the advertisers themselves, then pasted up on the page layout by the editor and printed, leading to an interior graphics disaster area, but the homemade quality was somehow part of the charm. It was *the* place to advertise old comic books, and some idea of the going prices for various issues of which titles at the time in the days before a quasi-official price guide standardized everything can be gleaned by looking at the various dealers' ads.

In not too many years, the venerable *RBCC* would be gone, outcompeted for the advertising dollar by *The Buyer's Guide for Comics Fandom*, a weekly tabloid newspaper that would endure for many more years until it in turn was rendered obsolete by the Internet and eBay.

In 1967, however, the *RBCC* pretty much *was* comics fandom, and one of the best things about it was that it was where all the other fanzines were advertised. A subscription to the *RBCC* was a bimonthly visit to the Land of Fandom where all your buddies hung out.

These days, your fellow comic-fan buddies may be hanging out on Facebook or holding forth in other on-line forums, but only the means of communication has changed. The spirit of the old comics fandom depicted in the stories in this book is alive and well even yet.

# Comic Book History in Brief

**Mid-1930s:** Modern comic books in familiar format emerge, mostly reprinting Sunday newspaper comic strips at first, later introducing original stories.

**1938:** Superman appears in *Action Comics* #1, inspiring a wave of imitations.

**Late 1930s to mid-1940s:** The "Golden Age" of superhero comic books, with literally hundreds of colorfully costumed Superman-type characters in addition to other genres. Few of the superdupers have Superman's staying power, however, and the fad comes to an end like any other.

**Mid-1940s to mid-1950s:** Few superhero comic books published, other genres (crime, horror, romance, funny animal, teenage humor, etc.) reign supreme.

**Early to mid-'50s:** Profusion of gory horror comic books and explicit crime comics lead to public backlash. Actual comic-book burnings in some places, Senate hearings held to determine among other things whether bad comic books lead to juvenile delinquency.

**1954:** Publication of alarmist book *Seduction of the Innocent* by psychiatrist Dr. Fredric Wertham, purporting to expose vile content of comic books and their baleful effect on children's minds. Overwrought and exaggerated, even deceptive, but not entirely wrong, either. Remembered long afterwards in the '60s by comics fans, with Dr. Wertham becoming symbolic of comics-hating authority figures.

**1955:** Panic-stricken by public outrage and possibility of government intervention if not censorship down the line, comic-book publishers band together to establish the Comics Code Authority, an independent body to review comic-book contents before publication to make sure they are non-violent and non-gory. Code-approved comic books with their distinctive postage-stamp like seal in the upper right-hand corner of the cover dominate newsstands for decades to come. The Code has been accused of making comic books a perpetually juvenile medium and choking the development of more adult comic books, but it probably saved the industry.

**Mid-'50s – late '50s:** Comic books flounder, many companies go out of business. The horror comics brouhaha, the adoption of the Comics Code, television becoming widespread, and the collapse of a major magazine distributor all have their effects.

**Circa 1960:** Superheroes start being revived as publishers look for something that will sell. DC Comics, publisher of famous WWII-era superheroes like Superman, Batman, and Wonder Woman, is prominent at first. The Silver Age begins, although it wasn't called that until much later.

**Circa 1961:** Organized comics fandom takes shape as fans find each other and publish fanzines. Most fans are young men who remember the WWII-era superhero comic books of their childhood. Early comics fandom collects Golden Age superheroes and little else, and even current comics are regarded somewhat dubiously as pale imitations of the greatness of the Forties.

**Early to mid-1960s:** Prices of Golden Age comic books in the collectors' market increase beyond the reach of younger fans. Newspaper articles about fabulous prices paid for old comics appear. Comics fandom grows, but new blood is heavily teenage Marvel Comics fans. Up to then a small-time publisher of mostly monster and "mystery" comics (i.e., what was left of horror comics after the Code), Marvel is finding its footing with new and original superheroes like Spider-Man and the Fantastic Four and revivals of its old '40s characters like Captain America. Marvel's output attracts a somewhat older audience, past the age when most comic-book readers had formerly given up reading them, and articles appear about how hip and with it Marvel is. Fandom's emphasis shifts from nostalgia of rapidly outnumbered thirty-something collectors to younger fans' interest in current comics, and interest in other genres than superheroes expands. Less obviously, sales of new comic books are declining and distribution to retail outlets is drying up.

**1966:** *Batman* TV show debuts. Instant hit, makes country comics-conscious like never before — for all the wrong reasons, some serious fans think.

**1966 – 1967:** Other companies besides Marvel and DC jump into superhero market in the wake of Batman's success, but most are soon gone. Batman's success has not translated into an enduring increase of overall comic-book sales. Casual readership of comics by average kids is in freefall, but the teenaged fans in comics fandom are increasing in number. In years to come, the lines on the graph will intersect, and the 2000 or so active fans in 1967 are the nucleus of what will become a majority of comic-book readership.

# About the Author

**Dwight R. Decker** has been enmeshed in the web of organized (ha!) comics fandom since he was fifteen. Over the years he has written for comics fanzines, published comics fanzines, and even dabbled on the professional side as a translator of foreign-produced Disney comics for a number of publishers on both sides of the Atlantic. The high point there was translating an Italian-produced comic book (or "graphic novel") featuring an adaptation of *Dante's Inferno* with Disney characters (published in *Walt Disney's Comics & Stories* #666). He has also tried his hand at prose: for the anthology *Steampunk* II: *Steampunk Reloaded*, he translated a 19th Century Danish story that can only be described as steampunk when steampunk was what was right outside your front door and not just a genre. Most recently, he translated and published a 1744 German story that may be the first fictional account ever written of a trip to Mars (or at least somewhere close by), *The Speedy Journey* by Eberhard Christian Kindermann. In addition, he writes lighthearted novels in a science-fictional vein, and has just published *Pleistocene Junior High*, with *The Napoleon of Time* coming soon, available from the usual online sources.

(Photo by Richard Pryor.)

Made in the USA
Charleston, SC
18 February 2015